The Silent Girl

Michael Hjorth is one of Sweden's best-known film and TV producers, and a well-renowned screenwriter whose work includes several screenplays of Henning Mankell's *Wallander*.

Hans Rosenfeldt has hosted both radio and television shows, and is Sweden's leading screenwriter and the creator of *The Bridge*, which is broadcast in more than 170 countries.

D854432

The Silent Girl

A Sebastian Bergman Thriller

Translated by
Marlaine Delargy

Hjorth & Rosenfeldt

arrow books

1 3 5 7 9 10 8 6 4 2

Arrow Books
20 Vauxhall Bridge Road
London SW1V 2SA

Arrow Books is part of the Penguin Random House group of companies
whose addresses can be found at global.penguinrandomhouse.com.

Text Copyright © Michael Hjorth and Hans Rosenfeldt 2014
Translation Copyright © Marlaine Delargy 2017

Michael Hjorth and Hans Rosenfeldt have asserted their right to be
identified as the author of this Work in accordance with the Copyright,
Designs and Patents Act 1988.

First published as *Den Stumma Flickan* by Norstedts in Sweden in 2014
This edition first published by Century in 2017
First published in paperback by Arrow books in 2017

www.penguin.co.uk

A CIP catalogue record for this book is available from the British Library.

ISBN 9781784752422

Introducing the national police homicide unit, based in Stockholm – also known as Riksmord...

Torkel Höglund – Chief Inspector

Ursula Andersson – police forensics expert

Vanja Lithner – investigative police officer

Billy Rosén – investigative police officer

Sebastian Bergman – psychologist and leading criminal profiler

Other police

Jennifer Holmgren – junior police officer in the small town of Sigtuna. Temporarily seconded to Riksmord.

He doesn't know what day it is.

But it's not a school day. He is still in his pyjamas, even though it is after nine o'clock.

Everyone is at home. He can hear the sound of SpongeBob SquarePants *coming from the living room.*

Mummy puts a bowl of yogurt on the table and asks him if he washed his hands after he went to the toilet. He nods. Would he like a sandwich too? He shakes his head. The yogurt will be enough. Banana and vanilla. He would have liked Frosties with his yogurt, but Fred has finished them, so he has to have Oat Krispies instead. However, that means he's allowed to watch a DVD straight after breakfast to make up for the disappointment. He decides on Transformers: Dark of the Moon.*

Again.

The doorbell rings.

'Who on earth can that be at this hour of the morning?' Mummy wonders as she heads for the front door. He doesn't even register the familiar noises as she pushes down the handle and opens it.

Then he hears a loud bang, and it sounds as if someone has fallen over in the hallway.

He gives a start, splashing yogurt all over the table, but he doesn't notice the mess. Daddy calls down anxiously from the bedroom. He's not up yet, but now rapid footsteps are crossing the landing.

Then someone appears in the kitchen doorway.

Holding a gun.

There were two of them now.

She was two separate individuals.

On the outside and on the inside.

★ ★ ★

On the outside she was still moving.

Reluctant but purposeful. The lesson she had learned in school about staying exactly where you were if you got lost went against her instinctive urge to run.

Was she lost?

She didn't really know where she was, but she knew where she was going. She made sure she could still hear the cars passing by on the road. She could go back to the road. Walk alongside it. Hide whenever someone came by. Keep walking until she reached a signpost, check that she was still going the right way, then disappear back into the forest. So she wasn't lost. There was no reason to stay where she was. Then there was the cold. The damp, bitter cold that persuaded her it was a good idea to keep on going. She was warmer when she was on the move. Less hungry. So she kept on going.

★ ★ ★

On the inside she was completely still.

For a while she had run. Both on the inside and on the outside. Racing blindly ahead. Now she couldn't really remember what she had been running away from, or recognise the place she had arrived at. It wasn't a place, or a room, it was more like . . . a feeling, perhaps.

She didn't know. But she was there and it was empty and she was still.

She was empty and it was still.

Silent.

That felt like the most important thing. As long as it remained silent, she was safe. In the place that wasn't a place, illuminated without light. Where no colours reminded her of the colours her staring eyes continued to register from the world outside. Open, but closed to everything. Except that feeling of safety. Which would disappear along with the silence. Instinctively she knew that. Words would give her away. Words would tear down the walls she couldn't see, make everything real again. Let in the terrible things that were waiting out there.

The bangs, the screams, the warm red liquid, the fear.

Her own and everyone else's.

On the inside she was still and silent.

★ ★ ★

On the outside she had to keep on going.

Go where no one could find her. Where no one would try to talk to her. The outside had to protect the inside.

She knew where to go.

There was a place they had been told about, warned about. A place where you would never be found, if you went inside. Never ever. That was what they had been told. No one would find her.

★ ★ ★

On the outside she pulled her thin, inadequate jacket more tightly around her body and increased her speed.

On the inside she curled up, became smaller and smaller, hoping that she would disappear completely.

Anna Eriksson was sitting in the car outside the pale yellow apartment block, waiting.

Vanja was late, which was very unusual. Anna assumed this was yet another of the ways in which her daughter had chosen to make her point over the past few months.

The worst thing was that she no longer called.

Anna could live with that. She understood why, and somewhere deep down perhaps she thought she deserved it. And to be honest, they had never had the kind of mother/daughter relationship that involved long chats on the phone.

But for Valdemar . . . He found the way Vanja had distanced herself unbearably painful, and it had reduced him to a shadow of his former self – more than the cancer, in fact. He couldn't stop talking about his daughter, and the truth they should never have kept from her. They should have done everything differently. He had cheated death, only to discover that life was full of grief and regret. Anna also found the whole situation difficult, of course, but it was easier for her to cope. She had always been stronger than her husband.

Valdemar had been out of hospital for over a month now, but she couldn't get him to leave the apartment. His body seemed to have fully accepted the new kidney, but Valdemar couldn't accept his new world. A world without Vanja. He simply pushed everything away.

Anna. The few colleagues who got in touch, in spite of what he had done. The even fewer friends who called less and less often.

Even the ongoing police investigation didn't seem to bother him these days. The accusations of tax evasion and fraud were serious, but they paled into insignificance compared with what he had put Vanja through.

She had hurled herself at him in a fury. It had been horrible. The yelling, the rows, the tears. Neither of them had ever seen Vanja like that.

So angry.

So terribly hurt.

The refrain was always the same: how could they do this? What kind of mother and father would do such a thing? What kind of people were they, for God's sake?

Anna understood. She would have felt exactly the same in Vanja's shoes. Her daughter's questions were justified and understandable. It was the answers Anna didn't like.

She was the kind of mother who would do such a thing.

Several times during the very worst quarrels Anna had been on the point of saying:

'Do you want to know who your father is? Do you really want to know?'

But she had bitten her tongue, refused to tell Vanja, insisted it was irrelevant.

Not because she wanted to protect Sebastian Bergman; she could see exactly what he wanted. He was trying to worm his way in, claim a right he didn't have, like a debt-collector determined to demand a payment that no one actually owed him.

Sebastian had never been Vanja's father. Valdemar had fulfilled that role, every single day, to the best of his ability. Whatever it said in the hospital notes Vanja had waved around in such a rage. The only positive aspect was that Sebastian couldn't exploit the situation to his own advantage. Like Anna, he was trapped by all the lies. If he told Vanja he had known the truth for quite some time but said nothing, he would reveal that he had let her down, just like Anna and Valdemar.

She would hate him too.

Freeze him out.

Sebastian was well aware of that. He had called Anna several times over the past few weeks, practically begging her to help him find a way to tell Vanja the truth. Anna refused. She would never enable him to take Vanja from Valdemar. Never. That was one of the few things she knew for sure; everything else was a complete mess.

Today, however, she was going to start regaining control of the situation. Today she was going to take the first step towards putting things right. She had a plan.

The door of the apartment block flew open and Vanja finally emerged, her hands thrust deep into her pockets, shoulders hunched. She had dark shadows under her eyes and looked washed out and exhausted; it was as if she had aged a couple of years over the last few months. She pushed back her lifeless, unwashed hair as she crossed the street. Anna gathered her thoughts, took a deep breath and got out of the car.

'Hi, sweetheart, I'm so glad you could come,' she said, trying to sound as positive as possible.

'What do you want?' came the response. 'I'm really busy.'

They hadn't spoken for three weeks, and it seemed to Anna that her daughter's tone was a fraction less sharp. That could be wishful thinking, of course.

'There's something I want to show you,' Anna said tentatively.

'What?'

'Let's go – I'll explain on the way.'

Vanja stared suspiciously at her. Anna knew that the longer they stood there, the more likely it was that Vanja would go with her. She had learned that during the course of all those rows; there was no point in attacking Vanja, or forcing her into a corner and trying to make her do something. If Vanja was going to get in the car, she had to do it without any kind of confrontation, and on her own terms.

'You'll think it's worth it,' Anna went on. 'I know you will.'

After a moment Vanja nodded. She got in the car without saying a word.

Anna joined her and they drove off. When they reached the petrol station down by the Freeport, she broke the silence and made her first mistake.

'Valdemar sends his love. He really misses you.'

'I miss my father too. My real father,'Vanja shot back.

'I'm quite worried about him, to be honest.'

'You only have yourselves to blame,'Vanja snapped. 'I'm not the one who's been lying all my life.'

Anna knew they were on the verge of another blazing row. It would have been so easy to cross the line. Vanja's anger was understandable, but Anna wished she could make her realise how much she was hurting those who really loved her, those who had always supported her, been there for her. They had lied to protect her, not to hurt her. She could tell that Vanja was just waiting for an excuse to explode, so she tried to defuse the situation.

'I know, I know. I'm sorry, I really don't want to argue. Not today . . .'

Vanja seemed to accept a temporary ceasefire, and they drove on in silence: along Valhallavägen and west towards Norrtull.

'Where are we going?'Vanja asked as they passed Stallmästargården.

'As I said, there's something I want to show you.'

'What?'

Anna didn't answer immediately, and Vanja turned to face her.

'You said you'd explain on the way, so start talking.'

Anna took a deep breath, keeping her eyes on the road and the traffic ahead.

'I'm taking you to your father.'

'You can go in now.'

Erik Flodin turned to glance up at the large, white-painted two-storey house where Fabian Hellström, the forensic technician who had travelled up from Karlstad with him, was standing on the veranda. 'We're almost done.'

Erik raised a hand to indicate that he'd heard, then looked back at the open countryside spread before him.

This was a beautiful spot. The fresh green lawn extended as far as the stone wall, and beyond it lay a meadow, waiting for spring to burst into life. The evergreen conifers now had competition from the delicate pale green attire of the deciduous trees as their leaves began to unfurl. A buzzard drifted high above the open field, breaking the silence with its plaintive cry.

Erik wondered whether to call Pia before he went inside. She was bound to find out what had happened, and she would be devastated. This was going to affect the whole community.

Her community.

But if he called her, she would start asking questions. Wanting to know more. Wanting to know everything, when in fact he knew only what his colleagues had told him when he arrived. So what would be the point in calling Pia? None at all.

She would have to wait, he decided. He glanced at the sandpit one last time. Traces of the weekend's downpour on a yellow plastic truck. A spade, a sandy Transformer and two dinosaurs.

Erik sighed and headed for the house and the deceased.

Fredrika Fransson was waiting by the patrol car, and came to join him. She had been first on the scene, and briefed him when he arrived. They had worked together in the past, when he was promoted to DI with special responsibilities in Karlstad. She was a good officer, conscientious and committed. She was almost twenty centimetres shorter than Erik's one metre eighty-five, and at least ten kilos heavier than his seventy-eight. Easier to jump over her than to run all the way around her, as one of his more poisonous colleagues had put it. Fredrika herself had never said a word about her weight – or much else, for that matter. She wasn't particularly chatty.

Erik thought he could smell the cordite as he stepped onto the veranda and saw the first victim. He couldn't, of course. He knew that. After a quick examination of the victims, the forensic pathologist had given him a preliminary time of death: approximately twenty-four hours ago. Even if the front door had been closed – which apparently it hadn't been when the nine-year-old from next door came round to see if she could find someone to play with – too much time had passed for any residual odour to remain in the air.

Erik put on shoe protectors and white plastic gloves before entering the property. He pushed aside the branches of pussy willow adorned with colourful Easter eggs displayed in a large vase by the shoe rack and knelt down next to the body of a woman, lying on her back on the rough stone floor. The first of four victims.

Four dead.

Two children.

A family.

They had yet to be formally identified, but Karin and Emil Carlsten owned and lived in the house with their two sons Georg and Fred, so Erik would be very surprised if this wasn't Karin Carlsten. Sometimes, when he spoke to colleagues from Stockholm and Gothenburg, or even from Karlstad, they were surprised that he didn't know everyone in Torsby. That was where he came from, wasn't it? Surely it was just some little dump in the middle of the forest? Erik would simply sigh wearily. There were almost twelve thousand people living in the community as a whole, with just over four thousand in the town centre. Did anyone in Stockholm know four thousand people? No.

He had never met the Carlstens, but he thought he had heard the name . . . in connection with police business quite recently?

'Do you know the Carlstens?' he asked Fredrika, who was still on the veranda, putting on her shoe protectors with some difficulty.

'No.'

'I seem to remember we came across them last winter.'

'Could be.'

'Would you check it out, please?'

Fredrika nodded, removed the one blue plastic protector she had managed to put on, and headed for the car. Erik turned his attention back to the brown-haired, thirty-five-year-old woman on the floor.

There was a hole in her chest, almost ten centimetres across. Too big for a pistol or a rifle – more like a double-barrelled shotgun. The amount of blood on the floor suggested a substantial exit wound. Erik guessed that the perpetrator had fired at point-blank range, with the barrel of the gun pressed up against the woman's body. The cordite residue had collected between the skin and the sternum, and the intense pressure had flayed the skin, causing charring to the woman's white woollen sweater around the entry hole. Death must have been instantaneous.

He glanced back at the door; she was less than a metre away from it, as if she had opened the door and someone had put a gun to her chest and fired before she had time to react. The impact had hurled her backwards.

Whoever shot her must have stepped over her and continued into the house.

Erik got to his feet and did the same.

The first room off the hallway was a large kitchen; no doubt an estate agent would have described it as a 'rustic farmhouse kitchen' if the house had been up for sale. An open brick fireplace in one corner. High-quality pine flooring, with a matching ceiling. A bread peel and some kind of kitchen tool he didn't recognise hanging on the wall above a traditional wooden sofa.

An old black wood-burning stove among the array of modern white goods.

The remains of breakfast were still on the big pine table. A bowl of what looked like yogurt with Oat Krispies. An overturned chair. A boy, eight or nine years old, lying on the floor. Still in his pyjamas.

It was the Easter holiday. No school. Unfortunately, Erik thought.

A closer look at the boy seemed to confirm his theory about the shotgun. One arm had more or less been ripped off at the shoulder. Minor perforations on the throat and one cheek. What was the distance if the killer had fired from the doorway? Two metres? Three? Enough for the deadly projectiles to spray outwards. The boy might not have died instantly, but it couldn't have taken more than a minute for him to bleed to death.

What next?

Someone had run through the room after the boy had been shot. A child. Small footprints in the blood around the chair. Erik looked towards the room beyond the kitchen: a small living room, with a television and a DVD player. Was the other boy watching TV when he heard the shots? Perhaps he got up when he heard the first bang. Stood in the doorway and saw his brother go down. Then he ran. Where? The trail led to the stairs.

Why wasn't he killed in the kitchen too? Was the gunman reloading? Erik checked the floor; no cartridges, as far as he could see. He must remember to ask Fabian if he had picked them up.

'Jan Ceder.'

Erik just managed to stop himself from jumping as Fredrika materialised behind him.

'The Carlstens reported him to the police in November,' she went on, her gaze fixed on the dead child on the floor.

'Why?'

'A breach of hunting regulations.'

'What kind of breach?' Erik persisted patiently.

'They handed in video footage of Ceder with a dead wolf on his property.'

'So he was convicted.'

A statement rather than a question.

'He was fined,' Fredrika confirmed.

Erik nodded to himself. A huntsman. A shotgun. It didn't prove anything, of course, there were plenty of people around here with guns and hunting permits, but it was a start.

'He threatened them last Tuesday.'

Erik's train of thought was broken. Had he understood Fredrika correctly? Sometimes it was difficult because she didn't give any more information than was absolutely necessary – often not even that.

'Ceder?' he asked, just to be on the safe side. 'Jan Ceder threatened the Carlstens last Tuesday?'

Fredrika nodded, looking directly at Erik for the first time since she had entered the kitchen.

'Outside the swimming baths. Several witnesses.'

Erik rapidly processed the information. Could it be that simple? Could someone be that stupid? The answer to both questions was yes. Just because this was a brutal, violent crime, it didn't necessarily have to be complex and carefully planned. Quite the reverse, in fact.

'I want to speak to him,' he said to Fredrika. 'Send someone to bring him in.'

Fredrika left the room, and Erik reviewed his decision as he followed the small bloody footprints to the staircase.

A threat.

A huntsman.

A shotgun.

He really hoped this was the answer. He had been in charge of the Violent Crimes Unit with the Värmland police for just over two months, and he had no desire to be landed with a long-running investigation. Pia would feel the same. She would demand a quick resolution, so that everyone in the community could put the whole thing behind them. Move on.

The footprints became fainter and fainter, and disappeared completely a few metres from the foot of the stairs. Erik began to climb. At the top he found a long, narrow landing with three doors, two of which were standing open. He glanced in the room on the left: bunk beds and toys strewn across the floor revealed that this was the boys' room. He walked to the end of the landing and stopped. Slumped against what Erik assumed was the bathroom door was Emil. He looked a few years older than Karin, or maybe it was just the sprinkling of grey in his hair. Dead, of course. Definitely a shotgun this time. Right in the middle of his chest. Erik pictured the man rushing out of the bedroom to find the gunman standing at the top of the stairs.

He looked around; it didn't seem as though Emil Carlsten had brought any kind of weapon with him. He must have heard what was going on downstairs, yet he had come out unarmed. He probably hadn't been thinking clearly. Erik couldn't even imagine how he would react if this happened at home. If it had been Pia and their daughter downstairs.

He stepped over the man's legs into the bedroom. A double bed dominated the space, at least two metres by two metres. Plenty of room for children having nightmares. The quilt and decorative pillows were neatly in place. Two bedside tables, a dressing table with a mirror. One wall was completely taken up by wardrobes; the doors of the middle closet were wide open.

Karin's.

Dresses, blouses and skirts on hangers.

Two thin bare legs protruded among the shoes on the floor. Erik moved closer.

The second son was sitting right at the back. He had crawled in as far as he could go, with a blanket on his knee. As if he were trying to hide. Was that why Emil didn't get any further? Had his son come running up the stairs, and Emil had tried to hide him? To save him?

If so, he had failed.

The gunman had found him. He must have stood exactly where Erik was standing now, just over a metre from the child.

The barrel of the gun even closer. The blast had practically torn off the boy's head.

Erik had to turn away. He had seen many things that human beings were capable of doing to one another, but this . . .

The children. The pyjamas. Those thin, bare legs . . .

He sat down on the bed and took several deep breaths, forcing back the tears. Perched on that big double bed, the tears scalding his eyes, he swore that he would catch whoever had done this. He couldn't remember ever articulating his goal so clearly before, but this was different. He was going to catch whoever had done this.

Whatever it took.

Sebastian had walked to work in Kungsholmen as usual.

It was his new routine. It took longer, and the more he was away from his apartment, the better. He was seriously considering finding a new place to live, but then again he spent very little time there. When he was at home he paced the floor until he got tired, then he tried to read the books he claimed he had already read. However, he was so restless that he started a new book before he'd finished the first one. A chapter here, another there, but still his thoughts floated around like driftwood.

Even women bored him. He still flirted, finding a certain relaxation in the process, but he was amazed at how rarely he had taken it all the way recently. That was very unusual for him.

But the image of Ursula on the floor . . .

He couldn't get it out of his head.

The pool of blood spreading, leaking from her right eye like a bag that had burst, her hair sticky and red. He still thought the sweet smell of blood lingered in the hallway, in spite of the amount of bleach he had used to scrub it down.

So he went to the office every day. He needed to work. An investigation, preferably complex and challenging, something that would demand every scrap of concentration.

But such a case was notable by its absence. None of the district police forces had asked for help from the National CID Murder Squad, known as Riksmord, so as usual the team were taking some leave in lieu of the overtime they had accrued. Billy, who was normally there whether they had a case or not, dropped in now and again to check his emails, but that was all.

Sebastian saw Torkel even less often, which was perhaps just as well. Torkel loved Ursula, and Ursula had been in Sebastian's apartment when the bullet penetrated her eye. Her lifeless body had been lying in Sebastian's hallway. He had a feeling that Torkel would always blame him for what had happened, even though they had made a point of avoiding the topic on the few occasions when they had met.

Did Sebastian love Ursula? Once upon a time, probably. But his first thought when he heard the shot and saw her lying there was terrible. It wasn't muddied by panic. It was crystal clear, and it was anything but loving.

What a fucking nuisance.

A woman he had known for many years. A woman to whom he had grown closer, with whom he had been more honest than anyone else, lay dying on his floor, and his first reaction was 'what a fucking nuisance'.

He recognised the thought very well.

It came into his head in connection with most things: conflict, importunate women, boring tasks at work, social events. In those contexts it was perfectly natural, possibly even a good thing.

But in this context . . .

In his hallway, after the shooting.

Even he found it frightening.

The only bright spot was that Vanja was around from time to time. She was the real reason why he still went into work. Their relationship had improved recently; the shock of discovering that Valdemar was not her biological father had turned her life upside down. It weakened her suspicion that Sebastian had somehow been involved when she lost her place on the FBI training course; it was as if she no longer had the energy to follow that particular fear to its conclusion.

It was understandable; few individuals would be able to cope with what she was dealing with at the moment. A war on several fronts. It was better to seal a fragile peace treaty with one person at least.

Besides which, Sebastian had persistently denied any involvement whatsoever. He had appealed to the selection committee twice, explaining how wrong their decision had been. Needless to say he had made sure by devious means that Vanja found out about his sterling efforts on both occasions. The committee had stood firm: Vanja Lithner was welcome to submit an application the next time a place at Quantico became available. However, Sebastian's intervention paid dividends in another way.

A few days after his final attempt, he had bumped into Vanja in the corridor. She was softer than she used to be. She seemed tired, not so keen to start a fight, not quite so ready to attack at the first opportunity. She even said hello. She told him she had heard about his efforts on her behalf, and then she went on to tell him about her father, who was no longer her father.

They had grown closer. Not as close as before, but it was a start, and from then on his thoughts of Ursula had begun to fade.

He had rediscovered his focus.

Vanja hadn't even considered getting back in the car with Anna. She had to keep her distance from the woman who was her mother, but who certainly hadn't behaved like a mother. No way.

Outside the taxi the spring was well advanced, even though it was only April. The days had been warm for over a week now, giving a taste of early summer. But Vanja felt frozen inside. Abandoned. Her father was no longer her father. As for her mother, she had no idea where they stood.

Who did she have left?

Not Billy. Not any more. They had been like brother and sister, but they had drifted apart. He was completely absorbed in his relationship with Maya, his fiancée; they had been together for a year, but Vanja had met her only in passing. And now they were getting married, apparently; Vanja didn't even know if she would be invited.

She didn't see much of Torkel, her boss and mentor, these days either. He wasn't in the office very often after what had happened to Ursula. She wondered if he was thinking of packing it in; sometimes it felt that way when she did see him.

Who else was close to her?

It was a short list.

Ridiculously short.

Jonathan, her ex-boyfriend, who called occasionally, hoping they might get back together, or at least that they might fall into bed.

Perhaps the odd colleague from her time at the academy; she saw them now and again, but they were all in the middle of building their families.

And then there was Sebastian Bergman.

If anyone had told her when they first met on a case in Västerås how much time they would spend together in the future, she would have laughed out loud. The idea would have been too absurd to contemplate. He drove her crazy, he wore her out. But these days she actually found herself missing him. How did that happen? How had a promiscuous, narcissistic criminal psychologist ended up on her ridiculously short list?

It wasn't just the lack of others that put him there, although it would presumably have been easier to shut him out if she'd been really close to someone else in her life.

There was another reason.

She enjoyed talking to him. He was impossible, rude and patronising with other people, but with her he was warm and gentle and perceptive. He chased women like trophies without any consideration for their feelings, but he cared about hers. She didn't understand why, but it was true. He couldn't hide it.

But could she trust him? He was often way too close when bad stuff happened.

Too close to the evidence that had brought Valdemar down.

Too close to Håkan Persson Riddarstolpe and the report that put an end to her hopes of training with the FBI.

But whichever way she looked at it, she couldn't find a single rational explanation as to why Sebastian would want to destroy her life. He insisted it was all a coincidence, and perhaps he was right. The problem was that if Vanja had learned anything from her job, it was that coincidences were extremely rare. Too many coincidences became circumstantial evidence. Possible became probable.

The coincidences around Sebastian were almost there. They were on the borderline, but maybe they hadn't crossed it yet.

She needed him. She was so lonely right now.

Erik Flodin parked outside the low, flat, and if truth were told, extremely ugly and boring building at Bergebyvägen 22, which had been his workplace until February. He got out of the car and headed for the main entrance. The three journalists who had been waiting on the wooden benches outside the police station got to their feet as soon as they saw him approaching. He recognised them all: two from *Värmlands Folkblad* and one from the local desk of *Nya Wermlands-Tidningen*.

They wanted to know what he could tell them about the murders. 'Nothing at all,' he said as he pushed open the door. He nodded to Kristina and Dennis on reception; he was taking out his pass card as his phone rang. He swiped the card and keyed in the four-digit code; once he was through the inner door he took the call from Pia.

No greeting, just: 'Is it true?' Erik thought he could hear a hint of reproach; why had she had to hear it from someone else and not from him? 'A family? An entire family has been shot?'

'Yes.'

'Where? Who are they?'

'Just outside Storbråten. Their name is Carlsten.'

'Do you know who did it?'

'We've got one . . . I wouldn't say suspect, but we have the name of someone who'd threatened the family.'

'Who?'

Erik didn't even hesitate. He usually shared most details of ongoing investigations with his wife, and so far nothing had ever leaked.

'Jan Ceder.'

'I don't know him.'

'We've had dealings with him before – I'm just going to talk to him now.'

Pia sighed deeply, and Erik could picture her standing at the window of her office in the council building, gazing out at the rowan trees in front of the Co-op on Tingshusgatan.

'It'll be all over the papers,' she said with another troubled sigh.

'Not necessarily – only *VF* and *Nya Wermlands* have turned up so far.' He said it because that was what he thought she wanted to hear, not because it was true.

Of course it would be all over the papers. Before long the three reporters outside the police station would be joined by their colleagues from Karlstad, and by their competitors from Stockholm. TV too, probably. Maybe even from Norway.

'Do you remember Åmsele?' Pia asked drily, immediately making it clear that she had seen through his attempt at reassurance. Erik couldn't help sighing too. Of course he remembered Åmsele. The triple murder of a family in and near a graveyard. Killed because of a stolen bicycle. Erik was in his first year at the police training academy back then; everyone followed the nationwide hunt for Juha Valjakkala and his girlfriend Marita across the media. 'That was over twenty-five years ago,' Pia went on in his ear, 'but that's still what people think of in connection with Åmsele. We want people to move here, not be frightened away.'

Erik stopped off at the coffee machine and pressed cappuccino. He was overcome by a sudden weariness. He was losing patience with Pia. She hadn't been there. Inside the house. She hadn't seen the little boy who was due to start school in the autumn, sitting right at the back of the wardrobe. His brother still in pyjamas, shot while he was eating his breakfast.

She hadn't seen them.

Hadn't seen the blood.

The pointlessness.

'I realise it's not ideal,' he said, trying hard to keep the irritation out of his voice. 'But four people are dead. Two children.

Perhaps the effect on whether or not people choose to move to the area shouldn't be our main priority right now, wouldn't you say?'

Silence. The coffee machine had done its work; he picked up his cup and sipped at his drink, which wasn't particularly hot, unfortunately. The coffee in Karlstad was better.

'You're right,' Pia said eventually. 'I'm sorry, I must have sounded incredibly self-obsessed.'

'You sounded committed to your job,' Erik replied. As always every trace of irritation disappeared, replaced by a pang of guilt as soon as she gave way and apologised. 'As usual,' he added.

'Are you bringing anyone in?' she asked, back to her usual efficient tone of voice.

'What do you mean?'

'Help. From outside.'

'No, I don't think so. Not yet, anyway.'

Further down the corridor, Fredrika stuck her head out of her office; the look she gave him made it clear that she thought it was time he said goodbye to whoever he was talking to. Erik complied.

'Listen, I have to go. We can discuss this later. Love you.'

He ended the call, slipped the phone in his pocket, put down his cup which was virtually still full, and quickly went along to Fredrika's office for an update.

Sebastian lowered the book with the lengthy academic title *The Psychopathology of Crime: Criminal Behavior as a Clinical Disorder* when he heard someone coming towards the glass doors. Vanja. She looked pale and drawn. She took out her pass card and pushed open the door, which seemed heavier than usual. Something had happened. Sebastian got to his feet and crossed the sterile, open-plan office. He tried a welcoming smile, but she didn't notice him at first.

'Hi, has something happened?' he asked, increasing his speed slightly. He was worried about her.

For a moment he thought she wasn't going to answer. She stood there in silence, staring at him. Her lovely blue eyes looked stronger than the rest of her. It was as if she had concentrated all her strength in those eyes, because when she did speak her words were weak and brittle, as if they had broken somewhere along the way.

'Mum . . . told me who my father was.'

An icy wave washed through Sebastian's body. He wasn't ready for this.

The impossible moment.

His mind was whirling.

Surely Anna wouldn't have told her the truth? Not long ago she had refused to help him; had she really told Vanja now?

'And who was he?' Sebastian managed, impressed that his voice sounded balanced and full of natural curiosity, in spite of everything.

'Do you know what she showed me?' Vanja went on, as if she hadn't even heard his question; her voice was a little stronger now.

23

'I've no idea.' The worst of the panic was subsiding; he must have got away with it this time. Vanja wouldn't be talking to him like this if Anna had revealed the truth. He knew Vanja well enough to be sure of that; unlike him, she was no liar.

'A grave. She showed me a grave.'

'A grave?'

'Yes. He's dead. He died in 1981, apparently. His name was Hans Åke Andersson.'

'Hans Åke Andersson?'

Sebastian was trying to adapt to this new situation. All credit to Anna: she had managed to provide Vanja with a father and prove he was dead at a single stroke. Creative. Vanja obviously didn't feel the same way.

'Apparently he was just some guy she met – he didn't want to know when she fell pregnant,' she went on, shaking her head. 'When Valdemar came along they decided not to tell me the truth.'

'Never?'

'Never. She claims she didn't want to hurt me, particularly as this Hans Åke Andersson died eight months after I was born, and he didn't have any relatives.'

Vanja suddenly looked furious. Her strength had returned; it wasn't only her eyes that were full of energy. He recognised her now.

'She must think I'm stupid. After several months she suddenly comes up with the name of some guy who conveniently turns out to be dead. Did she really think I'd fall for that load of crap?'

Sebastian sensed that the question was rhetorical, and chose to keep quiet. Not that Vanja waited for a response; the words came pouring out, a flood of pent-up fury that had been waiting to escape.

'Why couldn't she have shown me the fucking grave ages ago, if that's true? Why wait months?'

'I don't know,' Sebastian said truthfully.

'I do. Because it's a fucking lie. She's just trying to . . . close the door. Get me to make my peace with them.'

Sebastian remained silent, considering his strategy. Should he stick up for Anna? Help her to make Vanja believe the lie and move on, or should he encourage Vanja's scepticism? Drive another wedge into her relationship with Anna and Valdemar? What would serve him best in the long run? It was a difficult situation, but he had to make a choice. Vanja shook her head and took a deep, calming breath.

'The only thing that could make me even begin to think about forgiving them is if they're honest. If they stop lying. Do you understand?'

Sebastian decided to support Vanja. It felt like the right thing to do; it would buy him some time, and above all it would bring them closer together.

'Of course I do. This must be so hard for you,' he said sympathetically.

'I haven't got the strength to fight with you any more,' Vanja said quietly, gazing at him as her eyes began to fill with tears. 'I can't fight the whole world. I just can't.'

'You don't need to fight me,' he said as gently as he could.

Vanja nodded, then pleaded:

'Then you have to tell me: were you in any way involved in Riddarstolpe's report? Were you responsible for the fact that I wasn't put forward for the FBI training programme?'

Sebastian had to make a real effort to hide his surprise. How come they were back here?

'But I've already told you that was nothing to do with me,' he said, trying to pull himself together.

'Tell me again.' Vanja didn't take her eyes off him. 'And be honest. I'd find it easier to deal with if you were involved than if someone I care about keeps on lying to me.'

Sebastian adopted his most sincere expression and tried to look as genuine as Vanja's sorrow. With so much at stake, it wasn't difficult.

'No,' he lied, discovering to his joy that his voice was breaking slightly due to the gravity of the moment. 'I promise you, I had nothing to do with Riddarstolpe's report.'

He saw her exhale, saw her shoulders drop with relief, and he felt a warm glow of pride. With the right focus, he was a brilliant liar. He could probably have convinced her that the earth was flat.

'How you could even think . . .' he began, his voice suffused with sorrow, but she held up a hand to stop him.

'You don't have to say any more. I choose to believe you.'

Sebastian quickly emerged from his cocoon of smugness. What did she say? She had *chosen* to believe him?

'What does that mean?' he said, genuinely curious.

'Exactly what it says. I choose to believe you, because that's what I need to do right now.'

Sebastian looked at his daughter, who once again seemed to be on the verge of tears. She really did need someone after everything that had happened, and he was the person she had selected. Choosing to believe him was not the same as trusting him, but Sebastian assumed that was as far as she could go. Now it was up to him to prove that she had made the right decision.

'I won't let you down,' he said.

'Good.' She broke into a smile, stepped forward and gave him a hug. She held him for longer and more tightly than he would ever have dared hope.

Erik was informed that Jan Ceder was in one of the interview rooms down the corridor. Not that interviews were held in them very often; they were mostly used for staff appraisals, private telephone conversations, small meetings and occasionally for a quick nap.

According to Fredrika, Ceder hadn't seemed at all surprised when they came to pick him up. Nor had he raised any objections; he had been happy to accompany them. They hadn't told him why they wanted to speak to him, even though he had asked several times. They had merely said they wanted to clear up one or two things, without going into detail. Fredrika had gathered all the information they had on Ceder; there was a copy waiting for Erik on her desk. She had also been in touch with Malin Åkerblad, the prosecutor who was in charge of the preliminary investigation, and had obtained a search warrant for Ceder's property. A team was already on its way.

Erik was impressed, and asked for a few minutes to read through the material. Was there any chance of a cup of coffee that was slightly above room temperature? Apparently not. The machine was due to be serviced next week.

So he sat down without his coffee, and opened the thin folder.

Jan Ceder, born 1961. Five years older than Erik. Still lived in the relatively small house his parents had owned, just a few kilometres from the Carlsten family. On sickness benefits since 2001. Married and divorced twice; both exes were Thai. Currently single after a Russian woman – whom he referred to as 'the one I sent for' – had left him before Christmas following a row which ended up with her reporting him to the police for domestic violence. The complaint had later been withdrawn.

Erik moved on to Ceder's police record. Several instances of driving illegally, drink driving, picked up twice for being drunk and disorderly, lost his driving licence, illegal home distilling of alcohol, bootlegging, offences against the laws on hunting, plus another complaint of domestic violence from one of his wives, also subsequently withdrawn.

Erik closed the folder. Alcohol and a lack of self-control. It was definitely time to talk to Jan Ceder.

★ ★ ★

He was slumped at the table in a plain white T-shirt and scruffy jeans. With his unshaven, sunken cheeks, the red hair that needed a wash and a visit to the barber, and the fine blood vessels clearly visible beneath the dry skin of his slightly knobbly nose, Ceder looked considerably older than he was, Erik thought. The bloodshot eyes followed the uniformed officer as he left the room. Erik and Fredrika sat down and Fredrika started the recording, giving the date and stating that this was an interview with Jan Ceder, and that Detective Inspector Erik Flodin was also present. Erik cleared his throat and met Ceder's weary gaze.

'We'd like to talk about the Carlsten family.'

Jan gave a deep and apparently heartfelt sigh.

'What are they saying I've done this time?'

'What have you done?'

'Nothing, but a guy came in here and took . . .' He held up a trembling hand. 'He took fingerprints, and he wanted my jacket, shirt and shoes. What the hell is this about?'

Erik chose not to answer his questions. Not yet.

'You threatened Emil and Fred Carlsten outside the pool in Torsby the day before yesterday after Fred's swimming lesson,' he went on, without taking his eyes off Ceder.

'I didn't threaten them.'

Erik turned to Fredrika, who opened the folder in front of her, found the relevant document and read it out loud:

'You told them to . . . be careful none of them got in the way of the next fucking bullet.'

'Sounds like a threat to me,' Erik interjected.

Jan Ceder shrugged. 'I'd had a few drinks.'

'It's still a threat.'

'I was pissed.'

'Do you know what I think when people like you defend their unacceptable behaviour by saying they were drunk?'

Silence. No doubt Ceder was expecting Erik to continue without any input from him, but after ten seconds he realised this wasn't going to happen.

'No, I don't know what you think.'

'I think: Does he take me for an idiot?' Erik leaned forward – not far, but enough for Ceder to recoil slightly. 'Alcohol doesn't give you new ideas, it simply allows you to say what's already in your mind, the things that you're sensible enough to keep your mouth shut about when you're sober. You threatened their lives.'

Jan cleared his throat, suddenly looking a little less comfortable. He ran a hand over his grey stubble.

'I can apologise, if that's what you want. If I scared the kid or something.'

Before Erik had time to reply, Fredrika's mobile started vibrating on the table. He glared at her, but she successfully ignored him, glancing at the display and then taking the call, to Erik's great surprise. The two men waited for her to finish the conversation; all they could hear was the odd 'hmm' and a couple of monosyllabic questions.

'Any chance of a coffee?' Ceder asked after clearing his throat once more.

'It's lukewarm,' Erik said just as Fredrika ended the call. He was just about to make an acid comment and resume the interview when she leaned over and whispered in his ear.

She didn't say much, but when Erik turned his attention back to Ceder, he seemed to have acquired a fresh burst of energy.

'You have a licence for two rifles and a shotgun,' he began, opening his folder. 'A . . . twelve-calibre Benelli SuperNova. Is that correct?'

Ceder nodded.

'Could you please answer verbally – for the tape,' Fredrika clarified.

'Yes,' Ceder stated in an unnecessarily loud, clear voice. 'I own a twelve-calibre Benelli SuperNova.'

'The team searching your house just called.' Erik paused, leaned forward again. Further this time. Slightly more aggressive. 'They can't find it. Could you tell us where it is?'

'It got nicked.'

No hesitation whatsoever. Erik couldn't tell whether it was an honest answer, or just well rehearsed, but he had four dead bodies, four people executed with a shotgun, and Jan Ceder didn't know where his shotgun was.

What a coincidence.

He had no intention of letting this go.

'When was this?'

'A few months ago maybe. Some time before Christmas.'

'I don't see a report about the theft,' Erik said, gesturing towards the folder.

'I didn't report it.'

'Why not?'

Jan Ceder's lips cracked into a small smile for the first time. He could do with seeing a dentist after he'd been to the barber's, Erik thought.

'Why would I bother? You haven't cleared up a single burglary in the past ten years!'

It was true, the clear-up rate for burglaries was embarrassingly low, Erik thought, but most law-abiding citizens still reported any incident, particularly if guns were involved. But not Ceder. Then again, he couldn't exactly be described as law-abiding.

'A gun like that must cost around ten thousand kronor.' Erik sat back, his tone of voice suggesting they were just having a little chat.

'Something like that.' Ceder shrugged, underlining the fact that he didn't really know what a 12-calibre Benelli SuperNova cost these days.

'That's a lot of money. Didn't you want to claim on the insurance? You need a police incident number for that.'

'I don't have any insurance.'

'None at all?' Fredrika couldn't help asking. Ceder turned to her.

'It's not against the law, is it?'

'No. It's a bit stupid, but it's not illegal.'

Ceder shrugged yet again, then he scratched his nose and folded his arms. His body language made it clear that there was no more to say on the subject as far as he was concerned. Erik was inclined to agree; they weren't going to get any further with the gun. Time to go back to the Carlstens.

'Where were you yesterday?' he asked, once again in that relaxed, chatty tone of voice.

★ ★ ★

Erik Flodin slammed his fist against the useless coffee machine. The stress had got to him. The interview had been terminated when Ceder demanded a solicitor. He didn't have one, of course, so now they were waiting for a duty solicitor to get to Torsby. Fredrika had gone over to Ceder's house; she had just called to tell him that they hadn't found anything to link Ceder to the murders. However, one of the team had discovered a wolf skin in an outbuilding. The animal had been shot comparatively recently, because the skin was pegged out and salted to speed the drying process. Fredrika had said drily that they might be able to charge Ceder with another infringement of the laws on hunting if they couldn't come up with anything else.

They were getting nowhere, and there was no coffee. They had the threat Ceder had made outside the swimming pool, but nothing else. If they couldn't find a connection, they were going to have to start all over again. This was Erik's first major investigation since his promotion; he mustn't mess it up, but the clock was ticking. Soon the killer would have a head start of thirty-six hours; everyone knew the first twenty-four hours were critical, and they were long gone.

They were going to need help.

He needed help.

There weren't many people he could turn to. He immediately dismissed Hans Olander, his boss in Karlstad. Olander had made it crystal clear that he supported the other candidate, Per Karlsson. When Erik got the job, Olander's first words were: 'Oh, well, let's see how it goes'. He definitely wasn't the right person to ask for help just two months later. In addition, Olander had already intimated in a phone call that he would be happy to take over the case, as its complexity demanded what he referred to as 'seniority'. It was only the confidence that Anna Bredholm, the Chief of Police, had in Erik's abilities that had kept him in charge, for the time being at least. But he didn't want to call her either; Anna was one of Pia's closest friends, and it would look as if he was advancing his career on the back of his wife's contacts. There was already a certain amount of malicious gossip, and he certainly didn't want to provide any further ammunition. No, he needed someone who was completely removed from the political arena of Värmland.

'There's no shame in not being able to do everything yourself' – that's what his mother always used to say. It was true, of course, but what kind of signal would it send out if he brought in outside help on the second day of his first major case? Working out what Olander would think wasn't exactly rocket science, but what about everyone else? Would he be undermining his authority, making things more difficult for himself in the future? Would it make him look weak?

Whatever, he thought. If the Carlsten murder wasn't solved, he would be seen as incompetent, and that was worse.

In his mind's eye he saw that little boy, shot in the wardrobe.

It was time to call in the best.

He had never found it difficult to look at her.

Quite the reverse – he loved to gaze at her mouth, her nose, her cheeks, and finally her eyes. Sometimes he would secretly watch her in the office. There was something special about observing her when she was unaware of his scrutiny. Of course she had usually realised, and then he would quickly look away, try to appear unconcerned, but when he glanced back she would be smiling.

But just before the incident the smile had disappeared, replaced by a troubled expression on her face.

That was the way their relationship had been developing: in the wrong direction. He wasn't sure how it had happened.

She and Micke were divorcing, and Torkel had hoped that he would progress from being her lover to becoming her lifelong companion, but things didn't turn out like that. Not at all. Instead they met less and less often, and she had started avoiding him. He missed her.

It was hard for him to accept that she didn't want him as anything other than a lover, but now he was facing an even greater challenge than his disappointment at being rejected.

He could no longer look at her face.

She was lying on the sofa in the living room, under the speckled red woollen blanket. However hard he tried, he saw only the white compress covering her right eye, taking over the face he loved. He knew he needed to meet her gaze, but somehow he just couldn't do it. The bullet had ripped through her right eyeball, destroying the optical nerve, but according to the doctors the angle of the shot meant that it had exited through her temple without causing too much damage. But her right eye was gone for good.

He stood up; he had to get away from the compress for a while. He headed for her kitchen.

'Would you like another coffee?'

'I'm fine,' Ursula said. 'You help yourself.'

Torkel looked down at the cup in his hand, feeling stupid; he had hardly touched his drink. Was it obvious that he was running away? He couldn't turn back now; he walked into the kitchen.

'I'll just top mine up,' he said, mostly to himself. Ursula's voice followed him.

'How's Vanja?'

Torkel stopped at the black coffee machine next to the cooker.

To be honest, he had no idea. He hadn't thought about any-one except Ursula lately. He had hardly been into the office, and was hoping that no one would call on the team for quite some time. He wanted to be able to focus on Ursula.

'Fine, I think,' he said eventually.

'Are you sure?' Ursula sounded dubious. 'She called round the day before yesterday, and I thought she seemed pretty low.'

Torkel listened as he added a few drops of fresh coffee to his cup.

'I haven't seen much of her,' he admitted. 'She's got some kind of problem going on at home, or so I've heard. But to be per-fectly honest, I don't know.'

I've been thinking about you, he wanted to say. He went back into the living room and sat down.

'That's because you've been spending so much time with me,' Ursula said, smiling at him for the first time in ages. 'And I really want to thank you for that.'

Slowly she reached out and took his hand. Hers was warmer than usual, but just as soft as always. He had missed her touch.

It took so little; it was ridiculous. He tried to focus on the eye that was still there. The blue-grey iris. It looked tired, but it was still Ursula. She was in there. For a second he managed to forget that compress.

'You came to see me every single day in hospital, and you're here so often. I really do appreciate it, but it's . . .' Ursula hesitated. 'It feels a bit strange.'

'It's difficult for you?'

'Can I be honest?'

She gently let go of his hand and turned away. That told Torkel everything he needed to know, but she kept on going anyway.

'There's a dichotomy. You want more than me, which makes things complicated. You care about me, and I just disappoint you.'

'You don't disappoint me.'

'That's not true. Is it?'

Torkel shook his head. She was right; there was no point in pretending. He had so many questions, but one overshadowed all the rest.

What had she been doing in Sebastian's apartment?

It couldn't be a coincidence, he was sure of it.

He had meticulously gone through every single interview with Ellinor Bergkvist and Sebastian during the course of the police investigation – 149 pages of dense print. Time and time again Ellinor insisted that she and Sebastian had had a long and intimate affair. They had fallen in love at first sight, and he had begged her to move in with him. On page after page Ellinor explained how she and Sebastian had enjoyed what could best be described as a 1950s relationship. She had cooked and kept the apartment looking nice, she had bought flowers every Friday, while he had worked and taken care of the finances, coming home to dinner on the table and a willing sexual partner. This had gone on for months, until the day when he threw her out and changed the locks, which led to her firing a gun through the peephole in his front door. Her aim had been to show Sebastian that he couldn't treat her like that. She had wanted to injure or kill him. Over and over again she repeated that she didn't know there was anyone else in the apartment.

The Sebastian Bergman who emerged through these 149 pages surprised Torkel. The man he had once called a friend was completely unrecognisable. The man he still thought he knew well. To begin with, when he had read only Ellinor's interviews, Torkel was convinced she was lying. It was obvious she had a screw loose. The result of a major psychological assessment hadn't yet come through, but Torkel was pretty sure Ellinor would be sent to a secure psychiatric unit once the trial got under way in a month or so.

But the interviews with Sebastian confirmed much of what she had said, even if he gave a different reason for her ending up in his apartment. She had moved in when it seemed she might be in danger from the serial killer Edward Hinde, and she had somehow stayed put, but otherwise Sebastian's story more or less matched Ellinor's. Sebastian, who as a general rule never wanted to see a woman more than once, had had a long-term live-in partner.

Sebastian had felt terrible about what had happened, and had expressed great remorse in his interviews, but he had never visited Ursula in hospital. Not as far as Torkel was aware, anyway. Perhaps the shame was too great, and he couldn't cope with seeing her? Or perhaps he just didn't care. Torkel had no idea. Reading the interviews merely underlined what he already knew: he didn't understand Sebastian Bergman at all.

He had to ask the question.

'Has Sebastian been to see you?'

'Once.'

It was obvious that Ursula wanted to change the subject, but he kept going. He couldn't just let it go.

'How come? I don't understand him at all.'

'I do,' she said, a little sadly. 'He's an expert when it comes to avoiding anything that's painful.'

'Not a particularly attractive quality.'

'I think it's more of a defence mechanism; my only consolation is that he's probably the one who suffers most.'

She took his hand again. Torkel's cheeks grew warm. At least she really saw him. He had lived on hope for a very long time where Ursula was concerned; he could go on living that way for a while longer.

Being seen was better than nothing.

But she had been in Sebastian's apartment. Not with him.

He tried to push away the thought, to concentrate on the warmth of her hand. Her touch ought to be calming, reassuring, but it wasn't. Without even being there, Sebastian was standing between them.

The sound of his mobile interrupted his train of thought.

They were heading west along the E20 in the SUV.

As always Billy was behind the wheel, and as always he was driving too fast. Torkel usually asked him to slow down, but not this time. Instead he sat gazing out of the window at the endless pine trees lining the road on both sides. That was what Sweden seemed to consist of as soon as you left the suburbs: forest, forest and more forest.

Sebastian and Vanja were at the back. Side by side. Torkel found this strange; Vanja had been very distant with Sebastian the last time he saw them together. Something must have happened.

In the middle, where Ursula usually sat, was their luggage.

He suddenly heard Sebastian laugh; Vanja must have said something funny. Their luggage was in Ursula's seat, but Sebastian was laughing as if nothing had happened. Torkel felt even more annoyed as he gazed out at those endless bloody trees again.

★ ★ ★

After a few hours they turned onto the road that would take them all the way to Torsby in northern Värmland. Billy had never been there, and suspected none of his colleagues had either. The town's home page proudly announced that Torsby was the place where Sven-Göran Eriksson and Markus Berg had dribbled their first footballs, and that it boasted Sweden's only tunnel for cross-country skiing. Billy knew about Eriksson, mainly because of all the stories about his love life in the tabloid press, but he hadn't a clue who Markus Berg was, and he hadn't been cross-country skiing since he was thirteen.

'I was joking. I was just joking, darling.'

Billy remembered the words very clearly. They had cleared up the case of the mass grave in the mountains of Jämtland. He had shot Charles Cederkvist. One morning he had given Maya a key to his apartment. When she hugged him she had whispered that the next step was to get married. In May. She had seen his expression, a mixture of surprise and terror, and she had given him another hug.

'I was joking. I was just joking, darling.'

That was exactly what she had said.

Word for word.

However, when she presented him with a list of 150 potential guests two months later, wondering if he'd like to help her cut it down a little, he realised the wedding in May was no longer a joke, but a solid reality.

Maya.

He loved her, he was sure of that. But everything was happening so fast.

By midsummer they would have known each other for a year. And been married for over a month.

His attempts to slow down the pace of their rush to the altar had been in vain, and seemed pathetic compared with her passionate conviction that this was the right thing for both of them. A refusal to affirm their future together seemed mean and petty, as if he didn't love her.

He loved her very much.

He loved everything, from her intensity to the way she looked at him when they were lying in bed. He loved the fact that she threw herself into whatever she did. He loved the way she made him grow as a person. When he was with her he felt like the only man in the world, and for someone who had always had the sense of being an outsider, an observer, it was a wonderful experience.

So he gave in, ashamed of his caution.

To tell the truth, he had never thought of himself as someone who would get married, probably because of his parents' divorce.

He had been nine years old, and many times he had got the impression that he was more mature than either his mother or his father when they played him off against each other. But his main objection was the speed of the whole thing. It didn't suit him. He liked to analyse, to reflect and plan, while Maya was always dashing off to look at a new venue, trying on new clothes, presenting him with new invitations on which he was supposed to express an opinion. In the end he had simply given up, realised that their big day together was more hers than his. Once again he was standing slightly to one side, assessing the situation rather than participating fully. That was just the way it was. He told himself he was OK with that. He still hoped that the murders in Torsby would be fairly straightforward so that he could get back and help Maya with the planning, but the signs weren't good. An entire family wiped out. Weak circumstantial evidence against the only suspect, as far as he could make out. He usually felt hungry and focused on his way to a new case, but this time he was torn, as if he was always in the wrong place, wherever he might be.

He tried to push away his thoughts, concentrate on the monotonous road ahead. There was very little traffic, and the speedometer had crept above 140 kilometres per hour. Billy slowed down; it was usually Torkel who pointed out such transgressions, but he had remained silent virtually all the way, staring out of the window. He had aged recently, Torkel. Perhaps that wasn't so surprising; Ursula's ordeal had shaken Billy too. She was Torkel's equal when it came to the leadership of the team, and Torkel wasn't the only one who would miss her; they all would, Billy especially. He would need to oversee all the forensic data himself, and he didn't know if he was quite ready to shoulder that important responsibility alone. In a way the team had also lost an eye.

However, those two at the back didn't seem particularly concerned. It was strange, Billy thought as he glanced in the mirror. The last time he saw Vanja she had been furious with Sebastian, certain that he was trying to ruin her life. Now they looked like two kids on the back seat, on their way to summer camp.

Lately Billy had become more and more convinced that Sebastian's constant efforts to build a close friendship with Vanja were based on a hidden agenda. It had started when Sebastian asked Billy to find the address of someone called Anna Eriksson, the very first time they met in Västerås. Anna Eriksson had written a letter to Sebastian's mother in December 1979, and Sebastian needed to track her down. Billy hadn't paid much attention at the time, but after a while he had realised that Vanja's mother was called Anna Eriksson. Then her name came up again, on a list of potential murder victims who had all slept with Sebastian. So he had had an affair with Vanja's mother, and Vanja was born in July 1980, around seven months after that letter was written.

But what finally made Billy sure that Sebastian was Vanja's real father was the discovery that Valdemar wasn't.

That was one coincidence too many.

The more he thought about it, the more it had to be true. Sebastian sought Vanja out whenever he had the chance, but never in a sexual way. Billy had seen Sebastian with other women; he was always very clear about what he wanted. He had even flirted with Ursula, but never with Vanja. Never. And yet he always wanted to be close to her.

Billy suddenly realised that he needed to know the truth. He couldn't go around with such a strong suspicion without doing something about it.

He noticed that the needle had crept above 140 again. This time he didn't bother slowing down; the sooner they reached Torsby and got started, the better.

★ ★ ★

As they turned off to park behind Bergebyvägen 22 as per instructions, they saw a group of a dozen or so people outside the building. Cameras and microphones – journalists, Torkel thought grimly. He recognised some of the faces – Axel Weber from *Expressen*, for example. Their eyes met briefly as the black SUV swung in through the open gates. Axel stepped aside, reaching into his pocket. Ten seconds later Torkel's phone rang. 'Yes?'

'Are you in Torsby?' Weber asked without preamble.

'Maybe.'

'So what can you tell me about the murder of the Carlsten family?'

'Nothing.'

Torkel pushed open the door and got out of the car. It was good to stretch his legs after the long journey, even though all four of them had had a comfortable trip. He saw a man in his fifties emerge from a back door and walk quickly towards them.

'I haven't even met the SIO yet, so you'll have to wait a while.'

'Will you call me when you've spoken to him?'

'I shouldn't think so.' Torkel ended the call and slipped the phone into his pocket as the other man reached them.

'Erik Flodin. Thank you for coming.' He nodded to everyone and held out his hand to Torkel.

'Torkel Höglund.'

The two men shook hands, then the rest of the team introduced themselves before accompanying Flodin into the building that at first glance Torkel had assumed was a derelict car-repair workshop.

★ ★ ★

Erik led them to the cramped staffroom, apologising for the lack of coffee. He went on to say how pleased he was that Riksmord were willing to help, then quickly summarised what they knew so far about the family and the four murders. Billy, Vanja and Torkel took it all in, giving the matter their full concentration and asking questions here and there. Sebastian switched off. It was during this phase, when the local police were handing over a case, that he usually sat in the background drinking coffee, listening with half an ear. But as this godforsaken dump couldn't even provide a decent hot drink, he decided not to bother listening at all, and sat there lost in his own thoughts.

'So how do you want to do this?' Erik Flodin's voice brought him back to reality. The handover was done, and from now on Torkel was in charge.

42

'So you have a suspect – this Jan Ceder?' Vanja just wanted to clarify the situation.

'Well . . .' Erik hesitated. 'He's threatened the family in the past, but it looks as if he might have an alibi.'

Torkel got to his feet. 'Vanja and Sebastian, you take Ceder. Billy and I will go out to the scene of the crime.'

'I'll ask Fredrika to go with you,' Erik said, leaving the room. Sebastian looked at Torkel, who was gathering up his papers from the table.

Torkel and Billy.

Sebastian and Vanja.

That suited him perfectly, but was Torkel deliberately drawing a line between them? They hadn't said much to one another during those hours in the car on the way to Torsby; they had exchanged perhaps ten sentences. Sebastian tried to remember whether they usually chatted on the way to a case, and concluded that no, they didn't. The last time had been very similar, he thought – travelling from Östersund to that mountain station, whatever it was called. Besides, Torkel's decision was perfectly correct in view of their areas of expertise. Sebastian was virtually no use at a crime scene, while he and Vanja were a crack team when it came to interviewing a suspect.

However, he still felt as if they would have to talk about what had actually happened that evening at some point.

Talk about Ursula.

But not now.

★ ★ ★

They were sitting in a room that was really too small to be called an open-plan office, but it did contain five desks: four over by the windows, facing one another in pairs, and one on its own to the left of the door. Sebastian chose the latter and sat gazing idly at pictures of someone's wife and kids and childish drawings as he listened to the recording of the earlier interview with Jan Ceder.

They had already talked about threatening behaviour and a stolen shotgun; now they had moved on to insurance. Nothing of interest so far. He picked up a pencil and added a large cock to one of the drawings in front of him. He smiled to himself. Infantile but satisfying.

'*Where were you yesterday?*' Erik asked in a pleasant tone of voice; Sebastian saw Vanja's face brighten. He dropped the pencil and leaned back in his chair. He wondered if anyone would mind if he put his feet up on the desk, decided he didn't care one way or the other, and immediately got a dirty look from Erik, which he ignored.

'*Yesterday?*'

'*Yesterday.*'

'*I was in Filipstad,*' Ceder replied immediately.

'*When did you go to Filipstad?*'

'*On Tuesday evening.*'

'*And when did you return?*'

'*Today. This morning. I'd only been home for an hour or so when she came and picked me up.*'

'He means Fredrika,' Erik clarified.

Vanja nodded and jotted something down in her notebook. If that was true, Jan Ceder had been nowhere near Torsby when the murders were committed.

'*How did you get there and back?*' Erik asked on the tape.

'*I caught the 303 to Hagfors, then the 302 to Filipstad.*'

'At this point he gave us this,' Erik said, holding out a plastic bag containing a piece of paper. Vanja took it: a crumpled ticket from Värmland Transport.

A return ticket.

Outward journey the day before yesterday, return today.

'*What were you doing there?*' the interview continued.

'*I was with friends.*'

'*The whole time?*'

'*Yes, we drank quite a bit and . . . yes, the whole time.*'

'*I'll need the names and telephone numbers of these friends.*'

There was a scraping sound as Fredrika pushed a pad and pen across to Ceder.

'*What's this about, anyway?*' he asked.

There was a brief pause, as if both officers were considering how to proceed, how much to reveal, but eventually they obviously concluded that sooner or later Ceder was going to have to be told why they had brought him in for questioning.

'*The Carlsten family are dead,*' Erik said. '*Killed with a shotgun. What do you have to say about that?*'

Erik switched off the tape.

'He had nothing to say about that, at least not without a solicitor.' He removed the tape and put it back in its case, then turned to Vanja.

'Fredrika called the friends he listed, and they confirmed his alibi.'

'So why is he still here?' Sebastian wanted to know. Erik looked at him, still with a certain amount of distaste. Sebastian removed his feet from the desk, got to his feet and started to wander around the small amount of floor space available.

'I thought you said Ceder was an alcoholic with poor self-control,' he went on. 'Is that correct?' He stopped in front of Erik.

'Yes.'

'And yet you think he planned this in detail, established a false alibi, and acquired bus tickets to and from Filipstad to back up his story?'

Erik didn't respond, so Sebastian kept going.

'If he's so meticulous, then surely he wouldn't have threatened the family in broad daylight the day before he intended to go round to their house and shoot them all dead?'

'All I'm saying is that at the moment he appears to have an alibi,' Erik said grimly, failing to hide his annoyance. 'But we could still find traces of cordite or blood on his hands or clothes. If we find the missing shotgun, we can see if it matches the cartridges from the house. We haven't spoken to the Carlstens' neighbours yet; someone might have seen Ceder nearby. Then we'll be back on track.'

Sebastian shook his head; he couldn't suppress a smile.

'Or we could just go back in time, stand outside the house and see who shoots them. That sounds more realistic!'

'That's enough, Sebastian!'

Vanja stood up and Sebastian turned to face her. There was something dark in her eyes, something he recognised all too well. She was angry with him. She nailed him to the spot for a few seconds, then turned to Erik.

'I apologise – he can be such an idiot sometimes.'

'I've seen this kind of thing before,' Erik said in a softer tone, his gaze fixed on Sebastian. 'People who think we're useless just because we're not from Stockholm.'

'It's nothing to do with the fact that you live in a dump,' Sebastian explained kindly. 'Incompetence isn't all that sexy in the big city either.'

Vanja sighed to herself. She wasn't really surprised, to be honest. She knew that Sebastian didn't give a toss what anyone thought of him, but it was usually Ursula who criticised the local cops as soon as she got the chance. Sebastian's job was to make himself impossible in his dealings with witnesses and relatives; it was as if they had divided the shit-stirring up between them. But with Ursula gone, it looked as if Sebastian was taking on full responsibility for making everyone loathe them.

She gave Erik a tight little smile.

'We'd like to speak to Ceder now, if that's OK.'

Without a word Erik marched past Sebastian and out into the corridor.

★ ★ ★

A woman of about forty stood up and held out her hand as they entered the interview room.

'Flavia Albrektsson. I'm Jan Ceder's solicitor.'

Vanja introduced herself and shook hands, then sat down on the opposite side of the table.

'Flavia – that's an unusual name,' Sebastian said, holding her hand for a fraction too long – in Vanja's opinion.

'Yes.'

'And a beautiful one,' he went on, finally letting go of her hand. 'Where does it come from?'

Vanja rolled her eyes. If they had been faced with a male solicitor called Flavius, Sebastian wouldn't have given a flying fuck where the name came from.

'Perhaps we could discuss that later,' she said, keeping her tone neutral as she fixed her gaze on Sebastian.

'Let's hope so,' Sebastian said, smiling at Flavia. This time she responded in kind, and they both sat down. Sebastian weighed her up: dark hair in a bob, framing a round, open face. Discreetly made-up eyes and lips. A pearl necklace over the collar of the thin grey woollen sweater under the the jacket of her suit. Small breasts. A wedding ring. That usually meant more work; greater resistance to begin with, the outcome less certain. If he really was going to screw someone in Torsby, maybe he should start with something easier.

Vanja glanced at Sebastian; he obviously had no intention of leading the interview, so she turned her attention to the slumped figure next to the smartly dressed solicitor. He looked tired.

'Tell us about the Carlstens.'

'Tell you what?' Ceder asked with a shrug.

'What did you think of them?'

Ceder snorted and shook his head, making his opinion clear, but he obliged by putting it into words as well.

'They were tree huggers, eco-warriors, friends of the wolf, demanding toxin-free this and ecological that. They acted like cops – you could hardly piss in the forest without them complaining.'

'So you threatened Emil Carlsten outside the swimming pool.'

'I was drunk.'

'Can you tell us what you did after that?' Vanja went on, opening her notebook. 'Until the police picked you up at home.'

'He's already done that,' Flavia interjected.

'He hasn't told us his story.'

Ceder folded his arms. Took a deep breath. Started speaking.

Vanja and Sebastian listened carefully; from time to time Vanja asked a question or sought clarification. Approximately fifteen minutes later Ceder fell silent, seemingly exhausted by his efforts. He flung his arms wide to indicate that he had nothing more to say, and his chin sank down towards his chest. Vanja consulted her notes; everything he had said appeared to match his previous interview.

She gave a start as Sebastian suddenly stood up.

'The gun.'

'What about the gun?' Flavia wondered.

'That's the only part of your story I don't believe,' Sebastian said, leaning on the windowsill. 'You said it was stolen, but you didn't report it.'

'He's explained his reasons,' Flavia countered.

'I know, but I still don't believe him.' Sebastian shifted focus from Ceder to his defender. He was probably about to scupper his chances with Flavia, but it couldn't be helped.

'You said that's the only thing you don't believe.' Flavia leaned back, looking pleased. 'Does that mean you think he's innocent?'

'Yes,' Sebastian said firmly.

'So why is he sitting here?'

'Because I don't have the authority to release him.'

Flavia broke into a smile; maybe it wasn't too late after all, Sebastian thought.

'Sebastian's opinion isn't necessarily the same as that of Riksmord,' Vanja said sharply. 'He's not a police officer.'

However, she did agree with him on one point: there was a big question mark next to the issue of the shotgun in her notes too. She had picked up something false in Ceder's tone of voice at that point; it was something she was good at. Nuances. Billy sometimes referred to her as a human lie detector.

'He has an alibi,' Flavia insisted.

'Sometimes people make sure they have an alibi when they know they're going to be suspected of some offence.' Vanja closed her notebook and met the solicitor's gaze. 'The gun could still be the murder weapon, even if your client wasn't holding it himself.'

Sebastian folded his arms and leaned back; he was impressed.

'And maybe, just maybe, your client knew it was going to be used.'

A contract killing. Or a favour, more likely. Sebastian nodded to himself. Even an alcoholic with self-control problems would be able to sort that out. Ceder had lived in the area all his life; he had taken over his parents' home. He must know plenty of hunters and landowners who felt exactly the same as he did about the Carlsten family. Someone was bound to owe him a favour. Shooting an entire family was one hell of a favour, but if the Carlstens had made enemies, upset a lot of people, it wasn't an impossible scenario.

Alcohol, testosterone, the male of the species pissing to mark out his territory. Sebastian had seen stranger things.

'So I think he'll be staying here for the time being,' Vanja concluded, getting to her feet and heading for the door. Sebastian stayed where he was and watched her leave the room.

She was good. She was very good.

His daughter.

They caught the last of the daylight as they arrived at the isolated two-storey house twenty minutes outside the town. The place was a good size, and looked well maintained. Only the blue-and-white police tape gently swaying in the breeze showed that the attractive exterior was hiding a tragedy. Fredrika parked next to what Torkel assumed to be the family's white Nissan. She got out and nodded in the direction of the house. Billy pulled up, jumped out and retrieved his bag from the back seat. Torkel stayed where he was, staring at the house.

It really did look idyllic, surrounded by a meadow and a number of deciduous trees that were just coming into leaf. Slightly further away, along a track that ran parallel to the meadow, he could see several red-painted outhouses and a large greenhouse. Apparently the Carlstens ran an eco-friendly smallholding, specialising in locally produced root vegetables.

He got out of the car and walked over to the stone wall that curved around the house and the lawn. Two small bicycles, one green and one blue, were propped up against the inside of the wall; they looked well used. To the side of the lawn was a sandpit with various plastic toys perched on the wooden frame. The family seemed to have had a good life here. Lots of space and freedom to play.

A man dressed in protective clothing emerged from the house and came towards them; Erik Flodin had said that the local forensic technician would probably still be there.

'Riksmord?' the man asked Fredrika.

'Yes. Can you take care of them? I've got things to do.'

'Of course.' The man turned to Billy and they shook hands.

'Billy Rosén. This is Torkel Höglund, SIO.'

The man gave them a friendly nod.

'Fabian Hellström. Welcome.'

At least he didn't seem to have any objection to Riksmord turning up, which was a good start. Torkel had been on the receiving end of far chillier receptions in the past.

The three men set off towards the house.

'We've removed the bodies, but I took lots of photographs.'

'We saw some of them down at the station; you seem to have done a very good job,' Torkel said, and meant it. So far Erik's team hadn't put a foot wrong, as far as he could see.

'Thanks. It's a pretty big area. The perpetrator was both downstairs and upstairs, so I'm far from finished.'

'How sure are you that we're looking at a single perp?'

'Fairly sure. We've found prints from a pair of size forty-four boots all over the place.'

'And it can't be the father?'

Fabian shook his head.

'He wore size forty-six or forty-seven, and we haven't found any boots with soles that match the prints among his belongings.'

They had reached the door, and stopped to pull on shoe protectors and gloves. As soon as they walked in, Torkel saw the amount of blood on the stone floor in front of them.

'Karin Carlsten, the mother, was lying here,' Fabian explained. 'We assume she was shot first, and that she opened the door to the killer.'

Torkel nodded and took a step back. He wanted to get an overview. The door, the hallway, the blood. He realised that he was missing Ursula. Not that Billy wasn't competent, quite the reverse; he had worked closely with Ursula and had learned a great deal. There was no one Torkel would rather have had on the case, but he wasn't Ursula. No one could match her when it came to seeing that connection, that little detail that could move an investigation forwards.

'The front door was open when the little girl from next door found Karin, is that correct?' he asked after a while.

'Yes, and we haven't found any signs of forced entry on the back door or the windows so we're working on the hypothesis that the perpetrator came and went this way.'

Fabian led the way inside. There was a large kitchen at the end of the hallway; they could see an overturned chair in front of a table laid for breakfast. Blood everywhere. On the table and on the floor, even splashed across the walls several metres away. It wasn't hard to see where the victim had been lying; the seeping blood had left the outline of a small body on the rug next to the chair.

'Georg Carlsten, eight years old,' Fabian said, his voice not quite as steady as before. He pointed to the bloody trail of little bare feet leading out of the room, growing fainter as they disappeared in the direction of the staircase.

'His younger brother was here too.'

'Who the fuck does something like this?' Billy said as he crouched down to look at the footprints. 'Did the family have a lot of enemies?'

'So far we've only found one – Jan Ceder. But a lot of people thought they were a bit odd, with their green lifestyle and their ideas on the environment,' Fabian replied.

Torkel took a deep breath; he suddenly felt terrible. There was something about the little bowl of cereal on the table, all that blood; it made what had happened seem perfectly ordinary, yet at the same time so horrific.

'Whenever we see something like this it's usually to do with family conflict and custody issues,' he said.

'We haven't found anything like that,' Fabian said. 'They'd been married for twelve years. No contact with social services. Karin has a sister in Stockholm – we haven't managed to get hold of her yet. Emil was an only child, and his parents are dead.'

He pointed to a dirty mark on the floor next to the rug.

'That's the first clear print we found. There are a couple upstairs that show the whole pattern on the sole.'

Billy took a closer look.

'What size shoes does Jan Ceder wear?'

'We're in the process of finding out. The search team are at his house right now, and I've sent them a picture of the prints.'

Torkel made up his mind; he didn't need to see any more.

'OK. I'd like you two to concentrate on this place, both inside and out. Widen the search area – the perpetrator got here somehow, and I want to know how.'

Fabian tried to protest.

'I promised Erik I'd try and take a look at Ceder's house too.'

'You won't have time. Ceder's not going anywhere. This is the most important place. Update Billy on everything you've found so far, and keep everyone else out. I don't want a whole lot of people trampling around in here.'

Fabian didn't look happy, but he nodded. Torkel attempted a friendly smile as he walked towards the front door.

'Don't you want to see upstairs?' Fabian couldn't hide his surprise. 'Emil and the other boy are up there.'

Torkel shook his head.

'Show Billy. I want to find out a bit more about the family.' He turned to his colleague. 'Billy, could I have a word, please?'

'Of course.'

They stepped outside. Torkel lowered his voice and leaned closer.

'He seems OK, but double-check his findings. I'm a bit worried that they homed in on Ceder right away. They might have missed something that would lead us in a different direction.'

Billy nodded. 'No problem.'

Torkel placed a hand on Billy's shoulder to show his appreciation. Vanja had always been the unspoken favourite of the two of them, but Billy had grown a lot over the past year. He was fairly quiet and definitely wasn't as intuitive as Vanja, but he was always there when Torkel needed him.

'I know you're carrying a lot of responsibility this time, but I'm going to call Ursula and ask if she can give us some support,' Torkel said.

'But surely she's signed off sick?'

'Yes, but I think it would do her good to get back in the swing of things – just a little bit.'

'I can set up a link so she has access to all the material.'

Torkel smiled at him. As always, Billy was there when you needed him.

★ ★ ★

Torkel asked Fabian for directions to the Torsson family house, and decided to walk. On the way he called Ursula, who sounded surprisingly pleased when he asked her if she could help them out with the investigation. She made him promise to make sure Billy set up a link as soon as possible.

It was liberating to hear Ursula's voice as they discussed the case. She came to life, as if all that pent-up energy had somewhere to go. However brutal the details might be, she was more comfortable talking about concrete matters than about her feelings.

That was just the way she was.

Better with the dead than the living.

Torkel said he would call her in the evening so that they could exchange their impressions of the first day. That was how they usually worked, and he was pleased that Ursula liked the idea. He stopped. Was this the way back? Returning to what was familiar, what they had once had together? Perhaps that was where he'd gone wrong; he'd tried to change their relationship into a normal man–woman liaison. Their intimacy was built on solving cases together, not on cohabiting and being a couple like everyone else.

That was what he wanted, but she most definitely didn't.

He had to accept the truth.

The Torssons' place lay to the north behind the grove of trees at the back of the Carlsten property, and according to Fabian there was a narrow path between the two houses. That was the route Cornelia Torsson had taken when she discovered the bodies.

He found it quickly, next to the abandoned drying rack, a well-used track disappearing among the dark trees. Torkel increased his speed. It was good to be in the fresh air, inhaling the scents of the forest and clearing his head of the stench of death. In here, only a few metres from the burgeoning greenery in the Carlstens' garden, spring was nowhere near as advanced. The ground was still damp from the winter, and here and there little piles of snow remained, particularly on the shaded side of the bigger trees. He went up a slope and stopped again. About thirty metres away he could just see a yellow house. The material he had been given hadn't included much information about the Torsson family; he knew they were a couple in their forties with one daughter. The father worked in the finance department at the local council, and the mother in the health service. Their daughter often played with the Carlsten boys. They had been away visiting relatives over Easter, and had come home on Wednesday evening. The following morning Cornelia had gone over to see her friends, and found the bodies. It was a pity they hadn't been home; it wasn't very far between the houses, and they would probably have heard the shots and been able to provide an exact time for the murders. Plus their daughter would have been spared the traumatic experience of finding Karin dead in the hallway. Then again, things could have been even worse if they'd gone running over to see what was going on, or if Cornelia had already been there with the boys.

Torkel concluded that on the whole it was fortunate that the Torssons had decided to celebrate Easter elsewhere. The killer had acted with such coldness that he would have had no problem in killing more people. A lot more.

★ ★ ★

Felix Torsson opened the door; Torkel proffered his ID and was shown into the living room where Hannah and her daughter were sitting. Cornelia was clinging to her mother so tightly it looked as if she would never let her go.

'So how old are you?' Torkel asked in a friendly tone of voice when he had been introduced. 'You're nine, aren't you, sweetheart?'

Cornelia neither confirmed nor denied her age; she simply buried her head in her mother's chest.

Torkel sat down opposite the family and apologised for disturbing them. The parents nodded, looking at Torkel with a level of anticipation that was hard to misinterpret: they wanted him to help them understand. The curtains were closed, and neither the flickering candles on the low black glass coffee table nor the small glowing lamps were able to chase away the darkness and the shadows.

The silence and the pockets of gloom made Torkel think about some of the paintings he had seen in the Rijksmuseum in Amsterdam when he was there with his daughters. They had gone there for a short break during the autumn half-term holiday last year, mainly to make up for all the times Torkel hadn't been able to see them. The museum had just reopened after a lengthy period of renovation, and Vilma had managed to drag along her sceptical older sister and her slightly less sceptical dad. Torkel had been pleasantly surprised by Rembrandt, above all because of his feeling for faces in the darkness: people who were clearly carrying something within themselves, barely visible in the surrounding blackness, yet their humanity shone through. Like the Torssons . . . Felix broke the silence.

'Is there anything you can tell us?' he asked anxiously. 'Do you know who did this?'

Torkel tried to respond as neutrally as possible; he spoke calmly, sticking to the truth.

'At the moment we're trying to gain an overall picture. We're waiting for the forensic examination to be completed, but we have secured a certain amount of evidence.'

'Against Jan Ceder?' Felix said immediately. Torkel knew that rumours spread more quickly in small towns than in cities, but it was important for him to kill off any speculation as quickly as possible, and to say nothing that could add fuel to the fire.

'I can't comment on any names. We're working on a number of leads.'

'We don't know him,' Felix went on; he obviously wasn't prepared to give up that easily. 'But he's not the kind of person you'd want to hang out with, if I can put it that way. We heard he'd been arrested.'

Torkel decided to change the subject, and turned to Hannah. 'How's Cornelia?'

When she heard her name, the child burrowed into her mother's body once again. Hannah gently stroked her long blonde hair.

'Not too bad. We've been given the name of a contact in the Children's Psychiatric Support Service in Karlstad, but for the moment we're just trying to take it step by step.'

Torkel gave Hannah an encouraging smile.

'That's good. You have to let these things take their time.' He turned his attention to Cornelia, even though she still refused to look at him.

'Cornelia, I'd like to speak to your mum or dad on their own for a little while — is that OK with you?'

The girl didn't move, but Felix got to his feet.

'Come on, Cornelia, let's go up to your room.'

He picked her up gently, and she immediately wrapped her arms tightly around his neck.

'Hannah was at home when it happened, and she knew the family better than I did,' he said over his daughter's shoulder. 'I can come back down if you need me.'

'That's fine,' Torkel said. He waited until Felix and Cornelia had reached the top of the stairs before he spoke to Hannah.

'I realise all these questions are difficult, but I need more information,' he began. 'For example, has Cornelia said anything since she spoke to the police?'

Hannah shook her head firmly. 'Like what?'

'Anything at all. Has she been wondering about something, had she seen anyone at the Carlstens', had the boys mentioned anything that had come back to her?'

'No, she's been very quiet.' Hannah's eyes filled with tears. 'I hate myself for not going with her. I used to, but since last summer we've let her go on her own. She wanted to feel grown up.'

Torkel remained silent; there wasn't much else he could do. Hannah had to work through this on her own. He was about to bring the conversation back to the Carlstens when Hannah went on:

'Do you think it's safe for us to stay here?' she said, anxiety etched on her face. She had managed to suppress her fear when her daughter was in her arms, but now she didn't need to be brave.

It was a difficult question to answer. Torkel's experience told him that the murders next door were specifically targeted at the Carlsten family; it was unlikely that the killer would return and attack the neighbours. But of course he couldn't give any guarantees.

'I really don't think you're in any danger, but I can't be sure. If it will make you feel better, you can go away for a few days – just let me know where I can reach you.'

He took out his card and passed it to Hannah. She looked relieved, and he knew that she would follow his advice. However, he couldn't let the family go just yet.

'Did you know the Carlstens well?'

'I was probably the neighbour who knew them best, mainly because Cornelia loved the boys. They were good people, but a little bit different.'

'In what way?'

'They were really nice, honestly they were, but they did rub some people up the wrong way. They stuck out, if you know what I mean. They were from Stockholm, and there was a feeling that they were too fond of sounding off about the environment and so on.' Hannah seemed to appreciate the opportunity to talk about something else; some of the colour had returned to her face. 'That business of filming Jan Ceder and the wolf, for ex- ample. You don't do that kind of thing if you live here. Even if you don't like the person. That put people's backs up.'

'Are you thinking of anyone other than Ceder?'

Hannah thought for a moment.

'I mean, I'm not suggesting he . . . murdered them, but Emil made a complaint to the police about the boatyard down by the lake. Ove Hanson's place. They could be a bit argumentative, particularly Emil, but we never had any problem with them. Never.'

Torkel took out his notebook and wrote down:

HANSON / BOATYARD / EMIL?

'OK, good. Anything else?'

'Not that I can remember, and now I've made it sound as if there was something wrong with them.'

'No, you haven't. You just told me what you know, and that's what I need.'

Hannah suddenly looked sad again.

'It's so difficult. I mean, when it comes down to it, we agreed with them. I love nature too, it's just that sometimes they were a bit naïve . . . You have to fit in, don't you?'

Torkel nodded. Hannah gazed into space for a moment before she went on. It was clear that she felt guilty for even thinking anything bad about the family that had been murdered.

'They were such good people. They worked so hard. Their place was really run down when they took it on – they reno-vated the house, improved the garden and so on. And now . . . now they're gone . . .'

Torkel didn't know what to say, but one thing he was sure of. He needed to find out more about the Carlstens.

★ ★ ★

Torkel took the long way back to the scene of the crime.

The gravel track between the houses had been laid quite recently, and the pale grey stones crunched beneath his feet. He called Eva Blomstedt in the records office and asked her to do a search on Emil and Karin Carlsten. She quickly found two con-victions from 1994 and 1995; both involved trespass and criminal damage, and had resulted in fines and an order to pay compensa-tion. Evidently Emil was – or had been – a member of the Animal Liberation Front, a fairly militant animal-rights organisation, and had taken part in two attacks on mink farms in Östergötland. On both occasions they had managed to release hundreds of mink from their cages. Emil was only twenty-one in 1995, and there was no record of any criminal activity since then. The sins of youth. Torkel thanked Eva for her help and decided to call Björn Nordström in Säpo, the national security police. They had met at a Christmas party a few years earlier, and Björn had told Torkel that he'd just been asked to monitor the activities of militant animal-rights groups in Sweden. Hopefully he would be able to provide information on Emil off the record, preferably some indication as to whether Torkel ought to request more details through the formal and much slower route.

Björn didn't pick up, so Torkel left him a brief message.

He had reached the crossroads where the main road to Torsby met the smaller dirt tracks that snaked around the area. Torsby was to the right, the Carlsten house to the left. He could see Billy and Fabian crouching at the bottom of the steps, and decided not to disturb them. With Billy on site he could be sure of getting a full report on anything they might find. Instead he headed over to another neighbour. The Bengtssons lived further along the road leading straight ahead. According to the report they had been at home, but had heard and seen nothing. However, the interview had been extremely brief, and there was no information about their relationship with the Carlstens.

The route led across several extensive fields surrounded by last year's long yellow grass; some had already been ploughed, and in an enclosed pasture a group of horses were kicking up their heels, throwing off the confines of winter. There was no sign of a house, but he assumed the horses belonged to the Bengtssons, so it couldn't be too far away.

Björn Nordström called him back just as Torkel spotted a group of buildings: a red house and two barns. The place looked a lot more run down than either the Torsson or Carlsten properties. Björn apologised; he was up in Härjedalen with his family, and didn't have access to his computer. However, he had never heard of Emil Carlsten, so it was unlikely that he was particularly active, or played a central role in any of the militant animal-rights movements. Björn promised to check once he was back – or was it urgent? Torkel thought for a moment. Carlsten's last conviction was in 1995, there was nothing in Erik Flodin's notes about animal rights . . . no, it probably wasn't urgent. They chatted for a little longer; Björn had heard about the brutal murders, and wished Torkel well with the investigation.

By the time they ended the call, Torkel had reached the yard. The house itself looked empty and in darkness, and there was no car outside. Well, not one that was fit to drive. There were a couple of wrecks next to the largest barn, with doors missing and windscreens shattered. The whole place was overgrown with nettles, and the closer he got to the house, the more evidence he saw of a total lack of maintenance. The white paint on the window frames was flaking off, and in several places there were clear signs of damp on the wooden facade.

He tried the bell, but it didn't seem to work; at any rate he couldn't hear anything when he pressed his ear to the door. He knocked, but to no avail. They weren't home. He jotted down a message on the back of his card and dropped it in the mailbox on passing.

It was dark now, and chilly. He should have brought the car, he thought. It was easy to make a mistake in the early spring; everyone forgot how cold it got as soon as the sun went down. He zipped up his jacket and set off for the Carlstens' house. With a bit of luck Billy would have finished and they could head back.

Sebastian opened the window and looked out into the garden. Riksmord had taken four of the seven rooms in the yellow fin-de-siècle hotel which, according to the talkative lady on reception, was originally built as an extensive private residence known locally as the Palm House, because there was a palm tree two storeys high in the foyer. It had then been divided between several families before becoming an officers' camp for a while; it was finally converted into a hotel at the end of the 1940s, blah blah blah. Sebastian couldn't even bring himself to feign interest.

With the clear night air pouring in, he sat down on the bed, picked up the remote and switched on the TV.

Someone was singing.

He had no idea who it was or what they were warbling, but he left it on and lay down, gazing at the wall at the foot of the bed. The wallpaper was covered in little blue flowers, but they were so close together and their outlines were somehow so blurred that it looked as if an alien with blue blood had exploded in the middle of the room. White curtains, a white bedside table with a brass lamp, a desk. A white door leading into the bathroom. Sebastian guessed that 'cosy' and 'family feeling' had been the keywords when the room was decorated.

He was restless.

That familiar sensation.

With a simple cure.

However, not even sex was sufficiently appealing. He would have to go out, find a restaurant, buy drinks, make small talk, possibly even go dancing. It was too much like hard work, with the risk that the return might not be worth the effort. If it had been straightforward, he might have gone for it, but when he had spoken to Flavia after the interview, asked her whether she knew of a good restaurant in the area and if she would perhaps like to join him there – if not for dinner then at least for an after-work drink – she had made it very clear that her husband was waiting for her at home.

He had sat through a brief meeting at the police station when Torkel and Billy got back, heard more about the scene of the crime and the Carlsten family, but they really had nothing to work on. They had decided to make a fresh start first thing tomorrow when they were due to see the prosecutor, then they had all come back to the hotel.

On the way Sebastian had observed Torkel a little more closely. He had seemed subdued; perhaps the crime scene had affected him, but it was more likely to be Ursula. When they were out on a job her absence became even more palpable. Torkel had also informed the team that he intended to involve her in the investigation by giving her access to all data and images.

He hadn't chatted much to anyone, but he hadn't said a single word to Sebastian. Was it time to tackle the situation? It was one thing not talking about what had happened when they hardly ever met, but now they were going to be in each other's company 24/7. Did he have anything to gain by bringing it up?

Whatever.

He couldn't just lie here staring at the wall. If he wasn't going to go out on the pull, he might as well go and speak to Torkel.

★ ★ ★

Torkel opened the door a second after Sebastian had knocked, as if he had been standing just inside. Without a word he turned away. Sebastian walked in, closed the door and stopped dead. He couldn't quite take in what he was seeing. The walls seemed to be attacking him.

Flowers, flowers and more flowers.

Everywhere.

Not small and discreet like the ones in his room, but great big gaudy bunches that made him think of the folk art of Dalarna. And they were so close together – as if a Carl Larsson wannabe on acid had gone crazy with his brush.

'This is lovely,' he said with a nod at the walls, guessing that 'personal' and perhaps 'summery' had been the keywords for this room.

'What do you want?' Torkel was unpacking the suitcase lying on his bed.

'What do you think I want?'

Torkel walked past Sebastian with two shirts and hung them in the wardrobe behind the door.

'I was wondering if you wanted to talk about Ursula,' Sebastian went on, addressing his back.

'With you?' Torkel closed the wardrobe door and turned to his colleague.

'She was shot in my apartment.'

'And what was she doing there?' Torkel almost spat out the words. He sounded more jealous than he had intended, but that was what he wanted to know.

That was what had been gnawing away at him.

Eating him up from the inside.

He loved Ursula. She was divorced now. Suddenly there was the chance of a proper relationship. He was no good at being alone, he never had been. He longed to be part of a couple.

He longed for Ursula.

And then she had been shot. Almost taken away from him. In Sebastian Bergman's apartment, for God's sake.

'We were just having dinner,' Sebastian said, wondering what Ursula had told Torkel about her reasons for being in his apartment. Surely she hadn't told him the truth? Not that there was much to tell; they hadn't slept together. But they were going to – that night. If only Ellinor hadn't turned up with her lunacy and her Glock. Ursula wouldn't have said anything to Torkel, would she? She was good at keeping secrets – on a par with Sebastian. Maybe even better.

'Was she in the habit of having dinner with you?' Torkel asked, trying to achieve a neutral tone. But there it was again, the jealousy. He just couldn't help it. All those times he had invited Ursula to dinner; she had always turned him down.

'No. Now and again, but no, it wasn't a regular thing.'

Sebastian fell silent. He was beginning to wish he'd gone to the pub instead, but this had to be done. It was time. Torkel stood there staring at him, clearly expecting Sebastian to continue.

'I think it was all that business of her divorce from Micke,' Sebastian ventured. 'I suppose she needed someone to talk to.'

'And she chose you instead of me.'

'It was easier, I guess. I mean, she's a smart woman. She must have known how you felt about her, and . . . nothing was ever going to happen with me. She was . . . safe.'

Sebastian gave a little shrug as if to accentuate how innocent it had all been. Ursula might be more adept at keeping secrets but nobody was a better liar than him, Sebastian thought smugly as he directed his most honest and open gaze at Torkel, who couldn't suppress a scornful smile.

'Dinner at your place? Safe?' He moved back to the bed to finish unpacking. 'Have you ever had dinner with a woman and not gone to bed with her afterwards? Or before? Or during?'

That was true, to be fair. Dinner was foreplay. Sometimes stimulating and enjoyable, sometimes a necessary evil. Sebastian glanced at Torkel. They had been friends once upon a time.

He didn't feel it was necessary to find their way back to that relationship, but it would be nice if Torkel wasn't quite so overtly hostile. When Sebastian had returned to Riksmord after an absence of many years, Torkel had sought openness and mutual trust; Sebastian decided to go for it.

'We once had a relationship, Ursula and I.' He saw Torkel stiffen. 'A relationship like the one you had. Years ago. Back in the nineties.'

Torkel carried on putting away his clothes in silence. Sebastian watched him. Had it been a mistake to bring this up? Once again, it was time.

'She was married to Micke, but . . .' Sebastian cleared his throat. 'She finished it when she found out I'd slept with her sister.'

Torkel turned around, his expression suggesting that he couldn't possibly have heard Sebastian correctly.

'You slept with her sister?'

'Barbro, yes.'

'Is that why they don't speak to each other?'

Sebastian nodded. 'You know Ursula,' he said, taking a step closer to Torkel. 'Do you really think she'd be interested in me in that way after what I'd done?'

Torkel didn't respond.

'You know how she reacted when I turned up in Västerås,' Sebastian went on. He was surer of himself now – definitely on the right track. 'The very fact that she was prepared to have dinner with me was more than I ever dared hope for.'

Torkel stared at him, looking for any sign of a lie. Sebastian was well aware that Torkel thought he had let him down many, many times, but there was no doubt that he would regard this as the worst betrayal of all; their fragile friendship would never survive.

'If you're lying about this I will never forgive you,' Torkel said, confirming Sebastian's conclusion. Sebastian nodded to show that he understood perfectly, and decided to take it one step further. He placed a heavy hand on Torkel's shoulder.

'I'm sorry,' he said, surprising himself with how sincere he sounded. 'For everything. For the way things have turned out.'

Torkel glanced down at the hand, then at Sebastian's face.

'Have you told Ursula that?'

'I've only seen her once since . . . well, you know.'

'Yes, I do know. She told me.'

When Sebastian had gone back to his room, Torkel sank down on the bed. That had been an unexpected conversation. Unexpected, but welcome. Riksmord hadn't led an active investigation since the discovery of the bodies in the mountain grave. The intervening period had given them time to think. A great deal. And it had given time for emotions to surface.

Rage.

Loss.

Jealousy.

Following Sebastian's short visit, Torkel realised that whatever he had gone through, it was still better than the burden Sebastian was so clearly carrying.

Guilt.

Billy was sitting at the computer, naked apart from a towel wrapped around his waist as he sweated off a ten-kilometre run. He had been in the shower when his phone rang: one missed call and a message from Maya. He called her back without listening to his voicemail; it turned out that she had put various suggestions for flower arrangements in his Dropbox, and wanted Billy's opinion.

As he waited for the connection to the hotel's Wi-Fi he had told her a little bit about the case, and she had asked about Vanja and Sebastian. Although she had met Vanja only in passing, she was very interested in her future husband's friend and colleague; she was convinced that Vanja would benefit from therapy costing approximately the same amount as a small country's GDP. Billy filled her in on the latest news, but didn't share his suspicions about the family tie between Sebastian and Vanja.

Then he had opened Dropbox. Thirteen pictures of different flower arrangements that all looked like . . . different flower arrangements. Did she really expect him to have an opinion on this kind of stuff? Sometimes he thought she asked him just to make him feel as if he was a part of it all, when in fact she was perfectly happy to make the decision herself. Like now. But they still went through the routine.

She said: 'Are you sure?'

He said: 'Absolutely.'

She said: 'I'll choose, then.'

He said: 'Good idea.'

She said: 'You're a star.'

He agreed.

When they had ended the call, Billy made all the necessary preparations to allow Ursula to be a part of the investigation. He downloaded all the relevant material, then created a page, encrypted and password protected. Then he sent the password to Ursula with a short message saying that they all missed her, and he hoped she was feeling better. He could have called her, of course, but for one thing he and Ursula didn't really have that kind of relationship, and for another he honestly didn't know what to say to her.

When he had finished he glanced at the clock at the bottom of the screen. Too early to go to bed. Early next morning he would sort out the room they had been allocated at the police station, but until then there wasn't much he could do.

His thoughts turned once again to Vanja. And Sebastian. Knowing was one thing, proving it was something else. Nor did he have any idea what he would do with the information if his suspicions were confirmed, but right now the feeling of knowing but not knowing was annoying him. Like an itch he couldn't quite reach. He wanted certainty, for his own sake.

He googled 'paternity test': 24,300 results. He clicked on the top link: 'DNA Paternity Test – 100% accurate! kr.1395' filled the screen. He began to read. You paid up front, then they sent out a test kit. Two oral swabs per subject, which must be rubbed on the inside of the mouth for thirty seconds to collect cheek cells. That was a problem; there could be no voluntary swabbing. Billy closed that page and clicked on another link; this one offered 99.9% accuracy thanks to the world's most renowned DNA laboratory, but the method was the same. Billy was just about to leave the page when he noticed a rubric on the side menu: 'Alternative methods'.

He clicked on the heading and the first line raised his spirits significantly. 'If you are not able to use the swabs included in our test kit, you can send in a DNA sample using an alternative method, for example a toothbrush, or a used cotton bud or tissue.'

Billy carried on reading with growing interest.

On the outside she was shivering.

Things had improved slightly after she had eaten, but the April night was not warm.

After dark she had stayed close to the road, and had seen the lights of a petrol station. Keeping her head down, she had gone inside and waited until the boy on the till was busy with a customer. She had grabbed two wraps and a yogurt drink from the chilled counter; when you were hungry you needed proper food, not sweets. She had shoved everything into her pockets and slipped out. No one had called out to her or tried to follow her as she disappeared into the darkness once more.

★ ★ ★

On the inside the emptiness and silence seemed to be growing.

Or perhaps she was getting smaller. In spite of the fact that she still didn't know where she was or how she had got there, she felt safe and secure. The cold couldn't reach her here. Not even the darkness had managed to penetrate whatever was protecting the place that was not a place.

And still there was silence.

She was silent. Somehow that seemed even more important now. Perhaps the place would be able to cope with words from outside, but not from her. It would collapse, and she would not survive. She would never say anything again. Never. Not to anyone. She made herself that promise.

On the inside.

★ ★ ★

70

On the outside it was difficult to make her way through the forest in the darkness. She tripped and fell several times.

Got back up again. Kept on going.

Then she reached a dirt road. The main road was to the left – and to the right? It must lead somewhere. She had spent last night outdoors; it would be nice if she didn't have to do that again.

She followed the road that was actually little more than a track churned up by the wheels of some vehicle, and after a few minutes she reached an iron gate between two posts. No fence on either side. Behind an enormous rhododendron she could just see a house. No lights on. No car parked outside.

She crept all the way around it twice, then picked up a stone and threw it through the window of the veranda door before slipping back into the gloom and waiting for a reaction that never came.

★ ★ ★

It was cold inside the house, but not as cold as outside.

She sat down on the floor and ate one of the wraps – roast beef. She would save the other one until morning, along with half the yogurt drink. Then she went into the kitchen. The fridge was empty, but she found some tins in one of the cupboards. Tuna, chopped tomatoes, glacé cherries. She put them in her jacket pocket.

She wasn't really thinking. Just acting. She wasn't thinking very much any more. For long periods she didn't think at all.

Good. She didn't want to think.

Didn't want to remember.

She went into one of the rooms and found two beds. It smelled of dust and summer cottage. She pulled off the duvet and the pillow and crawled right under one of the beds with them, pressing her back against the wall.

Made herself small.

As small as she was on the inside.

The dream.

That bloody dream.

He didn't have it quite so often these days; sometimes he even managed to convince himself that he'd shaken it off. That it had gone. But it always came back.

Just like now.

Sabine like a bundle of pure energy on his shoulders. Walking down towards the sea; she wanted to play in the cool water. The air was humid, sticky. There was a little girl with an inflatable dolphin. Sabine's last words:

'Daddy, I want one of those.'

The sea. Splashing around. Laughter.

The shouts from the beach.

The roar.

The wall of water.

Her little hand in his, the thought that he must never, ever let go. All his strength, all his concentration. Focus. His whole life, there in his right hand.

Sebastian threw back the covers and went into the bathroom. Screwed up his eyes at the harsh fluorescent light as he had a pee, and slowly, painfully straightened out the fingers of his right hand.

The hand that had suddenly been empty.

The hand that had let go of his daughter.

He flushed the toilet and went back into the bedroom. The clock on the TV showed 04:40. He knew sleep was out of the question, so he got dressed and went outside. The sun wouldn't rise for another hour or so; there wasn't a soul in sight. He crossed the street and walked down towards the water, following the shoreline until he reached a road, the E16 / E45. Carried on along the water's edge.

The dream.

That bloody dream.

He knew why it had come back. Even though he had done his best to stay away from the pictures of the crime scene, and tuned out during the handover, there was no getting away from the fact that this case involved murdered children.

Again.

Just like last time.

He shouldn't have anything to do with dead children. He couldn't handle it any more.

After about half an hour he turned and followed the same route back to the hotel. A quick shower, then down to the dining room. He helped himself from the buffet, then went into the inner room. Somebody certainly loved floral patterns on the walls; this time the blooms were black on a white background. He chose a table for two and sat down.

As he was pouring his second cup of coffee Vanja came in and glanced around, looking for a familiar face. She gave Sebastian a little smile, then went to get her breakfast. She looked tired, Sebastian thought. That seemed to be her default setting these days: exhausted and joyless. The rift with the person who had meant the most to her throughout her entire life had left its mark.

Sebastian ought to be pleased; he had wanted her to distance herself from Valdemar since the day he had found out she was his daughter, but he was keeping a low profile, very conscious of what she had said about choosing to trust him, about not being able to fight the whole world right now. That could change very quickly, particularly if she found out about all the things he'd done.

'Did you sleep well?' he asked as she sat down opposite him.

'Not bad. How about you?'

'Like a baby,' he lied.

They chatted about this and that while they ate breakfast. On the way out they met Billy on his way in; he had been to the station to set up 'the smallest room in the world', as he called it. He offered them a lift if they could wait ten minutes while he grabbed something to eat, but they declined; they had already decided to walk.

Had Billy given them a funny look when they said that, or was it just Sebastian's imagination? Billy was the member of the team he knew least. Admittedly Billy had accepted Sebastian's presence right from the start – unlike Vanja and Ursula – but they hadn't grown any closer during Sebastian's time with Riksmord.

Billy had had a tough time. He had killed two people – all in the line of duty, of course, but even so.

Two internal investigations. Completely vindicated both times.

However, Sebastian found it difficult to believe that Billy was as unaffected as he tried to appear. He wasn't exactly the strong, silent, hard man. Sebastian had offered his services as a counsellor after the second shooting, but Billy had turned him down.

As they headed towards Bergebyvägen 22, Sebastian asked Vanja if she had noticed anything odd about Billy.

'No, he's just the same as always. Why do you ask?'

Sebastian changed the subject.

Just the same as always.

That was what he was afraid of.

That was what seemed strange, given that Billy had killed two people.

★ ★ ★

Ursula was at St Erik's eye hospital by nine o'clock in the morning to meet the prosthetics specialist her consultant had recommended, and to try out possible medical aids. The term annoyed her; this was a cosmetic exercise after all, rather than something that would bring about a medical improvement. However, the doctor insisted that a prosthetic eye was preferable to the alternative, which was to stitch up the socket. According to him, an ocular prosthesis, to give it its fancy name, also helped to speed up the patient's psychological rehabilitation. Apparently he had had positive experiences with patients who, like her, had been vehemently opposed to the idea to begin with. Personally, Ursula thought he was exaggerating her negativity. She had lost an eye, and felt no need to hide that from the world; she had also started to get used to the idea of having her right eye covered. At first she had suffered from terrible headaches, but she didn't know if that was because of the injury, or because her left eye was having to work twice as hard. Probably a bit of both. Now she only got a headache occasionally, and she was able to read fairly easily, or at least for about an hour and a half before she felt tired. However, her consultant insisted, and in the end Ursula agreed at least to go and see the technician, who turned out to be a young woman named Zeineb. She spent fifteen minutes calmly measuring the volume, width and depth of Ursula's eye socket, then recommended an acrylic prosthesis. She explained that it would be both resilient and easy to look after. Ursula had no opinion on the material, but surprised herself by staying and chatting rather than taking her leave. There was something about Zeineb's direct approach that touched her. The consultant had given her a diagnosis, a precise clinical description of the effects of her injuries. Torkel was someone who tried to be there for her, but never dared to mention what was behind the white compress. Zeineb provided her with something different: a liberating, matter-of-fact approach to the situation, almost as if they were two friends chatting about hairstyles or earrings rather than the gaping hole in her face.

The longer they talked, the more she had to admit that her consultant might have had a point. Perhaps covering the wound with a bandage and assuming that life went on was not enough to find her way back completely. Perhaps that was why the prosthetic was referred to as a medical aid – because it helped people.

Ursula wasn't sure if that was true, but she did know that she was already looking forward to seeing Zeineb again in two weeks' time to start trying out her new eye.

She felt really happy when she got home, and had lots of energy. Torkel had called her mobile, which she had left at home. No message, but she suspected she knew what he wanted.

What he always wanted.

But it no longer bothered her. She actually liked the fact that he didn't do anything to surprise her.

Unlike Sebastian Bergman.

He had visited her once in the hospital. Once. In spite of the fact that she had been shot in his apartment, by his ex-girlfriend. Once.

Even though she knew he tried to avoid anything that was difficult or painful, she was surprised. Astonished. However, with hindsight she had to admit that she had surprised herself too. She had almost made the same mistake all over again, the mistake she had made all those years ago. She had started to develop feelings for him.

Last time it had ended when he slept with her sister.

This time she had nearly died.

There wouldn't be a third time, however much he tried; she would make sure of that. But she was the one who had let it happen. She was the one who had opened the door and let him. That was the first thing she had to face up to: there was something about him that she found incredibly attractive. They had a complex relationship; like everything else in life, it wasn't simply black or white. There were so many things she liked about Sebastian – his intellect, his unconventional way of looking at the world, his ability to find a way out of any problem. But above all, the two of them were so alike. Both equally lonely. Both constantly searching for a love they would destroy in minutes.

If he had been the one who was badly injured, maybe she would have visited him only once. Further visits would simply have increased the burden, and carrying burdens wasn't something either she or Sebastian went in for.

They moved on.

Ursula sat down at the computer and logged on. There was a lot of material; most of it must have been gathered before

Riksmord took over, but she recognised Billy's hand in the organisation of files and folders.

Clear, easily accessible.

She began with Erik Flodin's preliminary reports from the scene of the crime; they were pretty good. Admittedly she would have liked more wide-angle shots from the house; the photographer had tended to concentrate on close-ups, but on the other hand there were enough to give her a decent overview. She began with the first victim, Karin Carlsten.

Karin, the mother, with a huge hole in her chest.

Thirty-nine pictures of Karin alone.

Six hundred and ninety-five pictures in total, plus the written reports.

It was going to be a long day.

It might not be the world's smallest room, but it certainly wasn't large. Fourteen square metres. Sixteen, perhaps, Torkel guessed as he arrived with Malin Åkerblad. Six people gathered around the oval table in the centre felt like at least two too many. Torkel introduced Malin to everyone, then reached across for one of the cups of coffee from Statoil. Someone had had the sense to bring in coffee rather than relying on the useless machine in the staff-room. He glanced at the newspapers strewn across the surface of the table; the local morning papers and both national tabloids had the Carlsten family murders on the front page.

'I've given Malin a copy of our notes, but we'll just do a quick verbal run-through,' Torkel said when he had settled down. He nodded to Billy, who put down his cup and got to his feet. On the wall behind him they could see the results of his early-morning work: a timeline, photographs from the scene, extracts from the interviews with the neighbours, and a map.

'The girl from next door – Cornelia Torsson – came over to the Carlsten house, which is here. It was nine o'clock on Thursday morning. She found the door open, and Karin Carlsten lying dead just inside. She ran straight home, her parents called the police, and the whole family was found shot dead.'

'The preliminary report indicates that they were killed at some point during Wednesday morning,' Vanja added. 'Probably with a shotgun.'

Malin merely nodded, as if this confirmed what she already knew.

'The only forensic evidence so far is a shoeprint,' Billy went on. 'Size forty-four.'

'And it's not the father's?' Malin asked. Vanja was struck by her deep voice; on the phone she could easily have been mistaken for a man. She caught herself wondering if Sebastian found it sexy; she glanced at him, but there was no reaction. He was resting his chin on the palm of his hand, and appeared to be having a little nap.

'No, he's a size forty-seven,' Billy said, returning to his seat. 'That's what we've got so far.' He gave a little shrug, as if to apologise for the paucity of the material. Malin nodded again and made a note on the papers in front of her.

'We haven't got much out of the neighbours we've managed to speak to,' Torkel said, taking over. 'The Carlstens were well liked, but several people have mentioned that their commitment to environmental issues could sometimes be seen as a little . . . trying.'

'In what way?'

'There was a perception that they meddled with things that had nothing to do with them, that they were rather over-zealous. The fact that they were incomers didn't help, even though it's twelve years since they moved to Torsby.'

'But no direct threats?'

'Not as far as we can tell,' Billy replied. 'Apart from Jan Ceder, but we already know about him.'

'I will be releasing him immediately after this meeting.' Malin's statement was so matter-of-fact that she could have been telling them what she'd had for breakfast this morning; the silence that followed suggested that most people thought they must have misheard. Even Sebastian woke up and gave the prosecutor a dubious look. It was left to Torkel to vocalise their concerns.

'You're going to release him?'

'Yes.'

'We'd prefer to keep him for a while.' In his own special way, Torkel managed to make this sound like a humble request and an order at the same time.

'Why?' Malin had clearly chosen to ignore the order aspect.

'He has an alibi.'

'He also has a shotgun he's unable to account for,' Vanja said, pretending not to notice Torkel's frown. She knew perfectly well that he always spoke for the team when dealing with outsiders, but releasing Ceder was such an idiotic move that she couldn't keep quiet.

'It's been stolen,' Malin snapped, looking Vanja straight in the eye.

'He *says* it's been stolen.'

'You haven't come up with any evidence to the contrary.'

Vanja wondered what could possibly be behind such an ill-considered decision. Apart from sheer incompetence, and Malin didn't give the impression of being incompetent. Which left only one possibility; it wasn't her place to ask, it would undoubtedly come across as an accusation, and Torkel definitely wouldn't like it, but she couldn't help herself.

'Do you know him? Personally, I mean?' Vanja wondered.

'Are you insinuating that I would act unprofessionally, or do you think everybody knows everybody around here because this isn't Stockholm?'

'At least in Stockholm we would have been allowed to hold him for ninety-six hours,' Vanja persisted stubbornly.

'But not here. And to answer your question – no, I do not know Jan Ceder personally. If I did, I wouldn't be working on this investigation.'

Malin looked down at her papers again, then turned to Billy.

'Jan Ceder's shoe size is forty-one. The print you found in the house was size forty-four, is that correct?'

'Forty-three or forty-four,' he confirmed quietly, well aware that this didn't exactly improve their case. Malin nodded with satisfaction and glanced at Erik, who was sitting next to Sebastian and hadn't said a word so far.

'Erik, you know Ceder. Is there any risk that he might abscond?'

Erik had asked if he could sit in on the meeting, and had been delighted when Torkel said yes; the chance of seeing at close quarters how Riksmord worked was too good to miss. He didn't really want to upset anyone, but in this situation it was impossible to please both sides, so he cleared his throat and opted for the truth.

'I don't know him either, but I'd say with his limited resources, and taking everything else into account, the risk of him taking off is minimal.'

Once again Malin gave that smug little smile which Vanja already loathed. To be honest, there wasn't much she liked about Malin Åkerblad so far. Nothing, in fact.

'He could destroy evidence,' Billy spoke up.

'I gave you a search warrant for his home,' Malin shot back. 'You've had twenty-four hours. If there's any evidence left to destroy, that means you haven't done your job.'

Nobody answered. Malin Åkerblad obviously wasn't going for Miss Popularity, Torkel thought.

'So tell me what grounds we have to justify depriving him of his freedom at this stage.' Malin's gaze swept around the table. No one said a word.

'OK, in that case I shall release him.'

The fat cop who had picked him up the previous day drove him home. He couldn't remember her name, and it didn't really matter. She concentrated on the road, and hadn't said a word since asking whether he wanted to sit in the front or the back as they walked to the patrol car.

No, that was wrong.

She had said 'Face' and passed him a newspaper as they waited for the gates to open. He hadn't understood what she meant until he saw people running towards them from the front of the police station, several of them holding cameras. He could see the flashes long before they were anywhere near the car. He covered his face with the paper, hearing a barrage of questions mixed with the frantic clicking of the cameras as they slowly drove past the reporters. They turned onto the main road, and since then there had been silence inside the car.

Which suited him perfectly. His father had brought him up to distrust authority in general and the police in particular. Fucking bastards whose sole aim is to make life difficult for ordinary people. Of course what had happened was terrible.

The murders.

An entire family.

Two innocent little boys.

But there was no way Gustav Ceder's son was going to sit making small talk with a cop. And a woman cop, to add insult to injury. Jan stole a glance at her. A uniform and a gun. Not exactly feminine. She was probably a lesbian. The TV and the papers kept trying to convince him that girls could play football; lesbians, the lot of them. In the Ceder household men had been raised to be men, and the women knew their place. That was the natural order of things. Biology. If God had meant men and women to be equal, he wouldn't have made men so superior. But of course you couldn't say that in this country any more.

He gazed out of the side window. Where the fields came to an end, the sun was reflected in the deep blue water of Lake Velen, where he often went fishing. Not necessarily legally. He would soon be home; another ten minutes or so. He let his mind wander.

Everyone he had spoken to over the past twenty-four hours had gone on and on about the missing shotgun. The first two cops, the fat dyke and her boss or whoever he was, had thought it was a strange coincidence, but the two from Stockholm had come straight out and said they didn't believe him.

Obviously he wasn't quite such a good liar as he had thought.

Another reason to be glad of the silence.

★ ★ ★

Jan Ceder stood outside his house and watched the police car disappear. The dog had started barking as soon as they turned into the drive, and he walked across to the pen. The Norwegian elkhound hurled himself at the chicken wire as Jan approached. Hungry, of course. Jan opened the lid of the sand box he had stolen down in Torsby a few years earlier and took out the bucket of dog food.

When he had fed the dog and given him clean water, he went indoors, took off his heavy boots and hung up his jacket next to his snowmobile overalls. Then he went into the kitchen. He glanced at the pile of unwashed dishes on his way to the fridge and a cold beer, and decided to ignore it. He opened the bottle, took several swigs, and put it down on the scratched Formica table by the window. The curtains had been untouched since his mother died thirteen years ago.

He sat down and opened up his laptop. The thin, modern computer didn't really look as if it belonged in the cramped kitchen; the half-panelled walls, the patterned orange wallpaper and the dark green cupboard doors screamed 1970s.

Jan checked his emails; he had had an answer from russian-babes.ua. He took another swig of beer, then began to read. There were plenty of fake sites out there, plenty of con artists, but this site had been recommended by a friend, and he knew it was genuine. He had found Nesha there, and now he was in touch with Ludmila from Kiev. They had started corresponding just over two months ago, and now they were discussing the possibility of Ludmila coming over. She was the youngest of four, with three older brothers. She used to work in a paper factory, but had had to leave to look after her mother, who had died six months ago. Now she was unemployed, with nothing to keep her in the Ukraine. She wasn't afraid of hard work. She had run the household for many years even before her mother fell ill, and had looked after her brothers until they left home. She seemed to be made of different stuff from Nesha, who thought the house outside Torsby was too small, too old-fashioned, too far from town, and had constantly badgered him for money. Jan read through Ludmila's message: a brief summary of what she had been doing since she last wrote, followed by a few lines about how much she was longing to see him, how happy and grateful she was that they were in touch, how she hoped that they could be together very soon.

That was the problem.

The flight from Kiev wasn't exactly free. Jan had been putting it off for a while for that very reason, but perhaps an opportunity had arisen now.

His shotgun hadn't been stolen.

He had lent it to someone.

Before Christmas. He had no real use for it; he hunted almost exclusively with a rifle. Of course there was no reason to assume that his gun had been used in the murder of the Carlsten family – there were plenty of shotguns in the area. The killings could be to do with infidelity or gambling debts or drugs or whatever the hell else people got murdered for, but if someone local had simply had enough of them, then there weren't too many candidates.

And one of them had borrowed his shotgun before Christmas.

He would just have to feel his way. Take it step by step. Bring the conversation around to the murders, gauge the reaction. Find out if it might possibly be worth his while not to reveal who had borrowed his shotgun. Even if he was on the wrong track, the person concerned might pay to avoid being dragged into the police investigation.

His train of thought was interrupted by the sound of the dog barking again, and a few seconds later he heard a car pull up outside the house. He couldn't see it through the kitchen window, and not just because it hadn't been cleaned since Nesha did it eighteen months ago; in fact whoever it was had driven the car as close as possible to the house and parked around the corner. Had the fat cop forgotten something and come back? Jan went into the living room and looked out of the window. Speak of the devil . . . He recognised the car.

And the person walking towards his house.

Carrying Jan's borrowed shotgun.

'Have you let him go?'

Pia had called Erik three times before he had the chance to get back to her. Everybody wanted a piece of him after Malin Åkerblad's decision. Of course Pia had already heard about Ceder, and her voice made it very clear that she was stressed and angry.

'Yes,' he said, slipping out into the corridor to avoid the curious gaze of his colleagues.

'You said he did it,' Pia went on, almost accusingly.

'No, I said I wanted to speak to him in connection with the murders,' Erik replied, adopting a slightly exaggerated, pedagogical tone. 'He has an alibi, and we don't have enough evidence to hold him . . . not at the moment, anyway,' he added in an attempt to appease her.

He knew his wife well; it would take more convincing words than he had at his disposal to calm her down once she really got going. It was a side of her that most voters didn't see; in debates, meetings and local election campaigns she was the very epitome of serenity, but this external stability hid a volatile temperament and a challenging mixture of insecurity and a desperate desire to achieve. Only her nearest and dearest were privy to those aspects of Pia's character.

Or were affected by them.

Now she was worrying once again that Torsby would become known as the place where a crazed killer was at large, rather than the modern, forward-looking community for which she worked so hard. After a lengthy monologue, during which Erik was required only to make small noises of agreement at the appropriate junctures, she ran out of steam and he was able to end the call after hearing himself promise that he would arrange for Pia to have lunch with the SIO from Riksmord, so that she could form her own opinion of the level of competence the team had brought to the case.

He went to find Torkel straight away. The atmosphere in the room hadn't improved, and Vanja obviously hadn't let go of what she regarded as Åkerblad's pathetic decision. Erik thought she had gone a bit too far in the way she spoke to the prosecutor, but he couldn't help being impressed by her passion. He didn't think much of Sebastian; there was no sign so far of his alleged acuity. Insults and a total lack of interest appeared to be his defining characteristics.

As Erik had expected, Torkel wasn't exactly thrilled at the idea of lunch with Pia, wanting to know why he needed to meet the chair of the local council, but when he realised she was Erik's wife, he agreed.

Together they strolled along to Nya torget 8, which was quite nearby. The council building wasn't particularly striking; it looked more like two sugar lumps made of dirty red brick which had been stuck together in a way that was anything but harmonious. The woman on reception showed them to the dining room on the first floor. Pia was already there, and had chosen a table over by the wall. She got to her feet as soon as she saw them.

'Welcome to Torsby. Our season lasts all year round,' she said with a smile.

'Right,' was the only response Torkel could come up with.

'That's our slogan. I'm Pia, Pia Flodin. Nice to meet you.'

Erik smiled as he looked at his wife. Gone was the irritation that had dominated their conversation half an hour ago; right now she was the very picture of calm composure as she stood there in her pale skirt suit with her perfectly styled hair. She led them to the self-service counter where the dish of the day was baked cod with mashed potatoes.

'Thank you for taking the time to come over,' Pia said when they had sat down.

'No problem. I believe you want to ask me a few questions?' Torkel said pleasantly as he opened his mineral water.

'I feel a bit pushy, asking you to lunch like this, but I would have wanted to meet you even if Erik and I weren't married.'

'Although it might have taken you a bit longer,' Torkel said with a smile.

'True, but there have to be some advantages to sharing a bed with the local police,' Pia shot back. Torkel laughed; thank goodness they seemed to like one another, Erik thought. He had no desire to play the role of mediator; they both had very strong personalities.

'I don't suppose you've seen much of each other over the past few days,' Torkel went on.

'No, this has been hard on Erik,' Pia said, placing her hand on her husband's. 'He's only just been promoted, and this is his biggest case so far.'

Erik felt the need to say something, otherwise it looked as if he was twelve years old, with Mummy and Daddy chatting over his head.

'And the worst,' he said. 'But I'm convinced we'll solve it.'

'Is that what you think too?' Pia asked Torkel. She sounded genuinely worried.

'Cases like this always take longer than one would like, but yes, I'm sure we'll find the guilty party. It's only two days since the shootings, remember.'

Pia nodded, but she wasn't happy.

'I know, but how long does it usually take you to solve something like this, and what's your clear-up rate in percentage terms?'

'I'm sorry?' Torkel said, meeting Pia's gaze and putting down his knife and fork.

'I have to make a statement, partly to say that we're going to organise a memorial service and an anti-violence demonstration, and partly to inform everyone that we've brought in Riksmord to show how seriously we're taking the situation,' Pia explained in her 'official' tone of voice. 'It would be helpful if I could tell the community what they can expect.'

'They can expect us to do our best. As always.'

'Of course, but how long does something like this usually take?'

Torkel shrugged and turned his attention back to his fish.

'It's impossible to say.'

'Please try. I've worked so hard to put Torsby on the map, and now the papers are *finally* writing about us, the focus is on such terrible events. We need a counterbalance. This is an absolute disaster for the town.'

'A family has been murdered,' Torkel enunciated slowly and clearly. 'That's the real disaster, particularly for those close to them. I expect your town will survive.' There was no mistaking the coldness in his voice. Erik felt the change in the atmosphere around the table.

'It's a terrible tragedy, I know that, but someone needs to look at the bigger picture, and unfortunately that someone is me,' Pia persisted, her eyes fixed on Torkel. 'I don't care what you think – that's just the way it is.'

Erik realised that his wife had gone too far once again, but he still had to stick up for her.

'Pia's worked incredibly hard to make Torsby feel modern and attractive. She's just afraid all her efforts will have been for nothing.'

Torkel looked at the couple sitting opposite, both under stress for different reasons. Erik had only just been promoted, and had to make sure he did everything right in such a high-profile case, while Pia had to appear strong and proactive, when in fact she had no control over the situation whatsoever. This was an election year, so anything could become a political hot potato. He almost felt sorry for them.

'The media will focus exclusively on the horrific details for a while,' he said, a little more gently. 'That's just the way it is – none of us can change that.'

'I do understand,' Pia said calmly. 'But letting Jan Ceder go was really stupid. Isn't he the killer?'

Torkel took a deep breath. The prospect of an all-out row might have dwindled, but he would be actively avoiding any further lunch engagements with Pia Flodin.

'We don't know that. The prosecutor took the view that we didn't have enough evidence to hold him. I'm allowed to have an opinion on that, and so are you, but it is what it is. Our job is to find the evidence, and so far we have failed to do so.'

Back to his cod and mash.

'So when will you find it?' he heard from across the table, and decided to put an end to the conversation once and for all.

'I can't discuss an ongoing investigation with outsiders, and if you can't find anything else to talk about, then I suggest we finish our meal in silence.'

Pia didn't say a word.

Erik felt a pang of guilt, but couldn't help enjoying his wife's discomfort just a little. He loved her, but he didn't often see her lost for words. The last time was when she was nominated to join the party executive.

That was three years ago now, so it was hardly a frequent occurrence.

Clearly there were many hidden advantages to calling in Riksmord.

Sebastian was standing in the doorway of their little room, watching Vanja. She looked as if she needed something else to think about as she sat there irritably flicking through the transcripts of Jan Ceder's interviews.

'Come with me,' he said, taking a step closer and gently placing a hand on her shoulder. She shook it off.

'I really want to go through this.'

'You haven't missed a thing.' Sebastian was determined not to give up. 'Let's go for a walk.'

Vanja looked up at him.

'I know what you're trying to do, but I'll get over it. I just need to be left in peace for a while.'

Sebastian smiled at her. He loved it when she behaved like a teenager. It was unlikely that everyone around her felt the same, but he was her dad, after all, which meant it was his job to nag her.

'Come on, you need a bit of fresh air.'

Vanja sighed, but to his delight she got to her feet.

'OK, but with the emphasis on "a bit".'

They walked through the police station; it provided a stark contrast with Police HQ at Kronoberg in Stockholm, where it was possible to keep going for fifteen minutes without even getting anywhere near the next floor. In Torsby they were in the car park after ninety seconds.

'Where's Torkel gone?' Sebastian asked. Vanja suddenly looked amused.

'To meet Erik's wife.'

'Sounds like an odd choice of priority.'

Vanja shook her head. 'She's not just Erik's wife, she's the chair of the local council too. I'm guessing she thinks she deserves a personal briefing.'

Sebastian actually felt a little sorry for Torkel. Having to get involved with politicians connected by marriage to the local police wasn't something he would wish on anyone. The political game was hard enough as it was, especially in small towns, when Riksmord turned up; a council leader who shared a bed with one of the key investigating officers could well prove tricky. This kind of crisis management seemed to get worse with every passing year; sometimes it felt as if Riksmord's work was increasingly focused on dealing with politicians, various authorities and the mass media, rather than investigating the crimes they had come to solve. If things carried on like this, they would end up getting nothing done.

'What do you think of Ceder?' Vanja asked, interrupting his train of thought. She looked a bit more cheerful, which was something at least.

'He's hiding something, but he's not the killer,' Sebastian said firmly.

Vanja seemed to agree.

'I still don't understand why Åkerblad let him go. What difference would it have made if he'd stayed put for a little while longer?'

Sebastian suddenly had an idea.

'Let's do something about that instead of standing here complaining about that idiot of a prosecutor!'

'Like what? Question him again? We can't bring him in – we don't have any new information.'

'He's not the sharpest knife in the drawer, so he might do something as soon as he gets home.'

'Again, like what?'

'I don't know, but we both think he's hiding something. He might feel the need to act. We ought to be there.'

Vanja was grinning now. She understood exactly what he meant, and obviously found his suggestion entertaining.

'Are you saying we should put him under surveillance?' She could barely stop herself from bursting out laughing. 'You and me?'

Sebastian nodded eagerly.

'Have you ever been involved in a surveillance operation?' Vanja asked sceptically. 'I mean, you're more the type who comes swanning in afterwards and takes all the credit.'

He couldn't really argue with that, but he raised an eyebrow. 'There's always a first time.'

★ ★ ★

They borrowed an unmarked police car and drove west through the suburbs before crossing the E16 and continuing north-west. Soon fields and forest took over; significantly more of the former, so the expression 'the deep Värmland forests' didn't really seem to fit – at least not along Östmarksvägen. They crossed the lake just outside Kil, and in Rådom Vanja started paying as much attention to the sat nav as to the road itself, or so it seemed to Sebastian.

Twenty minutes later she pulled up behind a dilapidated barn at the side of the dirt track they had turned onto, and switched off the engine. Sebastian looked at her with raised eyebrows.

'If we get any closer there's a risk he might see us,' she said, pointing.

Through the trees Sebastian could just see a small house, perhaps 500 metres away. Vanja undid her seat belt and got out of the car; Sebastian stayed put.

'I thought we could keep an eye on him from the car,' he protested.

'Don't start. This was your idea,' Vanja said as she walked around the car and flung open the passenger door.

He had no choice but to get out and hope he wasn't going to get his feet wet. He wasn't exactly prepared for a ramble through the forest, and was wearing thin loafers as usual.

'Cheer up – you said you wanted some fresh air,' Vanja teased him as she set off.

They made their way through the dense forest towards Jan Ceder's house, fighting through the undergrowth. Sebastian regretted his suggestion almost immediately. It wasn't long before they heard the sound of a dog barking.

'Of course, he's got a dog. We won't be able to get much closer without being spotted,' Vanja said, crouching down behind a moss-covered rock.

'Does it matter? I mean, it's already barking – what else is it going to do?'

'It'll bark differently if someone is coming.'

Sebastian didn't argue; he knew absolutely nothing about dogs, apart from the fact that he didn't like them. He looked over towards the house: unimpressive, old, boring, badly maintained. The place was in darkness; there was no sign of a light from any-where inside. A green pick-up truck was parked outside, and he could just see the dog's pen next to a ditch. It was surrounded by a tall fence made of chicken wire, and contained a large home-made wooden kennel. The dog running back and forth was a shaggy grey creature with its tail curving up over its back in a semicircle. Some kind of Spitz, Vanja guessed. It was still barking.

'Ceder doesn't seem to be at home,' she said after taking a closer look through her binoculars.

'The car's there,' Sebastian pointed out.

'True, but maybe he's gone for a walk.'

'Without the dog?'

'Why not?'

Why not indeed, Sebastian thought. Although Ceder had been away from the dog for over twenty-four hours; shouldn't he have taken it with him? Given it some exercise, let it have a good run? Then again, the guy didn't seem to treat his women very well, so why should his dog fare any better? Nor did he seem to be the type to go for a walk. Were they too late? Had he gone off to dispose of evidence? There wasn't much they could do but wait. Sebastian leaned against the rock and sighed quietly, but obviously not quietly enough.

'Bored already? We've only been here five minutes.'

'I don't know how you do this. It's mind-numbing.'

'I'm not really involved in surveillance these days. I'm an investigator with Riksmord, as you might be aware.' Vanja suddenly looked at him with interest. 'How come you started working with the police anyway?'

Sebastian smiled at her and realised that surveillance had its advantages; it gave them time together.

'Do you want me to be honest?' he teased, enjoying the opportunity to have a conversation that would strengthen their relationship.

'If you know how.'

Sebastian nodded cheerfully, but he had already decided not to tell the truth. It was sordid and immoral, and not the kind of thing you share if you want someone to look up to you. He leaned closer, ready to confide.

'When I started reading psychology at university, I realised I needed to create my own unique profile, become an expert in one particular field so that I'd stand out. I wrote my thesis on the compulsive fantasies of the classic serial killer and the underlying causes,' he said; it sounded pretty convincing. 'It was an excellent piece of work, and I carried on researching that area. It was the end of the 1970s. The whole profiling thing had just started up in the USA, but it hadn't reached Sweden, so I was the first in this country.'

It sounded good, but it wasn't true.

He'd written a thesis, but not in order to gain a unique position. In fact he had chosen the topic because he had always been drawn to the darker side of the human psyche, and because serial killers had fascinated him for a long time.

He continued with his doctored version.

'When I got the chance to continue my studies with the FBI, I thought it was too good to be true. I took the opportunity right away, and then it was too late to do anything else. This was the only thing I knew.'

Another slight modification of the facts.

Training with the FBI had been his only way out. The complaints about his sexual misconduct had reached the top, and he was just one board meeting away from being thrown out. The trip to the USA saved him from being sacked. It was just like everything else in his life, he realised. There was always a hidden agenda with whatever he did. Even today, sitting here behind a rock and trying to make Vanja like him by telling her what he wanted her to hear. This was who he was: a man who was good at revising the truth so that it suited him.

'Well, at least one of us managed to follow the FBI programme,' Vanja said with a hint of bitterness in her voice.

Sebastian realised he had unwittingly touched a nerve; she had found her rejection deeply humiliating. He tried to repair the damage:

'You'll get there – it's only a matter of time.'

Vanja didn't reply; instead she stood up and brushed the pine needles off her jacket. She seemed to have lost interest in pursuing the conversation.

'I'm tired of this. Let's walk around the house,' she said, waving towards the back of the isolated dwelling.

Sebastian also got up, annoyed with himself; why the hell had he mentioned that bloody FBI programme?

They set off slowly in a wide circle, keeping well away from the building. Undergrowth, trees, bushes and a huge ditch made it very difficult to move sideways without being seen. When they were almost halfway round, they could see that the place looked equally deserted from this position. They waited for ten minutes; the only sound was the constant barking.

'Does that dog bark all day? How the hell does Ceder put up with it?'

Sebastian looked over at the pen; it was almost hidden by the house from this angle, but he thought he could see something in there.

Something he hadn't seen before.

Something large.

'We need to move closer so that we can get a better view of the pen,' he hissed.

Vanja glanced at him, then over at the pen. She spotted it too. There was a grey shape next to the kennel. Was it a sack? She wasn't sure.

Sebastian set off, moving quickly; he didn't care if anyone spotted him from the house. He needed to see what was lying in the pen. Vanja followed, catching up with him just as they got close enough to have a clear view.

There was definitely something in there.

Something that shouldn't be there.

A body.

★ ★ ★

Erik was the first to arrive. By that time Sebastian and Vanja had decided to let the dog out. They didn't touch his master, who was slumped against the scruffy kennel holding a pump-action shotgun in his hands. It looked exactly like the pictures they had seen of a 12-calibre Benelli SuperNova. The weapon was lying along the stiff body, with the stock between the legs and the barrel pointing to where the head had been. Now only parts of it remained; the right-hand side, the lower jaw and large parts of the neck were no longer there. The force of the blast had ripped everything away, and the concentrated injuries indicated that the distance between the barrel and the body had been minimal. Presumably it had been pushed right up against the lower jaw when it was fired.

However, they were pretty sure they were looking at Jan Ceder. Most of the face was missing, but the nose and the left eye had survived. The scalp was also more or less intact, and that tuft of red hair looked like a clown's wig perched on top of a sludgy mixture of blood, bits of brain, teeth and fragments of bone. It was a disturbing sight.

Erik walked over to the body. They had warned him about what he was going to see, but still the colour drained from his face.

'Is it Ceder?' he asked, even though he knew the answer.

That kind of thing often happens when we are faced with the truly macabre; only the obvious remains.

'Yes, we found him like this,' Sebastian replied. 'The dog was barking like mad.'

Erik gazed at the body. He was trying to appear rational, but with limited success.

'Shit,' he managed eventually. In his peripheral vision he saw Torkel arrive and park next to his car. 'Do you think it's suicide?' Erik went on, turning to Sebastian.

'I'm neither a technician nor a forensic pathologist. Would you like me to guess?' Sebastian said acidly.

'It's a bit too perfect in my opinion,' Vanja said as she joined them. She had just found a piece of rope and tied the dog to a tree a short distance away. It was still barking. Erik looked enquiringly at her. 'What do you mean?'

Vanja pointed to the gun in Ceder's deathly white hands.

'I'm assuming that's the gun that killed the Carlstens?'

Erik crouched down and examined the shotgun.

'Could be. It's the right make and model.'

'That bothers me for a start,' Vanja said. 'Why would he use the murder weapon to take his own life?'

'Maybe it's his way of confessing?'

Sebastian had intended to take a step back, let Vanja take care of this. They were a team now, and in a team you sometimes have to play second fiddle. Even though that wasn't a role he was used to. However, there was something about Erik Flodin that set him off, and he just couldn't keep quiet.

'So after taking the trouble to set up an alibi, and spending twenty-four hours in custody flatly denying everything, he comes home, gets out his shotgun, which he's hidden so well that we couldn't find it, and shoots himself. Does that sound likely to you?'

Erik didn't answer right away. He really didn't want to start arguing with Sebastian at this point, but after a quick glance at his so-called colleague's sceptical, condescending expression he decided he had to say something.

'We have no way of knowing what he was thinking,' he said defiantly. 'It's a possibility, isn't it?'

'It must be wonderful to be you,' Sebastian said, not even attempting to hold back on the sarcasm. 'Life is just full of possibilities . . .'

'It is a possibility.'Vanja stepped in. Allowing the two of them to carry on bickering was no help whatsoever. 'But it's unlikely. If we'd had evidence against him I might be more inclined to take that view – if he was under pressure and it was only a matter of time before we got him. But we had nothing. I'm sorry, Erik, but it just doesn't make sense.'

Erik nodded and turned to Torkel, who stopped dead when he saw Ceder and reacted exactly as Sebastian had expected.

He shook his head. Told them to cordon off the area. Took out his mobile to call Billy.

He didn't speculate at all.

★ ★ ★

Billy had never reflected on how much he and the Riksmord team relied on Ursula, but with four murders in one house and another body in a dog pen, he actually felt her absence on a physical level throughout his entire body. It wasn't so much that they were one person down – Fabian had proved himself a highly competent forensic technician – it was Ursula's instincts he missed, particularly when it came to deciding which clues to follow up immediately and which to leave until later. His approach was structured and meticulous, but Ursula had an intuitive feeling for what was important. Without her he felt as if all he had done was to gather and organise masses of information. He needed her to prioritise what they had found. She had a unique ability to cut through all those pages, all those reports and possible leads and to find a direction. Right now this was like baling water out of a boat without any time to look for the leak, let alone seal it up.

And it didn't feel good.

He was standing in front of another dead body, trying to appear calm and methodical, as if it was the same old Billy bending over the deceased, but inside a wriggling black snake of anxiety was increasingly making its presence felt.

The uniformed officers Erik had brought in were busy cordoning off the area, while Fabian had taken the initiative and called Karlstad to ask them to send over the coroner. They didn't really want to touch the body until he or she arrived; it was essential that everything was done correctly. There would be serious consequences if they were unable to establish the cause of death.

Either it was suicide, in which case the murders in Torsby would instantly be solved.

Or it was another murder, taking the investigation to a whole new level. That would mean the killer had struck again, demonstrating a cold, terrifying ruthlessness.

The third possibility, of course, was that the two cases weren't connected at all; Ceder could have been murdered for completely different reasons, and the killer had merely exploited the fact that he was under suspicion in order to muddy the waters.

So many options.

Too many.

God, how he missed Ursula and her sharp mind.

He decided to start with the gun. Fabian was asked to examine the ground in and near the dog pen. Billy checked whether the gate could be locked and unlocked from the inside; according to Sebastian, it had been closed and locked when he and Vanja discovered the body. The simplest way to work out whether another person had been involved was to find out whether Ceder could have shut himself in; Billy quickly established that this was entirely possible.

No luck there.

He then focused on the weapon. He took lots of photographs, too many perhaps, as if the extra pictures might calm him down, before gently trying to free the shotgun from the dead man's grasp. It wasn't difficult; rigor mortis had not yet set in, and the hands were still slightly warm, indicating that Ceder hadn't been dead for very long – an hour, two at the most. They knew exactly when he had been driven home, so he wouldn't have had time to do very much before he or someone else placed the barrel of the gun underneath his chin.

Billy went over to the SUV and carefully placed the shotgun on a sheet of thick plastic in the back. He dusted it and found five complete fingerprints; one on the guard below the trigger, two on the stock, and two more on the edge of the magazine. He secured them with film and transferred them to individual cards. He assumed they were Ceder's, because the prints on the stock were exactly where his left hand had been. Unfortunately he found only a partial print on the trigger itself, much too small and unclear to be of any use.

Back to the gun itself. He drew back the fore-end, allowing the empty cartridge to drop onto the plastic sheet. He picked it up with a pair of tweezers; it was matt black, with gold-coloured metal around the primer – the same kind of ammunition they had found at the Carlsten house. Saga 12.70 44 gr. His stomach turned to a block of ice.

He shouted to Torkel, who was talking to Sebastian and Vanja; all three of them came hurrying over. 'What have you found?' Torkel wanted to know immediately.

Billy showed them the cartridge. 'It's the same ammunition as we found at the house.'

'So this is the gun that was used?' Vanja asked eagerly. Billy shook his head.

'I can't say for sure. The National Forensics Lab will have to help us out there.' He pointed to the side of the cartridge. 'When the hammer strikes the primer, it makes a little dent in the metal just here. That dent is unique to each shotgun, and we have two cartridges – one from here, and one from the Carlsten house.'

Torkel nodded encouragingly.

'Good – in that case I'll ask Erik if someone can take the gun and the cartridges over to the lab in Linköping. We need to know as soon as possible if it's the same gun.' He went off to speak to Erik, who was talking to Fredrika.

'Well done,' Vanja said to Billy. He searched for signs of irony, but couldn't find any; it sounded as if she meant it. He gave her a little smile, but felt as if he'd only come up with the obvious, something that anyone with a pair of eyes could have spotted. He was no Ursula, not by a long way.

'Fingerprints?' Vanja went on.

'I need to double-check our records, but my gut feeling is they're Ceder's, and no one else's.'

Vanja turned to Sebastian.

'What do you think? What did Ceder do when he got home? Did he get in touch with the killer?'

'Billy!' Fabian shouted all of a sudden. His voice was shrill; he had found something. Billy, Sebastian and Vanja quickly went over to join Fabian, who was crouching down outside the gate of the dog pen.

'He was here.'

They could all see a clear footprint on the ground.

'Who?'

'The man who wears size forty-four boots.'

Ursula was starting to get a headache. She had been sitting in front of the computer for hours, concentrating hard – totally against doctor's orders. In spite of the steadily increasing pain, she wanted to carry on. It was incredibly liberating to focus on something other than herself, even though the material she had received from Billy was far from easy. It was a terrible crime – an entire family wiped out, by someone who could pull a trigger and watch as children were ripped apart. That was the strongest impression she had of the killer: coldness.

There was nothing in the pictures to indicate rage or any other motive apart from the need to kill. Nothing had been smashed, there was no sign that anything had been ransacked or thrown around. The bodies had simply been left where they were.

Ice cold. Methodical.

The other thing that struck her was how quickly everything must have happened. The mother had died instantly, the boy in the kitchen hadn't even had time to get up from his chair, the father hadn't made it down the stairs. The only one who seemed to have had the chance to react was the younger boy, Fred, who had run from the living room, through the kitchen, upstairs and into the wardrobe to try and hide.

Something was bothering Ursula.

The timing. It had all happened so fast as far as the rest of the family was concerned, but Fred's situation was different.

She got up, went into the kitchen and swallowed two pain-killers with a glass of cold water. Took a deep breath.

What was it that didn't fit?

She went back to the computer.

The police report concluded that the father hadn't got any further because he was helping Fred to hide. He had used his last minute to try to conceal his son, then he met the killer on his way to the stairs. It was an entirely credible scenario.

And yet . . . something didn't fit.

The perpetrator rings the bell. Karin Carlsten opens the door. Dies. The eight-year-old is in the kitchen. Dies. By this stage the killer should see the younger boy racing through the kitchen. Why didn't he shoot the child there and then? Fred must have run straight past him. Did he need to reload?

Ursula had checked: a fully loaded Benelli SuperNova held four cartridges, plus one in the bore. A person who displays such coldness should be completely prepared, carrying a fully loaded gun. Anything else would be unthinkable. Therefore, he must have had at least two cartridges left. He hadn't fired and missed; the forensic examination of the scene had established that beyond doubt. No shots that had missed their target had been fired in the house.

He was ice cold, focused.

He wanted to be certain.

He wanted to shoot them at close range. That suited him, Ursula felt.

So he sees the boy in the kitchen. Sees him run up the stairs. Perhaps Fred is calling to his father.

He lets him run. He knows that he will find him up there anyway.

Ursula clicked on the images of the bloody footprints. They led out of the kitchen towards the stairs, grew fainter, then disappeared completely before they reached the first step. The boy had been running for his life.

God, how he must have run.

She looked at the pictures again. Little bloody prints on the floor.

Then she saw it. Saw what she had been searching for.

The thing that didn't fit.

The boy hadn't run at all.

Fabian had lifted the print with a plaster cast.

The team gathered at the SUV for a quick run-through. Erik was standing next to Fredrika, his face ashen.

The same boots.

The wear on the left-hand side at the front was identical. There could be no doubt. This wasn't a coincidence.

Two crime scenes.

The same boots.

The same killer.

For a second they stood in silence, overcome by the seriousness of the realisation that the killer had struck again.

'Billy, check out the make and model of the boots, then everyone needs to pitch in to find out where they were sold,' Torkel said, bringing them back to the moment.

Vanja glanced over at the pen, where Jan Ceder was still slumped against the roughly hewn wall of the kennel, and put her thoughts into words:

'So Ceder was probably shot only an hour or so after we released him, with the gun he said had been stolen.'

'How many people knew we were letting him go?' Billy asked.

'Far too many, unfortunately,' Torkel said with a sigh. 'A crowd of reporters saw him leave, and the prosecutor made a statement in a radio interview half an hour later.'

Vanja shook her head wearily. 'Idiot.'

'To be fair, we usually let the media know when we release a suspect,' Torkel said in an attempt to salvage Malin Åkerblad's reputation. The look on Vanja's face told him he was wasting his time.

'So plenty of people knew he was out, but only a few could have done this.' Sebastian hadn't said anything for a long time, but now he stepped forward. These moments were the ones he enjoyed the most: when a case took a different turn, and instead of having too little to work on, they suddenly had too much. Everyone on the team felt the same, to a certain extent. You didn't apply to join Riksmord unless you liked a challenge and thrived under pressure. However, Sebastian was definitely the one who revelled in those instances where the ground opened up beneath their feet.

'How do you know that?' Erik asked, justifiably sceptical. It was obvious that he had some way to go before he could see the charm in these situations. Sebastian stared him down. If he wanted to challenge Sebastian, that was fine, but he needed to listen.

'The gun. This tells us that Ceder knew who had it. The killer knew that Ceder knew, but he didn't trust him to keep quiet.'

He was pleased to see everyone taking in what he had said and beginning to think along the same lines. Even Erik nodded. Either he really was listening, or he had got fed up of being difficult. Sebastian didn't really care which.

'Let's say he'd lent it to someone,' he went on, almost enjoying himself. 'It was a very expensive shotgun – he wouldn't lend it to just anyone. That's why his death had to look like suicide – so that we wouldn't start checking out his friends.'

He turned to Erik.

'He can't have had the biggest circle of acquaintances in the world – put them under pressure. Go for his friends.'

Torkel nodded.

'Good idea, Sebastian. We'll start there. Erik, we'll need your help – you know who he hung out with.'

It was a long time since Torkel had looked appreciatively at Sebastian, but he was clearly pleased. Sebastian felt quite proud; he could see that Vanja was impressed too.

Why wasn't he like this more often? he wondered. Focused, energetic, engaged – instead of bored and switched off.

Vanja liked him when he behaved this way, and what he wanted more than anything was her love and respect.

Why wasn't he like this more often?

She had even asked him why he had started working with the police. Nothing else. Nothing about all his women. Nothing about Ursula or Ellinor. No, when they had the chance to chat, her first question, in fact her only question, had been about the police.

Because that was what really mattered to her. She was a police officer, and it was a major part of her identity. Perhaps it formed the whole of her identity, particularly now she was no longer her father's daughter.

He needed to remember that. He would show her why he wanted to work with the police, he promised himself. He would be really good from now on.

Torkel's mobile rang; it was Ursula. They could all see from his expression that it was important.

Sebastian wasn't the only one who was good.

So was Ursula.

Really good.

Billy parked the SUV outside the white two-storey house and they got out. Everything was quiet, except for the blue-and-white police tape still fluttering in the breeze up on the veranda. Sebastian looked up dubiously at the building. He knew the bodies were no longer there, but he still found it difficult to enter a place where children had been executed.

'Are you coming?' Vanja called from the front door; Torkel and Billy had already gone inside. Sebastian nodded and took a deep breath. After all, he had seen the pictures already, and if he was going to keep the promise he had just made and make more of a contribution to this case, then he had to put in the effort.

Which included a visit to the scene of the crime, whether he liked it or not.

He ducked under the tape, went up the seven steps to join Vanja, then stopped. A metre or so inside the door was a huge patch of dried blood. He opened his folder and found the pictures the technicians had taken when they arrived. Karin Carlsten lying on her back, the charred black gunshot wound against her white sweater.

'What do you think?' Vanja asked, leaning over to see the photograph.

Sebastian looked up, examined the front door, turned to the steps and back again.

'It was planned,' he said. 'This wasn't done on a whim, or in a moment of anger.'

'How do you know?'

'I don't know, but there are plenty of indications.'

He turned around again and pointed to the spot where they had parked the SUV.

'If he'd got angry with the family somewhere else, he would have driven home, fetched the gun, parked the car, rushed up the steps, yanked open the door and stormed in. This . . .' He made a sweeping gesture. 'This tells us that he rang the bell, waited, got ready, and put the barrel of the gun to Karin's chest when she came to the door.'

They stepped around the blood and carried on into the house.

'Has he killed before?' Vanja wondered as they approached the kitchen. 'Is there any point in going back over unsolved murders?'

'Maybe. He certainly wouldn't have any problem in doing it again,' Sebastian replied. They passed Torkel and Billy, who had stopped in the kitchen. Sebastian glanced at the bloodstains by the table, where the child's footprints were still clearly visible. 'Not after this.'

'Jan Ceder proves that.'

'True . . .'

Torkel watched as Sebastian and Vanja made for the stairs; he took out his phone and called Ursula, who answered right away.

'We're in the house now. What have you found?'

'Are you in the kitchen?'

'Yes.'

Ursula leaned back in her chair and closed her eyes. She had stayed away from her screen while Torkel was driving to the scene, but her headache had still got worse.

'Are the footprints still there, or has some local bright spark decided to do a little cleaning?'

Torkel smiled. Whatever happened, Ursula retained her total lack of confidence in any police officer who didn't work for Riksmord.

'They're still there.'

'I want you to measure them – measure the length.'

'Why?'

'There's something I need to check,' Ursula replied, her tone making it very clear that there was no point in asking for further information at this stage. Torkel turned to Billy.

'Could you measure the footprints, please?'

Billy looked as if he would like to ask why, but held his tongue and went off to the SUV. Torkel waited until he was out of earshot, then resumed the conversation with Ursula.

'How are you?' he said gently. 'You sound tired.'

'I've got a splitting headache.'

'You should only be working if you can cope.'

'I've taken it easy for long enough.' Ursula leaned forward and clicked on a document in which she had marked several sections.

'I miss you,' she heard Torkel say softly.

'That's very sweet of you,' she said, enlarging the text on the screen. She knew she sounded slightly dismissive, but she really didn't have the energy to pander to Torkel and concentrate on the job, and the job was more important. 'According to the material I have, there was a pair of boots and a pair of shoes in the hallway, size thirty-two.'

'If that's what it says I'm sure it's correct – would you like me to check?' Torkel glanced at the shoe rack in the hallway. 'Nothing's been moved.'

'No, there's no need.' Torkel could hear Ursula tapping away on her keyboard. 'Approximately twenty point five centimetres.'

'Sorry?'

'If you wear size thirty-two shoes, the foot is approximately twenty point five centimetres long,' Ursula explained, closing her eyes once again as a stab of pain shot through her head. The tablets hadn't helped at all. 'How long are the footprints?'

'I don't know yet,' Torkel replied as Billy reappeared with a tape measure in his hand. Torkel nodded to the prints in the congealed blood, and Billy knelt down.

'The assumption is that the boy who was found in the wardrobe ran through the kitchen after the second shot, and trampled in his brother's blood,' Ursula said, getting up and going into the bathroom. 'But for a start the prints were made by someone who was walking, not running, and secondly the boy in the wardrobe has too little dried blood on his feet to have gone through the pool in the kitchen.'

She opened the bathroom cabinet and took out a bottle of a stronger analgesic, shook out a tablet and put it in her mouth. She bent down and filled her mouth with cold water from the tap, then threw back her head and swallowed it. She put the phone back to her ear as she left the bathroom.

'Even if most of it had been wiped off on the floor or on a rug or something on his way up to the bedroom, the soles of his feet should have looked different.'

She sat down and clicked on the photographs of the six-year-old who had tried to hide. The sight was equally painful each time she saw it. 'There are only odd flecks of blood, probably his own.'

Billy straightened up and Torkel looked at him enquiringly.

'Twenty-three centimetres, maybe a fraction over.'

'Twenty-three centimetres,' Torkel relayed to Ursula. She didn't answer immediately, but he could hear her tapping on the keyboard again.

'Size thirty-five or thirty-six.'

Suddenly Torkel realised what Ursula was saying, what she had seen, and what she had proved with their help.

The footprints in the blood didn't belong to the boy they had found in the wardrobe.

Someone else had been in the house.

★ ★ ★

'Who could do such a thing?'

Vanja and Sebastian were standing side by side, gazing into the wardrobe. Sebastian still had his folder open, but neither of them was looking at the pictures. The traces left in the wardrobe made that unnecessary. It was unbearable.

'Kill children, you mean?' Sebastian wondered.

'Yes.'

111

'More people than you'd think. In order to do this you have to dehumanise your victims, make them . . .' Sebastian fell silent. Outside they could hear the sound of birdsong.

The sound of spring.

Full of life.

'Once you've done that, the age of the victim doesn't really matter,' he went on, closing the folder.

They turned and left the bedroom. On the narrow landing Vanja glanced at the blood on the bathroom door.

'Does all this tell you anything about the person who did it?' She made a sweeping gesture that encompassed the entire house, but before Sebastian had time to answer, they heard Torkel calling to them.

Telling them to come downstairs.

Right now.

★ ★ ★

They had been wrong, apparently. It wasn't the younger brother who had run through the blood.

It was someone else.

The size of the prints suggested a child or a small woman – most probably a child, as no one had contacted the police. But who could it be?

'I spoke to Erik,' Billy said on his way back into the kitchen. 'No children reported missing since last Wednesday. No women either.'

Torkel turned to Vanja. 'Check with the neighbours, see if they know who might have been here.' She nodded and left the house.

'Search the house again,' Torkel told Billy. 'See if you can find any trace of a fifth person.'

Billy went upstairs while Sebastian stayed where he was, contemplating the footprints in the blood. He glanced over at the living room; what had actually happened here? The mother is shot. The older son is shot – but then what? Were there two of them watching TV? The younger brother and someone else?

112

Fred runs past the killer. Up the stairs. The murderer knows that the family consists of two adults and two boys; he has just shot one child and seen the other, so he doesn't even look in the living room where a third child is hiding.

Possible.

Credible, even.

But then what?

'Come with me,' Torkel said, interrupting his train of thought.

★ ★ ★

They followed the bloody footprints until they faded at the bottom of the stairs.

'Whoever it was didn't go up,' Torkel stated, considering the possibilities. On the right was a small study, and further along there were two more doors, one leading to a bathroom containing a bath, a double washbasin and a toilet.

The second door led to an L-shaped utility room. It was long and narrow, and the shelves crammed with everything from gardening tools to hockey equipment opposite a washing machine and tumble dryer made it feel even more cramped. There was another door at the far end. Torkel tried it; locked. He turned the latch above the handle, and suddenly they were looking out over the lawn, extending down to the meadow. He examined the door. It was the old-fashioned type that didn't need a key to lock it from the outside; you just pulled it shut. There was no reason why the police should have paid it any attention when they first arrived on the scene.

Torkel and Sebastian stepped out into the sunshine at the back of the house.

'You witness several murders,' Torkel said. 'You run out here . . .' He took in his surroundings. 'Where do you go?'

Sebastian sensed that the question was rhetorical, but chose to answer anyway.

'Everyone reacts differently.' He took a few steps across the lawn, turned to face the forest. No buildings in sight to offer the most obvious means of protection. 'Some people would just run away,' he went on, turning back to Torkel. 'Run as far as possible without thinking. Others would be surprisingly rational.'

'In what way?'

Sebastian looked up at the closed back door; in his mind's eye he saw it open and a child or a woman emerge. The cold must have struck them immediately.

'It was pretty cold just after nine o'clock in the morning. The others were still in their pyjamas, and we know that he or she was barefoot.'

'So he ran back inside?'

'But this door was locked.'

They set off back towards the front door. As they reached the corner of the house, Torkel stopped. The grass at the bottom of the drainpipe had been washed away, leaving loose, damp earth.

The imprint of a bare foot. The wet surface had made the print swell, but Torkel thought it was probably about the same size as the footprints in the blood in the kitchen.

The person ran back. Towards the front door.

Torkel moved fast, up the steps and onto the veranda. Once he reached the hallway he stopped and waited for Sebastian, then held out his hand. Sebastian assumed he wanted the folder, and passed it over.

Torkel quickly found the relevant page.

'They didn't find any size thirty-five or thirty-six shoes. So you think whoever ran away came back in to grab a coat and shoes?'

'That would be my guess.'

'There were five toothbrushes in the bathroom upstairs, and I found this.'

Torkel and Sebastian spun around; Billy was standing in the kitchen doorway with a small red suitcase in his gloved hand. 'It was in the boys' room.'

'Have you looked inside?'

Billy nodded. 'Mainly clothes. Size 146. Girl's clothes.'

She had made it.

Behind a low fence the mountain opened up, leading into oblivion. The gaping hole in the rock that would swallow her up. Hide her on the outside, just as she was already hidden on the inside.

She crouched down behind the bushes as close to the entrance as she could get without risking being seen, and scanned the open space in front of the cave.

No sign of anyone.

No cars, no sound of approaching voices.

She straightened up and ran over to the fence, across the little gravelled area. A dented yellow metal sign was fastened to the wire mesh; it showed a policeman with his hand raised in a 'Stop' gesture, with the words 'Authorised persons only. Parents or guardians are responsible for their children' printed below.

The fence seemed to be there to keep out those who were too small to read the sign. It was no more than a metre high, and in some places the posts had fallen down.

She had no difficulty climbing over.

She hesitated before stepping into the darkness. She was going to be hungry. She hadn't eaten anything since the morning when she devoured the Greek wrap – minus the red onion. She hadn't drunk anything except the yogurt. But it would be OK. She seemed to remember that water ran down through the earth and rock where it was purified, then it dripped down into caves and formed underground lakes.

She would sort something out as far as food was concerned. She had the tins she had taken from the cottage. She didn't want to wait any longer. She was so close now. Just a few more metres and she would disappear for ever. Become unreachable.

On the outside and on the inside.

The girl clambered over the fence and marched purposefully down into the old cave system.

Then she vanished into the darkness.

'Nicole Carlsten.'

Billy pinned a picture on the board in the incident room as Vanja looked up from the papers in front of her. A dark-haired ten-year-old girl smiled at them from a typical school photo. 'Aged ten, lives in Stockholm. She's a cousin of the two boys.'

'And you're sure it's her?' Erik wondered from his place by the door.

'Not completely,' Vanja replied. 'According to the Torssons she often stayed with the Carlstens in the holidays, but they didn't know if she'd been there this week.'

'So where are her parents?' Sebastian asked. He got to his feet and walked over to the board.

'We tried to contact the mother earlier to tell her about her sister's death, but she didn't answer. She works for the Swedish International Development Corporation. I spoke to her boss, and she's on her way home from Mali.'

'When will she be here?' Torkel demanded.

'Apparently both mobile coverage and the reliability of flights from Mali are a little hit and miss,' Vanja explained. 'Nobody really knows.'

'I want her brought here as soon as she lands,' Torkel said, getting to his feet. He looked as if he'd like to start pacing back and forth as he usually did, but the room was too small, so instead he went and stood by the window with his arms folded. 'The neighbours didn't mention the fact that another child sometimes came to visit, and if the mother's in Africa, that would explain why no one has reported Nicole missing,' he summarised. 'So we assume it's her, until we can prove otherwise.'

Everyone nodded in agreement.

'What else do we know about the girl?' Torkel went on, directing the question at Vanja. Once again she consulted her notes.

'Ten years old, as I said. Parents divorced, lives with her mother, father's in Brazil, little or no contact with him, as far as I can make out.'

Was it Sebastian's imagination, or was there a hint of sorrow in her voice?

'According to her teachers she's intelligent and mature for her age.' Vanja gathered up her papers with a shrug. 'She's only ten, so there's not much.'

'Are we sure she's missing?'

Everyone, even Sebastian, turned to Billy.

'I mean, she could have been abducted,' he went on. 'The killer could have grabbed her coat and shoes in the hallway so that we wouldn't look for her.'

'No,' Sebastian said. 'If he'd seen her, she would be dead.'

'And you know that for certain, do you?' Billy couldn't help a note of irritation creeping into his voice. Being put right by Sebastian wasn't a new experience, but there was still something incredibly annoying about that self-assured tone.

'Yes.'

'How?'

'That's my job, and I'm good at my job.'

Their eyes met. Billy gritted his teeth; this was an argument he couldn't possibly win. Whatever the rest of the team thought of Sebastian, no one would question his expertise.

'So she's definitely missing, she hasn't been kidnapped,' Torkel stated, confirming Billy's thoughts. Sebastian turned his attention back to the photograph.

The dark hair tied back in a ponytail, apart from two strands that hung down and framed the girl's face. A red sweatshirt worn over a white blouse. Nicole's smile reached her open brown eyes.

Sabine had also had dark hair and brown eyes.

'Sebastian . . .'

He was jerked back to reality. Torkel and the others were looking at him as if they were expecting an answer, but he had no idea what the question might have been.

'What?'

'The girl, Nicole. What are you thinking?'

Sebastian thought for a moment before he spoke.

'She hid in the living room, waited for the killer to leave. Went back to fetch her outdoor clothes so that she wouldn't freeze later.' He paused, gazing at the smiling child in the school photo again. 'She's not just running around like a headless chicken – she's in hiding.'

'Where?'

'I don't know, but she's not prepared to go to the police. She could easily have come here in the past forty-eight hours. She has a different plan.'

He reached out and touched the photograph as if that would help him work out what was going on in Nicole's mind.

'Whatever she's doing might not make sense to us, but as far as she's concerned, it's the obvious course of action. She's behaving rationally, but according to her own logic.'

'That's really helpful,' Billy said quietly, but not quietly enough to stop the others from hearing.

Erik contemplated the Riksmord team with a growing feeling of unease. They seemed rather dysfunctional, to say the least.

'So what do you want us to do?' he asked Torkel, who took a deep breath. Good question – what did he want them to do?

They had a girl. Presumably traumatised. Missing for over forty-eight hours. Normal procedure would be to bring in as many resources as possible to search for her, but if he did that, they risked letting the killer know that there was a witness, which could theoretically put Nicole in mortal danger.

The alternative was to keep it to themselves for as long as possible and not to ask for help – but then they risked not finding her.

He could see that everyone was waiting for an answer. The alternative wasn't really an alternative.

'We go all out to find her.'

★ ★ ★

Torkel estimated that there were about eighty people in front of the police station. Most had been mobilised from the local defence service and off-duty police officers who had been called in, but there were also quite a lot of volunteers. A spokeswoman for Missing People had assured him that she could provide twice as many the next day if required. They had decided to combine a summary of the situation with a brief press conference; those who would be actively searching for the girl gathered around Erik Flodin and the large map, while the reporters formed an outer circle.

Sebastian reminded them that it wasn't unusual for the killer to return to the scene of the crime, or to try to get close to the investigation, then Billy went around and photographed everyone who had turned up.

After a couple of minutes Torkel looked for Sebastian, but couldn't see him; he must have gone back inside. He had decided to take a back seat at this point; Erik knew the area and he knew the people who were here, so he was the best person to take the lead, even though he wasn't the SIO. Torkel recognised a face in the crowd: Pia Flodin. Her expression was grim. After five murders in two days, no doubt a missing ten-year-old was the last thing she needed. He was a little surprised to see her; shouldn't she be meeting the council's PR representative to work on a damage-limitation exercise? But of course this was where all the cameras were, and it was election year . . .

Axel Weber detached himself from his fellow journalists and came over to Torkel. The previous year Weber had broken the story of two Afghan asylum seekers who had mysteriously disappeared, highlighting links to the military intelligence service and a murdered family up in the mountains, but it had caused no more than a ripple on the surface of the media pond. Clearly certain people had done enough to shut it down.

Weber had his notebook at the ready.

'Do you think she saw the killer?'

'If you listen to Erik, you'll find out what we think.'

'If I say she saw the killer, will you deny it?'

'We don't know what she did or didn't see. We just want to find her.'

'So no denial, then?'

Torkel didn't reply; instead he turned his attention back to the briefing, which was coming to an end. They didn't have many hours of daylight left. Everyone had been given a picture of Nicole, and the house from which she had disappeared had been pointed out on the map. She had been missing for over fifty hours by now; they had worked out an average speed, taking into account the possibility that she might have been going around in circles, and had come up with five areas where they thought she could be. These areas were now allocated to search teams, each with a leader: Torkel, Vanja, Billy, a local defence officer and the Missing People representative. Everyone was issued with the relevant telephone numbers and given walkie-talkies, sandwiches and a Thermos flask.

In conclusion Erik explained that he would be staying behind to act as co-ordinator and to take overall responsibility for the search. The team leaders would report back to him.

Cars started up, and the area emptied in no time. Erik watched as the last vehicle turned left onto Bergebyvägen, then he headed inside. Pia appeared at his side.

'Have you spoken to Frank?'

'No.'

'Don't you think you should?'

Erik considered the question. There was definitely something in what Pia said. Frank Hedén was the local game ranger. No one knew the forests around Torsby better than Frank and his dogs, but a few months ago, not long after his sixtieth birthday, he had been diagnosed with bone cancer. Erik didn't feel entirely comfortable about asking for his help.

'If he'd wanted to get involved he would have been here,' he began.

'If you need him, he'll help if you give him my love,' Pia said, placing a hand on his forearm.

That was probably true.

Frank had worked in local government for the Social Democrats for many years. He had been the chair of the council when Pia started to get interested in politics, and had become something of a mentor to her as she climbed the ladder. They were very close. Erik gave the matter a little more thought, then nodded. It was worth a try.

'Good,' Pia said, leaning forward to kiss him on the lips. She watched him walk to the car; he waved as he drove off, and she waved back, wearing a smile that disappeared as soon as he was out of sight.

They had to find the girl.

They had to put an end to this.

She had googled 'Torsby' during her lunch break, and after the town's home page and Wikipedia, the first three pages had been exclusively about murder and violence. That really wasn't good for the town, and anything that wasn't good for the town wasn't good for her.

And she really wanted everything to be OK.

Sebastian was sitting in their temporary HQ. He had stayed outside and listened to Erik for a little while, but had found it fairly boring. He had given a less than polite response when he was asked whether he would like to join one of the search parties, and had come inside.

Sebastian Bergman did not wander through the forest shouting out someone's name. There were plenty of superannuated military types, bored schoolteachers, housewives and unemployed layabouts to do that kind of thing. Not one of Europe's leading criminal psychologists.

Too little stimulation.

Too much nature.

He looked up at the wall.

Nicole . . .

Who had done this?

Presumably a man; female mass murderers were extremely rare. But who walks up to a house with a shotgun, intent on killing four people, two of whom are children?

Someone who feels hatred. Someone who wants revenge, or can't see any other solution to his problems. There must be a personal connection, Sebastian was sure of it; that was why Torkel's suggestion that the neighbours might like to go away for a while just to be on the safe side was completely idiotic. This was no psycho, randomly going from house to house. This was focused, planned. The killer believed the Carlstens deserved to die.

Nicole . . .

Had the Carlstens done something to the killer on a personal level? Probably, or at least that was how he perceived it. But why did the entire family have to be punished? Why the children? It was important to him that they all died. He must have searched for the boy in the wardrobe . . .

Sebastian gazed at the timeline. CEDER THREATENS CARLSTEN OUTSIDE SWIMMING POOL. Jan Ceder was something else. He was a threat. He had to be disposed of so that the killer could get away with the Carlsten murders. The family was the primary target.

CARLSTENS SHOT.

Nicole . . .

Why now? Why had they been shot now? Had something happened or changed recently, or did the killer have to build up to the massacre? Did he have to convince himself, turn them into symbols rather than people in order to be able to do it? That could take time . . .

CORNELIA TORSSON'S STATEMENT. CLOSE-UPS OF EMPTY CART-RIDGE. PLASTER CAST OF BOOT PRINT.

Nicole . . .

The door was open when Cornelia arrived. No attempt whatsoever had been made to hide the bodies. What did that tell Sebastian? That it didn't matter when the bodies were found. Why? Because the killer hadn't fled. He was still in the area, or at least not far away. He killed Jan Ceder within two hours of the official notification that he had been released.

CEDER FOUND DEAD IN DOG PEN.

Nicole . . .

Sebastian kept coming back to the smiling child in the school photograph, with her dark hair and brown eyes.

Sabine would have been a few years older by now.

He had never thought of her that way.

Older.

He had never thought about what it would be like to take her to school on her first day, or pictured himself as the proud father at parents' evenings or sports days. He had never considered what joys, what challenges, what discoveries might lie beyond the age of four. Never reflected on the fact that he would be the father of a teenager now, with all that brought with it: the responsibility of guiding her closer and closer to independence in an adult world.

Was that why he kept coming back to the photograph? Was he seeing Sabine in Nicole? If so, he was crazy. He had met lots of dark-haired, brown-eyed girls since Boxing Day 2004 without reacting like this.

Nicole . . .

Sabine had never grown older as far as he was concerned. She was still that curious four-year-old whom he had loved more than he realised, who was always at the centre of his universe. She had seized life with both hands, she was bright and she would try anything – it hadn't taken her long to work out how to escape from her cot!

They had had a rule. Sabine must go to sleep in her own bed. Whether she stayed there all night or ended up in their bed was irrelevant. In the autumn of 2004, her last autumn, she came to them virtually every night. He usually woke up when he heard her scampering along the parquet flooring in the hallway, but if not he would wake when he heard her say: 'I want to sleep here,' just before she threw her pillow in between him and Lily, then clambered up. He would help her to snuggle under the covers and put his arm around her. She liked to grab his fingers in her left hand and squeeze them. She stuck her right thumb in her mouth, and she was fast asleep in seconds . . .

Sebastian gave a start when he heard a knock on the door; a second later Fredrika walked in.

'There was coffee left over – would you like some?'

Sebastian straightened up; he had been miles away. In fact, he felt as if he had just woken up. How long had he been sitting here? He looked at Fredrika and saw her expression change from polite enquiry to something else. Confusion? Distaste? Sympathy?

She put down the Thermos and two green-and-white mugs.

'It's a terrible thing,' she said, nodding towards the display board. Sebastian still didn't understand, then he realised his cheeks were wet. Had he been crying? He quickly ran a hand over his face. Apparently he had. That explained Fredrika's reaction when she came in; she hadn't expected to find Riksmord's criminal psychologist in tears. But here he was, a lonely, sensitive man weeping over the victims, the meaningless violence. She hadn't retreated in horror though; she was still here, behaving as if this kind of thing was perfectly normal.

Perhaps she liked sensitive men.

Perhaps she already had one.

'So many people turned up to help with the search,' Sebastian said, clearing his throat as if to make sure his voice was working properly. 'It's great to see such commitment in the middle of all this.' He looked up and met her gaze. 'Was your husband out there?' he asked, making every effort to keep his tone neutral and chatty.

'I'm not married.'

Sebastian nodded and gave her a faint smile. He had no intention of enquiring about a boyfriend, partly because that would make it clear what he was up to, and partly because he was pretty sure she was unattached. Most people would follow up her last comment with 'but my boyfriend's there', or 'and my boyfriend couldn't make it' if they had a partner.

'Would you like some coffee?' she said again, nodding towards the Thermos. 'It's still hot.'

Sebastian shuffled in his chair. He really did need to chase away those thoughts. Another lonely night surrounded by that blue floral wallpaper was anything but appealing. He fired off his most winning smile.

'Only if you join me . . .'

He looks old, Erik thought as Frank opened the door and let him in. He had lost weight; his trousers, obviously too big, were pulled tight around his waist with a belt, and his shirt hung loose. His cheeks were sunken and covered in stubble, and Erik couldn't remember him having such noticeable bags under his eyes before. The only thing that hadn't changed was the short steel-grey hair that stuck straight up, reminding Erik of a character in a comic he used to read when he was a child: Mike Nomad. Erik took off his shoes and followed the older man into the kitchen. Was it his imagination, or had Frank developed a slight limp? He had had prostate cancer for several years, but in October last year he had begun to experience back pain, and had eventually gone to the doctor. Metastasis from the prostate cancer was affecting the base of his spine. Chemotherapy and radiotherapy had slowed down the progress of the disease, but it was inoperable, and no one knew how much time he had left.

Erik declined the offer of coffee and sat down at the small table. There was an unfamiliar and not entirely pleasant smell in the kitchen: fried food and . . . illness, Erik thought as he watched Frank spoon coffee into the filter.

'How are you?' he asked, hoping the answer wouldn't be too detailed.

'Oh, you know – it is what it is. One day at a time.'

Erik wondered how he was supposed to respond to that. Frank switched on the machine and put the packet of coffee back in the cupboard.

'Pia sends her love,' Erik said in order to break the silence.

'Send her mine – I hope she'll come and see me before too long.'

'I'm sure she will, it's just that there's so much going on at the moment . . .'

Frank nodded, but Erik got the feeling he was disappointed that they didn't see each other more often.

Disappointed and lonely.

He realised he felt sorry for Frank. He and Pia had often talked about it; a cancer diagnosis was never welcome, of course, but in Frank's case it was a disaster.

He had already suffered a great deal. His wife Aina had died in a car accident just over eight years ago. They had only one child. Hampus was twenty-eight years old and still lived at home. He was severely disabled, and would never be able to live independently. Erik knew he had cerebral palsy, epilepsy and partial paralysis, but he thought there was something else as well. Help was provided for eighty-five hours a week, but the rest of the time Frank looked after Hampus on his own. Erik didn't want to think about what would happen when Frank passed away.

Nor did Frank, presumably.

'How can I help you?' Frank asked, sitting down opposite Erik and clasping his hands on the table.

'Have you heard about this missing girl?'

'The one who saw the Carlsten murders?' Frank shook his head. 'Dreadful. Just dreadful.'

'Did you know them?'

'I knew of them, but I'd never actually met them even though they lived only about five kilometres from here.' Frank shook his head again.

'We really need to find the girl,' Erik went on, leaning forward to add weight to his words.

'Of course.'

'I thought of . . . or rather, Pia thought of you,' Erik corrected himself. 'You know the forest so well, and she thought the dogs might be able to help.'

128

Frank met his gaze, and Erik was struck by how sceptical he looked.

'She's been missing for a while, hasn't she?' Frank said, rubbing his stubbly chin.

'More than two days – fifty, fifty-five hours maybe. But we have items of clothing belonging to her, if that's any use.'

'Two days . . . that's a long time if you're expecting the dogs to track her.'

Erik nodded. Frank got up and went over to the coffee machine, where the last of the brown liquid was dripping into the pot.

'I'd be happy to help, you know that, but the carer finishes in two hours, and I can't leave Hampus on his own.'

'No, of course not.' It was hard to argue against Hampus's needs, but then he had an idea. After all, he was married to the chair of the local council, and the council was responsible for the help Frank received. He straightened up and made his final attempt.

'If you think the dogs might be of some use, then I can make sure someone comes in to look after the boy.' Frank poured himself a cup of coffee in silence, then replaced the pot and switched off the machine with a sigh. 'If you feel up to it, of course,' Erik added.

'I'm up to it.' Frank turned and leaned against the draining board, sipping his coffee as he thought things over. 'What kind of person would I be if I didn't even try?'

'Thank you.'

'Give me fifteen minutes to sort myself out.'

Frank took his cup with him and headed upstairs. Erik leaned back, feeling pleased with himself. Admittedly it had been Pia's idea to go and see Frank, but he was the one who had persuaded him to join in the search – by thinking outside the box. Just imagine if he could go home tonight and tell Pia that Frank and his dogs had found the girl! How would she react? She would be pleased, of course, perhaps even grateful. Two states of mind he had seen very little of lately.

She worked too hard.

Torsby wasn't the biggest town in the country – it had been number 185 on the list the last time Pia checked – but there was a lot to do. A huge amount, in fact. The last few months had been unusually tough. It was the beginning of an election year, with all that implied in terms of planning and positioning. Then there was the scandal about the food at one of the council's care homes for the elderly back in February, a newspaper article about inadequate record keeping in official vehicles, FilboCorp and the endless protests, the debate on salaries, an aggressive opposition that had already attacked next year's budget even though it wasn't due to be discussed until June, and an outbreak of TB at one of the preschools. And now five murders and a missing child.

Erik didn't know how Pia coped. Day in, day out.

She was always a politician – maybe more of a politician than a wife and mother recently, to be honest. That situation was unlikely to improve if she got what she wanted. Last month the party leadership in the Värmland district had decided to put Pia's name forward as a member of the executive committee, which meant she would join the top rank of politicians. She was unlikely to devote less time to her career if that happened; there were only twenty-four hours in a day, and if she was going to spend more of those hours to her work, she would have to take them away from something else.

From him and the family.

He knew it was mean-spirited to think that way, but he couldn't help it. He was working in Karlstad, and the commute meant that they already saw too little of one another, in his opinion. At the same time, Pia was passionate about her role. She wanted to bring about change, and she really believed she could do it. Her aim was to make Torsby better for everyone. Her commitment and dedication far surpassed anything he had seen among her colleagues, and that was probably why she was on her way to Stockholm. She always put the interests of the party and the town first.

Maybe that was why he was sitting here hoping that Frank and the dogs would find the girl today – so that he would become the most important thing in Pia's life again.

Even if it was only for one night.

It was cold.

Much colder than she had expected it to be.

The still air inside the cave couldn't be far above zero. She curled up in the crevice she had found, drew her knees up to her chin and wrapped her arms around her shins. That helped a little, but it couldn't compensate for the icy chill coming from the damp rock. She realised her teeth were chattering. She took several deep breaths and tried to relax as best she could. That was a bit better . . .

She wondered if she should take off her jacket and lie on it, but decided against it. She was probably getting more benefit from wearing it.

She closed her eyes.

It didn't make any difference. The darkness was so dense that it didn't matter whether her eyes were open or not.

She closed them anyway.

The only thing she could hear was her own breathing. The silence was so complete that she might as well have been deaf. If she went blind and deaf in here, she wouldn't even notice. But the darkness and the silence suited her.

No one would find her.

No one found the boys, the ones who died in here.

She had no intention of dying.

So why was she here? So that no one would find her. Was she planning on staying here for ever? How would she survive? The boys had died. Had she come here to die?

She pushed aside the questions, feeling irritated. She had come here so that no one would find her. She didn't want to be found. It was that simple. Not now, anyway. In a while, maybe. She hadn't thought any further ahead than that. She just wanted to run away to a safe place. That was all. Eventually she was going to have to think about the next step.

She would probably try and get hold of her mum. She would know what to do.

But she didn't have her phone. She hadn't thought about that when she went back into the house; it had been on charge next to her bed when she and Fred were watching TV, when the doorbell rang, when the shot . . .

No!

She wasn't going to think about it. What happened back there. That was on the outside, it didn't exist on the inside. On the inside there was silence and stillness. That was where she must go. All of her. She must shut herself in completely. Now she was here she could focus on that. Eventually she would have to work out what to do, but not now.

Maybe never.

Maybe she had everything she needed on the inside. If only she could find her way there. All of her. Everything she was. Perhaps she would never have to leave the calm of the place that was not a place.

The stillness. The oblivion.

She didn't even notice when she fell asleep.

Sebastian emerged from the toilet and went back to the slightly claustrophobic incident room. He glanced into various offices on passing, and met Fredrika's gaze as she sat at her desk. A nod and a little smile, then he moved on. Even though he sensed that she would accept an invitation to dinner, and that it would probably lead to sex either at her place or in his flowery blue boudoir, he didn't ask. He couldn't be bothered.

She was too quiet. She had given him too little to go on while they were having coffee, made it impossible for him to work out whether he was on the right lines or not, forced him to make too many guesses, to go back, regroup, change his approach too many times. Seduction had to be a joint effort if he was going to stay interested; this was a one-man show. So he had let it go and made a serious attempt to contribute by doing what he was employed to do: profiling the perpetrator.

An hour later Erik had come in and told him what they had found out so far about Ceder's circle of acquaintances. There wasn't much. His friends down in Filipstad had no idea who he could have lent the shotgun to. They didn't hunt and never talked about such things, they said. The neighbours described him as a lone wolf; they had no social contact with him. They said hello if they happened to see him, but that was very rare. Erik went over to the map on the wall; the neighbours lived almost a kilometre from Ceder's place.

Sebastian merely nodded to himself. After considering the information at his disposal, he decided he needed to rethink. He wasn't convinced that Ceder had lied about the gun in order to protect someone he knew well; it could be that it was more important for him to avoid helping the police than to clear his own name.

The more Sebastian read about Jan Ceder, the more the man emerged as a classic, dyed-in-the-wool anti-authority figure.

Erik had explained that they had searched Ceder's property again; according to Fabian, there was nothing to indicate that the killer had been inside the house. The most likely scenario was that Ceder had met him outside. Nor was there any clue as to where the shotgun might have been.

They were waiting for a list of calls from the mobile-phone operator, but nothing was listed following Ceder's release. Admittedly he could have deleted a call; if that was the case, they would find out on Monday. The only person he had been in touch with online was a woman in the Ukraine, so if he had been thinking of blackmail, it looked as though he hadn't had time to put his plan into practice before he was murdered.

Sebastian had thanked Erik, but told him it was best if he went through everything with Torkel and the others when they got back. Erik's expression had darkened.

'Surely you can do that?' he had said without any attempt to hide his annoyance.

'You know those people who take messages and pass them on to other people? They're called secretaries, and I am not a secretary.'

Sebastian couldn't deny that he enjoyed winding Erik up; he made his displeasure so obvious. Erik had left the room without another word, and Sebastian had gone back to his work.

It had been dark for an hour when he heard the others return. He went out into the corridor; Vanja was leading the way, closely followed by Erik, Torkel and Billy. Sebastian didn't even need to ask; their weary expressions said it all.

They hadn't found Nicole.

He didn't want to be a mass murderer, but that was what he was, according to Wikipedia.

'A person who deliberately kills more than three people during one event.'

You do what you have to do, he thought as he sat there in front of the computer.

Surely it would have said online if they had found her?

He had surfed the Net, searched all the newspaper sites. Local, national and Norwegian.

Nothing.

The latest update in *Expressen* had been posted over three hours ago:

DARKNESS HALTS SEARCH

The text beneath provided no fresh information; it was just a summary of all the other articles that had appeared during the day.

The murders. The missing girl.

Once again, the police had not denied the possibility that the girl might have seen the killer.

The tabloids loved this kind of story, of course. First of all an entire family had been murdered, then a suspect released from police custody had also been found dead. The icing on the cake was an innocent child who had witnessed the horrific killings, and was now missing.

On the run?

Alone in the vast forests of Värmland.

He had even found an article in *Aftonbladet* where they had spoken to an 'expert' about the greatest dangers she would face out there.

- Hypothermia
- Thirst
- Broken bones as a result of a fall
- Shock, which could lead to irrational behaviour.

And the last one, which had made him laugh out loud:

- Wolves

Anything to heighten the tension surrounding the search, he assumed. Which was why there would be banner headlines if she'd been found.

Nicole Carlsten.

How could he have missed her?

That was irrelevant now. He had missed her. He hadn't even thought about whether the Carlstens might have visitors. No point in brooding over it. What was done was done.

He closed the laptop, leaned back in his chair and considered his next move. He went through the 'expert's' list in his head.

Hypothermia was unlikely at this time of year − well into April. Nor was dying of thirst a particularly realistic scenario − there were lakes and streams everywhere. It was of course possible that she might injure herself in the forest, and he had no idea what post-traumatic shock could do to a child. What did irrational behaviour mean? Was she likely to drown herself? Step out in front of a timber wagon? He couldn't rely on it, whatever it might be. It sounded too good to be true.

Which left wolves. No one, apart from that zookeeper in Kolmården, had been killed by a wolf in Sweden since the beginning of the nineteenth century, and he wasn't expecting Nicole to change that.

Therefore, she would probably survive.

Which meant she would be found. Sooner or later.

The fact that he hadn't seen her didn't necessarily mean that she hadn't seen him.

You do what you have to do, even if you don't always like it.

That's what his mother used to say. All the time. When she got up at five o'clock in the morning to start one of her three jobs, when they moved in with her sister after his father threw them out, when she carried on working in spite of the cancer diagnosis, when she had his dog put down because his aunt thought it was shedding hairs all over the place, every time life put obstacles in her way. You do what you have to do.

Life isn't fair.

Another of his mother's aphorisms, which meant she never even tried to change their situation.

He reached forward and switched off the desk lamp, then sat back in the darkness. Gazed out of the window at the night sky, studded with stars. It was going to be a cold night.

Maybe she would freeze to death after all?

He allowed his thoughts to wander.

The girl. If she had seen him, why didn't she go to the police? She was ten years old. Weren't all kids taught from a very young age to call 112 or to go and speak to a nice kind policeman? So where the hell was she? Could she be deliberately hiding? She hadn't made a sound when he was in the house, when he systematically killed every scrap of security around her. Shock, or considered behaviour?

She was the boys' cousin. Apparently she had been a frequent visitor, but it was unlikely that she knew the surrounding area all that well. So if she didn't want to go to the police, where could she have gone?

He sensed that the answer lay within reach. The final piece of the puzzle was right there in front of him, but he couldn't see it.

But it was there. The answer.

He would find it, there was no doubt about that. He just had to stop thinking about it. That was how he worked. He had to push the problem aside, allow it to marinate in the back of his mind without paying any attention to it. Allow his brain to function in peace. He would find the answer, and then he would have to take the appropriate action.

He had thought . . . no, that was wrong, he had *hoped* that Jan Ceder would be the last. Nicole Carlsten had nothing to do with anything.

But you do what you have to do.

And she had to die.

Life isn't fair.

Billy pushed the computer to one side. There wasn't much more he could do tonight. He had catalogued all the information from Fabian, updated the database, and printed out everything he wanted to put up on the wall the following day. He'd had a brief chat with Maya on Skype; she had asked how the investigation was going, and he had told her about his day.

'How awful,' she had said when she heard about the missing girl. Billy could only agree. Maya wondered when he was coming home; he said truthfully that he didn't know. They both said how much they loved and missed each other, and agreed to talk again tomorrow.

Tomorrow. Another day in the forest, Billy guessed. Organising and joining a search party wasn't his favourite aspect of police work; perhaps he could ask Torkel if he could do something else instead? If twice as many volunteers turned up from Missing People, they should be able to manage without him. Sebastian had got away with it today, after all.

Billy looked at his watch. It was too early to go to bed, and the thought of channel-hopping didn't appeal. He was restless. Should he get changed and go for a run? Clear his mind? Then again, he'd had enough fresh air and exercise in the forest today. He couldn't be the only person who was bored, could he?

★ ★ ★

She seemed surprised to see him when she opened the door.

He held up a bottle of chilled white wine which he had managed to acquire from the restaurant on the ground floor, with a certain amount of persuasion.

'Unexpected,' she said when she had taken the first sip.

'What is?'

'You turning up with a bottle.'

'I was bored,' Billy replied, shrugging his shoulders. 'And it's a long time since we . . . hung out, you and me.'

Vanja smiled to herself. She didn't know anyone else of Billy's age who used so many expressions normally associated with teenagers. The age difference between them was only three years, but he seemed so much younger than her in so many ways. He was on Instagram, Twitter, Tumblr, none of which she used. Not that she was against them in any way – she just didn't see the point of them. Who would she follow, and who would follow her? If there was one thing social media excelled at, it was high-lighting a lack of friends and acquaintances.

'So how's Maya?' she asked, taking another sip. It was Friday night, after all.

'Good. Completely obsessed with the wedding.'

Vanja nodded; it was nice sitting here like this, and she wasn't about to destroy the moment by questioning whether things were perhaps moving a little too fast, criticising him in any way, or making a comment that could be interpreted as unwelcome advice.

'So when do I get to meet her?' she said instead.

'You have met her.'

'I've said hello to her – that doesn't count.'

'You must come over for dinner.'

Vanja nodded. If she hadn't been invited round during the ten months they had been together, it was hardly likely to happen now, but she didn't say that. She emptied her glass and watched Billy as he topped it up.

'You look tired.'

'I miss Ursula,' Billy said honestly. 'I feel as if I'm not up to the job.' Vanja wondered if their old argument was still haunting Billy; she had said she was a much better police officer than he was. Surely not – they'd sorted all that out. Found their way back. But things weren't quite the same as they had been, they both knew that. There was no reason to bring it up again.

'You're doing a fantastic job,' she said, placing her hand on his arm. 'We all miss Ursula, but not because you're not up to the demands of this case.'

'Thanks,' he said with a faint smile.

He missed Jennifer too, but he kept that to himself.

Jennifer Holmgren had been seconded to Riksmord during their previous investigation, when everyone expected Vanja to be joining the FBI training programme at Quantico. That didn't happen, which meant Jennifer no longer had a place on the team. She and Billy had continued to meet up. She was fun to be with. Easy to understand. She had made it very clear that she wanted her career to offer excitement and an adrenaline rush; there wasn't much of that available in Sigtuna where she was based, so they got together at the firing range from time to time. She loved guns, and Billy had to admit that she was a much better shot than he was. What he did have, however, was the experience of shooting living beings.

People.

Edward Hinde and Charles Cederkvist. He had shot and killed both of them.

Billy wished he could say that this had put him off using his service weapon again, but unfortunately that wasn't the case. On both occasions a feeling had lingered in his body for several days afterwards. A positive feeling. It frightened him. Sometimes when he was shooting with Jennifer down in the basement of Police HQ at Kungsholmen, he caught himself picturing a person instead of a black silhouette on a sheet of cardboard. It heightened his senses, increased his pulse rate and gave him . . . yes, pleasure, for want of a better word.

He could never tell anyone that.

Never.

Not Jennifer, although he told her most things. Not even Maya; in spite of the fact that she worked with life coaching and personal development, and was going to be his wife, she knew very little about his darker sides. And definitely not Vanja. Maybe a year or so ago, when their relationship had been more like that of a

142

brother and sister, but not now. Not any more. Something had broken on that day when she said she was a better cop than him, and however much they tried to convince themselves that they'd fixed it, the crack was still there. Jennifer had taken Vanja's place as his confidante.

'How's your dad?' he asked, realising that he actually wanted to know.

'He's been given a new kidney and he seems to be doing well, but I don't see him or my mother these days,' Vanja answered honestly. She was struck by how little she and Billy had talked over the past few months.

'But you're friends with Sebastian again.'

'I don't know about friends . . .'

'OK, but you've stopped thinking he's trying to ruin your life.'

'Yes.'

Billy looked at her. Short answers. Was that because she didn't want to talk about it? If so, she was going to have to ask him to stop.

'You seemed pretty convinced at the hospital.'

'I know, but why would he want to do something like that?'

To keep you close, Billy thought, but he didn't say anything.

'He's a pig in many ways,' Vanja went on, 'but I've chosen to believe him.'

'Fine – I just hope he doesn't let you down again.'

'So do I.'

They sat in silence for a while. Vanja was convinced they were both thinking the same thing. This was Sebastian Bergman they were talking about. The chances of him letting her down again were overwhelming. Billy emptied his glass and put it down on the bedside table.

'Mind if I use the toilet?'

'Of course not.'

Billy went into the bathroom, which was identical with his. As he was having a pee he noticed the little glass shelf below the mirror. In one of the tooth mugs was a blue toothbrush. Vanja's toothbrush.

It felt as if the idea of taking it was pure impulse, as if the opportunity had created the thief, but was that really true? Wasn't this the reason he had come to see Vanja in the first place? She would wonder where the toothbrush had gone, of course, but she would never imagine that he could have taken it. Why would he do such a thing?

Billy flushed the toilet, washed his hands, and after a final brief altercation with himself he picked up the toothbrush, wrapped it in toilet paper and slipped it in his pocket.

He stayed with Vanja for another half-hour or so, then he went back to his room, placed the stolen toothbrush in an envelope and put it in his suitcase. What now? He still wasn't tired. He ought to try and get to sleep, but he knew he wouldn't be able to relax. He decided to go out for a walk; he pulled on his jacket, switched off the light, and closed the door behind him.

It wasn't the dream that woke him this time. It was the hand, wearing a ring, that suddenly landed on his face. It was a second or two before he worked out who it belonged to and how it had ended up in his bed, but then he remembered.

This was probably not a good thing.

Forget probably.

This was not a good thing.

He should have put a stop to it before they got this far, but it was too late now. The owner of the hand turned over in her sleep and the arm to which it was attached flopped across his chest. He had bumped into her in the car park after the evening briefing. Automatically asked if she'd like to go for dinner, not expecting her to say yes. Somehow they had ended up at a slightly dodgy Chinese restaurant, and to his delight he found she was both intelligent and easy to talk to. The place started to get rowdy as the consumption of beer by other customers far outstripped their interest in the food, and Sebastian and his companion decided to leave. She knew a good place; they went to Björnidet where she carried on drinking wine and he carried on seducing her. Hours later she announced that she couldn't possibly drive home. Was his hotel anywhere nearby? It was, as it turned out. Not far away at all.

The sex had been unusually satisfying – inventive and passionate. Perhaps it was because it had been a long time, or maybe they just worked well together. They had fallen asleep just after two.

And now he was wide awake.

The satisfaction was gone, the intimacy nauseating.

He had to get rid of her. They couldn't be seen together.

This wasn't good, but perhaps it didn't have to be the catastrophe it had seemed when he first woke up. He had slept with the mothers of suspects, even with suspects themselves on a number of occasions, so even if this wasn't the smartest thing he had done, you could say that screwing the person in charge of the preliminary investigation was a step in the right direction.

It was doubtful if Torkel would agree with him.

She had no idea what time it was.

She had woken up several times, but had managed to go back to sleep, telling herself it must still be night. Even if it wasn't, what was she going to do? Where would she go? This was where she needed to be right now.

It was no longer quite so cold. She felt better. With the protection of the darkness, she had managed to move more of herself inside. Shrunk on the outside, grown on the inside. She would have preferred to forget that anything existed outside herself. She lay there with her knees drawn up towards her chin. She didn't know how long for, but in the end she had to acknowledge the needs of her body.

She stood up, pressed her back against the wall of the cave, and squeezed out through the narrow fissure. Keeping her hand on the rough surface, she edged a few metres to the right, then squatted down for a pee. It was the first time in many hours. She wasn't drinking enough. The cave was cold and dry – no water trickling down the walls as she had hoped, and no underground lakes. None that she had found, anyway. Not even a puddle.

Should she go back out there? Find something to drink? Get hold of some more food, perhaps a torch? Or matches . . .

But she didn't want to do that. If she went out she would be forced to deal with the outside of herself. Move around, be on her guard, approach people. Someone might be looking for her. She wanted to stay here. She wanted to be on the inside.

She felt her way back along the wall until she reached the crevice, then squeezed back inside and got the things she had brought from the cottage out of her pockets. The label had said that the glacé cherries were in a sugar syrup. She didn't really know what that was, but when she shook the tin it sounded as if there was some kind of liquid inside. She needed a stone to smash it open. She felt around in front of her, but couldn't find anything suitable. Should she force herself out through the fissure to search there? No, it wasn't worth it, she decided.

On the inside she was neither hungry nor thirsty. All she had to do was find her way back there.

She lay down, drew her knees up towards her chin, and after less than a minute she was fast asleep once more.

He was out of bed minutes before the sun appeared behind the trees down by the lake. He didn't need an alarm clock; he always woke with the dawn.

The devil makes work for idle hands, as his mother used to say. Not that she was religious in any way; she probably said it because the early morning was the only time they had together. Then she went off to work, and he was already in bed when she got home. His mother had been dead for many years, but he still couldn't sleep in the mornings.

He pulled on his trousers, buttoned his shirt and ran a hand over his cheeks. It was three days since he had shaved; better do it now.

In front of the bathroom mirror he applied shaving foam, then opened the old-fashioned cut-throat razor as his thoughts circled around the key topic.

What did he know about the Carlstens?

Apart from their fanatical tree-hugging / toxin-free / eco-friendly crap and their general refusal to engage with anything that involved modernisation or progress, of course. What had they said to their young guest? Where had they taken her? A ten-year-old girl who didn't know the area and didn't want to go to the police – where would she hide?

The police were intending to resume the search at first light. Should he go along and join them? No – that might turn out to be counterproductive. What if he was in the group that found the girl, and she recognised him, pointed him out there and then? He had to find her before anyone else did, or everything would have been in vain. What were the odds on his being successful?

Very small, but he had to try. Not just for himself; there was too much at stake. Five people would have died for nothing if he failed.

He rinsed off the remaining white foam with cold water and dabbed at his cheeks with a towel.

What did he know about the Carlstens?

They spent a lot of time outdoors. Of course. Karin had thought Torsby lacked an 'all-weather' nursery, and had tried to change the ethos of the preschool Fred attended, but without success. However, they were always outdoors – presumably when cousin Nicole was visiting too. So they could have taken the girl just about anywhere. He had to work it out. He had to find her.

Find . . .

There was something there. He stopped in mid-movement. Find . . . He met his own gaze in the mirror. He was close now. Concentrate. The piece of the puzzle was within reach.

He had been thinking the wrong way. It was the fault of the newspapers and the police.

They were *searching*. The girl was *lost*. They were *looking for her*, because she was *missing*.

Wrong. She wasn't lost, and she wasn't missing.

She was staying away, she didn't want to be found.

That was the difference. If she just wanted to hide, there were endless possibilities, from crouching down behind a rock to breaking into a summer cottage that was still closed up for the winter. But that meant there was a risk of being found, and that wasn't part of her plan.

Where would a person never be found?

He knew.

The question was, did she know?

She had spent time with her cousins, who had lived here for several years, so of course they must have told her about it. As a ghost story in the evenings, perhaps. The tale of the boys who died. She would have wanted to go there, see where it happened. Hear the warning as she stood outside:

If you go in there, you'll never be found.

There were many parameters to consider, many uncertainties, but this was where his brain had taken him, and he trusted his instincts. It was definitely worth a try. Better than sitting at home and reading on the Internet that she'd been found. Waiting for the police to turn up on his doorstep.

It was within the girl's capabilities. She'd had three days to get there. He wouldn't need more than fifteen minutes. He decided to skip breakfast and head off right away.

To the Bear's Cave.

Almost one hundred and sixty people turned up outside the police station to join the search. Fresh destinations were allocated to the same team leaders as the previous day. Torkel had firmly dismissed any suggestion that Billy should stay behind, and he was given a new group and a new area – further away and bigger this time. Nicole had left the house approximately seventy hours ago; she could have covered a considerable distance. Erik had also decided that because they had almost twice as many volunteers, he would add two new areas that were less likely but still possible. Telephone number, walkie-talkies, sandwiches, Thermos flasks. Cars started up and the place emptied surprisingly quickly.

Almost emptied.

An elderly lady remained behind, leaning on a crutch. She must be getting on for eighty, Erik realised as she hobbled towards him, surprisingly quickly. She was wearing a hat and a thick coat that looked as if it was made of wool, and her scarf was wrapped closely around her neck. There was very little heat from the sun as yet, but there soon would be; not a cloud in the sky. Erik guessed that the old lady just wasn't inclined to perspire.

'All those people were blocking the door,' she said. 'What's going on?'

'We're organising search parties for a missing girl, and—'

'Yes, yes,' the old lady interrupted Erik, waving her free hand impatiently. 'I want to report a crime,' she said. 'A murder.'

★ ★ ★

Fifteen minutes later Erik escorted his visitor back to reception. Her name was Ingeborg Franzén, apparently, and her husband was the president of the local Rotary Club. As he guided her towards the door she repeated that her husband had 'connections', and would therefore find out if her report wasn't taken seriously. It would be, Erik promised, failing to mention that even reports that were taken seriously could be given a low priority. The victim's name was Fluffy; he had been a twelve-year-old moggy with something of the Sacred Birman in him. The starlings had been making a terrible noise when Ingeborg went out to fetch the newspaper that morning, and behind the house she had found Fluffy lying by the dustbins, with a broken neck. His tongue had been sticking out in a way that made Ingeborg certain that someone had strangled her precious little darling. Erik didn't mention that Fluffy could have been hit by a car; the driver might have got out, seen that the cat was beyond help, and simply chucked him into the garden. Callous, immoral, but not impossible or illegal. Instead he repeated his promise that they would do their very best as he more or less shoved her out through the door.

Good God, fifteen minutes on a dead cat, he thought as he went back inside. He didn't even work here any longer.

As he was taking out his pass card, Dennis called to him from the reception desk. Dennis was the only person who was still in the station, apart from Erik and Sebastian Bergman; everyone else was out searching.

Erik turned to see a man standing at the desk.

'Any chance you could take this?' Dennis asked, waving him over. 'It's a break-in.'

'Can't you deal with it?' Erik said, his smile very much at odds with the muted irritation in his voice.

'I'm on my own and I have to answer the phone and . . .'

As if by magic, the phone started ringing. Erik sighed and turned to the man who was waiting patiently.

'This way.'

The main door of the police station opened again as Dennis picked up the phone. The press had been given strict orders to remain outside, which was why most of them had volunteered to join in the hunt for the girl. If they found her, they would have an eyewitness account, perhaps even an exclusive interview. If they didn't find her, they would be able to write an insightful piece about the desperate search and the personal sacrifice they had made in order to be good citizens. A win–win situation, you could say.

The person who walked in wasn't a journalist. He was a young man aged about twenty-five who worked for Statoil, judging by the logo on his clothing. He looked around and strolled over to Dennis, who nodded to him while he dealt with the phone call, taking a number and promising that someone would be in touch. Dennis hung up and turned his attention to the new arrival.

'How can I help you?'

★ ★ ★

Sebastian went over to the whiteboard and wrote down the key points in his profile of the perpetrator:

- MALE
- OVER THIRTY
- KNOWLEDGE OF THE AREA / LOCAL RESIDENT
- PERSONAL CONNECTION TO THE CARLSTENS
- INTELLIGENT / SOCIALLY FUNCTIONAL, POSSIBLY IN A RELATIONSHIP
- PLANNED / NOT HATRED OR RAGE
- MOTIVE / BELIEVES HIS HAND WAS FORCED / NEEDED TO DISPOSE OF AN OBSTACLE OR THREAT

He thought he could hear Billy's voice at that point: *Does that mean he could have acted on someone else's instructions?*

The answer was no, for several reasons.

On the very rare occasions where a contract killer is brought in, the case always involves organised crime. There was nothing to indicate that the Carlsten family was mixed up in anything like that. A professional hit man wouldn't use a borrowed shotgun, and he would have made more of an effort to hide any possible evidence. He might even have burned down the house. Nor would he have stayed in the area or killed Jan Ceder; the police were convinced Ceder knew the perpetrator. There was so much he could throw at Billy if he asked the question; Sebastian almost hoped he would.

There was a knock on the door frame and a uniformed officer Sebastian had seen around came in. He hadn't a clue what the man was called.

'Could you speak to a member of the public, please?'

'I'd rather not – isn't Erik around?'

'He's with someone, and this is important. It's about the girl. He says he's seen her.'

'He's seen Nicole?'

'Yes – shall I bring him in here?'

'Good idea. I think as many people as possible should be confronted with photographs of a slaughtered family.'

The young officer immediately realised his mistake. 'I'll put him in the staffroom.'

Sebastian sighed. This place was a madhouse. Perhaps he would have been better out in the forest after all? Then again, it could have been worse. Malin Åkerblad could have been here. She had left for Karlstad this morning, and wouldn't be back until tomorrow evening, unless there were major developments. He hadn't woken her until five thirty, when he had shaken her and told her she had to go. She had wanted to know why, and for once he had chosen to tell the truth.

'I really don't want Torkel and the others to see you. He wouldn't like it one little bit.'

Tempered with one small lie:

'And I was hoping we could do this again . . .'

She had nodded, understood, and let him know that she too was looking forward to a repeat performance next time they met. Sebastian had somehow managed to produce a smile.

He hoped she wouldn't give him away when she came back, that she wouldn't be clingy or affectionate. His temporary cease-fire with Torkel was fragile.

He headed for the staffroom. A young man in beige and blue clothing was waiting for him. He was wearing a cap over his dark hair, and had a narrow, angular face. Brown eyes, quite close together. Skin badly scarred from acne.

'Tell me,' Sebastian said, sitting down opposite him without bothering to introduce himself.

'I saw in the paper this morning that you were looking for her,' the young man said, pointing to the picture of Nicole on the front page of the newspaper on the table.

'Yes.'

'I saw her. Yesterday.'

'I already know that. All I'm interested in is *where* you saw her.'

'At work. At the petrol station,' he said, pointing to the logo on his shirt. 'When she came in I thought she was with someone who was filling up, but then she hung around by the chilled counter. She didn't seem to know anyone.'

'OK, that's very interesting, but *where*?' Sebastian asked, becoming increasingly impatient.

'I'm not sure, but I think she stole some food,' the man went on as if he had rehearsed his story and had no intention of diverging from the script.

'I expect she did,' Sebastian agreed. '*Where*?' he asked again, hoping it would be third time lucky.

★ ★ ★

Back in the incident room it didn't take Sebastian long to find the petrol station. He pushed in a pin and added the date and time. He heard footsteps in the corridor, and saw a man walk past the door, closely followed by Erik.

'Erik!' Sebastian called out.

'Back in a minute – I'm just showing this gentleman out,' Erik replied.

Sebastian sat down and contemplated the map, as if it could tell him where Nicole had gone after her visit to the petrol station. She had headed north-west from the Carlstens' house. Had she carried on in the same direction? If so, how far had she gone? Did they have a search team in that area?

'What do you want?' Erik asked as he stuck his head round the door. Sebastian certainly wasn't imagining the animosity in his voice.

'She was here yesterday,' Sebastian replied, getting up and pointing. 'She stole some food from a petrol station.'

Erik came into the room, looking interested. 'The guy who just left came to report a break-in at his summer cottage about a kilometre from there,' he said, indicating the exact spot on the map. 'Broken window, nothing stolen apart from a small amount of food, and it looked as if someone had slept under one of the beds.'

'Under the bed?'

'Yes – the pillow and duvet were still there.'

Sebastian thought fast.

A frightened little girl.

Frightened of everything, but she had to sleep, had to eat. It could be someone else, but the cottage was in the right direction, and anything of value that was of no interest to a girl on the run had been left untouched.

'If this is Nicole, she's heading north-west. What's further on, if she keeps going?'

'Norway eventually . . .'

'I think we can assume she's not planning to emigrate,' Sebastian muttered. 'What's on the way to Norway, up here?' He drew a circle with his finger on the map; Erik took a closer look, then shook his head.

'Nothing, really. Well, there's the Bear's Cave, but I shouldn't think she'd know about that, and if she did she wouldn't go there.'

'Why not?'

'Two boys disappeared there back in the eighties. They were never found. All the kids around here have it drummed into them that if you go inside the Bear's Cave, you'll never be found.'

Everything fell into place.

'That's what she wants,' Sebastian said instinctively. 'That's where she is.' He saw Erik's sceptical expression, and pre-empted him. 'Yes, I am sure. Call the others and let's get up there.'

She suddenly woke up.

A noise. She must have heard a noise.

It was daylight outside, she noticed. A small amount had found its way into the hollow where she was lying, but not enough to wake her. So she hadn't gone far enough into the cave; the light could still reach her. She would have to move. Go further in. Into the darkness. Into oblivion.

It was cold. Her breath was white. But that hadn't woken her either; she had been chilled to the bone more or less all night. No, she was sure it was something else. A noise.

She held her breath and turned her head, listening hard. Her tummy rumbled; she was so hungry she felt slightly sick. However, she quickly pushed aside the feeling when she heard it again. A crunching sound. Footsteps on the loose gravel at the entrance to the cave.

★ ★ ★

He stopped.

The sound of the gravel shifting under his weight seemed unnaturally loud, bouncing off the bare walls of the cave. If she was here, she would probably hear him.

So far he had made sure that no one had seen him. He had parked the car on a forest track almost a kilometre away, then walked through the trees. Before leaving home he had chosen a Serbu Super-Shorty; it was only forty-two centimetres long, and easy to hide under his oilskin coat. Were the acoustics in the cave system going to be his downfall?

He stood very still as he took the head torch out of his pocket and put it on. The powerful beam lit up the nearest wall and the way in. The plan had been to creep inside, hoping that she had left some kind of trail, or that she would be forced to move when he came closer, so that he would hear her. He was an experienced hunter. But she had probably heard him already; the element of surprise was lost. Might as well go for it.

'Nicole!' he shouted, moving forward as he unhooked the compact shotgun from inside his coat. 'We know you're here. I'm with the police.'

★ ★ ★

'I'm here to help you.'

Nicole shuffled backwards in the tiny space and pressed her body against the wall as hard as she could. She wrapped her arms around her shins, put her head on her knees and made herself as small as possible. She didn't realise it, but her breathing was shallow, panting. The footsteps outside grew louder, they were coming closer.

'Nicole! Everything's OK, you can come out now. It's the police.'

Nicole looked up without letting go of her legs. Beyond the crevice she could see a beam of light playing across the walls. If he shone it in here, there was absolutely no chance that he wouldn't spot her.

'Nicole!'

Maybe if she sat right next to the narrow entrance? On the right there was a projecting wall, about fifteen centimetres wide. If she could press herself against it, it was just possible that he might miss her, even if he shone his torch inside.

Cautiously she straightened her legs, then shifted her weight so that she could crawl over there. She discovered that she was more or less hyperventilating, and forced herself to breathe more slowly. She groped in front of her with her hands, then followed with one knee. It wasn't far. Another three shuffles and she would be there. She kept on going. Just a little bit further, turn around, press her back up against the wall. She could do it. One last push . . .

She felt it before she heard it. One of the tins fell out of her pocket, landed with a thud and rolled away.

★ ★ ★

He was about to call out again when he heard a metallic thud, followed by the sound of something rolling over the rocky floor. He stopped, listened. Of course the cave could change the perception of sound, but it had seemed to come from close by. Very close by. He took one step forward, tightening his grip on the gun.

She was here.

He had been right.

All he had to do now was find her.

But she was a frightened little girl, and he had all the time in the world. This could only end one way. For a moment he felt something like sorrow over what he was going to have to do, but he had no choice. There was no way back. You do what you have to do, even if you don't always like it.

He swept the beam of the head torch from right to left. Further in, the track would divide, becoming a labyrinth of caves and shafts, but here there was only one route; she couldn't have gone any other way.

He stopped again. What was that? A shadow? But of what? There were no projections outside to block the light. No, it wasn't a shadow, it was a crevice. Not very big, but wide enough for a ten-year-old to squeeze through. He directed the beam at the gap and advanced purposefully.

★ ★ ★

She had made it. There was enough room for her. She didn't think he would be able to see her if he looked through the crevice. She could hear him outside. Getting closer. The torch beam flickered across the wall to her right. She held her breath. Perhaps he would miss the entrance altogether. Then the light stopped moving. It was fixed on the crevice. On her hiding place.

But he might still miss her. She pressed herself even harder against the wall. Sharp stones cut into her back through her jacket. Then she saw it. The tin. If he looked inside he couldn't help seeing it. If he'd heard it, he'd know she was there. She had to move it. But how? The steps came closer and closer and the beam never left the entrance.

She was just about to hurl herself forward and try to grab the tin when she heard them.

★ ★ ★

He heard them too. Noises. Easily identifiable. Tyres on gravel, car doors opening and closing, footsteps, voices . . . Impossible to say how many, but more than one. The police or one of the search parties, presumably. And why not – if he could work out where she was, so could they. Was she inside that crevice? Did he have time to kill her? They would hear the shot, but he could disappear inside the cave system, stay hidden. But for how long? And how would he get out? He had no idea what it looked like deep inside. They would use dogs. He was screwed. He had missed his chance. He switched off his head torch and moving rapidly, almost silently, he headed away from the entrance.

★ ★ ★

Erik switched on the powerful torch as they walked into the cave.

'How far does it go?' Sebastian asked as they took their first steps into the icy stillness.

'No one knows. No one has explored the whole system.'

That wasn't good news. If Nicole had come here to disappear, there was a possibility that she had gone as far as she could. Which meant she might be the third child who was never found. However, as far as they knew she had no source of light with her, so the dense darkness might make her think she was further in than she actually was. She might feel safe even though she wasn't far inside the mountain.

Behind them they heard another car arrive, and seconds later Billy joined them with four people Sebastian didn't recognise.

'Why do we think she's here?' Billy asked, shining his torch ahead of Erik and Sebastian.

'We just know,' Sebastian replied, and to his surprise Billy seemed satisfied.

'So what do we do now?'

'The passageway is fairly wide here,' Erik said, taking over. 'After thirty metres it splits into several narrow tracks, which in their turn divide again further along. We have to find a way of covering as much ground as possible.'

'OK, I'll call for more volunteers and ask them to bring ropes and lamps and all that kind of stuff,' Billy said with a nod, turning away.

'The rest of you wait here,' Erik ordered Billy's four companions. 'See if the others need any help when they arrive. Sebastian and I will carry on as far as the fork in the passageway.'

The two of them set off. The roof of the cave was quite high; four or five metres, Sebastian guessed. No stalactites or any of those other pretty things associated with caves. Just hard, bare, grey-brown walls.

'Nicole! My name is Erik and I'm a police officer. We're here to help you.'

'She won't answer,' Sebastian commented drily. 'She doesn't want to be found by anyone.'

'Nicole!' Erik shouted again as if he hadn't heard – or as if he was determined to ignore Sebastian.

They carried on going, and suddenly Sebastian pointed to the left and said: 'There!' Erik followed his finger with the beam of his torch, and saw something that looked like a slender shadow on the rock. 'What is it?'

'A crevice.'

They moved closer and Sebastian leaned forward. It wasn't very wide, no more than thirty centimetres at the narrowest point. Wide enough for a ten-year-old, perhaps. Erik directed the torch inside and they saw a small space, just a few square metres. The light picked up something on the floor over by the rough wall: a tin of chopped tomatoes.

But no girl.

'Quiet.' Sebastian turned his head so that his ear was against the opening. Erik lowered his head and they both stood there motionless and silent, for a long time. Sebastian was about to straighten up when he heard it. A faint exhalation. Almost a gasp.

He took the torch from Erik without a word, then moved as far to the right as he could, put his hand inside the gap and shone the beam to the left.

A shoe, a foot and part of a leg.

'She's here,' he said, stepping back. 'I'd like you to go outside. Take the others with you, and go right outside.'

Erik met Sebastian's gaze and realised there was no point in protesting or asking questions.

'I'll call an ambulance,' he said with a nod.

Sebastian waited until he could no longer hear footsteps, then he sank down on the cold floor. Might as well get as comfortable as possible. This could take a while.

'Nicole, my name is Sebastian and I work with the police,' he began. No reply. Not that he had expected one. This would probably be a monologue.

'We've been looking for you. We know what happened to your cousins and their parents.'

Not a sound. Not a movement.

'I realise you don't want to come out. I understand why you're here, but hiding away isn't going to make things better.'

He shuffled on the hard, uneven surface. He was already suffering; how was he going to feel if this went on as long as he feared it might? He pushed the thought away.

'Your mum, Maria, is on her way, but she won't be here for a while. We can wait here if you like, but it would be warmer and more comfortable if we went somewhere else. You must be hungry too – we can go and get something to eat. Anything you like.'

No sign that she had heard him.

'I know that what you saw was terrible, but you don't need to be afraid. Everyone is here to protect you.'

Silence.

This was definitely going to take a while.

★ ★ ★

Billy was standing by the entrance to the cave. He rubbed the two scratches on the back of his hand and looked over at the area beyond the cordon by the fence that was half-trampled down. There were a lot of people here now. Two ambulances; the paramedics were standing by a trolley having a smoke. Several reporters, of course. Two TV news teams – Torkel was talking to one of them – and a few photographers had climbed up the little hill to the left to get an overview of the proceedings. Billy recognised most faces from the briefings before the search parties set off, but some were new. He guessed there were around seventy people hoping to get a glimpse of the little girl when she emerged.

He took a deep breath. The air was clear and a little chilly, even though the sun was shining in an almost cloudless sky. His nostrils were filled with the smell of forest and dampness and earth. For a moment he was transported straight back to the forest behind the house where he had grown up; he had spent virtually all his spare time out there, playing games with Ray and Peter.

Vanja pushed her way through the crowd, nodded to one of the uniformed officers by the cordon and slipped under the blue-and-white tape as he held it up for her.

'I've spoken to the Swedish International Development Corporation,' she said before she even reached Billy. 'Nicole's mother is on a plane that's due to land at 16.25 this afternoon.'

'Does she know what's happened?'

'Yes, they told her.'

'Is someone picking her up, or shall I go?'

'Torkel can sort that out. How are things going?'

Billy shrugged. 'No idea.'

'How long has he been in there?'

Billy glanced at his watch. 'Almost forty-five minutes.'

'What the hell are they talking about for all this time?'

★ ★ ★

Nothing, at the moment.

Sebastian had talked about everything under the sun, trying to remember as much as he could about Nicole. He wanted to make her feel safe, make her understand that they knew who she was. Win her trust.

It obviously hadn't worked.

Sebastian stretched his legs out in front of him, pushed back his shoulders and tried to sit up straight. He was getting really, really uncomfortable now. He wanted to sort this, not just so that he could get to his feet and leave the icy darkness behind, but because it was what he was supposed to be good at. No one had questioned his authority when he ordered everyone out of the cave. A traumatised little girl on one side of a stone wall, a well-educated, highly competent psychologist on the other. He was expected to succeed. So far he had got nowhere. He hadn't managed to make that vital connection. Factual information, coaxing, assurances – none of it was enough. He was going to have to give more of himself if she was going to trust him.

He took a deep breath and lowered his voice in the hope that it would sound more sincere, more honest.

'Sometimes when something happens, when you're sad because you've lost something, people say they understand how you feel, but most of the time they haven't a clue, because they've never lost anything precious.'

He turned and fixed his gaze on the crevice, pictured the little girl from the photo in the police station sitting there listening to him.

'But I think I really do know how you feel. I know what it's like when people you love suddenly aren't there any more.' He paused. Was this the right way to go? Did he actually want to do this? What he wanted didn't matter, he told himself. This was about what had to be done. 'I lost my wife and daughter in the tsunami,' he went on. 'Do you know what that is? It's a massive wave that came racing ashore in Thailand on Boxing Day in 2004.'

He fell silent again. He very rarely allowed himself to revisit these memories when he was awake. There was a reason for that. It wasn't too late to turn back, try something else. Choose a simpler approach. But no. With his unseeing eyes gazing into the darkness, he went back there.

To 2004.

To the disaster.

'We were down on the beach, my daughter and I. Her name was Sabine. My wife, Sabine's mother, had gone for a run. We were playing in the water, when suddenly the wave came. It was several metres high. I grabbed hold of Sabine just before the water hit us. I held her hand in my right hand, told myself I mustn't let her go. But somehow she disappeared. I couldn't hold on to her. I dream about it almost every night. I clench my right hand so tightly that it hurts.'

He was doing it now, he realised. He took a few more deep breaths and forced his fingers open.

'Sabine was four years old. I never found her. I never found my wife either. They were just snatched away, like your cousins and Karin and Emil. One second everything was perfectly normal, and the next everything was shattered. It hurt so much that I thought I would never be able to feel anything but pain for the rest of my life.'

He took a moment; he could hardly tell a ten-year-old the truth. That the pain never went away, that it became part of his life, that all the bad choices he had made, all the one-night stands, all the successful attempts to alienate everyone around him stemmed from that pain. That it was slowly poisoning him, combined with the guilt he still felt. Instead he shuffled around so that he could reach in through the crevice with his right hand.

'I let go of my daughter, but . . . there's no giant wave here, Nicole. No natural disaster. Just . . . a bad guy, and I can protect you from the bad guys. If you take my hand, I will hold on to you. I won't let you go until you want me to. When you're whole again. When it doesn't hurt any more. I can do that, I promise. I can help you. Please, Nicole – let me help you . . .'

His voice was breaking; he had to stop. For the second time that week, he felt the tears pouring down his face. He reached in as far as he could. This was no longer about getting a little girl out of a cave; this was about the possibility of reconciliation.

At first he didn't notice the movement, but then he felt it.

A little cold hand in his.

★ ★ ★

He carried Nicole towards the ambulance. She weighed more than he had expected, and the ground was uneven and strewn with loose stones. Several times he stumbled and almost fell. Nicole's arms were wound tightly around his neck. She didn't make a sound, but he could feel her warm breath on his neck. It was as if it gave him oxygen.

He was going to save her.

This time he wouldn't let go.

They were getting closer to the ambulance, very slowly. Two of the paramedics caught sight of them and ran over.

'How is she?' the first one asked; he was a muscular man in his mid-thirties, with multiple tattoos.

'OK, I think, but she's in shock,' Sebastian replied, feeling the child's grip tighten as the paramedic touched her forehead. She turned away and buried her face in Sebastian's chest.

'Shall I take her?' the paramedic asked gently.

Sebastian shook his head, straightened his back and kept on going.

'No, it's fine. I've got her.'

He spoke mainly to reassure the small figure in his arms. He felt her body relax a little; not much, but enough for him to real-ise that she trusted him. A wonderful feeling that gave him strength. He increased his speed.

'I'll sort out the trolley,' the paramedic said, running back to the ambulance. Sebastian nodded, but thought it was unlikely that Nicole would let go even if they offered her the softest four-poster bed in the world.

'Nicole, you're safe now. Everyone here wants to help you,' he said. There was no reply, but he felt her relax a little more, and her breathing slowed down. Words were superfluous; her body told him what he needed to know.

She was listening. That was enough.

They reached the ambulance, and the paramedics wheeled the trolley forward. The onlookers had begun to gather close by, cameras and mobile phones at the ready. A number of police officers and five or six civilians, presumably from Missing People, formed a protective circle around them. Suddenly it infuriated him, the silent, motionless group waiting for them. They didn't care if the girl was alive or dead, they were just nosy. The public. He and Nicole were the entertainment they had been waiting for.

'Get out of the way!' he yelled. They took a few steps back, and he felt Nicole's arms tighten the closer they got, as if she sensed that someone would soon try to force her to let go. The paramedic was holding up a pale orange blanket.

'Nicole, I'm going to have to put you down. The paramedics need to check you over, make sure you're OK,' he said as gently as he could. He tried to stroke her hair. 'You'll be seeing your mum very soon – won't that be lovely?'

She reacted immediately.

A glimmer of hope in her eyes. The fear that had filled her was defeated for a second. He held her even closer, looked into her eyes, drowned her in tenderness. Repeated the words that had had such an effect.

'I'm going to take you to your mum. I promise. I'm going to take you to your mum.'

He knew that repetition healed, particularly loving assurances. Trauma was a wall, love a way through, repetition the hammer that broke down the barrier.

Torsby Hospital was surprisingly modern, and Dr Hansson and her team of four, who met them as soon as they arrived, gave an impression of calm competence. Nicole and Sebastian were quickly transferred to a private room. Dr Hansson was a woman aged about fifty-five, with glasses and short, curly hair. She spoke gently to Nicole but the girl didn't answer; she merely pressed herself closer to Sebastian's chest with every question she was asked.

The consultant gave up and turned to Sebastian.

'Has she been this uncommunicative all along?' she asked, her expression grave.

'Yes, and she's been holding on to me like this ever since I persuaded her to come out of the cave.'

The doctor nodded and stroked the child's hair.

'Nicole, you're safe here. We just want to check that you're OK,' she ventured in a motherly tone.

The caress and the soft words seemed to help. Sebastian felt Nicole's muscles relax slightly. Dr Hansson leaned closer to him.

'I'd like to give her a mild sedative – could you help me?' she whispered.

'No problem.' He looked down at the little girl, caught her eye. 'The doctor wants to give you some medicine. Would that be all right?'

Nicole gazed up at him enquiringly; the fact that she trusted him touched Sebastian deeply. He smiled at her.

'It's OK, Nicole. I'll make sure nothing bad happens to you.'

Hansson held out a pipette; Nicole didn't turn away, but allowed the doctor to slip it into her mouth and empty the contents.

'Good girl. It will take a little while for the drops to work – I'd like to do some tests in the meantime,' Dr Hansson said, turning to Sebastian. 'Could you help me with that too?'

Sebastian nodded, not taking his eyes off Nicole.

'Of course. Any news of her mother? Is she on her way?'

'I've no idea.'

'I can give you the number of the Senior Investigating Officer – he should know.'

'Give it to Sister Samira,' Dr Hansson said, pointing to a slender, dark-haired young woman in green scrubs. She looked as if she came from the Middle East, but answered in a broad Värmland accent. Sebastian gave her Torkel's number and she went off to make the call.

Meanwhile another nurse had brought over a small trolley so that she could take blood samples. Sebastian stroked Nicole's hair and got her to hold out her hand.

It took fifteen minutes for the sedative to work. Meanwhile the staff managed to take the samples they needed, and to check both her pulse and blood pressure. Nicole's grip gradually loosened, and after a few minutes she let go completely. It was as if all the anxiety flowed out of her, to be replaced by much-needed sleep. Now Sebastian was the one who didn't want to let go, but he knew that he must; there was a lot to do.

Samira returned; she had spoken to Torkel. He was about to hold a press conference and would then come over to the hospital, but Vanja was already on her way. Sebastian decided to lay the sleeping child on the bed. She was really sweet, especially now, without those anxious eyes following every movement, that tense jawline. Now she was just a little girl again, a sleeping ten-year-old. Only the grazed knees and her dirty face, hands and clothes betrayed something of what she had been through. Sebastian settled her gently, then picked up a compress from the bedside table, moistened it with cleanser and began to dab at her face. The white compress was grey in no time. He exchanged it for a fresh one; the same thing happened again.

He didn't notice Vanja standing in the doorway until she spoke. He had the feeling she'd been watching him for a while.

'How's she doing?'

'She's slightly dehydrated, but all her values are normal. She's sleeping now.'

'Good. Can I have a word?'

Sebastian straightened up; before he left he tucked an orange hospital blanket around Nicole. To tell the truth, he didn't want to leave her. The last hour had been so emotionally intense that he had no desire to return to reality. To the murder investigation. To a team groping in the darkness.

He went out into the long, empty corridor with Vanja. It could have been a hospital corridor anywhere in Sweden, with its green vinyl floor reflecting the fluorescent lights. Sebastian wondered if anyone had researched what a hospital corridor should look like in order to make the patients want to get out as quickly as possible. He couldn't remember seeing that unpleasant shade of green anywhere else.

From a room further along he could hear voices talking eagerly; presumably they were gossiping about the latest admission. About the police. About the crime, what they'd read and heard. That was how it worked. Events became real and important only when the newspapers and television took an interest. And now they were more than interested. Now they had a survivor. The girl from the 'House of Horror', as *Expressen* had so poetically described her.

'Has she said anything?'

'Nothing at all, I'm afraid.'

Vanja managed to look both surprised and annoyed at the same time.

'Nothing? Surely she must have said something?'

'Not a word. She's deeply traumatised.'

Vanja moved on to scepticism.

'So you're telling me we have no new information, in spite of the fact that we've found a possible eyewitness?'

'I'm afraid so. But we've done a good job – we've found Nicole. That's the most important thing, after all.'

Vanja didn't reply, but her expression made it clear that she didn't agree. She wanted to catch the killer. She was glad they'd found Nicole, of course, but as far as Vanja was concerned, the girl had only one function: she was a lead. A route to the perpetrator. Her possible contribution to the investigation was more important than her well-being. Sebastian understood perfectly; he usually felt the same.

'We're holding a press conference at the council offices,' she said. 'Do you want to be there?'

Sebastian shook his head. He'd been up since five. Sat in a cave. Carried a little girl in his arms. But the exhaustion had only just caught up with him. He sighed.

'What's the point of a press conference?'

'The fact that we've found her is already all over the Net,' Vanja explained. 'If we don't say something, they'll just start speculating.'

'Surely they'll speculate anyway?'

'It's Torkel's decision, and I think he's right.'

Sebastian had no intention of arguing with her over something they both knew was a necessary evil. It was just a fact of life.

'She must have seen something,' Vanja said, nodding towards Nicole's room. 'Get her to start talking. That's your job.'

With that she disappeared around the corner. He let her have the last word.

It no longer mattered to him.

Torkel stepped up to the pale wooden lectern, surrounded by microphones bearing company logos, clearly visible to the cameras: SVT, TV4, SR, TT, NRK.

He had intended to hold the press conference at the police station, but had changed his mind because there wasn't a room big enough. Erik had suggested asking Pia if they could use the council chamber, and now Torkel was about to speak in a room where political rather than police matters were normally discussed. Not that there would be a great deal of discussion; most of those gathered in front of him already knew more or less everything there was to know. This performance was more for form's sake – playing to the gallery, in a way. 'In order to show openness between the police and the media' as it had said in a message from on high in which senior officers were also encouraged to open a Twitter account.

Torkel waited until the hum of conversation died down, then briefly ran through the information known to the police.

The girl was related to the Carlsten family. She had probably been in the house when the family was shot, and since then had managed to remain hidden. She had been found – as everyone was no doubt aware – in the Bear's Cave, roughly ten kilometres north of the town, and was now in hospital. She was slightly dehydrated and there was some evidence of hypothermia, but there were no physical injuries. As far as the murders were concerned, the investigation was ongoing, but there were no suspects at present. Until forensic tests had been completed he couldn't confirm that Jan Ceder had been killed with the same gun, but a connection between the murders of Ceder and the Carlsten family could not be excluded.

Torkel fell silent and took a deep breath. This was the part he disliked the most.

'Any questions?' he said, his gaze sweeping the room as a forest of hands shot up, waving to attract his attention. He pointed to a red-haired woman he didn't recognise on the front row.

'Have you found a motive for the murder of the family?' she asked in melodic Norwegian.

'No, but there definitely was a motive – they weren't chosen at random.'

'How can you be sure of that?'

'I'd rather not say,' Torkel replied, and was immediately asked what he was prepared to say with regard to the motive.

Vanja was leaning on the wall at the back of the room. Torkel had offered her the opportunity not only to get involved, but to lead the press conference. She had declined, and she was very glad she had made that decision as she watched him calmly answering question after question. It was good to be working again, she thought, rather than having too much time on her hands, getting bogged down in illness and lies. Good to focus on something else. However, she knew she didn't have the patience to run a press conference; she became irritated and snappy far too easily these days.

As if to confirm her thoughts, her mood immediately dropped to freezing point as the heavy door of the chamber opened and Malin Åkerblad walked in. The prosecutor stopped just inside as the door closed behind her; she looked around, spotted Vanja and came over.

'You found her. The girl,' she said quietly in her husky voice.

'Obviously.' Vanja kept her eyes fixed on her boss.

'Can she identify the killer?'

'We don't know yet, we haven't questioned her.' She sensed Malin nodding to herself. 'I thought you weren't due back until tomorrow?' Vanja said, unable to hide the fact that this would have been preferable as far as she was concerned. Actually, she would have preferred it if Åkerblad hadn't come back at all.

'Is Sebastian here?' Malin asked, gazing around the chamber as though she hadn't heard Vanja's comment. Vanja turned and looked at her. No doubt Malin Åkerblad thought she had asked the question in an appropriately casual tone of voice, but there was something else, something more, and Vanja was good at picking up that kind of thing.

Sebastian.

First name, a hint of anticipation, that little unconscious smile. He'd slept with her.

Vanja really didn't care how many women Sebastian screwed, or who they were; he clearly had a problem, an addiction perhaps. But Malin Åkerblad?! The incompetent cow who had released the only person who could have moved the investigation forward?

He'd slept with her?!

Personally, Vanja would regard that as the worst punishment of all, but it was obvious that Malin didn't share her point of view. To her surprise she felt as if Sebastian had let her down. Things had been going well between them since their fresh start; he really seemed to be making an effort to regain her trust. Then he went and slept with their common enemy. In a strange way she felt as if he had rejected her.

'Is he here?' Malin repeated when Vanja didn't respond. 'I can't see him.'

'He's at the hospital.'

'Oh, right.'

'We've taken a closer look at Jan Ceder's circle of acquaintances,' Vanja went on quickly and quietly before Malin decided to leave. 'You remember him? He's the guy you released. The one who got shot.'

Malin didn't speak, but the look on her face said it all.

'Anyway, there aren't many of them. The local police have gone in hard, but those who don't have an alibi just aren't capable of doing something like this.'

Malin seemed genuinely puzzled. 'Why are you telling me this? I want to know when you get results, not when you don't.'

'Ceder knew who had his shotgun, and you let him go. It's a mystery to me why you're still in charge of the preliminary investigation.'

'I don't like your tone.'

'I don't like you.'

They weighed each other up. In the background Vanja could hear the question-and-answer session still going on:

'You said the girl was related to the Carlsten family – in what way?'

'We don't need to go into that.'

'She's the boys' cousin, isn't she?'

'Next question.'

'Did she see the killer?'

'We don't know, and the less speculation the better.'

Malin took a deep breath as if she was about to say something, then thought better of it. Instead she drew her jacket more tightly around her and got ready to leave. Vanja stopped her.

'Just one more thing . . .'

Malin's expression left no doubt about how little interest she had in anything Vanja had to say.

'He's a sex addict. Sebastian. He'll screw any woman with a pulse. Just so you know what you're getting into.'

Malin simply turned on her heel and marched out. Vanja couldn't suppress a satisfied little smile as she turned her attention to what was going on at the front of the room. Torkel was busy gathering up his papers, and a woman Vanja hadn't seen before took his place on the podium.

'Good afternoon, everyone, if you could just remain seated for a moment . . . My name is Pia Flodin, and for those of you who don't already know, I'm the chair of the council here in Torsby. I'd just like to take this opportunity to thank Torkel Högberg and his team for coming here . . .'

Vanja met Torkel by the door.

'Did I see you talking to the prosecutor?' he asked quietly.

'You did.'

'What did she want?'

'Sebastian, apparently.'

'Why?'

Torkel raised an eyebrow, but Vanja could see that he already knew the answer.

'I've no idea – what do you think, herr Högberg?'

'Shut up,' Torkel said, smiling in spite of himself as he pushed open the door.

Her mind was spinning as fast as the trees were racing by outside.

The police car was speeding, its blue lights casting a vivid reflection on other vehicles as they pulled over to let it through. The woman police officer at the wheel didn't say a word. Maria Carlsten was sitting in the back, surrounded by the smell of leather and disinfectant, but she couldn't quite remember how she had ended up there.

They had found Nicole.

She was alive.

That was all she knew right now.

She should be happy. Ecstatic. But that was impossible. Completely impossible.

The past twenty-four hours had been the worst day of Maria's life. She was cold, sweaty, exhausted and finding it difficult to focus with her eyes. She couldn't remember when she had last slept, but she was still finding it hard to sit still. She felt as if tiny creatures were crawling all over her body. The panic that had seized her when she got the call in Bamako was still there, twisting and turning inside her, making her feel sick. She opened the window to get some fresh air. The draught made a whistling sound; the gap was too small. She lowered the window a little further, and the noise stopped. She moved her head closer and the cold air blew onto her face. It was nice, although the interior of the car soon felt chilly. She closed her eyes and tried to suppress her fear.

She knew Nicole was alive.

She ought to be relieved, she realised that, but the guilt was in the way. Behind Nicole stood a family that had been wiped out.

Maria's little sister Karin, Emil and the boys. She had no idea how to reconcile her joy and her grief.

It was inhuman. A wave of nausea swept over her, leaving a nasty taste in her dry mouth. She fumbled for the bottle of water the police officer had given her, took a swig of the tepid liquid, letting it fill her mouth. Swilled it around, then swallowed. Looked out again at the trees. Felt the wind in her face. Shivered, but didn't do anything about it. It seemed somehow appropriate.

She was on her way to an inhuman place.

A place that held both the greatest sorrow and the greatest joy.

★ ★ ★

The large two-storey building with a sign reading 'Torsby Hospital' appeared all of a sudden. For a while it had seemed as if the police car would keep on driving for ever and ever, that she would be on the way to her daughter for all eternity, and never arrive.

Then all at once she was there.

Only a few metres from the person she longed to see.

What would happen now? Would she regain control, or would things continue to happen without her being able to influence them in any way?

Whatever. She couldn't wait; she surprised herself by opening the door before the car had stopped completely. She wanted to run inside, find her daughter, never leave her again. The policewoman leaned towards her and raised her voice for the first time.

'Wait! They want you to wait here. They're going to take you in through the back.'

Maria was furious, overcome with anger at everything that had happened. At last, she thought. It was high time. It gave her an energy she hadn't believed she could summon up.

'I'm not waiting any longer!' she said firmly, pushing the door wide open. She was going to find her child.

She ran towards the big glass doors. They would open, and Nicole would be there. Behind her she could hear the policewoman calling again:

'Wait! Maria, wait!'

Maria glanced over her shoulder to see if the woman was coming after her to try and stop her, but she was just standing there shouting. Maria hadn't expected it to be so easy. She increased her speed; the entrance was right in front of her. It was so good to get some oxygen in her lungs, feel the strength in her muscles. She didn't even feel sick any more. The reddish-brown building came closer; she could see people moving around behind the glass.

Nearly there.

Nothing could stop her.

Nothing.

'Maria Carlsten?'

Someone was calling her name. She tried to ignore the man who was getting up from a bench a few metres from the entrance. He was wearing a green parka that was rather too big for him, and brown trousers. She could see that he was going to cut her off, block her path. She speeded up even more; she had no intention of stopping.

'I don't have time,' she snapped. The man took two steps towards her. He was tall, slightly overweight, but she was sure she could get past him. Push him out of the way if necessary.

'I'm the one who found Nicole.' His voice was calm, tentative, and she immediately believed him. 'I need to speak to you,' he went on.

Maria lost her impetus. Her strength drained away in seconds. She turned to the man who was simply standing there waiting for her, utterly self-assured.

'My name is Sebastian Bergman,' he said, holding out his hand. 'I work as a psychologist with Riksmord. Your daughter is fine, I promise.'

'I have to see her,' she said, her tone almost pleading. 'That's all I want.'

'You will see her, but I need to have a word with you first.'

He glanced around, slipped a hand under her arm and led her away from the doors.

'Come with me. There are quite a few reporters in there.'

Maria obediently complied; she didn't have the energy to resist any more. She saw the policewoman over by the car give a nod of acknowledgement to the man who had taken over responsibility for her. The two of them cut across the turning area, heading for the entrance used by emergency vehicles. There was an ambulance parked outside at an odd angle, next to several green benches. One of the paramedics was having a smoke. That was something Maria could never understand; how could hospital staff, the very people who probably knew most about the damaging effects of nicotine, carry on smoking? Sebastian stopped at the first bench; they sat down, and he turned to face her.

'OK. The doctors have examined Nicole, and from a purely physical point of view, she's doing pretty well. She's tired and dehydrated, but nothing serious.'

She could tell from his tone that there was something else he wanted to say. Something he was keeping back.

'So why do you need to talk to me, if everything's fine?'

Sebastian took a deep breath before he went on:

'Because she won't talk. Nicole hasn't spoken at all since I found her.'

The words hurt. They were so heavy, in spite of the fact that there were so few of them. She removed his hand from her arm. She understood what he had said, and yet she didn't.

'What do you mean? Surely she must have said something?'

Sebastian shook his head.

'Not one word. The doctors can't find any physical cause.'

The anxiety and the nausea came flooding back.

'Maria, listen to me. It isn't unusual for traumatised individuals to retreat inside themselves, particularly children. It's a psychological reaction, a powerful flight mechanism, a way of protecting themselves from extreme experiences. And Nicole has lived through something truly horrific.'

'Did she see them being killed? My sister and . . . the others?'

Sebastian was afraid the information might be too much for her, but she had to find out at some point.

'Yes.'

He watched her carefully. At first it seemed as if she wanted to say something, but then she looked down at the ground instead. Sat there in silence. Then she began to cry. Silent sobs, shaking her whole body. Sebastian took her hand, pushed back her long dark hair and looked into her exhausted, red-rimmed eyes. The epitome of a person who couldn't take much more.

'Nicole will get better. She just needs time to heal in peace and quiet. And she needs the support of the person who loves her the most.'

Maria nodded cautiously. She wanted that to be true, but there was so much guilt in the way.

'It's my fault. I left her. I wasn't here when it happened.'

Sebastian squeezed her hand.

'But you're here now. That's the most important thing. You can't change what's happened, and if you had been there, you'd be dead too. Do you understand that?'

Maria took in what he had said. It seemed to help a little; she looked up at him with slightly more focus than before.

'But how long will it be?' she asked after a while. 'Before she starts talking?' Sebastian tried to put a positive spin on things, even though he hadn't a clue.

'It could take a few hours. A few days. A few weeks.' He decided he couldn't lie; he knew far too little at the moment. 'Even longer if we're really unlucky, but that's not very likely. What we need to find out now is whether her mutism, which is the correct term, is selective or total.'

'I don't understand.'

'She might talk to someone with whom she feels safe. That's called selective mutism, and it's much more common than total mutism. Does that make sense?'

There was a glimmer of hope in Maria's eyes.

'You mean she might talk to me? But no one else?'

Sebastian nodded encouragingly. 'That might well be the case.'

This seemed to give Maria a fresh burst of restless energy.

'When can I see her?'

'Soon,' Sebastian said, but then he hesitated. Should he tell her about their suspicions, or not? Once again, he came to the conclusion that she had to know. There was no way around it.

'We're working on the theory that Nicole might well have seen the killer.'

Maria nodded slowly, as if the quota of shocks had now been filled, and nothing could surprise her any more.

'So if she tells you anything, you have to tell me,' Sebastian went on calmly.

Another nod. 'I really need to see my daughter now.'

'OK, let's go,' he said, getting to his feet.

★ ★ ★

They walked in silence along the hospital corridor, passing room after room with identical doors. The only sound was the rustle of their clothing. Sebastian slowed down as they reached the end of the corridor and turned the corner. Outside the next room a uniformed police officer was sitting on a chair that appeared to have been borrowed from one of the waiting areas. Sebastian recognised him from the station in Torsby. Dennis, was that his name? He got to his feet as soon as he saw them.

'Is this the mother?' he asked, far too loudly. Sebastian looked at him with displeasure.

'Yes. She's to have free access to this room. And by the way, an order has gone out stating that her anonymity is to be protected, so perhaps you could avoid yelling at the top of your voice next time you see her.' Dennis lowered his eyes, clearly embarrassed, and apologised. He stepped aside to let them in.

The room contained four beds, but only the one nearest the window was in use. The girl seemed to be asleep; she was curled up in a little ball under the blanket Sebastian had placed over her, and all he could see was a few strands of her dark hair. Nicole's body signalled anxiety and vulnerability, as if she was trying to make herself as small and invisible as possible, even in her sleep. Maria moved uncertainly towards the bed. Sebastian could see that she was finding it difficult to work out what to do; part of her wanted nothing more than to dash forward and hug her daughter, but the fragility of the sleeping child held her back. She turned to Sebastian.

'Are you sure she's all right?' she asked nervously. 'She doesn't usually sleep like that.'

Sebastian merely nodded. What could he say? Maria would have to discover for herself the consequences of what had happened to her daughter.

She edged closer to the bed, then slowly bent down. Pulled back the blanket just a fraction, so that she could see Nicole's face. With gentle, loving caresses she smoothed back the child's hair, getting as close as she dared without waking her.

'I was terrified I'd never see you again, sweetheart. I was so scared.' Her fingertips were just touching Nicole's mouth and cheeks; she was clearly enjoying the feeling of skin on skin.

'But here you are. Here you are,' she went on, as if every repetition made the girl more real, more alive. She leaned over and kissed her forehead – for a long time, as if she didn't want her lips to leave her daughter. Maria's body suddenly started shaking, and Sebastian heard muted sobs as all the tension and fear ebbed away. Nicole really was alive. The proof was there in front of her; she could actually touch her.

Sebastian knew that he ought to withdraw, leave the intimate scene being played out in front of him. Not only would it be respectful, it was the reasonable thing to do. Maria needed some privacy with Nicole after everything that had happened. Instead he moved forward. The encounter touched him deeply, and he couldn't walk away. This was what he had hoped to experience. Admittedly with a different parent and a different daughter, but in this hospital room in northern Värmland he saw the reunion for real. He felt a stab of envy.

No one had come to his aid and saved Sabine.

No one had led him into a room to be reunited with his child.

No one.

He tried to push away the unpleasant feelings. He wanted to keep the purity of this moment. It was too beautiful to be distorted into something painful. He could see hope right there in front of him, and he needed hope in his life. He was already all too familiar with sorrow and grief.

Maria climbed onto the bed and got as close to Nicole as she possibly could, still taking care not to wake her.

Sebastian decided that he really ought to do what anyone else would, and give Maria her privacy. He wanted to stay, like a stowaway on a voyage he had only dreamt of, but he was beginning to feel like something of a parasite. He had to do the right thing. He turned away and was about to open the door when Nicole woke up.

She tried to disentangle herself from Maria before she opened her eyes, still heavy with sleep. For a second she seemed disorientated, then she jerked away violently, searching for an escape route. Sebastian came back to the bed; he could clearly see the instincts that were uppermost in her subconscious.

Escape.

Flight.

Run.

Maria stiffened and let go of her daughter, totally unprepared for the powerful reaction.

'Sweetheart, it's me,' she said, trying to calm the child by holding on to her.

The effect of the words spoken in that familiar voice was instant. Nicole stiffened in surprise, somewhere between sleep and wakefulness. It didn't last long; in seconds she was fully awake, eyes wide open. She turned to Maria, shock written all over her face.

As if she didn't believe what she had just heard. Didn't dare to trust in what she could see.

Maria gave her a big hug.

At first Nicole didn't respond, as if she still couldn't rely on her senses, but soon her arms were wrapped around her mother. Maria squeezed and caressed her daughter, every movement accompanied by a torrent of words, words of reassurance and love. Safety and security, promises never to leave her again.

Nicole offered no words in return.

Not one.

Sebastian doubted that Nicole would say anything now. The encounter between mother and child had been so emotionally intense that the odd word should have made it across the internal threshold, through the barrier that was preventing Nicole from speaking.

It was possible that Nicole would abandon her mutism if she spent more time with her mother, but Sebastian was a realist. The trauma was probably more deep-seated than they had thought. He decided to try something: he stepped forward and placed a hand on the girl's shoulder.

'Nicole? It's me. Do you remember me?'

She looked up at him from her mother's arms. She recognised him, he was sure of it.

'I told you I'd take you to see your mum. I promised. And here she is.'

Nicole looked deep into his eyes; Sebastian saw trust.

'We're a bit concerned because you haven't said anything,' he went on, squeezing her shoulder. She seemed to be thinking about what he had said. She glanced at her mother, then at Sebastian, then back at her mother.

'I'm here now – you can talk to me, Nicole,' Maria whispered. Nicole's expression was tormented; it wasn't that she was trying to talk and nothing would come, more that she was incapable of even making the attempt. She understood what they were saying, but not what she was supposed to do to please them. She buried her face in her mother's chest, and a tear trickled down from her left eye. Sebastian decided to leave the room after all. Perhaps his presence was making it harder for Nicole to pluck up the courage to speak, and that was his main reason for being there: to find out what she had seen. That was his job. Nothing else. Even if a part of him wanted to carry on being a stowaway.

'I'll wait outside,' he said, heading for the door. Maria nodded, but Nicole's reaction was astonishing. She twisted free of her mother's embrace and stared at him, her eyes full of pleading. He stopped.

'Do you want me to stay?'

She carried on staring, and Sebastian interpreted this as a yes.

'I'll be back in a minute. I'm just going to fetch something. I won't be long.'

He walked out without turning around. It was easier that way.

He had disappeared very quickly. The man who had saved her.

He was coming back.

He had said he was coming back, and she believed him.

But on the outside she felt unprotected again.

Unprotected and vulnerable.

On the inside the walls were holding, in spite of the words. They seeped in, and although she had been afraid, they had in fact strengthened her defences, bathed her in a sense of security.

But on the outside. The room was too light to hide in.

The blanket was too thin to conceal her.

So many people could see her, lying there in the middle of the bed.

In the middle of the room.

She was too visible. Too easy to find.

But her mother had come. Just as the man who had saved her had said. She smelled wonderful, even though she was hot and sweaty.

She allowed herself to be hugged.

That made her feel a bit better.

But she could still be seen. Her mother couldn't protect her.

She couldn't protect her mother.

She hadn't even been able to protect Fred, and he was only little.

No one would be able to protect the two of them if it happened again.

No one.

She hoped he would come back.

The man who had saved her.

Sebastian.

Sebastian sent Dennis off to find some drawing paper and coloured pens, then he called Vanja to update her on the situation. She sounded disappointed that Nicole was still mute, in spite of the fact that she had been reunited with her mother.

'They're alone now. I'm going to leave them for a little while, see if it makes any difference.'

'And if it doesn't?' Vanja sounded sceptical.

'Then it's going to take a while. But I thought I might try and get her drawing.'

'Drawing?'

'It's a classic method. It can be easier to deal with traumatic memories if you draw what you've been through.'

Vanja managed a humourless laugh.

'So our only hope lies in persuading a ten-year-old to draw pictures?'

Sebastian understood her frustration; he wished things had been more straightforward.

'Yes. Unless you've got a better idea?'

Vanja didn't say anything for a moment; he knew her well enough by now to realise that she was trying to come up with a cutting remark, something that would improve the situation and make her feel clever. She obviously failed.

'OK, call me if anything happens,' she said after a long pause, then hung up. Sebastian slipped his phone back into his pocket and went to the corner to see if Dennis was on his way.

No sign of him.

Typical – the guy couldn't even find a few felt-tips. Sebastian went back to Nicole's room feeling irritated. He gently pushed open the door and peered in. Nicole and her mother were sitting exactly as he had left them.

He heard footsteps and closed the door. Dennis appeared with Fredrika; he was carrying a sketch pad and a big box of coloured pens.

'Did it take two of you?' Sebastian said acidly. Dennis shook his head.

'We're changing over. I'm taking the night shift.'

Sebastian took the pad and the pens and turned to Fredrika.

'You don't let anyone in, OK?' She nodded in response; he had expected nothing else. She was one of the least sociable individuals he had ever met.

Maria and Nicole looked up as he went back into the room. He smiled encouragingly.

'Only me!' he said cheerfully.

He placed the pad and pens on the bed.

'Do you like drawing, Nicole?'

He left a space for the answer he knew wouldn't come, then went on:

'Sometimes it's nice to draw instead of talking. But maybe it's not something you enjoy?'

'She loves drawing, don't you, sweetheart?' Maria said, doing her best to support Sebastian's efforts.

'I'll leave the pad here, then you can use it whenever you feel like it.' Nicole looked, but made no move to touch it. Sebastian turned to Maria.

'I'll have a word with the hospital, tell them you'll be staying here tonight with Nicole.'

'Thank you.'

'Just say if there's anything you need – food, drink, a change of clothes, whatever. It's important that you take care of yourself.'

She nodded gratefully.

'Thank you. I just want my daughter back. The way she was before.'

'It will happen – don't give up.'

'I won't.'

'Good, because you're the most important person in her life. Which is why you must tell me if you need anything.'

He couldn't help noticing that Maria looked pretty good now that the worst of the stress had passed and she was beginning to relax. He knew he had already made a good impression; most people found calm assurance in extreme situations attractive. And he had rescued her daughter. If it happened, it wouldn't be the first time gratitude manifested itself as physical attraction. His expression was tender as he looked at her.

'Thank you,' she said again.

'You're welcome.'

In his peripheral vision he noticed that Nicole had picked up the pad and started sketching.

'What are you drawing, Nicole?'

The child showed him. She had only just started, but he immediately saw what it was. A yellow vehicle with green markings. The back doors wide open.

'That's good – is it the ambulance we came here in, you and I?'

She carried on drawing: a well-built figure in a green coat, carrying someone.

Nicole was talented; there was no mistaking who the figure was.

'Is that me?'

The child looked up; he thought he could see a 'yes' in her eyes. She bent over her picture, filling in the details on the person being carried.

Big eyes.

No mouth.

Nicole.

★ ★ ★

Sebastian was feeling quite positive by the time he left the hospital.

Nicole had an impressive visual memory. The drawing of her and Sebastian had been simple, but with a surprising number of accurate details.

One of the paramedics had tattoos.

Sebastian was wearing brown shoes.

There was a police car parked a short distance away from the ambulance.

It was a good picture, and he and Maria had decided that they would carry on tomorrow.

In spite of this success, he still felt worn out when he got back to his hotel room. He lay down on the bed and fell asleep, but was woken by someone hammering on the door.

Sebastian estimated that a maximum of three seconds elapsed between opening the door and Torkel starting to yell at him. No pleasantries, he just marched right in. Sebastian didn't even have time to ask him what he wanted. Not that it mattered, as it turned out; Torkel got straight to the point.

'Tell me you haven't slept with the prosecutor.'

Sebastian closed the door.

'I haven't slept with the prosecutor.'

Obviously it sounded just as unconvincing as he had intended. Torkel spun around, and Sebastian could see a small vein throbbing at his temple. That couldn't possibly be good for his heart.

'What the hell were you thinking?'

'You know me,' Sebastian said lightly, with a disarming shrug. 'I don't think.'

'Well, it's time you started! You're working for me now, which means you follow my rules.'

Torkel looked as if he was a hair's breadth from a coronary, so Sebastian was prepared to meet him halfway and discuss the matter, in spite of the fact that being yelled at did nothing for him.

'I can understand your being upset when I've ended up in bed with witnesses and suspects, but what difference does it make if I screw our prosecutor?'

'It's unprofessional. And to be perfectly honest, you and all your women, the fact that you just take what you want, you don't care whether they're in a relationship, you don't care about anybody else – it makes me sick.'

Sebastian stared at his boss, whose dark eyes were fixed on him.

'This is about Ursula,' he stated matter-of-factly, sitting down on the bed.

'This is about you being totally incapable of keeping your cock in your pants. Your behaviour damages Riksmord, and it damages me.'

'It's because Ursula was in my apartment . . .'

Torkel took a step closer; he seemed to be fighting to stop himself from poking Sebastian in the chest with an accusing finger.

'Stop what you've started with Malin Åkerblad right now. Tonight! That's an order.'

'I'm not very good at taking orders.'

'I could have asked you, for the sake of our friendship, but as you're constantly demonstrating how little that means to you, I don't really have a choice.'

With that he was gone.

As the door slammed behind him, the room seemed more silent than it had been before he arrived.

Sebastian exhaled slowly. He really hadn't expected this. Following their conversation in Torkel's room he had thought it was all sorted, finished, done. Ursula had been having dinner with a colleague when she was shot. It was a terrible tragedy, the result of a series of unfortunate circumstances, pure chance, nothing more. But it clearly wasn't over as far as Torkel was concerned. Presumably the only thing that would enable him to put the whole thing behind him would be if Ursula got together with him. Properly. Went public with their relationship. Marriage, even. However, if Sebastian knew Ursula as well as he thought he did, that was never going to happen.

So now he had to decide what he was going to do with the rest of his evening.

He had spent quite a lot of time coming up with excuses not to see Malin tonight. She had come back to Torsby a day early and had asked about him as soon as she arrived; that was all a bit too much for Sebastian. He usually tried to avoid a repeat of any sexual encounter, and he couldn't possibly go anywhere near a woman who was actively seeking out his company.

Once doesn't count.

Twice is once too often.

Although . . .

He was torn between his reluctance to encourage Malin in any way, and his urge to defy Torkel; if Torkel hadn't been so angry, he would have realised that a direct order was guaranteed to make Sebastian want to do the exact opposite. That was how Sebastian Bergman worked – like an obstinate child. An express ban could make things he didn't even want seem desirable and important.

Sebastian made up his mind. He would probably be leaving Torsby and Malin Åkerblad within the next few days, but Torkel would be around all the time. He simply couldn't let him win.

Decision made.

A quick shower and then sex with the prosecutor.

'Who were you talking to?' Maya asked as soon as Billy answered. 'I've been trying to call you for ages.'

'Jennifer,' Billy replied as he strolled onto the neatly mown lawn in front of the hotel. He liked to walk around while he was on the phone, and his room felt too small and confined. He glanced at his watch; Maya couldn't really have been trying for ages, but he was surprised to see that he had been chatting to Jennifer for over an hour.

'What were you talking about for such a long time?' Maya demanded; if Billy hadn't known better, he would have thought there was a hint of suspicion in her voice. But that was one of the things he really liked about Maya: there wasn't a trace of jealousy in their relationship. She knew that his friendship with Vanja was – or at least had been – special. She knew that he met up with Jennifer on a regular basis. She was cool with the fact that female friends from school or the police training academy turned up occasionally, and he had never given her any reason to doubt him. He simply wasn't the unfaithful type. Never had been.

'I was going over the case – it's good to have an outsider's point of view.'

That was true, but it wasn't the whole truth. It had started that way, just catching up; Jennifer had chatted about what she had been doing at work, all completely pointless according to her, while Billy had told her how the mind-numbingly boring hours in the Värmland forests had led to the discovery of the missing girl. Well, to be perfectly honest, Sebastian had worked out where she was and managed to get her out of the cave.

'Do you remember when we first met?' Jennifer asked. 'I was looking for a missing child back then – Lukas Ryd.'

When we first met . . . Billy thought that sounded like something a girlfriend might say. Or a really close friend. There was something intimate about it, and Billy realised Jennifer had taken over from Vanja as his best friend.

'I do remember, out at the gravel pit,' he replied; he could have sworn that Jennifer was smiling, just like him. 'It was so hot, and Vanja had a hangover.'

'How's she doing after all that business with her dad?'

'OK, I think – she doesn't say much about it.'

They had gone on to discuss the case in more detail, and Billy had confessed that he felt inadequate. It was nice to admit it to someone who – unlike Maya – didn't immediately come up with tips and ideas on how to get over it, how he should alter his mindset, what he should do. Someone who understood him on a personal level, who had been in situations where she felt exactly the same. Not many, of course – most things that happened in Sigtuna were well below Jennifer's level of competence – but she had been there too. A conversation, mutual understanding, without an insistence on finding 'solutions'.

And now he was talking to Maya.

Or rather listening. She had sent out the save-the-date invitations today, and made decisions with regard to a few more details about the wedding which she hoped he was OK with, otherwise everything, or most things anyway, could be changed. She had looked at a venue she thought was perfect; there were pictures in Dropbox so if he could check them out over the weekend that would be great, she had to give them a definite answer on Monday.

Billy promised to get back to her. Then they talked about personal matters, how her day had been; they both said how much they missed each other, as usual.

'Have you ever had phone sex?'

Billy stopped dead. Surprised to say the least.

'No . . . Have you?'

'No. Would you like to try it?'

'I'm not in the hotel.'

'When will you be back there?'

'Soon – in a few minutes,' Billy said, gazing up at the facade.

'Call me then.'

'OK.'

Maya ended the call, and Billy slipped the phone in his pocket. This was something new. He actually had no idea how it worked, and it felt a bit . . . embarrassing. Were they just going to talk, or was Maya thinking of Skype? Maybe she had an idea, and all he had to do was go along with her.

As he reached the steps leading up to the main door, he met Sebastian coming out.

'Hi, where are you off to?' Billy asked as he grabbed the open door.

'Why?'

'No reason, I was just wondering.'

'Carry on wondering.'

Down the steps, off down the well-tended path, out onto the street and he was gone.

Billy stared after him.

Sebastian had gone out. His room was empty. The opportunity might not arise again; no one knew how long they would be staying here. He couldn't turn up on Sebastian's doorstep with a bottle of wine and pinch some DNA when he went to the bathroom – partly because Sebastian didn't drink, and partly because, unlike Vanja, he would think it was seriously weird. They didn't have that kind of relationship.

Billy thought about what he was planning to do. What would happen if he got caught? There wasn't much of a friendship to wreck, they were definitely no more than colleagues. Which was a bit strange, really, because Billy was the only member of the team who hadn't had a negative attitude towards Sebastian when he first turned up, and yet Sebastian was much closer to both Ursula and Vanja, both of whom had wanted rid of him at any price from the start. Then again, maybe it wasn't so strange. They were women. Billy didn't know how it worked, but Sebastian seemed to have an almost magical touch when it came to the opposite sex – at least when it came to getting them into bed. It wasn't something to admire; he abused women the way other people abused alcohol. Presumably he felt just as bad the morning after as an alcoholic did after a bender. Or did he? Billy didn't know, and he didn't really care. The only thing of interest right now as far as Sebastian Bergman was concerned was whether or not he was Vanja's father, and in order to find that out, Billy needed a sample of his DNA.

He went over to the reception desk.

'Hi – my colleague has just gone out and I've left my laptop in his room. Any chance I could borrow the key for a couple of minutes?'

No problem.

It was dark in the forest, and he was crawling along the narrow track at a snail's pace. He had killed the car's headlights when he turned off the main road, and now he was forced to navigate by moonlight. He leaned forward as far as he could, trying to make something out. He wanted to park as close as possible so that he could get in and out quickly, but he didn't want anyone to see the car. He spotted a little opening by the side of the track, a field of last year's tall grass. He didn't want to be facing the wrong way when he was leaving, so he turned the car around, then got out. It couldn't be more than fifteen minutes' walk to the hospital. He planned to head down to the main road, which ran parallel with the track a few hundred metres away, keeping to the edge of the forest so that he could duck in among the trees if anyone came. Not that anyone was likely to be around at 02:45.

The whole of Torsby was sleeping.

Apart from him.

He retrieved his small rucksack from the back seat and set off. It was a clear, chilly night, and the bright moon cast a dreamlike glow on the trees surrounding him. The rucksack felt heavy, although it shouldn't. Guilt weighed things down, he had realised lately. It was as if other physical laws applied if you did things you would never have thought you were capable of.

Certain things weighed more.

Others less.

Killing children.

That weighed most of all.

He pushed away that last thought; it always affected him more than he wanted it to. It hurt.

The main road below him was deserted, just as he had expected, but he still stayed on the edge of the forest even though he could have made significantly faster progress if he'd gone down to the verge.

But he stuck to the plan. Didn't change a thing. Plans were made to be followed.

★ ★ ★

After about ten minutes he caught a glimpse of the upper part of the hospital, half-hidden behind a grassy slope that he knew led to the car park at the back. The slope was densely planted with shrubs, which he intended to use as cover. The hospital had two entrances, the one for ambulances and the main one at the front. He wasn't going to use either of them. He was going to get in via one of the emergency exits. There were several on every side of the building, and he had often seen both staff and patients standing outside smoking with the doors wide open, even at night. With a bit of luck, that meant they weren't alarmed. It was worth a try, anyway. He cut through the bushes and was suddenly struck by a strong, sweet perfume – a scent that reminded him of the summer, of long walks. As he reached the top of the slope he crouched down and peered at the car park, which was almost empty – only four cars in a space that was big enough for twenty times that number. He waited for a little while just to make sure that no one was on their way to one of the cars, then ran across the tarmac as fast as he could to the nearest door. He took out his black leather gloves and put them on. Tried the door. Locked. It gave a little when he pulled at it, and he briefly wondered whether to try breaking it open with his knife, but instead he decided to try the next emergency exit, where he had definitely seen members of staff smoking. He moved fast, keeping close to the wall. When he reached the door, he saw that he was in luck for once. One of the smokers had forgotten to move the little stone that was used to hold the door open. He stepped into the dark corridor and closed the door behind him.

Stage one completed. Things would be more difficult from now on. He saw a reddish-orange button for the lights glowing in the gloom, but decided to use his little LED torch instead. He got it out of the side pocket of his rucksack and switched it on. Saw that he was in a yellow basement. He passed a hospital trolley and several doors marked 'STOREROOM'. He stopped and went back; perhaps he could find a change of clothes that would make it easier for him to move around upstairs.

That was the weakness in his plan: the risk of being discovered and identified. He might just be able to minimise that risk.

The first storeroom contained cloths, rolls of protective paper and bandages. He looked in a few boxes and found one containing masks. He took one out and put it on over his nose and mouth. He could feel his warm breath on his lips and cheeks; he felt better already. At least his face was partly covered.

The second room was a linen store, but in the third room his luck was in once more: boxes and boxes of clothes, all marked with different sizes. He gathered together the best combination he could find: green scrubs, including a cap. It felt like something that would be worn in theatre, and no doubt it would look odd if anyone saw him, prepped for an operation at three o'clock in the morning, but it did make him virtually unrecognisable. He put down his torch and got changed. He folded up his coat and hid it in one of the boxes, then pulled on the scrubs over his shirt and trousers. He covered his head with the cap, and found a pair of sterile gloves. He took what he needed out of his rucksack, then hid it in a box next to the one containing his coat. Unfortunately there were no pockets in his scrubs, and he had to find somewhere to conceal the knife and the small Taser he had brought with him. He would have preferred a pistol, but he needed something significantly quieter this time. The last time any possible witnesses had been far away; this time they would be in the adjoining rooms.

He went back out into the corridor and returned to the trolley he had passed earlier. He unlocked the wheels and tried pushing it backwards and forwards a few times. It moved easily and quietly, although one wheel seemed to pull to the side a little.

He slipped the hunting knife and the Taser under the pillow, then checked out the area in his new outfit, looking for alternative escape routes. He found two staircases and a lift, plus four emergency exits in addition to the one he had used to get in. Good.

He wheeled the trolley over to the lift. He would go up in the lift, back down the stairs. That was the plan. He pressed the call button and heard the machinery whirr into action. He would begin on the ground floor, where the general wards were; the girl should be there.

The lift arrived and he stepped inside. Looked at the control panel: three buttons, B, G and 1. He pulled the trolley in after him, checked the items under the pillow one more time, then pressed G. The metal doors closed and the lift rose slowly and smoothly. He felt the tension return.

This was his last chance.

The lift stopped. He had arrived.

★ ★ ★

The man wheeled the trolley along in front of him. So far he hadn't seen a soul. The corridor with its shiny green floor was deserted. He stopped, listened. The staff on the night shift must be around somewhere, and he would prefer to know where they were before they saw him. A short distance away he heard voices coming from a room with the door open. At least two people. Women. He decided to go in the opposite direction. The corridor went all the way around the building in a square, so he would be able to check out the entire floor whichever route he took. He was happier with the voices behind him; he didn't really want to walk past the door. They died away after a little while, and soon the only sound was the muted metallic click of the trolley's wheels. He glanced at each door as he passed by. They were all identical: white, windowless, closed. No names or patient details on display, which was what he had been hoping for. That

203

made things a lot more complicated. He really didn't want to open every single door; that would seriously increase the risk of being caught. It might be necessary eventually, but he wasn't going to start that way. The first thing was to get an overview, go right the way round this floor if the worst came to the worst, and then search each room if there was no other option. Difficult things became easier if you had an overview. He knew that from experience.

A little way ahead, one of the doors was ajar. He moved forward, stopped, listened. The room was as silent as the grave. He decided to look inside. He was sure it wouldn't be the girl's room – he couldn't be that lucky – but it would give him the chance to see what the rooms looked like. The doors were all the same, so that probably applied to the interiors as well. He considered taking the knife with him, but thought better of it.

Overview first.

Action only once the target has been located.

Cautiously he pushed open the door.

It was in darkness; the only light came from the corridor behind him. Four beds. Three in use. Women, he thought, all asleep. He made up his mind to keep going, but with a fresh insight. He had been so focused on the girl that it hadn't crossed his mind that there might be more than one patient in a room. It wasn't exactly news to him, but it annoyed him. It didn't change anything, but he didn't like the realisation that he hadn't thought of everything.

He set off again, pushing the trolley. He felt more comfortable that way. Soon he reached the corner; he slowed down and carefully manoeuvred the trolley. The faulty wheel made it heavier than he had expected, and it slid over to the left. He had to make a real effort to stop it crashing into the wall. He straightened it up, and at the same time saw a figure in his peripheral vision. A man in police uniform, sitting on a chair.

The man felt a shiver run down his spine; suddenly all his senses were on full alert. There could be only one patient with a police officer stationed outside her door.

He had arrived.

The policeman glanced at his watch, then leaned his head back against the wall and closed his eyes. Perhaps he was going to have a little nap. The man pushed the trolley along, and the policeman turned drowsily towards the sound. He's just seeing a hospital employee in scrubs, the man told himself, but picked up speed to give the policeman less time to wonder why someone was pushing a trolley around at this time of night.

The officer nodded as the trolley drew level with his chair.

The man reached under the pillow, took out the Taser, pressed it against the officer's neck and fired in one fluid movement. The compact black-and-yellow object crackled with electricity. Too loud, he thought, but it was too late. The policeman's body jerked spasmodically several times, his arms flew up and his legs flailed horribly. For a second it looked as if the power of the electric charge would bring him to his feet, but instead he thudded down on the floor. And stayed there. Out cold.

According to the Internet, it would be ten or fifteen minutes before the paralysis eased. He remained standing there for a few seconds just to be on the safe side, hoping no one had heard anything. The voices from the staffroom were faintly audible, but only if he listened really hard. To him the brief interlude had seemed incredibly noisy, but the lack of shouts or footsteps heading in his direction reassured him. The coast was clear. He stepped over the other man's body, opened the door and looked inside.

A lamp glowed in the corner. Only one bed was occupied. Good.

Or not. Instead of a little girl, there was a woman lying on top of the covers. She seemed to be wearing her own clothes rather than a hospital gown.

It must be the wrong room.

But there had been a police officer sitting outside. There couldn't possibly be someone else in the hospital who needed a police guard. This was Torsby. It had to be the right room.

He had to get rid of the unconscious body anyway, so he slipped back outside, grabbed the man's legs, pulled him into the room and dumped him by the bed next to the door. Then he closed the door and moved towards the sleeping woman.

There was a coat draped over the end of the bed, and a pair of dark-coloured shoes below it. He took a closer look. Long, dark, almost black hair, a round, attractive face. She definitely didn't appear to be a patient. She wasn't dressed like a patient, and she was lying on top of the covers, very close to the edge of the bed with both arms outstretched towards the middle, as if someone had been lying in her arms.

Hadn't he read in the paper that the girl's mother was abroad? Difficult to get hold of?

Presumably the police had found her. But where was the girl? Was she being examined? Had she been whisked away because of some emergency? But then the mother wouldn't be lying here fast asleep. It didn't make sense.

Nothing made sense.

He was starting to worry about the amount of time that was passing as he stood there feeling confused and indecisive. He needed to make up his mind about what to do. The problem was that he had only theories. He was guessing. He had nothing to go on.

On the pale wooden bedside table he saw something that lessened his confusion. Next to two glasses, one half full of juice and one empty, lay a sketch pad and some coloured pens. Someone had been drawing. He moved silently around the bed, picked up the first picture. An ambulance parked next to some trees, a man carrying a little girl. A little girl with long dark hair and big eyes. They were emerging from something that must be a cave.

He was in the right room.

The girl had been here. He headed for the door.

She ought to be nearby. She must be nearby. Sometimes there was a simple answer to something that seemed inexplicable. There were no toilets in the rooms; if you wanted to pee in the middle of the night, you would have to go somewhere else.

He quickly opened the door and looked out. It was just as quiet and deserted as before. The bathroom wasn't far from the policeman's chair. He had to move fast now. He had very little time left. He stopped about a metre from the toilet door.

He had been right.

The locking mechanism showed red.

Someone was in there.

He quickly turned back to the trolley, reached under the pillow and grabbed the knife. How much time had elapsed? The policeman would need a little while to recover once he came round, but the woman would be wide awake as soon as the uniformed man on the floor started moaning and groaning. It had been stupid to drag him in there. Stupid to stand around for so long.

He had made some mistakes.

But he had found her.

He gripped the handle of the knife more tightly and got ready. Edged towards the locked door. Placed his ear against it and listened. Nothing. He pressed closer until it almost hurt. Still nothing.

Could the red display mean that the toilet was closed, out of order? Was he standing here with his knife poised, listening to an empty room? He was just about to try and pick the lock with the point of the knife when he heard the familiar sound of flushing water. He quickly positioned himself against the wall next to the door on the hinge side, so that he would be hidden when it opened. Best to remain concealed as long as possible. He would look terrifying, with his mask, his surgical cap and his great big hunting knife; she would probably start screaming at the top of her voice as soon as she saw him. Better to let her come out first; with a bit of luck she would have her back to him. He would have time to cover her mouth with his left hand before she saw him, then he could stab her hard between the shoulder blades with his right hand. All the way to her heart with a single blow, hopefully. Unfortunately both the spine and the ribcage were in the way, so he was prepared for the possibility that he might need several blows in order to achieve the desired result. Actually it would be safer to cut her throat, but he had discounted that idea from the start. There was something about the slender neck of a girl. The soft skin. The neat throat. She would be too close to the child she was. It was a strange thought, but that was how he felt. And he knew you had to listen to your internal voice in situations like this, otherwise you could be beset by doubts and lose focus. That couldn't happen. He had to carry this through without hesitation. He couldn't afford to get it wrong.

There was a click as the lock turned and the door opened. Faster than he had expected, but not fast enough for him to lose the initiative.

He stepped forward and was about to cover the girl's mouth and bring down the hand holding the knife with all the force he could muster.

There was just one problem.

The person standing with her back to him wasn't the girl.

It was an old lady in a hospital gown that was practically tripping her up.

He tried to stop the forward motion, but he had put so much energy into it that he didn't have a chance. He managed to twist to one side so that only his hand made contact with her back rather than the knife, but the woman went down like a felled tree. He realised he was losing the plot. The woman looked up at him and started screaming. For a second he thought maybe he ought to stab her anyway just to shut her up, but he hesitated. Glanced around. Heard footsteps hurrying towards him. Voices. The situation wasn't improved when another person started screaming, even louder than the old lady on the floor.

The woman in the room.

She was screeching like a lunatic. At least he had been right about one thing: she was the girl's mother.

'Nicole!' he heard her yell.

He turned and ran.

As fast as his legs would carry him.

Sebastian had never driven so fast, at least not in a densely populated area. Twelve minutes ago he had been in bed with Malin Åkerblad in her hotel room. He had answered his mobile, still half asleep, but when he heard Maria's voice he was wide awake in a second. After a minute or so he managed to get her to give the phone to one of the nurses, whom he asked to contact the police immediately. Malin woke up, and Sebastian briefly outlined what had happened. He more or less forced her to lend him her car, and as soon as he left the car park he called Vanja. He had obviously woken her, but she was soon firing on all cylinders.

'Someone's kidnapped the girl!' he yelled.

'What?'

'Nicole, someone's kidnapped Nicole! She's gone!'

Vanja's surprise immediately shifted to razor-sharp focus, and he thought he could hear her leap out of bed.

'From the hospital?'

'Yes, I've just arrived there,' he said as he turned into the car park.

'I'm on my way.'

'Tell Torkel,' he tried to say, but Vanja had already hung up. He knew he didn't need to worry; she would make sure everyone was there. Vanja was a professional, much better than him in a situation like this. She should be first on the scene, really; he usually turned up last, when the deed had been done and the team was already gathered. But not this time. This time he was first, and there wasn't a second to lose. He jumped out of the car, ran in through the main doors and into reception. There were quite a lot of people standing around, people with anxious eyes, patients in night clothes with tousled hair. They looked at him enquiringly as if he could provide them with answers, but he had none. He ignored them all and rushed towards the doors leading to the ward.

The adrenaline was coursing around his body. Had they lost her? The whole thing felt like a nightmare. He saw the empty chair outside the room, the open door, a couple of curious patients standing in the corridor.

'Go back to your rooms!' he snapped before he went in. Two members of staff were standing next to a sobbing Maria, who was sitting on a chair next to the bed. A nurse was attending to Dennis; he was slumped on one of the beds and looked terrible. Sebastian reached Maria in two strides.

'What happened?' he said as gently as he could. He knew that the most important thing right now was to exude balance and calm, regardless of how panic-stricken he actually felt. A calm approach made others stop and focus; it strengthened their ability to try to see clearly. However, Maria was anything but calm.

'She's gone! Nicole's gone!'

Sebastian crouched down and took her hands in his.

'I know. But you have to tell me what happened.'

Despair was etched on Maria's face.

'I don't know what happened. I fell asleep with her . . . When I woke up she was gone, and he was lying on the floor over there.' She pointed to Dennis, who was now on his feet.

'What the fuck were you doing?' Sebastian demanded. 'You were supposed to be on guard duty!'

Dennis looked embarrassed.

'I was sitting out there when this guy in scrubs came along, pushing a trolley. He had a Taser.'

This wasn't good. Night-time, armed, the right kit, dressed to fit in. That suggested determination, someone totally focused on their goal. He suppressed the feeling of anxiety that came bubbling up, and turned back to Maria.

'We'll search the entire hospital. We'll find her.'

'But someone's taken her – don't you understand?'

He did understand. Probably better than she did. But he had to remain calm.

Somehow.

★ ★ ★

Vanja had woken both Torkel and Billy. Torkel had promised to sort out backup from Karlstad while Billy accompanied her to the hospital. A patrol car had already arrived when they got there, and two uniformed officers were in reception trying to find out what was going on. Vanja asked them to watch the main entrance so that only authorised personnel could come and go. She asked Billy to gather all the staff in reception and to inform them of the situation. There were too few police officers to search the place effectively, so they were going to need the help of the staff. Billy would quickly divide them into pairs and explain that they were to observe and report back; they were not to approach anyone they found, or touch anything. He nodded and set off; Vanja could hear him talking to people as she ran towards Nicole's room.

She found Sebastian there and he provided a rapid, almost feverish summary. The more she found out, the less she liked what she was hearing.

An elderly lady and the officer who had been guarding Nicole's room had been attacked by a man wearing scrubs and a face mask. According to the lady who had been in the toilet, he had been brandishing a knife.

Several members of staff had seen a man in green scrubs running away. He had been moving very fast, and had disappeared down the stairs to the basement.

No one had seen Nicole. She had vanished without a trace.

Sebastian looked paler than usual, and seemed to appreciate her presence.

'Can we talk outside?' he asked with a discreet nod in the direction of Nicole's mother, who was ashen and exhausted. Vanja thought that was a good idea, and they left the room.

211

'What do you think?' she asked quietly. Sebastian gazed at her for a moment before he spoke.

'I think we're fucked, to be honest. He beat us to it again.'

'First Ceder, and now Nicole. We look like idiots . . .'

'We don't just look like idiots, we are idiots,' Sebastian said drily. 'We're responsible for this. We took our eye off the ball again.'

Vanja had to agree. The fact that someone had managed to abduct a key witness under police protection, and a child to boot, was nothing less than a disaster. For the case, for the girl, for her mother, and for Vanja's career, although she certainly wasn't proud of that thought. She knew it was in no way comparable with Nicole's fate, but she felt as if the faint hope she had nurtured of reapplying for the FBI training programme at Quantico was fading. She wasn't the SIO, but even so . . . this wouldn't look good. Feeling ashamed of herself, she focused on what was important. The girl. The girl. The girl.

'Billy's co-ordinating a search of the entire building – you and I will take the basement,' she said firmly. 'I believe that's where he was last seen?'

Sebastian nodded. 'Well, he was heading in that direction.'

'Let's start there.'

★ ★ ★

They set off down the stone stairs. Not too quickly – they didn't want to miss anything. The stairwell was narrow, with yellow walls and a green handrail. Vanja's phone rang; Torkel had arrived with Erik Flodin and wanted an update. Vanja outlined her plan for the search: two police officers on each floor, plus hospital staff in pairs. Billy would be able to provide more detail.

'Perhaps Erik could talk to Dennis?' she suggested. 'Then you could concentrate on the old lady – she's the only one who's seen our perpetrator at close quarters.'

Torkel agreed, and said he would deal with the reinforcements who were on their way. There was a risk that they would go from too few officers to too many, and without clear

212

leadership they might all end up running around like headless chickens.

'One of the nurses said she thought the trolley the man was pushing came from down here,' Sebastian said when Vanja had ended the call.

'How could she tell? There must be dozens of trolleys in this place.'

'Apparently they'd done an inventory last week, marked the ones that needed repairing and put them down in the basement. The trolley outside Nicole's room was marked.'

Vanja thought for a moment.

'So he went up in the lift.'

At the bottom of the stairs they were faced with a yellow, somewhat battered metal door that looked as if it had had a hard life.

'Are there any entrances to the building down here?' Sebastian asked.

'Emergency exits. Several.'

Vanja was about to open the heavy door, then she paused. Reached for her gun and drew back the slide. The moving parts of the Sig Sauer clicked into place. Sebastian gave her a sceptical look.

'I don't think he's still here. He's been much cleverer than that so far,' he said as he pulled open the door, revealing the dimly lit corridor beyond. Vanja followed him and pressed the orange button. The fluorescent lights flickered into life, illuminating a series of three storage rooms and bare cement walls. Immediately on their right was the lift; Vanja made a mental note to ask the CSIs to check it for fingerprints. They set off quietly, listening for any indication that there might be someone else down here. The only sound was the faint monotonous hum of the air-conditioning system, and their own footsteps.

They stopped at the first storeroom; Vanja raised her gun and Sebastian pushed the door open. It was dark inside; he fumbled for the light button, found it. They saw cardboard boxes that had been torn open, with green scrubs and white hospital uniforms strewn all over the floor, mainly shirts and trousers.

'This is where he got his clothes,' Sebastian said.

'Mm. Don't touch anything – I'll ask Billy to see if they can find any traces of DNA.'

They moved on to the next room, which contained sheets and blankets, all neatly folded and stacked on shelves. All perfectly tidy, which strengthened their suspicions about what had happened in the previous room.

The last room also seemed untouched; it was full of boxes of bandages, nappies and rolls of protective paper. They relaxed a little, and Vanja began to feel that her loaded gun was in the way more than anything. She slipped it back into its holster with a practised movement.

'He was in a hurry to get out of here,' she said. 'He's acted so professionally in the past – if he'd had time, I'm sure he would have tidied up after himself.'

Sebastian nodded. 'I don't understand his behaviour at all right now. Why would he kidnap Nicole? It doesn't make sense.'

Vanja looked at him, her expression grave. Put into words what they had both been thinking ever since they got to the hospital, but hadn't dared to say:

'So we're looking for her body.'

Sebastian nodded again. An image came into his mind: Nicole, pale and covered in blood. Stabbed. Disposed of. Dumped under a pile of cardboard boxes somewhere.

He tried to push the image away, but it refused to go.

Some images do that. In the worst-case scenario, you have to live with them for the rest of your life.

Nicole's dead body would be one of those. He knew it.

His train of thought was interrupted as the metal door at the bottom of the stairs flew open and a nurse appeared. They could see she had something important to tell them before she spoke.

'We've found her! We've found her!' she shouted.

The image was there to stay.

★ ★ ★

214

He recognised it immediately. The location was different, of course, as were the items she had used, but the way she had arranged them was the same. The blanket draped over the boxes. She had made herself a little hiding place. Somewhere she felt secure, safe from everything she was running away from. In a linen storeroom on the second floor, Nicole had recreated the cramped refuge in the Bear's Cave.

An auxiliary had noticed that two boxes were in the wrong place. They were on the floor in front of a shelf full of sheets, as if they had fallen down. A blanket had been draped over them, and there was a pillow on each side to stop anyone seeing inside. She was a mother herself, and recognised a den when she saw one. She moved one of the boxes a fraction, peered in and saw Nicole's terrified eyes shining, right at the back below the bottom shelf.

By the time Sebastian arrived, Maria had managed to get her out. She was in her mother's arms, pale and frightened. Maria was sobbing with joy.

Nicole didn't say a word. But the way she looked at him said it all. She wanted to go back. Back to her hiding place. Sebastian understood perfectly. The grown-ups hadn't been able to protect her.

Not her mother. Not the police. Not Sebastian.

Only Nicole.

Sebastian felt both relieved and proud of her; she really was a survivor. He smiled at her.

'Hello, Nicole – we were worried about you.'

She didn't answer, but she made a faint movement towards him. Maria noticed, and looked in surprise at her daughter. Sebastian held out his hand.

'Do you want to come to me?' he asked softly.

Nicole freed herself from her mother's arms and reached out to him. Sebastian could see that it was hard for Maria to let go of the daughter she had just found. He tried to calm her.

'I'll just carry her back to her room.' Maria nodded, and Sebastian took the child. Her body was warm and slightly sweaty, her muscles tense, but not like the last time he had carried her. He felt her relax as soon as she was in his arms. It was a powerful feeling, the realisation that he was so important to her. That she had chosen him, trusted him.

But he had to ask the question. He tried to do it as gently as possible:

'Did you see him? Is that why you hid in here?'

Nicole looked at him blankly, as if she didn't understand. He tried again.

'The man who was here – did you see him?' His tone was a little more urgent this time, but the response was the same; she obviously had no idea what he was talking about. He was relieved that she didn't know how close to danger she had been. He stroked her soft hair.

'Or did you just come here to sleep? Because it felt better?'

She looked away, as if she was ashamed. He tried to reassure her with a smile.

'You haven't done anything wrong.' The words were so inadequate; he really wanted to tell her how happy he was that she had escaped not only the danger, but also the knowledge of that danger.

He adjusted her position so that her head was resting on his shoulder, then turned around and spoke to Maria and Vanja:

'I'll carry her downstairs, then we can talk about what to do next.'

'I don't want to stay in that room,' Maria said as they set off. 'I don't feel safe there.'

'I understand. We'll find you somewhere else,' Sebastian replied. He chose the stairs, meeting the gaze of the staff who were watching them with a certain amount of curiosity.

The man and the little girl in his arms.

The mother following on behind.

Like a family. But not a family.

★ ★ ★

216

He put Nicole down on the bed next to the window, and was surprised at how easily she let go of him. She really did trust him, which was why she was no longer so clingy. She knew he would come back to her. He looked around and understood exactly what Maria meant. He noticed the sketch pad and coloured pens on the bedside table; Nicole had done another drawing. He could just see it under the top one; he picked it up and took a closer look.

Lots of black and shades of brown. Broad strokes. A little girl in a cave. Several adults nearby, searching for her. The girl was very small, hidden away. The other figures were much too big. The proportions were all wrong, but that was how tiny she had felt inside the cave. He turned to Maria.

'When did she do this?'

'Yesterday, just after you left.'

Sebastian glanced over at Nicole, who was sitting motionless on the bed gazing up at him. He felt a wave of relief. In the midst of all the chaos, this was a small breakthrough.

'It's working,' he said.

Maria looked enquiringly at him. 'What's working?'

Sebastian lowered his voice so that Nicole wouldn't hear.

'She's drawing her memories. This is just before we found her in the cave. She's working backwards. First me and the ambulance, now the cave . . .'

'You mean she might . . .' Maria began anxiously, but Sebastian stopped her with a discreet gesture.

'Shh . . . We'll see. The main thing is for her to carry on,' he said encouragingly.

Maria didn't seem convinced. The thought of the drawings that were still to come clearly frightened her.

'Because that will tell you what you need to know,' she said expressionlessly. 'She'll draw her dead cousins and you'll be able to solve the case.'

Sebastian wasn't sure how to respond. What she said was both true and false. He cared about Nicole, but they also needed to solve the case. For her sake.

'I don't think any of us wants this guy running around on the loose.'

Maria didn't say anything, but after a few seconds she nodded. It was important that Nicole carried on drawing. It was the only way they would ever find peace.

Torkel had increased security following the events of the previous night. Two uniformed officers accompanied them in the lift up to Nicole's new room, away from the ground floor. Nicole was in a wheelchair, silent and somehow smaller than ever, with Sebastian by her side and Maria behind. The double doors leading to a corridor identical to the one they had just left swung open automatically as the little group approached. Torkel and Vanja were waiting further along; Sebastian glanced in through the open door of Nicole's new room. Same off-white walls, same scratched grey-green vinyl floor. Two beds. But there was also an orange two-seater sofa and an armchair arranged around a small table in one corner, with big windows overlooking the corridor.

'I need to have a word with my colleagues,' Sebastian said, turning to Nicole. 'But we'll stay here, so you'll be able to see me through the window all the time.'

There was no reaction from the girl, nor had he expected one, but she was obviously happy with the arrangement because she went with Maria without protesting or clinging on to him.

'Leave the curtains open, please,' Torkel said to Maria's back, and she nodded in response. The two uniformed officers stationed themselves on either side of the door.

'So what do we know about last night?' Sebastian asked as soon as the door closed.

'The hospital has CCTV cameras in the main foyer and outside the entrance for those who are brought in by ambulance. Billy's gone to see if he can get hold of the films,' Torkel replied. 'How's Nicole?'

'Hard to say, but she's started drawing, which is a step in the right direction.' Sebastian gestured with his right hand, in which he was carrying Nicole's pictures.

'Can I have a look?' Vanja said, and Sebastian passed her the drawings.

'But she's still not talking?' Torkel went on.

'She hasn't said a word.'

'Do we know how she got past Dennis?'

'He says he went to get a cup of coffee at eleven thirty, but it's not impossible that he might have nodded off at some point.'

Sebastian sighed. He looked into the room where Nicole had just got out of the wheelchair and climbed into bed. Maria tucked her in, took a book out of the bag hanging on the back of the wheelchair and sat down on the edge of the bed. Nicole was lying on her side, her eyes fixed on Sebastian. He gave her a little wave.

'How's Ursula, by the way?' Vanja wondered, looking up from the drawings.

'She's having a new eye fitted, so I guess . . . she's as well as can be expected,' Torkel replied, turning to Sebastian. He should have been the one to enquire, to show interest and concern, but needless to say that was too much to ask. 'Nothing unusual about the Carlstens' finances so far either – we haven't been able to find any major deposits or withdrawals.'

'What's this?' Vanja said, holding up one of the pictures.

'It's the cave,' Sebastian explained. 'She's started with what happened most recently, and she's moving backwards. You've got the ambulance in the first one, and the second one is inside the cave. She's gradually getting closer to the house and what happened there.'

Vanja nodded, and looked at the drawing again. Torkel noticed that she was frowning slightly.

'What's the matter?'

'I was at the cave, but I must have missed . . .' She held up the piece of paper again and pointed to a man with a yellow 'V' beaming from his head. 'Who was wearing a head torch?'

★ ★ ★

'Erik confirmed that none of his team was wearing a head torch at the cave.'

Torkel's expression was grim as they gathered outside Nicole's room fifteen minutes later. 'Our killer was in the cave, and he was here in the hospital. He seems to have decided to silence Nicole.'

'How did he know she was in the cave?' Vanja asked no one in particular.

'He knows the area, he's local,' Sebastian said, looking in through the window. Nicole was lying on her back with her eyes closed. Maria put down the book and went over to the sofa. 'Just as I said,' he added.

'So is Erik Flodin, and the rest of his team,' Vanja said. 'They didn't work it out.'

'Flodin is a klutz,' Sebastian said, turning back to his colleagues. 'We're dealing with an intelligent and very determined individual here.'

'If he's local, then I suggest we get Nicole out of here,' Torkel said firmly. 'We'll move her to one of our safe houses in Stockholm.'

'Can she be moved?' Vanja wondered, glancing at the pale, thin figure in the bed.

'I'll check with the doctors, but as I understand it there's nothing physically wrong with her, and after all she comes from Stockholm, so in a way she'll be going home.'

'I'll go with her,' Sebastian stated in a tone which he hoped made it clear that this was not a matter for discussion. However, Torkel raised an eyebrow.

'She's a traumatised witness, I'm a psychologist,' Sebastian clarified in an exaggeratedly pedagogical voice, as if he was explaining something to a small child. 'She came out of the cave because she trusts me. I can do more good by spending time with her than by sitting in an office checking bank accounts or going through CCTV tapes or searching for footprints in caves, or whatever it is you're planning on doing.' He turned back to the window. Nicole's dark hair spread across the pillow. Her little hands resting on her stomach, the fingertips almost touching.

Even, steady breathing. He was filled with an indescribable ten-derness as he gazed at her — tenderness and a desire to protect her. He could do that only if he was where she was.

'She trusts me, even more than she trusts her mother right now. And I promised I wouldn't leave her,' he said in conclusion, surprising himself with how emotional he sounded.

In spite of the fact that he had just been spoken to as if he was an idiot, Torkel recognised the logic in what Sebastian was saying.

The priority was to remove the girl from Torsby.

★ ★ ★

She had fallen asleep with her head on his shoulder.

Sebastian had intended to sit in the front passenger seat, leav-ing Maria and Nicole to spread out in the back of the car, but as they were about to get in it became clear that Nicole wanted both of them beside her. So now they were all squashed in the back of the brown Opel Zafira Tourer, heading for Stockholm.

Once they decided to move Nicole, everything else moved fast. Just after nine o'clock an unmarked police car had pulled into the ambulance bay, which had a roof and was partially hidden from view from the rest of the hospital. Sebastian, Maria and Nicole had quickly got in, and no reporters had noticed their departure, as far as they could tell.

They had been travelling for about an hour. Fredrika was driving, sticking to a steady 110 kilometres per hour as they headed east along the E18. Just after Sunne she had asked if any-one minded if she put the radio on, but otherwise she hadn't said a word. Sebastian thanked his lucky stars that he hadn't slept with her; that would have made the silence uncomfortable rather than welcome.

Billy had offered to take them to Stockholm, but Torkel wanted him to stay in Torsby. They had got nowhere with the tapes from the CCTV cameras at the hospital, but at least they had a time frame to work on; Dennis had glanced at his watch just before he was attacked.

They were now working on retrieving images from the cameras covering the roads leading to the hospital in the hope of spotting a car within the relevant period. There were unlikely to be many vehicles around at that time of night. Unfortunately Torsby didn't have all that many cameras either, and if the person they were looking for had excellent local knowledge, as Sebastian believed, he had probably managed to avoid the cameras that were in place – but they had to try.

Vanja and Fabian, the forensic technician, were going back to the cave to see if they could find any trace of the man who had been there before Erik and Sebastian arrived. Both of them were adamant that they hadn't seen a car parked nearby, so whoever it was must have made their way to the cave on foot. Partly, at least. An appeal had been issued, asking for anyone who had seen a parked car within a few kilometres of the cave last Saturday morning to contact the police. Nothing so far.

'Anyone need me to stop?' Fredrika asked as they passed a sign showing that there was a service station coming up in one kilometre. Sebastian and Maria looked at one another, and Maria shook her head.

'We're fine, thanks,' Sebastian said, adjusting his position a fraction while taking care not to disturb Nicole. He was tired; he had had only a couple of hours' sleep last night. The good thing about the eventful night and their hasty departure was that he hadn't seen anything of Malin Åkerblad.

When he nipped back to the hotel to pack his things, he had something of a surprise. As he was going up the stairs to his room, the receptionist had spoken to him.

'I hope it was OK to let your colleague into your room last night.'

Sebastian had stopped dead, completely taken aback; the young man on the desk had realised he needed to explain.

'Your colleague, Billy Rosén – he said he'd left his laptop in your room, and you'd gone out.'

Sebastian tried to make sense of what he had just heard, but without success. Billy hadn't even been in his room since they arrived, let alone left his laptop there. However, there was no point in making a big thing of it with the receptionist, so Sebastian had merely nodded emphatically.

'That's perfectly OK. Absolutely. No problem at all.'

As he quickly gathered up his things, he tried to work out why Billy would have wanted to get into his room. He couldn't think of any reason. Nothing seemed to be missing. Had he planted a bug? A hidden camera? But why? The only thing Billy could expect to see or hear was the odd bout of hotel-room sex, and that seemed highly unlikely. So why had Billy been in here?

He didn't have time to worry about that now; at least he knew it had happened, and he could think about the reason at a later stage.

Now he started to wonder once more, but he was too tired to concentrate. The temperature inside the car was a steady twenty-one degrees, the engine was purring, the music was playing quietly and Nicole's head was resting on his shoulder.

Sebastian leaned against the window and fell asleep.

★ ★ ★

Three hours later they stopped on Sofielundsvägen in Enskededalen, south of Stockholm. Fredrika informed them that this was the first time she had seen the Globe arena in real life, and for a moment Sebastian was worried that she might crash as she leaned forward over the wheel to see as much of the building as possible for as long as possible.

When they arrived she waited in the car while Sebastian, Maria and Nicole went up to the first-floor apartment. Three rooms, light and fresh, with parquet flooring in the hallway which continued into the living room on the left, beyond two white closets with sliding doors, and a seat upholstered in green corduroy.

'Just bring what you need for the next day or so,' Sebastian said as he slipped off his shoes and went inside. 'Then you can make a list and we'll send someone over.'

Maria nodded and took Nicole by the hand.

'Shall we start in my room?' she suggested, and they disappeared into the room at the end on the right. Sebastian went into the living room. Bookshelves along one wall. A beige corner sofa with brightly coloured cushions under the large window, on a shaggy brown rug. A round coffee table with metal legs. A flatscreen TV on the wall opposite. Books and DVDs along the shelves, interspersed with photographs in IKEA frames. Sebastian picked up one of them: a younger Nicole, perhaps four or five years old, standing between Maria and a man with a Latin-American appearance. Her father, presumably. The separation obviously hadn't been unpleasant enough for Maria to want to erase him from their everyday lives. On the other hand, she hadn't contacted him since she came back to Sweden, as far as Sebastian knew, so he guessed that their relationship could best be described as neutral.

He put down the photograph and left the room. He could hear Maria's voice, and walked past the bright kitchen towards the sound.

He stopped in the doorway of Nicole's room. She was standing by the bed putting three books into a small rucksack, while Maria was taking clothes out of the wardrobe. The images came from nowhere, without warning, taking him back ten years.

To another little girl, another bed, another rucksack.

With Bamse the bear on it.

Sabine, packing for the holiday in Thailand with the concentration and care only a four-year-old could summon up. Books, hair slides, pink hairbrush, plastic tiara with a picture of Cinderella on it, surrounded by plastic diamonds, a little purse containing the ice-cream money Grandma had given her, plus Dragon, her favourite cuddly toy. He was orange with green spines all along his back and down his tail; he had been a present on her second birthday, and she never went anywhere without him.

Sebastian hadn't thought about Dragon since . . . since when? Since Boxing Day 2004. Dragon had stayed in the hotel room when Sebastian and Sabine went down to the beach. He didn't like swimming. 'He breathes fire, you see,' Sabine had explained, her voice full of a four-year-old's wisdom as she tucked Dragon up in her bed. 'So it's not good for him if he gets wet.' Then they had left the room.

Gone down to the beach.

To the wave.

'I'll wait in the car,' Sebastian managed to say, in spite of the lump in his throat. Nicole looked up at him, immediately anxious. She glanced at Maria, then back at Sebastian, as if she couldn't decide where she wanted to be.

'Actually,' Sebastian began when he saw the child's reaction, 'I might as well wait in the living room. I'm not going anywhere.' He smiled at Nicole. 'You finish off your packing.'

In fact he ended up in the kitchen. A table and four chairs, fridge, freezer, built-in microwave at a comfortable height. Photographs, drawings and Post-it notes stuck on with brightly coloured magnets. Neat and tidy shelves. A kettle and a milk frother in one corner, several cookery books in another. The draining board had been wiped clean, and there were no dirty dishes in the sink. A kitchen that had been prepared for a lengthy absence. Sebastian opened the shiny white cupboard doors until he found a glass. He let the cold water run for a little while, then filled the glass and drank deeply. He leaned against the sink and gazed at the poster on the wall above the table: the animals of Scandinavia. In his head he started to go through the ones he recognised and could name.

Ten minutes later they were back in the car.

★ ★ ★

The 'safe house' in Farsta was also a three-room apartment, but that was where the similarities ended. Maria and Nicole's place was a home – personal, well thought out, cosy. This was functional at best. There was a stale smell as they opened the door, and as soon as they walked in the sense of dilapidation increased, mainly due to a big hole in the plaster on one wall, presumably because something far too heavy had been hung up and come crashing down. Nicole slipped her hand into her mother's as they went from room to room.

The furniture was clean and nothing appeared to be broken, but it was just a collection of random pieces, giving the impression that whoever had lived there before had gradually thought of things they needed, and bought whatever it was without paying any attention to what was already in the apartment. The whole place looked a bit like a car boot sale.

A female plain-clothes officer who introduced herself as Sofia had met them outside the block and escorted them up the three flights of stairs. She was now sitting in the armchair opposite the sofa, where Nicole was curled up next to Maria. Sofia explained that the threat to their safety was now regarded as low level, since they had moved to a secret address in Stockholm, but that the police would patrol the area every two hours around the clock. They had decided it was best not to draw attention to the situation by visiting on a regular basis, or posting a guard outside the building or in the stairwell.

Maria was given an alarm to wear around her wrist, and a pre-programmed mobile; she only had to press one button and the police would respond, 24/7.

After taking a short tour of the apartment and visiting the bathroom, Sebastian came into the living room just as Sofia stood up to leave. She shook hands with Maria and nodded to Sebastian in passing.

'You need to do some shopping,' Sebastian said when the front door had closed. 'There's not much in the kitchen.'

Maria nodded wearily, then leaned back on the sofa with a deep sigh.

Sebastian could see that the events of the past couple of days were beginning to hit home. She hadn't had a minute's peace since she landed at Landvetter. Learning about the deaths of her sister's family, the worry about her missing daughter, the events at the hospital and then their abrupt departure, as if they were on the run. At last she had the chance to sit back and process what had happened.

'How do you feel?' Sebastian asked, taking a step closer as he realised she was fighting back the tears.

'I feel as if . . . as if the whole thing is totally unreal.' Maria let out a joyless laugh. 'My sister has been murdered and Nicole saw who did it.' She drew her daughter closer. 'And now she won't talk.'

'She will,' Sebastian said, sitting down beside her. 'I promise.'

Maria merely nodded and stroked Nicole's hair. Sebastian wondered what to say, what he could say, and realised there wasn't much that hadn't already been said, or would make a difference. This was something Maria had to get through, and if she needed to talk he would be there, but offering words of consolation without being asked could easily appear clichéd and intrusive. Particularly as they didn't know each other very well – or at all, to be honest.

'I'll go and do some shopping, then I'll cook dinner,' Sebastian said, getting to his feet. 'I won't be long,' he added reassuringly as Nicole raised her head from Maria's chest. He could feel her eyes following him as he left the room, but at least she stayed put, with Maria's arm around her.

'Thanks,' Maria called out as he pulled on his shoes. She doesn't need to thank me, he thought. This definitely wasn't some kind of sacrifice. On the contrary – he was looking forward to the evening.

Erik Flodin was in the kitchen frying rösti. The schnitzels had been dipped in egg, flour and breadcrumbs and were drying off on a plate, while the caper and anchovy butter was ready in the fridge. He had plugged his phone into the kitchen stereo and was singing along to Lars Winnerbäck from his Spotify playlist. He enjoyed cooking – he always had. To him it was the perfect form of relaxation. It didn't matter what his day had been like; an hour's total focus on his pots and pans was all he needed to make him feel better. It might take a bit longer tonight; today had been crazy. The craziest ever. The murders of the Carlsten family and Jan Ceder were bad enough, but a killer who dresses up in scrubs to get at a witness in hospital during the night . . . It was like an American action movie. From the moment he had been woken at three o'clock this morning he had thanked his lucky stars that he was no longer in charge of the case.

'Dad.'

He turned around and reached out to turn down the stereo at the same time. Winnerbäck faded away, and Erik could see from the look on his daughter's face that it wasn't a second too soon. Alma had turned twelve just a few weeks ago, and at the moment almost everything Erik and Pia did was either *sooo* embarrassing or totally, like, hopeless. Erik guessed that his duet with Lars Winnerbäck ticked both boxes.

'Didn't you hear the doorbell?' Alma said, making it perfectly clear that she held Erik responsible for the fact that she had had to leave her room and answer the door.

'Who is it?' Erik wondered, turning down the heat under the rösti. Alma merely shrugged and headed back to her room. Erik wiped his hands and went into the hallway; Frank was standing just inside the door looking apologetic.

'I'm so sorry to disturb you – are you in the middle of dinner?'

'No, it's fine, come on in,' Erik said, shaking Frank's hand. 'I'll give Pia a shout.'

'It's actually you I want to see,' Frank said, kicking off his boots and following Erik into the kitchen.

'OK – would you like to stay for dinner? It'll be ready in ten minutes.'

'No, thanks, I have to get back to the boy.'

Frank sat down at the kitchen table while Erik went back to his cooking. 'So how can I help you?' he asked, flipping over the rösti. Perfect.

'I heard you were looking for a car parked near the Bear's Cave yesterday.'

'That's right.'

'I saw one.'

Erik turned around as Frank leaned forward and clasped his hands on the table.

'Someone called the council in the morning and said they'd hit a deer, so I drove up there and parked . . . have you got a map?'

Erik nodded and left the room. A minute later he was back, spreading a map on the table in front of his guest.

'I parked here.' Frank pointed to a spot about a kilometre from the Bear's Cave. 'There was another car down this little track.' Frank took out his handkerchief and wiped his nose, which was running slightly from being out in the chilly April evening. 'At first I thought it was the car that had hit the deer, but there was no one in it, or anywhere nearby.'

'Do you remember what kind of car it was?' Erik asked as he busied himself with dinner once more.

'It was a Mercedes, I noticed the logo, but I've no idea what model it was.'

'Colour?'

'Dark blue, almost black.'

'Would you recognise it if you saw a picture?'

'Maybe – I'm not sure.'

'And you don't remember the registration number?'

'Sorry, no.'

Erik quickly considered what to do with this information. Get in touch with Torkel, of course. Riksmord had to be told. They would probably want to speak to Frank, see if they could work out what model the Mercedes was, then run a check against the database hoping to find one or more possible vehicles registered to someone living in the area.

'How long can you be away from Hampus?' Erik asked, trying to come up with a timescale in his head. Frank glanced at his watch.

'His carer leaves in half an hour. Why?'

'You need to speak to Riksmord. They'll want to try and identify the car.'

'They're welcome to come and see me at home,' Frank said as he got to his feet. 'You can tell them where I live.'

Erik showed him out, then turned his attention to the schnitzel.

Sebastian was sitting on the worn grey-green sofa with Nicole by his side, reading aloud from one of the books she had brought with her.

Gregor the Overlander.

Something about two siblings who had apparently fallen into the underworld, where one of them was worshipped as a princess by the cockroaches and had to save the subterranean kingdom from war, while both of them searched for their missing father and tried to find their way back to the real world. Maria had said it was a fantasy story.

Sebastian thought it was utter crap.

But he had to admit they'd had a very pleasant evening.

He had cooked dinner for all three of them, with Maria and Nicole keeping him company and acting as his kitchen assistants. Nicole had diced onions and grated carrots for his spaghetti bolognese, while Maria set the table and lit candles; she had found two spectacularly ugly dark green candlesticks on the window ledge. Nicole seemed to have enjoyed her meal; Sebastian had kept the conversation going, hoping to make everything seem as normal as possible. He had asked Maria about her work and her stay in Mali, but he had focused mainly on Nicole. Wondered if she liked school, what her favourite and least favourite subjects were, who her friends were and so on. Although Nicole hadn't spoken, of course, Sebastian had directed all his questions to her. Maria had given her daughter the opportunity to respond, then answered herself, always concluding with 'Isn't that right, sweetheart?' or something along those lines so that Nicole would feel involved.

After dinner Sebastian and Maria had cleared away and washed up, while Nicole sat at the table with her pad and coloured pens.

'She got very anxious when you were out shopping,' Maria had said quietly, nodding in the child's direction. 'She stuck to me like glue the whole time.'

Sebastian turned to look at Nicole; once again he was surprised by the tenderness he felt towards her. She put down her pen and sat back.

'Can I have a look?' Sebastian moved around the table and looked down at the drawing. A house in a forest. A broken window in a door on a veranda. Even though he hadn't seen the place, Sebastian assumed this was the house she had broken into on her way to the Bear's Cave and what she believed would be a safe haven. Only half the house had outside walls, the rest was a kind of cross section. A living room, a kitchen and a bedroom, with a dark-haired girl lying underneath a bed.

'Is it OK if I keep this one too?' Nicole met Sebastian's gaze; there were no words, of course, not even a nod to indicate that she had heard what he said. On the other hand, there were no protests either when he picked up the drawing and rolled it up.

'Could you possibly stay while I have a shower?' Maria had asked, and Sebastian had admitted that he had all the time in the world. No one was waiting for him.

★ ★ ★

Maria stood there for a long time, letting the hot water flow over her body in the hope that it might miraculously wash away some of her grief and despair.

It didn't.

She had witnessed suffering at close quarters through her work. She had got involved, empathised with victims and their families, but she had always managed to maintain the professional distance necessary to avoid being swallowed up, going under.

But right now she was definitely going under.

She rested her forehead against the tiles, her body shaking with silent sobs; for the first time since she got home she realised how tired and empty she felt when she didn't have to be strong for Nicole. Her legs refused to hold her up. She sank down on the floor and sat there with the water pouring down on her.

She wasn't sure if she would ever be able to get up again.

★ ★ ★

When she emerged from the bathroom after a good half-hour, Sebastian was sitting on the sofa with Nicole, reading aloud from one of the books she had brought with her. Maria stopped in the doorway, watching them.

Sebastian Bergman really did have endless patience with the child. In the midst of all the darkness, all the uncertainty and turbulence, he was the fixed point that Nicole needed. And not only Nicole, she realised. She would never have got through the last couple of days without him. She leaned against the door frame listening as his voice altered in both tone and accent for the different characters in the story. She was drawn in just like Nicole, who was utterly absorbed. Maria was even a little disappointed when the chapter came to an end, and Sebastian closed the book and put it down on the coffee table.

'Time I made a move,' he said, getting to his feet. Nicole immediately looked anxious. She jumped up, hurried over to Maria and clung to her. 'Will you be OK?' Sebastian said as he retrieved his coat from the hallway.

Maria nodded, but heard herself say: 'Can you stay?'

Sebastian stopped and looked enquiringly at her.

'Nicole will be sharing with me anyway, so you could have the other room,' Maria went on. 'If you want to, that is.'

He barely had time to formulate the answer in his head before he spoke.

'No problem – of course I can stay,' Sebastian said, hanging up his coat once more.

Torkel opened his laptop and was about to write a brief report on his conversation with Gunilla and Kent Bengtsson when there was a knock on the door.

It had been an eventful evening.

Erik Flodin had called at about eight o'clock to tell him that a witness had seen a parked car in the right area at the relevant time, but just as Torkel was about to ask Billy to go with him to meet Erik and speak to the witness, he got another call from a man called Kent Bengtsson, the Carlstens' neighbour, who had found Torkel's card in his mailbox when he got home. Torkel had quickly changed his plans: Vanja and Billy could go with Erik, while he went over to see the Bengtssons, who welcomed him warmly in spite of the late hour.

He had got back to the hotel about half an hour ago. When he answered the door, he found Vanja standing there with a white box; the contents immediately filled Torkel's room with the smell of fast food.

'Want some?' Vanja asked as she opened the box to reveal a cheeseburger and chips.

'No, thanks – I managed to get the kitchen to make me a sandwich when I got back.' Torkel opened the window, although Vanja didn't seem to see the connection with her not-so-fragrant meal.

'How did it go? What did the Bengtssons have to say?' she asked as she took a big bite of her burger.

Yes, what did they have to say? Torkel thought. Neither Gunilla nor Kent had been particularly talkative; their answers had been brief, and they hadn't really said anything that changed the picture the police already had of the Carlsten family. Pleasant, popular, with a burning commitment to environmental issues; Gunilla and Kent didn't really have a view on such things, although they knew that others had found it irritating.

'What others?' Torkel had asked, and had received the same answer as before. Jan Ceder and Ove Hanson were the individuals who had been most vociferously opposed to the family, but then they were also the two who had been reported to the police. Otherwise it was just a matter of odd comments and gossip. Nothing serious. And the Bengtssons certainly couldn't imagine who would want to kill their neighbours. It was just dreadful, particularly the murders of the two little boys. The two of them had often come over to say hello to the horses.

'Nothing we didn't already know, to be honest,' Torkel concluded. Vanja nodded. 'So where had they been since Thursday?' she asked, dipping a chip in a pool of tomato ketchup.

'They went to a sixtieth birthday party in Karlstad on Friday, and stayed the weekend.'

'So they weren't too upset to go to a party.'

'I got the feeling they didn't know the Carlstens all that well. They hadn't fallen out or anything, they just weren't very interested.' Torkel shrugged. 'How did you get on?'

'OK. Billy showed Frank Hedén pictures of just about every Mercedes that's been produced since 1970 – that's what it felt like, anyway.'

'And?'

'He wasn't sure of anything apart from the fact that it was a Merc. Billy's writing up a report. Are you sure you don't want some?' She pushed the white box towards Torkel, who held up a defensive hand. There was another knock on the door, and Billy walked in with his laptop.

'Hi. Vanja's just been telling me that your little outing wasn't much use,' Torkel said by way of a greeting.

'I wouldn't say that,' Billy replied, looking unusually pleased with himself for someone who had got nowhere. He sat down on Torkel's bed and turned the laptop so that his colleagues could see the screen.

'Frank wasn't sure, but the indications were that it was a later model.' Billy brought up a homepage with a slide show, and a series of Mercedes passed across the screen. 'It could be an A-class sedan, a C-class sedan, a coupé or an estate car, a CL, a CLA, a CLS—'

'OK, I get it,' Torkel interrupted him. 'It could be any one of a long list of cars. Move on.'

Billy looked a little disappointed that he wasn't allowed to carry on with his parade of possible cars, but he closed down the slide show and opened a new page.

'There were too many options to be of much help, but then I ran all the relevant models against the database anyway to see if any are registered to owners in this area, and if so, how many.'

Billy pushed back his shoulders; he couldn't suppress a smile, which told Torkel that he'd found something. The evening hadn't been wasted after all.

'Guess who owns a 2011 CLS 350?'

'Who?' Torkel asked, making it perfectly clear that he wasn't interested in guessing games right now.

'Ove Hanson.' Billy brought up the information on his computer.

'Why does that name seem familiar?' Vanja mumbled with her mouth full of the last chunk of her burger.

'He owns the boatyard down by the lake. Emil Carlsten made a formal complaint to the police because Hanson was using illegal anti-fouling paint on the hulls of his boats,' Torkel said, leaning forward to take a closer look.

'The local police spoke to him briefly on Friday – there's a summary in the shared folder, along with Carlsten's complaint,' Billy concluded. 'What do you want us to do?'

Torkel straightened up and moved away.

'Does he hunt?'

'He has a licence for two shotguns, so I assume he does.'

Torkel paced around the room for a moment. This was good. It could be the breakthrough they needed. He glanced at his watch: just after eleven. It was unlikely that anything would change if they had a few hours' well-earned rest.

'We'll read through what we've got and bring him in first thing in the morning,' he decided.

Billy and Vanja nodded, and after a brief chat about the plan for the following day, they went off to their respective rooms.

When he was alone Torkel closed the window and wondered whether to call Ursula. He wanted to, he longed to hear her voice, but it was too late. It would have to wait until tomorrow, and with a bit of luck he might be able to tell her that they were a little closer to solving the case.

He was on his way to the bathroom when his phone rang. Ursula, he thought optimistically, but it was a different number, a different name.

'It's late,' he said.

'I know, sorry about that,' Axel Weber said, sounding as if he actually meant it. 'I just wanted to tell you something.'

'What?' Torkel's tone was anything but friendly.

'I have some younger colleagues up in Stockholm . . .' Weber paused as if he wasn't quite sure how to continue. 'You've moved the girl, haven't you?'

'No comment. Goodnight,' Torkel said, determined to end the call.

'Wait, wait, that's not why I called.' Weber took a deep breath, as if he wanted to make absolutely sure he was doing the right thing. 'They know where she is. We're publishing the details tomorrow.'

THIS IS WHERE SHE'S HIDING

Capital letters.

Followed by a smaller but equally eye-catching subheading:

SHE SURVIVED THE HOUSE OF HORROR

The rest of the page was taken up by a grainy image that appeared to have been taken with a telephoto lens from a considerable distance away; this was probably a deliberate choice aimed at increasing the sensationalism and the air of a major revelation, Torkel assumed. Given the photographic techniques available these days, he could see no reason why the picture wasn't in sharp focus. It showed a section of the apartment block where Nicole and Maria had arrived less than twenty-four hours ago. Easily identifiable in spite of the poor quality. A pale oval that could well be a child's face at a window on the third floor. A red ring around the window so that no one could miss it, or doubt the accuracy of the headline.

'It's already out,' Torkel said after describing the front page to Sebastian over the phone.

'Have they said exactly where we are?' Sebastian asked, trying to absorb the enormity of what he had just heard. They would have to move. But where would they go? To his surprise the answer came into his mind immediately.

'It says *in an anonymous apartment block in Farsta*,' Torkel replied, skimming the article once more. 'But with the picture it won't be difficult to find for anyone who's interested.'

'Someone's tried to kill Nicole twice – what the fuck are they thinking?' Sebastian lowered his voice to a whisper; he was in the living room.

'I presume they're not thinking at all, but I've increased your security – there will be two officers in the stairwell.'

Sebastian nodded to himself, but his increasing anger made it impossible for him to stand still. He started pacing around the room as he hissed down the phone:

'She needs peace and quiet right now, and as normal a life as possible.'

'No one will get near you,' Torkel assured him.

'A normal life doesn't mean isolation and a constant threat.' Sebastian realised he was overemphasising his words once more. 'She has to have the chance to go out if she wants to, without reporters and photographers hiding in the bushes, and without someone trying to shoot her.'

Torkel wondered whether to inform Sebastian that the days of photographers lurking in the bushes were long gone, but he understood what his colleague meant.

'We'll move you again,' he decided. 'We have several safe houses.'

'I'm guessing that's the problem,' Sebastian said, surprised that Torkel hadn't put two and two together. 'You have *no* safe houses – there's a leak.'

'How do you know?' Torkel realised he had immediately adopted a defensive stance, as always when his organisation was criticised.

'You just read the proof out loud to me.'

In an instant Torkel realised Sebastian was right. The information about where Maria and Nicole were could only have come from someone within the police service. There weren't many names to choose from, and he made a mental note to find out exactly who the guilty party was, and to make sure they were out on their ear in no time.

But that wasn't the immediate problem.

'So what do you suggest?' he asked Sebastian, tossing the offending newspaper on the bed.

Sebastian allowed himself to share the thought that had come into his mind as soon as Torkel revealed that their hiding place was no longer a secret.

'They can stay with me.' Torkel didn't respond right away; Sebastian interpreted his silence as an initial resistance to the idea. 'I've got plenty of space, they'll have their own room, and no one – apart from you and me and the team – needs to know where they are.'

Somewhere deep down, Torkel felt he ought to say no, that it was out of the question, it was a terrible suggestion, it went against every rule in the book. However, the problem was that it actually wasn't a bad idea. Not at all.

Quite the reverse.

The girl seemed to have formed a bond with Sebastian, and Torkel was convinced he could be good for her. After all, they were dealing with a traumatised psyche, and that was Sebastian's area of expertise. He didn't trust Sebastian on a whole range of things, but he had complete confidence in him when it came to Nicole. They had an urgent problem, and Sebastian had given him a solution which could work, and at least give them a breathing space.

'I'll send a car,' he said. 'How soon can you be ready?'

'Wow, this place is huge!'

Sebastian gave a start at Maria's words. After taking their out-door clothes and telling them to have a look around and make themselves at home, his eyes had fallen on that spot on the wall in the hallway.

Again.

It had been a few days, but had he really thought it was over? That he'd have forgotten?

That he'd be able to walk into his apartment without thinking he could see traces of red, pick up the iron-rich smell of blood?

Yes, he probably had, he realised. Deep down he had hoped that company, other living beings, would dispel the memories and somehow cleanse the home in which he was finding it more and more difficult to spend time. Clearly it hadn't worked.

Not yet, anyway.

He turned away from the wall and saw Maria standing in the living-room doorway with Nicole's arms wrapped tightly around her waist.

'Sorry, what did you say?'

'This is a huge apartment.'

'Yes. Yes, it is.'

Sebastian reached for a hanger and hung up Maria's coat.

'Do you live here on your own?' Maria asked as she and Nicole carried on along the passageway to the rest of the apartment.

'Yes,' Sebastian replied as he hung Nicole's jacket on a hook.

Maria stopped in front of a white-painted door. 'What's in here?'

'Open it and see.'

Maria did as she was told.

'I thought this could be your room,' Sebastian said as he joined them.

'It's a beautiful room.'

Sebastian looked around and realised Maria was right. It was a beautiful room, if a little narrow. Lily had insisted that they needed a guest room, and had furnished it from a single extremely expensive visit to an auction in Norrtälje. Pale blue wallpaper, a stylish white rococo chest of drawers and a desk along one wall. Black-and-white portrait photographs in black frames. White curtains. Beneath the window a wide bed with a heavy wrought iron frame. All from the same estate, even the pictures. They had no idea who these people were who had once got dressed up and posed for a photographer, but Lily had thought they should stay with the rest of the furniture. Lovely things that went together perfectly, but they needed a living presence to become something more than a pretty room, to become part of a home.

'Will you be OK sharing the bed, or shall I bring in another mattress?'

'We'll be fine,' Maria assured him. 'Thank you so much for . . . for all you've done. I really appreciate it.'

Sebastian didn't respond immediately. It struck him how unused he was to receiving compliments. He was good at giving them, automatically and without an ounce of sincerity, but it was a long time since someone had genuinely expressed their appreciation to him. That was probably his own fault, but even so . . . it felt good.

'It's nothing,' he said honestly, meeting her gaze. 'I'm happy to help.'

'Thanks anyway. I don't know how we would have coped without you.'

There was another brief silence before Sebastian took a deep breath and stepped back.

'I haven't got much in, so I'll go and do some shopping while you two find your way around,' he said in a slightly louder voice, efficiently breaking the moment of intimacy that had arisen between them. At the same time he jerked his thumb in the vague direction of the front door.

'When I get back maybe Nicole and I could have a little chat.' He turned to the child, who was studying the photographs on the chest of drawers. 'What do you think?'

Nicole turned and met his gaze. Then she gave a faint nod. It was a tiny gesture, a blink-and-you'd-miss-it moment, but it was there. A reaction. The door to her self-imposed prison had opened, just a fraction.

Sebastian gave her a warm smile, and for the first time since that evening he didn't glance at the wall in the hallway as he left the apartment a few minutes later.

Ove Hanson was a giant of a man.

Torkel saw him in the corridor as the local uniformed officers led him to one of the interview rooms. Well over six feet tall, and if he got on the scales, Torkel thought they would show over 140 kilos. Maybe more. A series of tattoos was visible above the neckline of his sweatshirt. Earrings. Huge hands with tattoos on the backs, and an unkempt black beard which completed the image of a potential thug. Torkel knew it was wrong to judge people by their appearance, but he had no difficulty picturing Ove Hanson walking around inside the Carlsten house with a shotgun.

His train of thought was interrupted as Erik stuck his head around the door.

'They've put Ove Hanson in room one.'

'Thanks. Are we waiting for legal representation?'

Erik shook his head. 'He doesn't want anyone.'

'What did you say to him?' Torkel asked as he gathered up the printout of Hanson's first interview, which he had been reading.

'I just told him we wanted to talk to him in connection with the Carlsten murders.'

'And he still didn't want a solicitor?'

Erik shook his head again, and disappeared. Torkel glanced at his watch. He had time to grab a coffee while he was waiting for Vanja. He had seen a service technician working on the coffee machine when he came in this morning, so with a bit of luck he would be able to get a hot drink.

★ ★ ★

245

Vanja let the cold water drip off her face as she studied her reflection in the mirror.

Dark circles under her eyes. She was sleeping badly these days. She would wake only an hour or so after falling asleep, then she would lie there, doze for a little while, then wake again. She didn't really know why; she didn't feel anxious when she woke up, there were no conscious thoughts demanding her attention, no unsolved problems.

She just couldn't sleep.

Last night she had dreamt about walking with Valdemar – she didn't even think of him as Dad in her dreams any more – out on Djurgården. They had stopped at the lake she had never known the name of, where herons nested in the trees. They had talked. About everything, just like they used to do. When he had been the most important man in her life.

Before the lies that had torn everything apart . . .

In the dream he had put his arm around her shoulders as they strolled along by the water. She had been aware of the warmth of his hand through her thin jacket. She had felt safe. Loved.

It had been a good feeling.

In her dream.

With an irritated sigh she yanked two paper towels out of the holder on the wall and dried her face. She had never thought she would admit this to herself, particularly after the events of recent months, but she missed Sebastian. She had no problem with Torkel or Billy, but if she was ever going to talk to anyone about the way Valdemar and Anna had betrayed her, it would be Sebastian.

Strange, but true.

She didn't like him.

She didn't even trust him.

But on those occasions when she had toyed with the idea of actually talking to someone, of letting everything out rather than carrying the burden all by herself, it was Sebastian who had come into her mind.

246

However, right now he was in Stockholm, and she had an interview to take care of. She threw the paper towels in the bin, and with a final glance in the mirror she went to find Torkel.

★ ★ ★

'This is Vanja Lithner, my name is Torkel Höglund and we're from Riksmord.'

Ove Hanson merely nodded as Vanja and Torkel sat down opposite him. Vanja pressed 'Record' on the little tape recorder beside her and gave the date, time, and the names of those present, then glanced at Torkel to see if he wanted to go first. Which he did.

'Tell me about the Carlsten family,' he said, leaning forward and clasping his hands on the table.

'What do you want me to say about them?' Hanson replied in a quiet and surprisingly well-modulated voice which didn't seem to go with his huge, almost brutal body. 'I didn't like them – they reported me to the police for next to nothing. But I didn't kill them.'

'Why did they report you to the police?'

'I was selling anti-fouling paint that can't be used for environmental reasons,' Hanson said patiently. The look he gave Torkel made it clear that he was well aware that Torkel already had this information. 'But selling it isn't illegal,' he concluded, looking directly at both his interrogators.

Vanja opened her folder and glanced down at the contents – mainly for appearances' sake; she had already memorised Hanson's previous interview, but it gave the questions extra weight if the person being interviewed believed they were based on documented facts.

'You have no alibi for the day of the murders,' she stated, looking into those brown eyes beneath bushy brows.

'I have an alibi for some parts of the day,' he said calmly, holding her gaze. 'As I recall you were unable to say exactly when the murders took place.'

Which was true. Ove Hanson had given a fairly detailed account of his activities on the Wednesday. There were gaps here and there when no one could corroborate his story, but as they didn't have an exact time of death for the victims, they had been unable to link those gaps to the murders.

Vanja let it go, changed tack.

'What were you doing on Saturday between nine and eleven?'

'Saturday just gone? The day before yesterday?'

'Yes.'

'Between nine and eleven in the morning?'

'Yes.'

'I suppose I was in the shop. We open at ten on Saturdays.'

'You *suppose* you were in the shop?' Torkel interjected.

'I was in the shop,' Ove corrected himself, with a weary look at Torkel.

'Were you alone?' Vanja wanted to know.

'I open up on my own, then there are two of us from lunchtime until we close at four.'

'So you were alone in the shop on Saturday morning?'

'Yes.'

'Did you have any customers? Did anyone see you there?'

'What happened on Saturday?'

Torkel and Vanja exchanged a glance. Torkel nodded. Vanja consulted the folder again as if she was searching for facts with which to confront Ove, but in this case there weren't any. Only guesses. Circumstantial evidence, if you were feeling generous.

'Your car was seen in the vicinity of the Bear's Cave, where we later found Nicole Carlsten,' Vanja lied blithely.

The truth was that a car which *could* have been Ove Hanson's had been seen near the cave, but the truth was no help in the current situation.

'The girl who was in the house?' Ove said, genuinely taken aback. 'I was nowhere near the Bear's Cave on Saturday,' he went on when he got no reaction to his question.

'So how do you explain the fact that your car was there?' Vanja demanded, slowly closing the folder.

'It wasn't.'

'Are you sure? You hadn't lent it to someone else? Could someone have taken the keys without your knowing?' Torkel spread his hands wide in a gesture that said he had heard stranger things. Vanja waited; the tension was unbearable. If it was Ove's car that the witness had seen in the forest, and if Ove had put it there, Torkel was giving him the chance to explain how it got there without admitting any personal involvement. At least that would confirm that they were on the right track, then all they had to do was expose the lie.

'No. I took the car to work in the morning, and nobody drove it all day.'

Vanja breathed out; she was so disappointed. He hadn't taken the bait, and she couldn't detect any falseness in his tone. Weariness, perhaps; she had the feeling that Ove Hanson had been questioned and accused many times over the years just because of his size and daunting appearance. She made one last attempt.

'So you can't explain how your car ended up near the Bear's Cave on Saturday?'

'It wasn't there,' Hanson stated firmly.

Torkel and Vanja exchanged another glance and remained silent. Most Swedes don't like silence. They feel the need to fill it. Sometimes this tactic produced results as the interviewee tied himself up in explanations and hypotheses the police hadn't even asked for. After only a few seconds it seemed as if this might be the case with Ove Hanson as he shuffled uncomfortably and took a deep breath.

'What was the registration number of the car up there?'

Another glance. Not an explanation. Not a hypothesis aimed at helping them along the way. A question.

They had three options.

Lie – they knew Ove's registration number.

Ignore the question completely.

Tell the truth – they didn't know the number of the car the witness had seen.

Vanja thought it best to leave the decision to Torkel.

'Listen to me,' he said with a sigh that suggested he was running out of patience. 'You're part of this investigation because you had a motive.'

Option two, Vanja noted.

'A complaint to the police that went nowhere? That's not a motive.' Ove Hanson leaned across the table. 'I know several people who have better motives than me. A million times better.'

It was time to take a more defensive approach.

He didn't like it, but he had been lying awake since sunrise, and he couldn't come up with an alternative solution. He was still furious when he thought about how close to success he had been in the cave. If only he'd got there five minutes earlier, the girl would no longer be a problem. She had been right there, in the little space inside the crevice.

He had been on the right lines.

In the right place.

But at the wrong time.

He wouldn't even have needed five minutes – three would have been enough. Or two. Then all his troubles would have been over.

He had briefly considered shooting both of them, the girl and the slightly overweight cop or whoever he was, who had sat down to talk to her and eventually persuaded her to leave her hiding place. Killing them would have been easy, but how would he have got away? The shots would have been amplified by the cave and would have been heard outside; the area was crawling with police. He could have run the other way, into the darkness, deeper into the cave system, but no one knew if there was another way out. He had been trapped.

So he had been forced to let them go. Watch them disappear. And then there was the hospital.

It should have been simple, but he couldn't find her.

So far he had been proactive, but as he got up and went down to the kitchen to put the coffee on, he had realised the truth: twice he had been so close, twice she had got away. There would be no third chance. It would be impossible to get to her now.

The girl was alive. According to the papers she wasn't talking; no doubt that was true, otherwise the police would have come knocking on his door by now.

Because she must have seen him, mustn't she?

He was working on the assumption that she had, so what could he do now? Make sure there was as little forensic evidence as possible if – or when – she decided to tell the police what she had witnessed. There must be nothing in his home that could link him to the crimes.

He thought he had already dealt with most things. He had chosen routes that weren't covered by CCTV cameras on his way to and from the hospital, he had parked far enough away so that anyone who happened to notice and recognise his car wouldn't make the connection – just as he had done at the Bear's Cave – and he had entered the hospital through a back door with no security cameras anywhere near.

He was pretty sure no one would be able to prove that he had been at the cave or the hospital.

The shotgun he had used at the Carlstens' was back with Jan Ceder. He had changed his tyres down in Filipstad, so that any possible tyre tracks couldn't be traced back to him.

What else?

He had to think.

He opened a drawer and took out a little notebook and a pen. It was important to be meticulous. Not to forget anything. Write everything down methodically. He sat down at the kitchen table, finished off his coffee and put pen to paper.

Burn the clothes I was wearing at the Carlstens'
Burn the clothes from the cave
Burn my boots

That hurt. He loved those boots, besides which they were nearly new.

But you do what you have to do.

He had read somewhere that steam cleaning was the best way to get rid of stains. But was that really necessary? Could Ceder's shotgun have left any traces? There was nothing strange about having guns in the car; he had a licence for several weapons. He left it on the list, but added a question mark.

Low priority.

What else could prove his downfall?

Shotgun, car, clothes, boots . . . He couldn't think of anything.

Burn list he added, then left the notebook on the table and went upstairs to get changed and start the day properly.

He glanced at the computer as he passed the door of the study, and quickly decided not to wake it up. He could easily spend an hour or more sitting there once he got sucked in. On the other hand, it had proved invaluable when it came to finding out how the investigation into the crimes he had committed was progressing. The tabloids were alarmingly well informed.

He told himself it was for his own good, and he would just have a quick look at the websites he had bookmarked. Nothing else. With two strides he reached the machine and moved the mouse, waking the screen from sleep mode. He leaned forward; he wasn't even going to sit down, this would only take a second. He clicked on *Expressen*'s homepage. His broadband connection wasn't too bad, and in no time the page had refreshed.

He sat down.

THIS IS WHERE SHE'S HIDING

Capital letters.

Followed by a smaller but equally eye-catching subheading:

SHE SURVIVED THE HOUSE OF HORROR

He read through the article with interest, looking closely at the grainy image with the pale oval at the window.

The girl who got away.

He would need to add something to the list on the kitchen table.

Go to Farsta

★ ★ ★

It had taken longer than expected to do the shopping, mainly because he wasn't used to catering for anyone other than himself. Admittedly when Ellinor had been around he had started venturing beyond the 7-Eleven and the Östermalm Food Hall, but this was different. He was shopping for a little girl and her mother, and he didn't know where to start. What did a ten-year-old like? He went for brightly coloured packs of fruit yogurt and cereal, then he added a sliced loaf, butter, liver pâté, cream cheese, smoked ham, milk, O'Boy drinking chocolate and orange juice. That was breakfast sorted; now for lunch and dinner. There was far too much choice on the shelves, and the fact that he wasn't sure whether he or Maria was doing the cooking didn't exactly help. Nicole and her mother were his guests, and it would feel odd if he simply dumped a pile of carrier bags in the kitchen and assumed that Maria would whip something up. That's what he was hoping for, of course, but he had to have a Plan B just in case.

He moved on to the freezer aisle and picked up plenty of ready meals and ice cream, then added instant mashed potato, frankfurters, ketchup, waffles and cream. By the time he reached the checkout the bill came to almost 1,500 kronor, and he had four heavy bags to carry home.

He cut across Östermalmstorg; the handles of the plastic bags were cutting into his palms, but he felt positive, inspired. There was someone waiting for him at home.

Two people who needed him.

As he walked along he looked at everyone around him, hurrying home perhaps, or to a meeting somewhere, and suddenly he felt part of it all. They weren't just bodies in motion; they all had a destination.

So this was what it felt like to be needed. Life had a direction. He allowed himself to be swept along, and increased his speed. He was going home.

Five minutes later he turned into Grev Magnigatan, then stopped and put down the bags, his hands aching. He looked up at his apartment, and realised that he hadn't given a thought to the ever-present smell of detergent in the hallway, or felt any reluctance to return. On the contrary: for the first time in ages he longed to open his new front door.

He noticed a movement at one of the living-room windows; a pale little face was just visible behind the glass. Nicole. She had seen him; she pressed closer, presumably to get a better view. This worried him; she ought to stay away from the windows. He didn't want to encourage her, so he didn't acknowledge her. At the same time he felt a burst of fresh energy in his legs, and he hardly noticed the pain in his hands.

Not only was he needed.

Someone was longing to see him.

★ ★ ★

'You need to make sure Nicole stays away from the windows,' Sebastian said when he came in and put down the bags in the hallway.

'I only left her for a second.' Maria's voice came from the kitchen, and a second later she ran into the living room clutching a Melitta filter.

'Nicole! Come away from there!' she shouted, sounding almost angry. Sebastian heard Nicole jump down; it sounded as if she was barefoot, and that little detail pleased him. If you were barefoot it meant you were comfortable, he thought. It meant you felt at home.

He left the bags and followed Maria into the living room. Nicole was standing next to her mother; one of the antique

255

armchairs behind her was facing the window, so she had presumably climbed on it to see out. He walked past her and demonstratively drew the heavy green curtains. Ellinor had put them up, and at first he had hated their pretentious luxury, but he had learned to appreciate something that so effectively shut out the outside world.

'Let's not do that any more, OK?' he said, trying to sound kind but firm. 'I've bought lots of food – I didn't know what you liked.'

They followed him into the hallway and Maria picked up two of the bags.

'This is exciting,' she said with a smile, heading for the kitchen. 'I'm starving!' She dumped the bags on the table and started unpacking them; Sebastian grabbed the other two and followed suit.

'Look, Nicole! O'Boy. Spaghetti. Meatballs. Isn't that great?' She came to three bright red boxes of frozen food, which didn't please her quite so much.

'Beef hotpot? I guess you've never had kids?' she said, pretending to be sceptical. She was obviously enjoying the ordinariness of the situation, the banality of the conversation. Which was hardly surprising after the tension of the past few days.

'No, never.'

The lie came automatically. He never talked about Sabine and Lily. Women had a tendency to home in on the subject, wanting to know more. Wanting to know what had happened, and when they found out, insisting on talking about how terrible it must have been. However, with Maria he didn't feel the same kind of emotional pressure; perhaps he would even be able to tell her the truth. But not right now.

'I've got ice cream and waffles if you'd like some,' he said, changing the subject.

'We love waffles, don't we, sweetheart?'

'In that case all I have to do is find the waffle iron,' Sebastian said, wondering where to look. He had a feeling he had seen a waffle iron around the place a long time ago; he couldn't ever remember using it, but he had definitely seen it. He knelt down and started with the cupboard to the right of the cooker. That was where people usually kept larger items of kitchen equipment, wasn't it? At least that was what his mother had done, and if he had put a waffle iron away somewhere, surely his subconscious would have made him shove it in there. He opened the door and saw three shelves containing a mixer and several large pans and frying pans. Where had all this stuff come from? Perhaps Ellinor was responsible for some of it, but not all of it. Lily? But they hadn't spent much time here; they had lived mainly in Cologne. Behind him he could hear Maria continuing to unpack the shopping, chatting away to Nicole, who was perched on one of the chairs by the table, as she brought out sweets and biscuits, ice cream and fruit. Nicole seemed to be enjoying herself; she was certainly participating with her eyes at least. The atmosphere was good, and he shuffled along to the next cupboard. Behind a fondue set he had absolutely no recollection of, he saw an electric cable so old that it had some sort of fabric outer casing. He tugged, and there it was at last: the waffle iron. It was an unwieldy object made of Bakelite, and it looked ancient. Now he remembered where it had come from: his uncle's house. When he died Sebastian had filled several boxes, mainly to irritate his father, who had clearly set his heart on taking the lot. The question was whether it actually worked. He plonked it on the draining board and turned to Maria. He was about to say something when the sound of a mobile phone sliced through the apartment.

'It's mine, I switched it on so I could check my messages,' Maria said, getting the phone out of her pocket and glancing at the screen.

'I don't recognise the number.'

Sebastian felt a pang of anxiety.

'Shall I answer it?' Maria went on, moving closer to him. Sebastian hesitated for a second.

'OK, but don't say where you are. That's the most important thing.'

Maria swiped the screen. 'Hello? Yes, it's me.'

257

Sebastian could just hear the voice of a man on the other end of the line, but he couldn't make out what he was saying.

'Yes, that's right.' Maria looked surprised. Not scared or anxious, which reassured Sebastian; at least the conversation wasn't threatening. He was curious though, particularly when Maria suddenly got upset.

'I can't think about that right now.' All at once she was angry.

'No, I don't understand why you think it's OK to call me!'

She ended the call and looked at Sebastian; she was clearly furious.

'Was it a newspaper? They can be pretty inconsiderate,' he said, wanting to put his arm around her shoulders to calm her down.

'It was a solicitor, wondering if I wanted to sell the house.'

'What house?'

'My sister's house.'

Sebastian felt as if he couldn't quite grasp what she was saying.

'Someone wants to buy your sister's house? Just days after the whole family was murdered?'

'Yes, some company or other. Filbo, I think he said. Cold-hearted bastards!'

Sebastian reached out his hand. This meant something, he was sure of it. He had to find out exactly what that might be.

'Can I borrow your phone?' Maria passed it over, and Sebastian immediately realised he couldn't cope with this level of new technology.

'How do I find the last incoming call?' he asked, handing it back. Two clicks and a swipe, and there it was.

08.

A Stockholm number.

A man's voice answered after two rings.

'Lex Legali, Rickard Häger.'

Sebastian recognised the tone and range of the deep voice; this was the man who had spoken to Maria.

★ ★ ★

Sebastian had gone into his study and closed the door. He had tried not to worry Maria too much, but suspected that his grim conversation with Rickard Häger had proved anything but reassuring. He had made every effort to remain professional, but Häger had ducked and weaved, refusing to answer his questions. He had passed the phone to Maria so that she could give Häger her mandate to discuss the matter with a third party, but when that didn't work either, Sebastian had threatened him with a full-scale police investigation, which finally produced an answer.

Häger was representing Filbo Sweden AB, a subsidiary of FilboCorp Ltd, a mining company registered with the Toronto stock exchange. He had apologised for making enquiries so soon after the tragedy, but his client wanted to express an interest in the property at the earliest possible moment. If he had understood correctly, Maria was now the sole owner, and to him it seemed perfectly normal to contact the person in that position.

It was just business.

Sebastian tried to elicit further information: had Häger discussed a possible deal with Maria's sister?

Häger refused to answer.

Sebastian had threatened him again, both with his colleagues and with the press, but he had got no further. Rickard Häger was obviously a highly skilled solicitor.

But he was about to be faced with a highly skilled Riksmord team. The only question was how Sebastian could get Torkel to show an interest in this lead rather than dismissing it out of hand.

It was probably best to tell the truth. Torkel was bound to be frustrated by the lack of an apparent motive so far, and the call from Lex Legali was the best thing that had turned up.

Perhaps others had been interested in the Carlsten property.

Perhaps there was more to be found out about FilboCorp.

Time to call Torkel.

The little room at Torsby police station didn't have a projector on the ceiling, so Billy turned his laptop around, enabling everyone to see the image on the screen. Three pickaxes that Torkel associated with America and the gold rushes in the nineteenth century were arranged to form a triangle, with an 'F' and a 'C' in green inside; presumably the colour had been chosen to indicate commitment to environmental issues. Above the whole thing was a transparent gear-wheel, or something that looked like one.

'FilboCorp,' Billy began. 'A Canadian mining company. Founded in 1918, branches all over the world. Principal shareholder is John Filbo, the grandson of Edwin Filbo, who started the company.'

'Less history, more current information,' Torkel said, waving his hand to emphasise that he wanted to hurry things along.

'At the moment they have two projects in Sweden – one mining copper and pyrrhotite near Röjträsk just north of Sorsele, and one around Kurravaara outside Kiruna,' Billy went on, leaning forward to bring up a map with two red dots. Just as well, Vanja thought. She might just about have put Kiruna in the right place – way up north in the middle somewhere. As for Sorsele, she hadn't a clue. Not to mention Röjträsk and that other place she'd already forgotten the name of.

Torkel's mobile began to vibrate, and he glanced down at the display. Sebastian.

'I need to take this,' he said, picking up the phone and leaving the room. 'I'm in the middle of a meeting,' was the first thing he said as he took the call. 'Is this important?'

'A lawyer just called Maria. A mining company wants to buy her sister's place in Torsby.'

'FilboCorp – yes, we're already on to them.'

Torkel could almost hear Sebastian deflating. No doubt he had thought he was passing on something vital, a breakthrough in the investigation for which he would be able to take the credit, but they already had the information. That probably said something about their relationship right now, but he couldn't help feeling a rush of pure *Schadenfreude* as he sensed Sebastian's disappointment.

'What's it all about?' Sebastian asked.

'We don't know yet, but according to Ove Hanson, FilboCorp wanted to start mining in the area where the Carlstens lived, but they refused to sell their land.'

'Is that a motive for murder?'

'We're talking about a hell of a lot of money.'

That was enough of an answer. Love, jealousy and sometimes custody disputes were the most common motives, but money was right up there too. Greed was definitely the one of the seven deadly sins that claimed the most victims. A large amount of money within reach could drive certain people beyond all normal boundaries.

'Listen, if there's nothing else . . .' Torkel said, glancing into the room where Vanja, Erik and Billy were waiting for him.

'No, I just wanted to tell you about the call.'

'Thanks.' Torkel hesitated, then decided the others could wait a little longer. 'How's Nicole?'

'OK – things are going well.'

'Good. You'll let me know if she tells you anything?'

'What do you think?'

Torkel was about to reply when he realised the quality of the call had changed. There was less static. It was quieter. Sebastian had hung up. He sighed and rejoined his colleagues.

'The mine in Kurravaara,' Billy went on, ignoring the brief interruption. 'Something similar happened there.'

'What do you mean?'

'Well, I say similar, but . . .' Billy turned the laptop around and with a few clicks found what he was looking for. He read from the screen: 'Someone called Matti Pejok opposed the plans and refused to sell his land. He objected to every proposal, stirred up opposition to FilboCorp in the press.'

'Like the Carlstens, perhaps?' Torkel wondered, looking to Erik for confirmation that he had understood how their objection to the mine might have been expressed. Erik nodded.

'After causing trouble for over two years, Matti Pejok disappeared,' Billy went on, glancing up at the others above the screen.

'Dead?' Vanja said.

Billy shook his head.

'Missing. The mining company had the documentation to prove he'd sold his land to them, but his brother Per is convinced the signature is a forgery.'

Torkel absorbed this new information in silence.

There was no doubt that they would have to investigate FilboCorp more closely, but so far no one in the company knew that it figured in a murder case in Värmland. A multinational mining company.

Torkel was under no illusions; they would be faced with slick corporate legal advisers, but the more facts they had to begin with, the harder it would be for FilboCorp to obstruct the inquiry.

They needed to know more. A lot more.

He thought their local colleague would be able to help them on that score.

★ ★ ★

'How much do you know about mining?'

Pia placed four cups of coffee on the table. If she felt any trace of animosity towards Torkel after his previous visit, she was hiding it well. She was a welcoming burst of sunshine.

Torkel and Vanja were sitting on the sofa, Billy on the armchair in one corner of her spacious office on the second floor of the council building. Pia wheeled over a desk chair and sat down opposite the sofa, while Erik remained standing.

Vanja glanced around the room. A large Persian rug under and in front of the desk. A dark, polished wooden floor. Green wallpaper which gave the room a certain gravitas; it reminded her of the state rooms in some old castle. Two big windows with green curtains. Artwork in heavy frames; Vanja presumed it remained in situ whoever won the election. On the wall behind the desk were more personal items: a signed photograph of Pia with Göran Persson, the former Prime Minister, and one with the football manager Sven-Göran Eriksson; a framed placard from *Sport-Expressen* about the ski tunnel. More photographs of hands being shaken, smiles directed at the camera. A child's drawing that had faded in the sun, but the words 'The best mummy in the world' were still visible in big, sprawling letters. Vanja was no expert in interior design − in her apartment there was strict hierarchy where function always took precedence over aesthetics and personal touches − but she got the feeling that this room exuded a mixture of narcissism and power. Then again, Pia was a politician, so it was only to be expected.

'Nothing really,' Torkel replied to Pia's introductory question. He leaned forward and sipped his coffee, which was much hotter than the liquid that emerged from the machine back at the station, in spite of the fact that it was supposed to have been repaired. This was how coffee ought to be.

'A few years ago I didn't know anything either, but I've had to learn. Starting up a mine isn't straightforward, let me tell you. Milk?'

She held out a small white jug. Torkel and Vanja shook their heads, but Billy accepted. Torkel noticed that Pia hadn't brought a cup of coffee for her husband. Presumably she knew he wouldn't want one, or she'd simply decided that he'd had enough caffeine for one day. Bearing in mind what he had seen of the couple so far, he thought the latter was more likely.

'How long have FilboCorp been interested in this area?' he asked.

'Let me see, when were they granted permission to start prospecting . . .?' Pia looked to her husband for his help. 'Six or seven years ago, maybe,' she went on, and Erik nodded in agreement. 'The plans have been on ice for over two years, so it never crossed my mind that they could have anything to do with the Carlstens.'

'Nor me,' Erik said. 'Absolutely not.'

'Did they really call that poor woman asking to buy the place?' Pia sounded indignant, as if it were a personal insult to her.

'They did.'

'That's in very poor taste, I must say.' Pia shook her beautifully coiffured head. 'Very poor taste indeed.'

Once again Erik nodded in agreement, and Torkel didn't feel any need to pursue the subject.

'FilboCorp,' he said, bringing the conversation back to the matter in hand.

'Yes, they applied for an exploration permit for the land up there about eight or nine years ago.'

'What's an exploration permit?' Vanja wondered, putting down her cup.

'It gives a company permission to investigate the bedrock with the aim of finding exploitable deposits in the search for certain minerals,' Pia replied, and Vanja got the feeling that particular formula was in an official document somewhere.

'And they can do this even if they don't own the land?' Torkel asked.

'Yes, according to the law you can be granted permission to prospect for minerals regardless of who owns the land. But that's not down to us – there's a national authority that makes those decisions.'

'So FilboCorp was granted one of these . . .' Torkel struggled to remember the correct term.

'Exploration permits, yes. The Mining Inspectorate of Sweden, the county and the Environmental Court all approved the application.'

'And this was when?' Billy had the laptop on his knee; it was his job to enter all the information on the timeline, and he wanted to be sure of his facts.

'Six or seven years ago, as I said. I can find out the exact date if you like.'

'Please.'

'OK, so they got their permit – what happened next?' Torkel wanted to push on; he was well aware that this new lead would involve a considerable amount of work. They didn't have time to sit around drinking coffee in the council offices.

'Before starting work, the person or company who has been given the permit has to produce a schedule outlining how the work will proceed. This is passed on to the landowners, who then have the opportunity to object.'

'And the Carlstens did just that,' Torkel stated.

'Yes, but it didn't stop the project. They objected to everything, so in the end the company just decided to move the prospecting area to outside the Carlstens' land.'

'I don't understand,' Vanja said. 'When did they decide to shelve the idea?'

'Much later. As I said, starting up a mine isn't straightforward.' Pia gave a little smile, indicating that she had learned the hard way how difficult it was and how much time it took.

'The exploration showed that there were enough deposits to make it worthwhile proceeding, but it was clear that the main vein ran under the Carlstens' land. The company had to be able to access that vein in order to fulfil the community benefits of the project, and to make it financially viable.'

'So then they pulled out,' Vanja said. Like Torkel she had heard enough about mining, but Pia shook her head emphatically, and Vanja realised they still had some way to go.

'No, FilboCorp carried on and won the permission they needed to start a new mine.'

'Why did they do that if they knew the Carlstens weren't going to budge?' Billy asked.

'I suppose they hoped the situation would resolve itself during the time it took to go through the process – they wanted to have everything in place *if* they managed to reach an agreement with the Carlstens so that they could get started right away. They were given a concession by the Mining Inspectorate, a permit subject to certain conditions according to the environmental laws, and the council granted their planning application as per their original work schedule, so all they needed was to acquire the land by reaching an agreement with the various landowners.'

'But the Carlstens still refused.' Torkel, Vanja and Billy almost gave a start when they heard Erik's voice; they had more or less forgotten he was there. 'Dug in their heels and said no.'

Pia nodded. 'Without their land the project just wasn't financially viable. FilboCorp kept trying, but when they started mentioning a compulsory purchase order, the Carlstens threatened to go to the European Commission and other international bodies. It's possible that FilboCorp might have won, but the whole thing would take for ever, so they pulled out about . . . yes, two years ago.' Pia spread her hands to show that she had reached the end of her account. She picked up her coffee cup, the contents of which must be as tepid as the beverage on offer at the station, Torkel thought.

He leaned back and considered what they had heard.

The mining company gets its permit and the green light from all the relevant political bodies to start up a new mine. One family says no. The company loses the chance to make a significant profit.

A Class A motive for murder.

And they hadn't pulled out. The call to Maria Carlsten proved that they were still extremely interested.

However, FilboCorp probably weren't the only ones who had lost money when the plans were put on ice.

'How many landowners would the company have had to reach an agreement with?' Vanja asked, just as Torkel was about to say the very same thing.

'All of them,' Pia said with a shrug, making it clear that they should have been able to work that out for themselves.

'And how many was that?'

'Five, including the Carlstens.'

'We need a list of the other four, please.'

★ ★ ★

Billy was standing at the whiteboard wondering whether to cross 'Carlsten' off his short list. They were dead, and therefore of no interest in the investigation in the same way as the other four names, but then everyone would know that. If he left the name there, it would be a more complete list of those affected by FilboCorp's plans. Decisions, decisions.

He decided to leave it.

He took a step back. He had updated the timeline with the information about FilboCorp's activities in the area according to the documentation provided by Pia Flodin. On the left-hand side he had written the names of the five landowners and the details he had about them. Apart from the Carlstens, he had listed:

HEDÉN – FRANK & SON, HAMPUS
BENGTSSON – GUNILLA & KENT
TORSSON – FELIX, HANNAH & DAUGHTER, CORNELIA
ANDRÉN – STEFAN

He had added what they already knew, plus anything that was easily accessible through various databases. Erik had told them about Frank Hedén, a widower with a disabled son. He was a former colleague of Pia's, and was now a gamekeeper in the area. He was suffering from cancer.

Torkel had passed on what he knew about the Bengtssons and the Torssons, since he had interviewed both families, although there wasn't much to say; they would have to go and talk to all of them again. In one afternoon they had gone from being neighbours and possible witnesses to potential suspects.

They knew virtually nothing about Stefan Andrén. They hadn't spoken to him in connection with the murders because he didn't live near the Carlstens; in fact he didn't even live in Torsby. He owned a tract of forest in the relevant area, but he was based in London. Forty-five years old, single. A risk analyst with an investment bank. And that was all they had.

Torkel came in carrying several folders, and before Billy could tell him the timeline had been updated, and ask what he should do next, Torkel pre-empted him.

'I want you to go to Kiruna,' he said, pulling out a chair and sitting down.

Billy hoped he had misheard. Kiruna? A few days in Torsby was bad enough, but Kiruna? In April? Was it even light up there yet? The snow certainly wouldn't have disappeared.

'To do what?' he asked, reluctance in every syllable.

'Take a closer look at this business with FilboCorp,' Torkel replied, giving no sign that he had picked up on Billy's distaste.

'Can't I just read up on the case?'

'I want you to talk to Matti Pejok's brother, and I want you to look at the contract he's supposed to have signed.'

'You do know there are things called scanners,' Billy tried again. 'And telephones. Skype . . .'

'Scanners and Skype don't let you talk to people face to face,' Torkel said, demonstratively opening the top folder and beginning to read. The conversation was over.

'Skype does. Kind of.'

'You're going to Kiruna.'

Billy gave a resigned sigh. The boss had issued an order; there wasn't much he could do about it.

'Can I at least take Vanja with me? Then we could share the work so that I don't need to stay as long.'

'No, I need her here.'

'Well, can I take someone else?'

'Fine.' It was Torkel's turn to sigh. 'Take whoever you like, just go as soon as possible.'

Billy nodded and left the room, glancing at the time on his mobile.

Check out. Travel back to Stockholm. He might manage to get up to Kiruna today; otherwise he would spend the night in Stockholm. At home. With Maya. The phone sex hadn't worked at all; he didn't even want to think about that. It had been incredibly embarrassing and . . . No, he really didn't want to think about it.

'Call Gunilla and she'll sort out tickets for you and the person who's going with you,' Torkel called after him.

Way ahead of you, Billy thought as Gunilla's phone began to ring. Torkel's PA would have the pleasure of finding out the fastest way he could leave a place he didn't want to be in order to get to the place he definitely didn't want to visit.

★ ★ ★

He had learned a lot during his years with Riksmord, and one of them was how to pack quickly. Fifteen minutes after arriving in his room he was ready to leave. He had gathered up his things and made several calls.

The first was to Jennifer.

As always she had sounded cheerful when she answered, and she was even happier when he asked her if she'd like to go up to Kiruna.

On a job.

With Riksmord.

'Why isn't Vanja going with you, or someone else on the team?' she wondered when she had pulled herself together after delightedly saying yes, in spite of the tight schedule.

The question wasn't exactly a surprise. It was no secret that Jennifer had been bitterly disappointed when Vanja's FBI training fell through and Jennifer lost her temporary post with Riksmord. Jennifer was too smart to blame Vanja – she knew it wasn't Vanja's fault she was back in Sigtuna – but feelings were feelings; they might be irrational, but she still resented Vanja just a little, perhaps subconsciously. The way she overemphasised the other woman's name reminded Billy that it was a sensitive situation.

'Torkel needs her here, and Ursula is still on leave, so there's no one else,' Billy replied truthfully. 'And to be perfectly honest, I'd rather go with you.'

She had laughed at him.

'I bet you say that to all the girls!'

Then they had got down to details; Jennifer wasn't sure she would be allowed to go at such short notice, but Billy promised to fix it.

His next call had been to Jennifer's boss, Magnus Skogsberg in Sigtuna. Billy had quickly explained the situation: Riksmord needed Jennifer Holmgren to assist in an important inquiry.

Yes, it was to do with the murdered family in Torsby.

No, she would be going to Kiruna.

No, Billy couldn't give him any more details about why they would be going to Kiruna.

Yes, Billy understood this created difficulties for the Sigtuna police, yes, he knew his request came far too late and not via the correct channels.

Yes, he understood that it took time to reorganise rotas, but was it possible that they could spare Jennifer for a few days? Torkel Höglund would really appreciate it.

Billy never ceased to be amazed at the power of Torkel's name in police circles. Billy knew him only as the boss who ran Riksmord with a firm but almost invisible hand; he never made a big deal of his role. He didn't need to; there was never any doubt about who was in charge. But every time Billy mentioned Torkel to police officers outside the team, he got the feeling he was working for a completely different person. A legend. Someone who was simultaneously respected, admired and feared. Someone whose words carried real weight, and whose friendship, or at least appreciation, was much sought after. Magnus Skogsberg was no exception. Apparently he could spare Jennifer after all. He was happy for her to join Billy. Could Billy pass on his best wishes to Torkel?

Then Gunilla had called back to tell him he couldn't fly to Kiruna until early tomorrow morning. She had rented him a car from the Hertz depot on Bergebyvägen in Torsby; all he had to do was pick it up. She was about to sort out tickets, a hotel and a hire car for him in Kiruna; was he taking anyone with him?

Billy had explained about Jennifer, thanked Gunilla and ended the call as he closed his suitcase. She was good. Fast, efficient and focused on finding solutions. Vanja was convinced that Gunilla was a little bit in love with Torkel; she claimed to have seen the signs, without specifying what these signs might be. Billy had pointed out that Gunilla was married with three children, as far as he knew; Vanja had wondered what that had to do with anything. They had never found out for sure.

Billy picked up his case; time to go.

His glance fell on the padded envelope lying on the desk. Sealed, addressed and ready to drop in the postbox. Inside lay Vanja's toothbrush in a plastic bag, and in another some hairs from Sebastian's comb, along with a piece of toilet paper with his blood on it which Billy had found in the bin in his bathroom. Presumably he had cut himself shaving.

When he stole Vanja's toothbrush and lied his way into Sebastian's room, he had been hell bent on pursuing his little project right through to the end, but when he had put everything he needed in the envelope, he wasn't so sure, which was why it was still sitting there. He had to make a decision. Did he really want to know? What good would the information do him if his suspicions were confirmed? Should he forget the whole thing?

He grabbed the envelope on his way out. Whatever he decided to do, he couldn't leave it there. He had a long car journey to Stockholm during which he could think things over. And he had one more call to make.

He didn't call Maya until he was in the car – a Ford Focus ST. It was fairly new, with only 1,790 kilometres on the clock when he picked it up. Not bad to drive. Billy was travelling at a steady 130 kilometres per hour on the E45 heading towards Sunne when he switched from Spotify on his phone and pressed Maya's number. Xzibit's 'The Gambler' disappeared and was replaced on the speakers by the single note of the ringtone. Maya answered almost right away.

'Hi, darling.'

'Hi, what are you up to?' Billy realised he was speaking unnecessarily loudly. It was impossible to hold a normal conversation when you were using the car's built-in microphone. It was one of the laws of nature.

'I have a client arriving in five minutes,' Maya said; Billy could picture her glancing at her little gold wristwatch. That was the only thing he could picture; he had never been to her office. According to Maya it was nothing special: two very comfortable armchairs facing one another, with a coffee table in between. A desk at the other end of the room, a rug from IKEA, and a fairly basic coffee machine from Nescafé. That was all. She rented the space in an office block, and the room was no more than twelve square metres.

She referred to her customers as clients. In Billy's eyes they were more like patients. They fell into two main groups: company directors who needed help with their leadership skills, and 'Seekers' who wanted to 'fulfil their true potential' and 'be true to themselves'. Billy knew she was doing something useful, that she made people feel better, gave them a sense of having developed when they had been to see her, but he didn't know how she could stand it.

'Was there something special, or can we talk later?' she asked.

'I've got bad news and good news,' Billy went on, pretending he hadn't realised that she didn't have time for him. Five minutes to the next client; this would take two.

'Start with the bad news,' she said with a little sigh, as if she was expecting the worst.

'I'm going to Kiruna tomorrow.'

'Kiruna?'

'Kiruna.'

'What for?'

'Work.'

'OK.' A note of resignation in her voice. The fact that he had been in Torsby since Thursday was bad enough. 'So what's the good news then?'

'I'm on my way home right now. I'm flying from Arlanda in the morning, so I'll be at home tonight.'

'You're coming home?'

Genuine pleasure. He could hear that she was smiling; so was he.

'I'm on my way – I'm just outside Sunne.'

'I've missed you so much! And guess what – I can come with you tomorrow.'

Billy's smile stiffened. What did she mean? Was she offering to drive him to the airport? No, her tone made him think she meant something else. Something more.

'What do you mean?'

'I can come with you to Kiruna. I have no more clients this week. I was going to take a few days off so that I could really focus on the wedding, but now we can do that together. In Kiruna.'

He should have been pleased, but this wasn't the way he had planned things. This wasn't what he wanted, but he couldn't tell her that. He had to think fast.

'That's not a good idea,' he managed while he tried to come up with a suitable response.

'Why not?' she shot back as expected.

Because he was going with Jennifer. Because he had been looking forward to going with Jennifer. Because the plan was to go with Jennifer. He played his safest card: work.

'I'll be working.'

'Not all the time, surely?'

'Virtually, yes.'

'In the evenings and at night?'

He sensed that she was beginning to realise he didn't want her there. She was a skilled listener, adept at picking up nuances, what lay behind the words, what they really meant. That was part of her job, and she was good at her job.

'I'm really sorry, I would have loved you to come up to Kiruna with me, but it's not a good idea.' He thought he had achieved the perfect balance of gentleness and regret. 'I'm being sent there by Riksmord.'

'I'll pay my own way if that's what's bothering you.'

'It's not that, it's just . . . I'm working, and I don't think I should have my girlfriend with me.'

There was a brief silence. Billy assumed she was wondering whether to try again, or let it go. She chose the latter option.

'OK, it was just a suggestion.'

'I'm really sorry, but it wouldn't work,' Billy said again, sounding genuinely upset.

'Anyway, my client is here, so . . .' She didn't complete the sentence, but she didn't need to; the conversation was over.

'See you later. I love you.'

'Love you too. Drive carefully.'

With that she was gone. Billy subconsciously eased up on the accelerator. That hadn't gone as he'd expected at all. He would be working in Kiruna, more or less all the time, and he didn't know anyone in the police who took their other half with them when they went away because of the job. Everything he had said to Maya was true, and yet he felt as if he had lied to her.

He clicked on Spotify and Xzibit carried on from where he had been interrupted. Man vs. Machine. The best album he had ever made, in Billy's opinion. He turned up the volume and put his foot down.

★ ★ ★

Torkel was standing by one of the cars at the back of the police station waiting for everyone to sort themselves out. The additional staff they had brought in had been briefed and divided into groups, and now they were busy packing the equipment they needed into the vehicles that would take them to the various addresses. Torkel would accompany one team to the Bengtssons, while Vanja and Erik would start with Frank Hedén. Whoever finished first would move on to the Torssons.

The back door of the station opened and Vanja walked out into the sunshine. She blinked a few times as her eyes got used to the brightness. She looked exhausted, Torkel thought. Dark shadows under her eyes, her hair lank and greasy, her face pale and washed out. Holding her hand up to her forehead to block out the setting sun, she came over to him.

'Nearly ready?' she asked, glancing around.

'I think so. How are you?'

Vanja turned to him with an enquiring look.

'I'm fine – why do you ask?'

'You look tired.'

'I'm not sleeping very well, that's all.'

'Are you eating properly?'

Vanja hesitated. Torkel didn't know, she told herself. That wasn't why he had asked. He didn't know anything about her old demons, the ones that were sleeping now. No one knew. No one except Valdemar. He had helped her through a tough time, remaining staunchly by her side every step of the way. Just as a father should do. He had never stopped believing that they would make it. Together. And they had. In spite of everything that she had been through over the past few months, she had never felt the need to stop eating. She had never stood in front of the mirror and thought she would feel better if only she looked different. She had never connected her unhappiness and her pain with her body. She had no desire to punish herself. Others, yes, but not herself.

'Absolutely. I'm fine,' she repeated truthfully. She was fine. When it came to her eating habits anyway.

'You know where I am if you need to talk.'

Vanja nodded and gave him a little smile. Torkel realised it was a long time since he'd seen her smile.

'Thanks, but it really isn't necessary. Things have been difficult, but I'm OK.'

She left him with another smile and went over to join Erik. Torkel watched her go. Things didn't feel right. Not just with Vanja, but with the whole team. Things hadn't even felt right at the beginning of this investigation, and they definitely hadn't improved.

Sebastian was in Stockholm with their key witness.

Billy was reluctantly on his way to Kiruna.

And then there was Ursula, of course.

Perhaps that was why it was all so difficult. They were a team of four – five if you counted Sebastian, which Torkel did approximately fifty per cent of the times he thought about his group – who had developed together. Grown together. Become a close-knit unit. The sum had become greater than its parts. If one member of the team was missing, the balance was disturbed. That was probably the explanation; that was why it all felt so different. They were all slightly out of balance. Torkel really hoped this exercise would give them the breakthrough they so badly needed.

He wanted to get away from here.

He didn't often feel that way when he was out on a job, but right now he just wanted to go home. To get away from Torsby, away from FilboCorp, away from dead families and away from Malin Åkerblad.

After the meeting at the council offices Torkel had called the prosecutor and told her what they were planning to do: re-interview the four landowners who had been affected by the Carlstens' refusal to sell to the mining company, and carry out a search at all four properties at the same time. He had expected her to agree that this was the logical next step in the investigation, but fru Åkerblad was full of surprises.

'Do you really have enough for a search warrant at this stage?' she had asked as soon as Torkel had informed her of his decision.

'When the Carlstens said no to the mining company, it cost their neighbours millions. What else do you need?' Torkel had asked, unable to keep the annoyance out of his voice.

'I'd like to hear your reasons for undertaking such a major invasion of their privacy.'

'I've just told you. The Carlstens turned down the mining company's offer, which cost these other families millions. That's my reason.'

'That's not sufficient to invade their homes.'

Torkel closed his eyes. A property search was a necessary measure as far as the police were concerned, not an invasion of privacy. He had decided that was the next step in their investigation. *My* investigation, he corrected himself. It was time to show Malin Åkerblad who was in charge.

'I wasn't asking for permission,' he said with such authority in his voice that it was impossible to misunderstand the message even if you didn't understand the language. 'I was merely informing you of what we are intending to do.'

'I'm still in charge of the preliminary investigation,' Malin said in an attempt to regain control, but Torkel interrupted her.

'With respect, I couldn't give a toss what you think are sufficient grounds for further action.' He didn't raise his voice, but there was an added sharpness to his tone. 'I am the Senior Investigating Officer, and whether or not to carry out a house search is my decision. It would have been nice to have you on our side, but as you have a different view of the situation from mine, I suggest you regard this conversation as an update, nothing more.'

He had ended the call, and rejected two further calls from her. He then received a text; he saw only the word 'unacceptable' before he deleted it. He had heard nothing from her since then. She might cause problems, but he didn't think so. He could always bring up Jan Ceder; Åkerblad's insistence on releasing him had made their job considerably more difficult, and had led to a further death. The prosecutor was the least of his worries.

Torkel looked around; everyone seemed to be ready to go.

Erik and Vanja set off with two cars following on behind. Fabian waved to indicate that he was all set to follow Torkel, who waved back and got into his car.

He definitely wanted to get away from here.

★ ★ ★

Erik wasn't particularly happy either, sitting behind the wheel with Vanja beside him.

Partly because they were on the way to see Frank Hedén, a man Erik regarded as a friend of the family; now they were supposed to treat him as a suspect. Question him. Search his home.

That was the second reason for Erik's unease.

Torkel had made it very clear that he didn't just want to talk to the people on the list; every property was to be searched. That would require additional personnel from neighbouring districts; Karlstad and Arvika were the closest.

Torkel had offered to call and request the extra resources, but Erik had thought it was best to do it himself. Otherwise there was a risk that he would be seen as having lost control, hiding behind Riksmord.

Arvika wasn't a problem; Regina Hult was easy to work with. He explained what he needed and why, and she immediately sent over four officers who were suitable for the task. That left Karlstad.

And Hans Olander.

'How's it going?' Olander asked as soon as he heard who was on the other end of the line. A perfectly reasonable question from a senior officer, but to Erik it sounded like *I guess things aren't going too well, then*.

'The investigation is moving forward, that's why I'm calling. I need some extra personnel right away – just for a little while.'

'Extra personnel? What for?'

Erik hesitated. Torkel had told him not to mention FilboCorp, or to reveal which properties were to be searched, because the more people who knew, the greater the chance of a leak.

'We need to carry out a number of house searches today,' he said. He had to give Olander that information at least, to ensure that he sent the right officers.

'So you're close to solving the case?'

'We hope so.'

'I hope so too. We're not coming over all that well in the press.'

Erik didn't respond. He had known that Olander would use this conversation to get at him in some way, and he was about to find out how.

'I've been wondering whether to send Per over to give you a hand.'

Aha. Per Karlsson, the other candidate for Erik's job, comes up to Torsby when the investigation has been under way for a week; he's there when the case is closed, and Olander points out that this happened only when Karlsson joined the team. His candidate for Erik's job. Thus proving that the board had made the wrong choice when they appointed Erik.

'It's Riksmord's case – we're only assisting,' Erik said without raising his voice. He wasn't going to give Olander the satisfaction. 'I don't know what contribution Per could make.'

'Whatever you're doing, but hopefully he would do it better.'

'It's Riksmord's case . . .'

'You said that already.'

'They haven't asked for another DI,' Erik went on, ignoring Olander's interjection. 'They need people who can carry out a number of house searches.'

'I haven't exactly got officers standing around doing nothing here.'

Erik couldn't believe his ears. Was Olander going to refuse? Was his dislike of Erik so strong that he would obstruct the inquiry? Erik was beginning to get angry. Personal antipathy was one thing, but unprofessional behaviour was something else.

'You can't spare three people?' he asked, his tone making it clear that he didn't believe this for a minute.

'Things are difficult, there's a lot of illness going around,' Olander insisted.

Erik closed his eyes. At some point in the future he was going to have to face up to it. Confront Olander. He had hoped he would be more settled by the time the situation arose, have achieved more in his new role so that his words would carry more weight, perhaps have senior officers backing him up, but right now he didn't have the energy to play Olander's ridiculous game any longer.

'Hans, I know what you're trying to do,' he said calmly and clearly. 'But this isn't going to look as if I've failed. Everyone will be informed that you have refused to send extra resources. This will come back to bite you, not me.'

Silence. It went on for so long that Erik wondered if the connection had been lost, or if Olander had hung up.

'Hans?'

'How many bodies do you need?' There was no mistaking the suppressed rage in Olander's voice.

'Three, preferably four.'

'On their way.'

'Thank you.'

Erik was about to end the call when he heard Olander's voice again, low and ominous.

'Listen to me, Erik. I'll give you the rest of this week, then I am going to take over myself, and then it *will* look as if you've failed. Not even your wife's friends in high places will be able to do anything about that.'

Silence again; this time the superintendent had hung up.

Erik had slipped his phone into his pocket. There it was. Pia's friendship with the Chief Constable. Perhaps challenging Olander had been a mistake. A mistake that could affect his future career in the police.

Those were his thoughts as he pulled up outside Frank Hedén's house.

'Here we are,' he said, realising as he heard his own voice that he hadn't said a word since they left the station. Vanja was peering curiously at the house through the windscreen. Torkel had once told Erik she was the best he had ever worked with; Erik hoped that was true.

He hoped that the next few hours would give them the breakthrough they so desperately needed.

He really didn't want to be removed from Torsby.

They had more or less avoided talking about Maria's call from Lex Legali for the rest of the day. It had been difficult at first, but when they noticed how anxious Nicole became when they discussed the matter, they decided to stop. The last thing they wanted was to cause her any further stress. Instead Maria told Sebastian more about her sister and her relationship with Karin and the house in Värmland. They had bought it together; at the time the place had stood empty for many years, and was in quite a state. It would take a lot of work to turn it into the summer retreat they had always dreamt of, but the price was right. The idea was that they would go there to relax and enjoy life in the future. Together. With the families they might one day have – husbands, children, dogs and the Carlsten sisters. Sharing meals at a long table outdoors, summer dresses, bare feet and sunshine. But it had never really become that shared project; it soon became clear that Karin wanted more. She wanted to do more work, get the place sorted out more quickly, put in more effort. Maria just wanted to turn up and relax. It was a summer cottage, it didn't have to be perfect. Eventually they decided they would go there at different times, divide the best weeks of the summer between them, but that didn't put an end to the problems. Karin still wanted to invest, and demanded that Maria pay half the cost of any repairs or renovations. The house certainly wasn't bringing them closer, and when Karin met Emil and asked if they could buy Maria out, she agreed straight away. Karin and Emil decided to make their home in Torsby on a permanent basis, and the geographical distance meant that the emotional distance between the sisters also increased.

However, over the last few years they had found their way back to each other, thanks mainly to the children; Nicole was always welcome in Torsby. Karin had never mentioned that someone was trying to buy the house from them.

While Maria made a start on lunch, Sebastian took Nicole into the guest room. Together they made up the bed in the pretty little pale blue room, and opened the window to let in some fresh air for a while. When Sebastian looked at the empty bed he wished he had bought some cuddly toys for her; he would definitely do that the next time he went shopping. She would be here for a while. Maria called to tell them lunch was ready, and they joined her in the kitchen.

After macaroni with meatballs, they settled down in the living room. Nicole picked up her pad and her coloured pens and immediately began to draw.

Sebastian was enjoying himself. It was good to shut out the world for a while, to sit in his living room and allow himself simply to be. Nicole came over and placed a drawing on his knee. Shutting out the world was no longer an option. He had to deal with a closed-in world that was on its way out.

And what a world it was.

A little girl in a big forest.

Huge trees, darkness.

Narrow paths and small feet.

Nicole produced one picture after another; she was really in the swing of things now. Each one was basically the same, but her need to express herself seemed to have increased since those first tentative strokes of her pen in Torsby.

Sebastian found it difficult to hide how moved he was by the vulnerability he saw before him. A little girl all alone in the forest, fleeing for her life. He could see that Maria was struggling too. Her eyes filled with tears as each drawing was completed and each new one was begun. The repetition showed the scars that Nicole needed to process. She seemed to have got stuck in the forest. Maria must have been thinking along the same lines, because she leaned forward and gently touched her daughter's hand.

'I'll never leave you again,' she said tenderly.

'This is good, Nicole,' Sebastian said, trying to sound as reassuring as possible. 'Carry on drawing the forest, but remember you're not there any more.'

Nicole looked up at both of them. For a second it seemed as if she wanted to say something, but couldn't. She went back to her picture.

Sebastian picked up the last image she had placed on his knee. Still the dark forest, but something else was just visible over to one side.

The outline of a house. A white two-storey house. Sebastian recognised it right away.

Nicole was no longer fleeing through the dark forest.

She was outside the house.

The house where it all began.

Torkel rang the Bengtssons' doorbell, and when they answered he explained why he was there. He wanted to ask them a few more questions about the Carlsten family, and the officers who were with him would be carrying out a search of the property. The reaction was exactly as he had expected; first of all they wanted to see a search warrant.

Torkel didn't have one, because it wasn't necessary. It was only in American films that the cops had to wave a piece of paper in order to gain access.

But if they didn't have a warrant, did that really mean they had the right to search the house?

Yes, it did. The Swedish Code of Judicial Procedure chapter 28 paragraph 1 gave them that right.

Kent and Gunilla Bengtsson stepped aside, wearing the slightly bewildered expression that Torkel had seen so many times before, when people were forced to let in several police officers, knowing that they were about to go through their entire house. Not exactly an enjoyable experience.

'Perhaps we could sit down and have a chat?' Torkel said in a friendly tone of voice as he steered the couple inside.

They ended up in the kitchen. Gunilla offered him coffee, but Torkel declined. He looked around the pleasant room. Pale birch-veneer cupboard doors that looked new, unlike the old, scratched Formica worktop that ended at an induction hob. The scruffy grey-green vinyl flooring actually had little holes in it here and there; it was as if two completely different timelines criss-crossed within the limited space. Torkel recalled a similar feeling in the living room, where he had interviewed the couple on his previous visit. He had sat on a modern three-seater sofa in front of a bulky old TV that must have been around for ever. It was as if the Bengtssons played spin the bottle as far as their home was concerned, replacing whichever item it pointed to without much planning.

'Why didn't you say anything about the mine?' Torkel asked when he had told them what he had found out earlier.

Kent and Gunilla exchanged a glance which Torkel would have described as uneasy.

'It's a long time ago – we didn't think about it,' Gunilla replied.

'You didn't think about the fact that the family who were murdered were responsible for several people losing the chance to make millions?'

'It did cross my mind,' Kent admitted, his eyes fixed on the table. 'But it seemed stupid to mention it. I mean, it would just make us suspects.'

'Finding out from elsewhere has hardly allayed our suspicions.'

Kent shrugged, suggesting that he had hoped the police wouldn't find out at all.

'And we weren't annoyed with the Carlstens,' Gunilla said. 'This is the house where Kent grew up. It wasn't an easy decision to sell, knowing that it would be pulled down.'

'We're happy here.' Kent raised his head, meeting Torkel's gaze. 'OK, we're talking about a lot of money, but money isn't everything.'

'But you agreed to the sale.'

Once again the Bengtssons exchanged a look. This time Torkel had the feeling they were both a little ashamed. Gunilla gently placed her hand on Kent's.

'Yes, we did,' Kent said, nodding. 'Everybody said we'd be stupid not to take the opportunity. For that kind of money, we could buy more or less whatever we wanted.'

Gunilla took over, in the way that happens only when you've been married for a long time, Torkel thought; he had never got to the finishing-each-other's-sentences stage with either of his wives. 'But when the Carlstens said no and the whole thing fell through . . .'

'We were quite pleased,' Kent supplied.

'Relieved.'

'Because the decision hadn't been made by us.' Kent fell silent.

Torkel understood. There are many times when we want to be in control, to decide things for ourselves, but sometimes it's nice when a decision is taken by someone else, so that we can just sit back and say that we had no choice. It's easier that way, particularly in situations where both options are acceptable. Or unacceptable.

The search team still had a lot to do, but Torkel was convinced they wouldn't find anything. There was nothing in the Bengtssons' behaviour, body language or tone of voice to indicate that they had lied to him with regard to their feelings about either the sale or the Carlsten family.

He wondered if it was too late to ask for that cup of coffee.

★ ★ ★

The strawberry yogurt dribbled down Hampus's chin; Frank Hedén scooped up most of it on the spoon with a practised hand, while the rest ended up on the white bib.

Vanja didn't really know where to look. She was surprised, and slightly disappointed, at how difficult she found it to handle the situation. She knew that Frank had a severely disabled son who lived at home, but she hadn't met him when she was here with Billy, and she hadn't expected . . . well, she didn't really know what she had expected, but obviously not the young man sitting opposite her. A wide belt kept him sitting upright in the heavy wheelchair. His head leaned to the left at an unnatural angle, jerking at regular intervals as if his body wanted to straighten it up, but it was too heavy and always fell back. Three of the thin fingers on one hand were sticking out in different directions, and from time to time the arm waved in what appeared to be completely uncontrolled movements. The other hand lay motionless on his knee. Paralysed down one side, Vanja guessed. Black, spiky hair and blue eyes gazing into the distance without focus; no words emerged from the permanently half-open mouth, but occasionally there was a sound which Frank seemed able to interpret as a request for another spoonful of yogurt.

Vanja looked away.

Frank had let them in with a nod of recognition to her, a warmer greeting to Erik. Vanja had explained that the accompanying officers would be searching the house and Frank had simply acquiesced; no questions about papers or their right to do such a thing. When she asked if they could have a chat with him about the mining company's plans, he had said that it was time for Hampus to have a snack – could they talk while he fed his son?

He had fetched a tray from the kitchen and led them into one of the rooms on the ground floor.

'This is Vanja, and you know Erik already,' Frank had said as they walked in. 'Vanja is a police officer too.'

'Hi, Hampus,' Erik had said, and Vanja had also managed a faint 'hi'.

This was a sick room more than anything. It was dominated by an adjustable bed with a hoist, and metal bars on the sides. The bedside table was crowded with assorted tablets, creams and other medical necessities. A machine that Vanja assumed supplied Hampus with oxygen when necessary stood by the far side of the bed. Along one wall was a range of exercise equipment that looked more like instruments of torture, with all those shiny metal parts, harnesses, ropes and counter-weights.

Vanja had never imagined herself as a mother. She wasn't sure that she wanted children at all, even though her friends who had started families told her that the love they felt for their children, and the joy they brought, was deeper and more real than anything they had ever felt for anyone else. Vanja couldn't help wondering if this was also true of Frank and Hampus. Love, yes, but joy? Wouldn't Frank just feel a constant anxiety, facing a never-ending round of work without getting anything in return? Did the joy really outweigh the effort, or was she simply too analytical, too calculating? She definitely lacked the emotional dimension that having a child of one's own involved.

Once they had sat down and Frank had started feeding his son, Vanja had brought up the issue of the mine. Frank had nodded. Yes, he was one of those who had wanted to sell. He didn't have much time left, as Erik knew, and Hampus wouldn't be able to stay here alone when Frank was gone. The mining company was offering far more for the land than he would get anywhere else, so why not?

'But the sale fell through,' Vanja said.

'It did.'

'So how did you feel about that?'

Frank shrugged. Brought the spoon with its pink cargo up to the young man's mouth once more. Most of it ended up down his chin.

'When I'm gone, friends I can rely on will sell the land for as much as possible. The council has promised that Hampus will be able to keep his carers – he'll be fine. That's all that matters.'

'Did you know Jan Ceder?' Vanja suddenly asked.

'We didn't have much to do with one another, but we've both lived here for a long time. I had reason to call on him occasionally in my role as gamekeeper – he had what you might call a flexible approach to the laws on hunting.'

'Have you ever borrowed a shotgun from him?'

'Why would I do that?' Frank shook his head. 'I have my own guns.'

Vanja didn't say anything. Something had happened there. In that last response.

Frank's voice had become slightly strained. A tension in the vocal cords raised the tone a fraction. Not very much – a less skilled listener would have missed it completely, but not Vanja. Frank cleared his throat. Had he noticed it too? Was he trying to cover it up, or did he just have a frog in his throat?

Vanja waited, hoping Frank was the type who disliked silence, and would feel the need to fill it. Perhaps he would try to distance himself even more from Jan Ceder. Start talking about what he had 'heard', provide them with an alibi for the time of Ceder's murder even though they hadn't asked for one.

Unfortunately she didn't find out how Frank handled silence, because Erik jumped in and started burbling about the up-and-coming first of May celebrations, wondering if Frank would like to join him and Pia for dinner in the evening, after the procession.

The moment, if it had been there, was lost.

'We'd like you to stay in the area, or contact us if you're intending to go away,' Vanja said, getting to her feet.

'Am I a suspect?' Frank wanted to know, sounding almost amused. For the first time since the conversation began he took his eyes off his son and looked at Vanja.

'No, but we'd still like to know.'

'I'm supposed to be going to Västerås tomorrow – there's a two-day conference on new laws relating to game. Can I still go?'

Vanja thought for a moment. Whatever she might have heard, it wasn't reason enough to keep him here. Not by a long way. If she'd had a child with that level of disability, she would have needed to get away now and again. However much Frank loved his son, he probably felt the same.

'That's fine. Two days, you said?'

'Yes – I'll be back on Wednesday evening.'

'Where will you be staying?'

'At the Best Western, I think.'

'Good. Thanks for your help,' Vanja said, holding out her hand. Frank put down the spoon and shook it. 'Bye, Hampus,' Vanja added before she left the room.

★ ★ ★

Frank stood in the window watching as Erik reversed, spun the wheel and drove away. Through the closed door he could hear the four police officers searching his home. Behind him Hampus jerked in his wheelchair and let out a protracted wail that rapidly grew louder. Frank didn't turn around. It wasn't an epileptic fit. He had learned to tell the difference between the normal if somewhat violent movements, and an attack. Hampus wanted a shower. That was the highlight of his day. He would happily sit under the warm water for hours. Frank glanced at his watch. The visit from the police had upset his schedule a little, but he would still have time to get Hampus washed and into bed before Monica came to take over for the night.

He saw Erik's rear lights grow smaller and smaller, then disappear completely, but he stayed where he was, gazing out into the spring evening.

Vanja Lithner.

She had found Hampus difficult to cope with; he had noticed that as soon as she walked in. Everyone reacted differently, and he didn't hold it against her. Nor did he object to her intrusive and perhaps slightly aggressive questions about FilboCorp, the Carlsten family and the murders. But she had suddenly fallen silent when they were talking about Jan Ceder.

He didn't know her.

He didn't know what it meant when she stopped driving the conversation forward and sat back. Did it mean that she suspected him? Was he going to be dragged into their murder inquiry?

He knew Erik.

Knew him and liked him.

Erik was no alpha male – God knows there were enough of those around here; he was more accommodating, willing to compromise. At home he had no problem with letting Pia wear the trousers. Frank had no doubt that was essential if the marriage was going to work, but even so. Erik knew his own worth, in spite of the fact that he appeared to play second fiddle at times. He had brought in Riksmord. Someone more intent on making a name for himself would have been reluctant to let go of a case that could be pivotal in terms of his career, but not Erik. It didn't matter to him who did the job, as long as it was done well. Aina had been very fond of Erik; she had always said he was too good for Pia.

No doubt she had been right.

He allowed himself a moment to miss her. They came less frequently now, they were more fleeting, but he let the memories of Aina fill his mind. The image of her was crystal clear. He remembered every line on her face, every strand of hair, the sound of her voice, her laughter.

God, how he had loved her.

He had grieved for her, a grief so deep he had been afraid he would never climb out of it. A darkness so immense that it threatened to swallow him up. If he had been alone he would probably have given in, let himself be swept away. But he had Hampus, and half of Hampus was Aina. The boy was totally dependent on Frank, so becoming bogged down in his grief wasn't an option. Slowly but surely he had found his way back. He pushed away the picture of Aina out there on the lawn in her summer dress, wiped away a single tear from his eyelashes, and turned to his son.

He didn't have time to wallow in sorrow.

He didn't have the energy either.

There was no room in his life for such luxuries.

★ ★ ★

By the time Torkel left the Bengtssons, twilight was falling.

The warmth of the spring day disappeared quickly as soon as the sun was gone, and Torkel zipped up his jacket as he walked to the car. At the same time, he was struck by how cool and fresh the evening was. The clean air, the faint breeze carrying the odour of manure spread over the fields, mingled with the smells of the forest. He stopped and took a deep breath, then decided to walk over to the Torssons. Vanja hadn't been in touch, so he assumed she was still busy with Frank Hedén. He wondered whether to tell the Bengtssons that he was leaving his car there for a little while, but concluded that there was probably no need.

He set off, amusing himself by trying to identify the songs of various birds as they made use of the remaining daylight to try to attract a partner. When the girls were young they had spent a lot of time outdoors. Torkel thought it was important for them to get to know the forest, not just playgrounds, bouncy castles and ball pools. A picnic basket, a little pond with tadpoles swimming around, a grass snake wriggling away, tiny boats made of bark bobbing along a stream towards their carefully constructed dam, picking berries and edible leaves, learning to recognise droppings, to work out whether it was a dormouse or a squirrel that had been nibbling pine cones. There was always plenty to do and to learn in the forest. Simple pleasures, but he realised he experienced those things less and less often these days. Yvonne had once pointed out that the person who had the most fun on their forest excursions was Torkel himself, and she might well have been right, but he was still glad he had been able to give his daughters that kind of childhood. Today kids weren't allowed to go anywhere where they might possibly hurt themselves. Everything had to be safe, controlled – all the time.

He left the fields and meadows behind and carried on along the gravel track. Ten minutes later he spotted the yellow house behind the trees, and soon he was in the garden. He had enjoyed every single step of the way, but now it was time to return to harsh reality. His phone rang and he glanced at the display: Vanja. It was a brief conversation; she and Erik had just finished with Frank, and were wondering whether to come over to the Torssons. Torkel explained that he was already there; she and Erik could go back to the station, and he would see them later.

He had only just ended the call when his phone rang again. This time it was Fabian; the search team had more or less finished at the Bengtssons' place and he could spare two men if Torkel had anything else for them to do. Torkel told him to send them over to the Torssons'. At the same time he picked up the heavy door knocker – a gilded horseshoe. No response. He tried again, a little harder and for longer this time. Nothing. He peered through the nearest window; there were no lights on, no sign that anyone was home. Had the family followed his advice and gone away?

He called Fredrika at the station and got hold of both Felix and Hannah's mobile numbers. Felix answered almost right away, and Torkel introduced himself, then asked: 'Where are you?'

'We've gone away for a few days, as you suggested. We're at Hannah's sister's.'

'When will you be back?'

'I don't know – in a couple of days I should think. Cornelia has to go back to school.'

Torkel heard a car approaching, and saw Fabian's car turn into the drive.

'I need to talk to you. Where does Hannah's sister live?'

'Outside Falun. What do you want to talk to us about?'

Torkel hesitated. How much should he say? Fabian had got out of the car and was walking towards him; he gestured towards the house, but Torkel shook his head and pointed to his phone. Fabian nodded to show he understood.

'We've heard about the mining plans,' Torkel said to Felix.

'Yes?'

'You lost a great deal of money when the Carlstens refused to sell and the whole thing fell through.'

'We didn't lose anything,' Felix said, as if it was obvious. Torkel didn't understand. 'On the contrary, we gained.'

'We were told that everyone except the Carlstens wanted to sell.'

'That's true, but we don't own the land or the house. We rent the place, and the fact that the Carlstens said no meant we could stay.'

Slowly Torkel realised the significance of what he had just been told, and he cursed Erik and his colleagues. This was something that should have emerged as soon as the four landowners affected by FilboCorp's plans became relevant to the investigation. He shouldn't be finding out over the phone from someone else. Still, better late than never, he thought, taking care to keep the anger out of his voice as he asked for the information he should already have had.

'So who owns the land?'

★ ★ ★

'Thomas Nordgren,' Erik said, putting up a picture of a man in his forties. It was an enlargement of a passport photograph, and like ninety-five per cent of the population, he didn't look his best in it. Poor focus, harsh lighting, a desire to look relaxed that actually achieved the opposite effect and a manic stare which was the result of being afraid to blink as the shutter clicked combined to produce an image that could have been taken from a criminal records database.

However, Thomas Nordgren was not on a criminal records database.

They had no idea where he was.

When his name came up, Torkel tried the two numbers they had – a mobile and a landline. The mobile barely rang once before a message came on: *The person you are trying to reach cannot take your call at the moment. Please try later.*

The landline rang four times, then a male voice with a broad Värmland accent spoke: *Thomas Nordgren. I'm not at home. Leave a message.*

When they eventually got hold of his employer, they were informed that Thomas had been off for just under a week, and wasn't due back until after the weekend. She had no idea what he was doing, or who might know.

So the closest they had got to Thomas Nordgren was the photograph on the wall.

Vanja and Torkel stared at it as Erik consulted his notebook.

'As you know, he works as a gardener in Rottneros Park and lives alone in a two-room apartment in Sunne. He and his wife bought the land where the Torssons now live back in 2001. They divorced in 2009, no children.' Erik looked up, his expression almost apologetic. 'That's all we've got so far.'

'The Torssons moved in in 2009,' Torkel said. 'On their contract Thomas appears as the sole owner.'

'He probably bought out his ex-wife,' Vanja speculated.

'That must have cost quite a bit,' Torkel went on. 'How much does a gardener earn? Twenty thousand a month? Twenty-two maybe?'

'But in 2009 the plans for the mine were still viable,' Vanja pointed out, realising where Torkel was going with this. 'So he must have counted on getting his money back, and then some.'

'We haven't finished looking into his finances yet,' Erik said. 'We'll know more tomorrow.'

'I want to know about everyone's finances,' Torkel said, getting up and walking over to the display board. 'Everyone on this list,' he said, tapping the names Billy had written up. 'We'll all work on it in the morning. I still think money is our motive.'

Vanja and Erik both nodded. Vanja glanced at her watch and stood up, interpreting Torkel's final comments as an indication that the working day was over. Wrong.

'One more thing, Vanja,' he said as she started to gather up her things. 'I want you to go back to Stockholm.'

'Now?' Vanja asked, automatically checking her watch even though she knew what it said.

'As soon as possible. It's time we contacted FilboCorp.'

'Are they based in Stockholm?'

'That's where they have their Swedish HQ,' Erik interjected helpfully.

'And I want you to talk to him.' Torkel pointed to the last name on the list: Stefan Andrén.

'I thought he lived in London?'

'He's on a business trip to Oslo – he'll be in Stockholm tomorrow evening,' Erik informed her, clearly pleased to have so much information at his fingertips. 'I've got his number here.'

'Sebastian's already in Stockholm – can't he do it?'

Torkel sighed. What the hell was wrong with everybody? Why couldn't they just go where he sent them, where he needed them most?

'Sebastian isn't a police officer, and if he was he would be a very bad police officer, and I need someone good.'

'Flattery will get you nowhere,' Vanja said with a little smile that she hoped would hide her genuine annoyance at being packed off to the city.

'I don't need to flatter you, because I can give orders,' Torkel said, returning her smile as he left the room and any further objections.

★ ★ ★

Erik mopped up the last of the dip from his plate with a piece of bread and sat back. He didn't usually eat this late, but he had been starving when he got home, and he had found a salmon kebab and a pot of wasabi dip left over from dinner on Saturday. He had warmed the kebab in the microwave while he put together a simple salad, and had washed down his impromptu meal with a low-alcohol beer. The recipe was from a TV cookery programme, and he actually thought it tasted better now than when it was freshly made. The chilli and ginger marinade had intensified, and the fish had taken on the flavour of the lemongrass stalks he had used as skewers.

He put his plate and cutlery in the dishwasher, connected his phone to the stereo in the kitchen and started up his playlist while he filled the sink with water. Neither Pia nor Alma had sussed out how the combination of sink, hot water, washing-up liquid and brush actually worked, and Erik was the one who always dealt with anything that didn't go in the dishwasher. He didn't mind; sometimes he enjoyed the sense of achievement as he listened to music and produced a spotless sink, draining board and hob. He much preferred this task to vacuuming and ironing, for example, which he found tedious beyond belief.

He had almost finished and was looking forward to settling down on the sofa with the Discovery channel for an hour or so before bed when he felt a pair of hands slide around his waist.

'You could scare a person, doing that kind of thing,' he said as he turned.

'How was your day?' Pia asked, standing on tiptoe to kiss him on the lips.

'Good. I've just been out to see Frank.'

'Because of this business with FilboCorp?'

'Yes. Torkel thinks that's where the motive lies.'

'Does he suspect Frank?' Both Pia's expression and her tone made it clear how absurd she found the very idea.

'I don't think so. The other two, Vanja and Billy, are looking into the company right now, so I reckon that's their main focus. That and Thomas Nordgren.'

'Thomas Nordgren?' Pia raised an eyebrow.

Erik shook his head, slightly annoyed with himself. He really ought to be more careful about what he shared with regard to the case, but he couldn't help himself. Not when it came to Pia. She always got what she wanted.

'He owns one of the properties up there, but we can't get hold of him, and he's been away since last week, so . . .'

'So he's a suspect,' Pia finished the sentence for him.

'I shouldn't really be discussing this with you,' Erik said with a smile, then gave her a kiss.

'So don't,' Pia said, taking a step back and looking as if she was trying to suppress a smile. 'Ask me about my day instead.'

'How was your day?'

'Pretty ordinary − I've fixed a date for the memorial service and set up a working party to sort it out. Things were quite boring, actually, until half an hour ago.'

She paused, gazed expectantly at him. She was obviously waiting. Whatever she was going to tell him, she was determined to spin it out for as long as possible. She seemed happy, relaxed and fully present in a way that he didn't see her very often, so he had no problem playing along.

'What happened half an hour ago?'

'I got a phone call.'

'Who from?'

'From Stockholm.' She couldn't hold back any longer; a great big smile spread across her face. 'They want me to go down there. They want to see me at Sveavägen sixty-eight.'

Erik knew exactly what that meant. Sveavägen 68 was an almost legendary address in the Flodin household, a kind of political Shangri-La. The headquarters of the Social Democratic Party.

'Why do they want to see you?' he asked obligingly, even though he thought he knew the answer.

'Why do you think? They want to talk to me about a seat on the executive committee.' Pia was bubbling over with joy and anticipation. She probably didn't even know she was doing it, but she was actually jumping up and down, and her smile couldn't get any broader. Her girlish, unaffected joy was infectious. 'I called Mia in the district admin office and she said it's more or less a formality – they've already decided.'

She threw her arms around him, hugged him tight and ran her hands over his back.

'So if you like you can have sex with an aspiring member of the executive committee.'

To his surprise Erik discovered that the offer sounded considerably more arousing than he would have expected.

Maria was bathing Nicole while Sebastian cleared away after dinner. They had decided on sandwiches; none of them had the energy to cook a meal, and Nicole didn't seem to mind. Quite the reverse; she had eaten three cheese-and-pickle sandwiches. There had been no more drawings since the one where the Carlstens' house was just visible to one side, and neither of them had pushed her. They both knew what was waiting in there. They were all happy to stay outside for a little while longer. Sebastian was impressed by the speed with which Nicole was working backwards. The trickiest thing was when trauma patients got stuck, brooding on a particular event, and were unable to move either backwards or forwards. Nicole didn't seem to have that problem; she was demonstrating an impressive inner strength and maturity. She had the courage to remember.

Sebastian went into the living room, gathered up the drawings and placed them in the middle of the table. He heard the bathroom door open and went to meet his guests. Maria was carrying Nicole, who was wrapped in a big white towel. The scent of soap and warm dampness followed them from the bathroom.

'Could you get my case?' Maria asked.

'It's already in your room,' Sebastian said, leading the way. Maria put her daughter down on the bed and dug a pair of blue-and-white pyjamas out of her big black suitcase. They were kind of old-fashioned; stylish in a classic way.

'Do you need anything before you go to bed?'

'Just a glass of water, please.'

'No problem.'

When he came back, Nicole was already tucked up in bed. Maria was lying next to her with her arms around her. Sebastian placed the glass on the chest of drawers and turned to say goodnight. Nicole looked up at him with her big dark eyes.

'I just want to say that you've been such a good girl today, Nicole,' he said, perching beside her. 'Both your mum and I are very, very proud of you.'

Nicole nodded; she looked proud too. He smiled at her and gently stroked her cheek, then got to his feet and turned to Maria.

'You only have to say if you need anything else – I'm just out there.'

'There is one thing . . .' she began tentatively.

'What?'

'It's just . . . Nicole is much calmer when you're in the room.'

Sebastian waited for her to go on; he had known that ever since they were at the hospital in Torsby. Maria took a deep breath.

'I think she'd like it if you lay down next to her while she falls asleep,' she went on shyly, almost as if she had made an indecent suggestion.

'Is your mum right?' Sebastian wondered, glancing over at Nicole. A faint nod, but that was enough.

He lay down cautiously on the narrow bed. He immediately noticed Nicole's reaction. He looked up at Maria, but this time he was frowning.

'There's only one problem,' he said.

'What?'

'There's no room. Come with me.'

★ ★ ★

It was a strange feeling. As if someone had ripped a hole in the curtain of time, transporting him back ten years.

He had a family again. A woman lying on one side of the double bed in his room, with him on the other side.

A child between them.

He had had many women in his bed over the past ten years. But never a ten-year-old girl.

And yet it felt perfectly natural. That was the strangest thing of all. Perhaps it was because Nicole reminded him more and more of Sabine. Perhaps it was because for the first time in an eternity he understood what the trust of a child meant.

A trust that demanded nothing more than to be reciprocated.

A trust that had no hidden purpose, no ulterior motive.

A trust that, unlike him, was totally honest.

Perhaps it was because he was experiencing love. Tenderness. Without any trace of sex or lust.

He had felt much of the same tenderness towards Vanja, at least when things were going well between them. But the lies were always there, always in the way.

She didn't know. He did.

It was perfectly simple, and immensely complicated.

He realised he wasn't going to be able to sleep, so he simply lay there, enjoying Nicole's closeness and her soft, even breathing.

It felt wonderful.

Maria's voice came through the half-light: 'Are you asleep?'

He didn't want to answer her. He wanted to stay where he was, in the waking dream, but she was a part of it. An important part, so he had to respond.

'No,' he said quietly.

He heard her turn slightly; she obviously wanted to talk. Let the words and the thoughts come. She had kept everything inside for so long.

'Things haven't been easy for Nicole and me,' she began tentatively. 'She has virtually no contact with her father, so there haven't been many men in her life.'

He didn't say anything. There was no need.

'That's why I felt it was important for her to spend time with her cousins, to see how a family works.'

She paused. It was painful to contemplate what she had lost.

'It's really strange,' she went on, speaking even more quietly. Sebastian wasn't sure if it was because she didn't want to wake Nicole, or because the emotion was taking its toll on her voice. 'I was so envious of Karin. So angry. We didn't even speak to each other for years. I thought she always got what she wanted. I thought she was selfish and spoilt.'

Maria turned a little more, and for the first time she met his gaze above the sleeping child's head.

'But she didn't get anything for free. She worked hard, but I think she made me feel . . .' Maria hesitated, groping for the right words. 'I don't know . . . I suppose I was envious because she seemed so happy.'

A glint of tears in her eyes.

'Are you ashamed of feeling that way?'

'A little, maybe. But mostly I'm sad for Nicole. Now she's all alone again. The way I've always felt.'

She fell silent.

Sebastian didn't say a word.

'Why don't you have any children?'

The question took him by surprise. He had been expecting and looking forward to finding out more about the woman in his bed, not this sudden change of subject, with the conversation focused on him.

'It just didn't happen,' he replied automatically.

'You seem to like children. You're good with them.'

'Yes.'

'Have you never been married?'

'No.'

The lies.

They came so easily.

Without any thought for the possible consequences. Without any thought at all.

'Hm . . .' she said, with the hint of a smile on her lips.

'What does that mean? Hm?'

'It's just strange.' She edged a fraction closer. 'You're a wonderful person.'

'Thanks.' No one had ever called him wonderful before. No one. Ever. His hand edged over towards hers, and she took it; her touch was warm and gentle. He moved closer to Nicole and felt her soft skin against his cheek.

The mother's hand in his.

The daughter between them.

He never wanted to fall asleep.

Erik called just as Torkel left the hotel, heading for his car. He sounded excited, almost elated. Something had happened.

'I've just spoken to Thomas Nordgren's ex-wife, Sofie. She was working last night.'

'Good.'

'Better than good. She knew about the situation with the Carlstens. Apparently Thomas was furious when they refused to sell – he had tried to put one over on her, but failed.'

'I don't understand,' Torkel said as he opened the car door.

'Thomas bought her out in 2009, even though he couldn't really afford it. He took out a sizeable loan on the house. It was only afterwards that Sofie realised he had been planning to sell the place on to FilboCorp right away, making a huge profit.'

Torkel could see a motive emerging from the shadows.

'And that's not all,' Erik went on.

'Go on,' Torkel said, settling down behind the wheel. He heard Erik take a deep breath.

'Thomas knew Jan Ceder.'

'Are you sure?'

'According to Sofie, they were members of the same hunting club when the Nordgrens were living in Torsby from 2002 to 2009. She remembered Ceder very well – she thought he was a nasty piece of work.'

'So why didn't Thomas appear on Ceder's list of friends and acquaintances?' Torkel demanded crossly.

'Because he left the club when he moved to Sunne in 2009. They haven't had any contact since then, but they did know one another.'

Torkel nodded to himself. A motive and a direct link to the man who owned the murder weapon. That was more than they'd had up to now; he could understand why Erik was so excited.

'Where are you now?' he asked.

'At the station.'

'I'll come and pick you up – we'll go over to Sunne and search the house.'

'Right now?'

'Right now.'

Torkel ended the call and started the car.

★ ★ ★

Torkel and Erik arrived at the same time as the locksmith.

Arnebyvägen 27 in Sunne was a drab, grey, three-storey apartment block. Thomas Nordgren lived on the second floor; there was no lift, so they had to take the stairs. There were four identical doors, and they quickly found the right one. Torkel rang the bell several times, but he had no intention of waiting longer than thirty seconds; he wasn't expecting anyone to answer.

He turned to the locksmith.

'Open the door, please, but don't go inside.'

The locksmith nodded; he was a fit-looking man wearing glasses, dungarees and a polo shirt with the company logo on the pocket. He put down his toolbox and opened it while Torkel pulled on his shoe protectors.

'I'll go in first, decide if we need to bring in Fabian.'

Erik stepped back, trying to manage his expectations. This could be a blind alley. However, there had been no sign of Nordgren for a week, and he had links to all those involved. They might solve the case here and now, several days before Hans Olander was due to march in and take over.

The locksmith started work. Torkel was about to put on his gloves when his phone rang. His first thought was to ignore it, but he glanced at the display and saw that it was one of the last people he wanted to talk to: Malin Åkerblad.

He gave Erik a weary look.

'Did you tell Malin we were coming here?'

Erik was taken aback. 'No.'

'Good.'

He took the call; she was responsible for the preliminary investigation after all.

'Torkel Höglund.'

'It's Malin Åkerblad.'

'I know that. Is it something important? I'm rather busy.' He had no intention of telling her what he was doing unless it was absolutely necessary.

'Yes, it is.' Her tone was sharper than usual; she sounded as if she was already angry about something. Torkel got ready to defend himself. 'I have to step down from this investigation.'

Torkel didn't know what to say; he certainly hadn't been expecting this. He should have been delighted, but he just felt tired. A new person meant more work. Surely she wasn't walking away because they'd had one or two differences of opinion? Perhaps he should do a bit of grovelling; it might be worth it to avoid the hassle of bringing someone new up to speed on the case.

'What's happened?'

'I've done some thinking, and I've come to the conclusion that I can't be in a situation that involves a conflict of interests.'

'What are you talking about?'

'My brother owns land that the mining company is interested in, and with this new lead I—'

Torkel interrupted her.

'Hang on, what the hell are you saying? Your brother owns land up there? What's his name?'

'Thomas Nordgren. I mean, we're not close, but I've—'

The world tilted on its axis, and Torkel interrupted her again, with some force.

'Thomas Nordgren is your brother?'

'Yes.' Malin sounded vaguely embarrassed. Torkel glanced at Erik and couldn't help smiling. The whole thing was too absurd to do anything else.

'Shall I tell you where we are, Malin?' he went on, slowly and icily. He didn't bother waiting for a reply. 'We're standing outside your brother's apartment in Sunne, and we're about to carry out a search.'

A sharp intake of breath told him how shocked she was.

'What does that mean?' she asked faintly.

'It means we are no longer talking about a conflict of interests as far as you're concerned – you've just become a suspect. I want to see you at the police station in Torsby as soon as possible.'

He ended the call. His assertion that Malin was now a suspect wasn't strictly true, but he really did want to speak to her, and a slight exaggeration would make her more inclined to come in and explain herself. And she really did have a great deal to explain. First things first, however.

'Get this bloody door open right now.'

Billy and Jennifer walked out of the red, barn-like building that was Kiruna airport, straight into at least half a metre of snow. May was just over a week away, and Billy honestly didn't understand how the residents of Kiruna could stand it.

He hated snow.

In Billy's world, snow made cycling difficult and running impossible; it was slippery and horrible, you couldn't park the car, you were always cold and wet, and you brought in half a litre of water every time you stepped through the front door. A year or so ago there had been snow in Stockholm from the middle of November until the end of April, and Billy had seriously thought he would go mad. Most people who talked about the winter as far north as Kiruna were worried about the lack of daylight, but Billy would choose darkness over snow any day.

Bastard white stuff covering the ground for more than half the year.

Every bloody year. Year after year after year.

He would kill himself.

'Have you been this far north before?' Jennifer wondered as they headed for the car park to pick up the Citroën C3 that Gunilla had rented for them, to Billy's horror. Getting in such a tiny car would feel like pulling on a rucksack.

'Yes, I did Kungsleden a while ago.'

'What's that?'

'It's a hiking trail. I walked from Abisko to Kebnekaise, and up onto Sydtoppen.'

They found the car, put their overnight bags in the tiny boot and set off on the nine-kilometre drive into the centre of town.

As they turned left onto the E10 and Billy put his foot down, Jennifer mentioned the only thing she actually knew about Kiruna.

Apparently they were going to move it.

Neither of them was familiar with the details; they'd just heard that the town centre was going to be relocated several kilometres to the east because of the extensive iron-ore mine that was causing subsidence, threatening homes and public buildings. Billy thought he'd read somewhere that LKAB, the mining company, were putting in something in the region of fifteen billion kronor in order to carry out the relocation, which would enable them to continue mining. That gave some kind of perspective on the sums involved in the industry. The deposit outside Torsby couldn't be compared with the amount of iron ore under Kiruna, but if they could move an entire town, it didn't seem unlikely that someone might decide to move a family who were in the way.

They didn't talk much for the final part of the journey, although Jennifer gazed out of the window with interest and commented approximately every 500 metres on how beautiful it was. Billy made vague noises of agreement, but his thoughts were elsewhere.

In Stockholm.

With Maya.

She hadn't been able to let go of the fact that he didn't want her to accompany him to Kiruna. Yesterday evening hadn't worked out the way he had hoped or imagined at all. As soon as he walked in he had been required to sit down and discuss the wedding plans. Many decisions had to be made now he was finally home for a few hours. Things had got a little tetchy; they had gone to bed late and had bad sex. Neither of them had really been interested. As they were having breakfast Billy had asked if she could drive him to the airport as she had a day off, but she had said she had a lot to do, so he had to catch the Arlanda Express from the central station.

However, his bad mood had evaporated as soon as he met Jennifer in the departures hall; she was so openly delighted to see him. She had run towards him as if they were in a romcom, hugging him and giving him a warm kiss on the cheek.

'I've missed you!' she'd said, in case her welcome hadn't made that clear, and he realised he had missed her too.

More than he had thought.

They hadn't chatted a great deal on the plane; Jennifer had studied the case notes while Billy had got out his iPad and read the new issue of one of the gadget magazines he subscribed to. Apparently there was a new vacuum cleaner that shone a UV-light onto the floor as it worked; according to the manufacturer, it would kill bacteria, viruses, fleas and lice by breaking down the DNA structure of their cells. Billy had no idea whether that was even possible, but it made him think about the padded envelope he had finally dropped in the postbox in the departures hall. He had made up his mind on the train. If there was a relationship between Vanja and Sebastian, he wanted to know. What he would do with that knowledge was a separate issue, but when had it ever been a disadvantage to have as much information as possible? Never.

They arrived on the outskirts of the town that would soon be moved. Gunilla had booked them into the Railway Hotel, which according to Billy's satnav lay one and a half kilometres from the railway station, for some inexplicable reason. They decided to check in, find something to eat, then travel the twenty kilometres or so up to Kurravaara and Matti Pejok's brother.

She didn't recognise the room right away.

But she did feel safe.

Her mother on one side.

The man who had saved her from the darkness on the other.

Part of her still wanted to run. The apartment was big. Plenty of places to hide.

But she didn't need to. She didn't need to run away any more.

She sat up. There was something else she needed to do.

She needed to open the door of the house.

The house she had run away from.

But the blood frightened her. The blood that had stuck to her feet, oozed up between her toes, found its way under her nails.

She didn't want to open the door. She didn't want to.

She lay down again. Between them. She wanted to stay here. Feel safe.

The blood could wait.

The house could wait.

The others were dead anyway. They didn't exist any more. Opening the door wouldn't change that.

But the person who had killed them. The man with the shotgun.

The man who had found her in the cave.

The man who apparently had almost found her at the hospital.

He was still out there. With his gun. The gun that tore bodies apart, let the blood come pouring out.

He was still out there.

The man who had saved her had promised to catch him, but he needed help. Her help.

He needed that open door.

She sat up again, shuffled down to the foot of the bed and left the safe place behind her.

Sebastian woke up at nine o'clock. It was a long time since he had slept so well. He discovered that he was holding Nicole's little hand in his; that must be why he hadn't woken in a panic. He hadn't had the dream, because he had managed to hold on to her this time. Sabine.

He had been searching for a little girl's hand to hold every night for ten years.

Now he had found one.

Maria was facing away from him, breathing softly. He gazed at her long dark hair, realised that the occasions when he had contemplated a sleeping woman in the morning without wanting to leave were few and far between. Perhaps it was because they hadn't had sex, but it was more likely that the answer was lying between them.

He stretched and heard something fall on the floor at the foot of the bed. He sat up cautiously and looked down. The pad and the pens.

They had been in the living room at bedtime; he stiffened. Had Nicole got up during the night?

He glanced at her; she looked so peaceful. There was nothing to indicate that she had sat there on her own, drawing in the middle of the night. And yet it was the only scenario that made sense, the only logical explanation. He pushed back the covers, swung his legs over the side of the bed and got up. Crept over to the picture lying on the floor. He recognised it immediately. He had seen the crime-scene photographs from the Carlstens' house.

She had seen the reality.

Karin Carlsten lying in her own blood in the hallway.

He picked up the sheet of paper. Studied it. The image was incredibly powerful in its simplicity. The precise but childish lines made the terrible subject even more horrific. A little girl was standing by an open front door. Inside, the body lay twisted on the floor. Karin's brown hair in a sea of red, coloured in with violent strokes.

The girl lying in his bed was braver than anyone he had ever met in his entire life.

She had found the courage to face her demons alone.

In the middle of the night, when the adults preferred to forget. Preferred to dream.

His mobile rang. He gave a start, reached the bedside table in two strides and grabbed it. Vanja. He rejected the call in order to avoid waking Nicole and Maria.

He picked up the pad and the pens and left the room, closing the door quietly behind him.

He decided to hide the drawing. He needed to prepare Maria; this could be too much for her. She wasn't as ready as Nicole. His phone rang again; he knew Vanja never gave up.

'Hi, sorry, I couldn't really answer just now.'

'So you haven't heard?' Straight in, no pleasantries.

'Heard what?'

'About your extremely poor judgement.' Vanja sound almost hostile; he was completely unprepared for her tone, and started to feel annoyed.

'What the hell are you talking about?'

'Your fuck buddy Malin Åkerblad is now one of our suspects,' Vanja explained with unmistakable relish. Sebastian tried to understand what she meant, but to no avail.

'I still don't get it.'

'Her brother owns land up in Storbråten, and he knew Jan Ceder. Now do you understand? The Jan Ceder she insisted on releasing!' The words came flooding out. Sebastian was totally confused.

'Are you sure?'

'I'm sure. Torkel is just about to interview her.'

'That sounds crazy.'

'Indeed. How do you do it? You slept with Ellinor too. The woman who shot Ursula. And you slept with the mother of the murderer in Västerås, if I remember rightly.'

'That's enough—'

'Perhaps we should start all our new investigations with you choosing someone to screw, then we just arrest them,' Vanja went on without any indication that she was thinking of stopping. 'That would make our job so much easier.'

'Very funny, but I need to call Torkel,' Sebastian said, feeling stressed.

'Believe me, he's no more impressed than I am.'

'Vanja, I have to—'

'I can tell you exactly what he's going to say. You're not to go anywhere near Malin, you're to help me here in Stockholm, and I will be picking you up in twenty-five minutes. Make sure you're ready.'

With that she was gone.

Sebastian stood there, still trying to get his head around what Vanja had just told him. Could it be true? Was Malin involved? Could he really have been so unlucky?

He glanced towards the bedroom. Realised he probably ought to get Maria up before Vanja arrived. It wouldn't look good if she was lying in his double bed when Vanja walked into the apartment. Not after the conversation they'd just had.

Vanja was annoyed that she was no longer in Torsby. It might be childish, but she couldn't help feeling that she had been sent away from the heart of events. To the periphery.

She hated being on the periphery.

The very thought of missing the interview with Malin Åkerblad infuriated her. She had found the prosecutor's attitude unacceptable right from the start, and would have loved the chance to put the squeeze on her. Torkel had promised to do his best on her behalf, and she knew he was good. But it wasn't the same as being able to do it herself.

At the same time, she was well aware that the leads they had needed to be followed up, and that it was time to confront FilboCorp with their suspicions that the Torsby murders were linked to the planned mining development. And then there was Stefan Andrén, the man from London who also owned land in the area. He would be arriving in Stockholm that evening, and had promised to call her. But FilboCorp was definitely first on the list; she and Sebastian would be there in half an hour.

She double-parked outside his apartment block on Grev Magnigatan, keyed in the entry code and ran upstairs to collect him. Perhaps she had been a little hard on him on the phone, but he really had messed things up. Nobody had forced him into bed with Åkerblad, and he deserved to be given a hard time over it. However, she also knew that if he was going to be of any use to her, she had to calm down, otherwise he would act like an offended prima donna all day, which would be counterproductive. They had a lot to do.

She took the stairs three at a time and rang the doorbell. He answered more quickly than usual.

'Morning – nearly ready,' he said as he let her in.

The apartment smelled of coffee and toast. Unexpectedly homely. A door opened and a woman emerged from the bathroom wearing a dressing gown. Vanja was about to make a cutting remark, but she suddenly recognised her.

Maria Carlsten. Nicole's mother.

Nicole came out of the kitchen in her pyjamas, wearing a milky moustache and clutching a half-eaten piece of toast in her hand.

'What the hell are they doing here?' Vanja whispered when mother and daughter had disappeared into the kitchen. Sebastian looked at her in surprise.

'They're staying here. The apartment in Farsta was compromised. We decided this was the safest place.'

'Who's we?'

'Torkel and I, so don't go thinking this was just my idea,' he said. There was a defensive note in his voice; it was obvious that he didn't want to discuss the suitability of this little family living in his apartment. Vanja felt completely out of the loop. She had had no idea that Nicole and her mother were here; why hadn't she been informed? Didn't Torkel trust her, or was he just trying to avoid her objections?

'We've made quite a lot of progress with Nicole since they came here,' Sebastian said as if he could read her mind. 'A calm, homely environment has helped her.'

'Good.' Vanja thought she probably meant that; Nicole was potentially their only witness. 'What kind of progress? Anything you can share?'

'Absolutely.'

Sebastian showed Vanja to his study. She glanced into the kitchen on passing; Nicole and Maria were happily eating breakfast. Sebastian was probably right; this place was much better than any of the police safe houses for a ten-year-old girl who needed to rest and recuperate; they were impersonal and usually not very nice.

Sebastian closed the study door, went over to one of the bookshelves and picked up a pile of papers.

'Nicole did these drawings yesterday.'

Slowly he began to show Vanja the pictures, one at a time. She saw a girl in a forest.

'I told you she was moving backwards, working towards the moment. When she was in Torsby she drew the scene outside the cave when she'd been found, then inside the cave. Now she's in the forest.'

The images were emotionally powerful, with strong colours. Vanja was struck by how talented Nicole was when it came to expressing herself. The childish strokes emphasised the sense of vulnerability; the huge forest really did seem threatening, the little girl totally isolated. Vanja could feel her flight in picture after picture.

'In this one we reach the house – just on the edge, see?'

Vanja nodded. He was right; she recognised the Carlstens' white house.

Sebastian handed her the last drawing.

'She did this one last night. I haven't shown it to Maria yet.'

Vanja understood why when she saw the body with the brown hair, surrounded by blood.

'So she saw everything?'

Sebastian nodded, and Vanja looked up at him; she was overwhelmed.

'Well done.'

'There's more to come.' Sebastian went and put the drawings face down on the bookshelf. 'She hasn't finished yet.'

'In that case I have to admit you're right – it's obviously good for her to be here with you.' The words were rather more conciliatory than she had planned, but she was actually quite impressed by him right now.

'Thank you.'

'Although I did think it was a bit odd when I first saw them here.'

'I can understand that. I've made a complete cock-up of things with Malin.'

Vanja couldn't help smiling. 'To say the least. Torkel has really got his teeth into her now.'

'Have you tracked down her brother? What's his name, by the way?'

'Thomas Nordgren. No, he's been away since the murders. No one's seen him. I think Torkel is going to put out a call for him.'

Sebastian smiled too, almost playfully.

'But he's over thirty, he has a personal connection to the Carlstens, and he knows the area?'

Vanja nodded. Sebastian continued, exuding confidence:

'Socially functional, and he is or has been in a relationship? Am I right?'

Vanja realised where he was going with this.

'Yes, he fits your profile of the perpetrator,' she said drily.

'I just wanted to hear you say it.'

Vanja shook her head and laughed. Sebastian opened the study door.

'Shall we go? They'll be fine without me for a few hours.'

Vanja nodded. 'It's always better if there are two of us. We're starting with FilboCorp.'

Sebastian went into the kitchen to say goodbye; he patted Nicole on the head.

'I have to go to work for a while, but I'll be back soon.' Nicole looked resigned, but after a moment she gave a little nod. Sebastian turned to Maria: 'Any problems, just call me. Don't open the door to anyone.'

Vanja watched the three of them, wondering if she ought to let him stay. Perhaps he would be of more use here with Nicole. Then again, there was something about the little tableau that bothered her. It didn't feel entirely healthy. Sebastian wasn't acting only as an investigator; there was a sense that they were a family, somehow. Daddy's off to work.

'Nicole really likes you,' she said when he rejoined her. 'She seems to trust you.'

'She's probably the only person in the whole world who does,' he answered honestly.

Vanja shook her head. That was just typical of him, reading too much into every situation.

'She's a child, Sebastian. A traumatised child. She needs you, but she doesn't know you,' she said, a little more sharply than she might have wished.

'So you're saying that anyone who knows me can't possibly like me or trust me?'

'Well, it's certainly more difficult,' Vanja replied honestly.

Sebastian put on his shoes, making it clear that the discussion about the child in his kitchen was over.

They left the apartment in silence.

Torkel was standing by the coffee machine waiting for his fourth cup of the day when Erik appeared.

'Nordgren's financial details,' he said, handing over a print-out to Torkel who quickly read through it and nodded when he discovered that the information confirmed their theories from the previous day. Thomas Nordgren's personal finances were, to put it politely, under a certain amount of strain. He was still paying off the substantial loan he had taken out in 2009 in order to buy his wife out of the house when they divorced. The interest rate wasn't great, and he also had a comparatively large bank loan, a number of credit-card debts, and several unsecured loans. His monthly income was 22,400 kronor before tax. Even Torkel, with his relatively limited knowledge of such matters, realised that Thomas must have ended up in the red every month. Selling the land to FilboCorp would literally have changed his life.

It was useful information, but it wasn't evidence. However, it did help to establish a motive.

They didn't have much in the way of proof.

They had nothing, to be honest.

Nothing had been found in Thomas Nordgren's apartment or his storeroom in the cellar that might link him in any way to the five murders. None of the neighbours had anything useful to say about Thomas as a person, his circle of acquaintances, his recent activities or where he was right now. No one had seen him for over a week.

'She's been in there for nearly an hour,' Erik said, glancing at his watch.

Torkel knew exactly who he was referring to. 'She' was Malin Åkerblad. She had made herself available immediately and had voluntarily come in for questioning; she had now been waiting longer than was either necessary or acceptable.

'I know, I'm on my way,' Torkel said, lifting his cup from the metal grid. 'I just wanted to wait for this,' he said, waving the printout Erik had given him. 'Thanks – well done.'

He set off along the corridor, wondering whether to apologise to the prosecutor for keeping her waiting. However, he didn't like Malin Åkerblad, and he was pretty sure the feeling was mutual. Vanja had asked him to put her under pressure, and that was exactly what he intended to do. Starting with an apology was not an option.

★ ★ ★

Malin Åkerblad was in the same room where they had interviewed Jan Ceder. Poetic justice, Torkel thought.

'I'm perfectly willing to help you,' Malin said with a mixture of weariness and anger in her husky voice. 'There's no reason to treat me badly.'

Torkel didn't reply; he simply went over to the table and put down his coffee cup. He hoped she would take note of the fact that he hadn't brought one for her, nor was he offering to go and fetch one. He pulled out the chair and sat down. Placed his elbows on the table, rested his chin on his clasped hands.

'Your brother . . .' he began, leaving the rest of the sentence hanging in the air.

'Yes?' Malin's tone made it clear that she needed a little more to go on.

'Tell me about him.'

'What do you want to know?'

'What do you want to tell me?'

Malin shrugged. 'Thomas is eight years older than me, so we didn't hang out much when we were growing up. He left home when he was seventeen and I was only nine, so . . .' She spread her hands wide as if she was hoping that would explain

323

the significance of the age gap for their relationship. 'We had sporadic contact, I saw him when there was a family birthday, at Christmas and so on while our parents were still alive, but since they died . . .' Again she clearly hoped that no further explanation was necessary.

'And what about the property the Torssons rent from him?' Torkel wondered, cutting to the chase.

'Thomas and Sofie bought the place two years after they got married. Sofie and I didn't get on, and we had virtually nothing to do with each other during their marriage.'

'And now?'

'We're in touch occasionally.'

'Do you know where he is?'

'No, I haven't spoken to him for weeks.'

Torkel nodded to himself and took a sip of coffee. Sat back and clasped his hands behind his head.

'Thomas and Jan Ceder were members of the same hunting club while he was living in that house,' he stated in a conversational tone of voice. Malin looked genuinely surprised.

'I didn't know that.'

Torkel didn't respond; he merely tipped his chair a fraction, balancing on the back legs. Totally at ease. Apparently.

'I don't know any of Thomas's friends,' Malin went on, suddenly a lot more keen to convince him. 'And as I said, I didn't have anything to do with him while he was married to Sofie.'

'So you weren't aware that he knew Jan Ceder?'

'No.'

'So that's not why you were so reluctant to help us hold Ceder?' No hint of an accusation, no anger, no attack. A dignified discussion. A perfectly simple question.

'No, I released him because you didn't have enough evidence to warrant keeping him in custody.'

'We thought we had.'

'You thought wrong.' She was absolutely sure of her ground, and Torkel realised how convincing she could be when she was standing up in court. That was the voice of a winner, but she

324

wasn't presenting her argument to the jury right now. In fact, you could say she was in the dock.

'Your brother didn't like the Carlstens,' he said, getting up and going over to the window. He leaned on the sill facing the glass, even though you couldn't see either out or in through it.

'I didn't know that either.'

'He never told you that he regarded them as the reason for his financial troubles, or said that he'd be rich if only they would agree to sell their land?'

'No.'

'So when the Carlstens were murdered and this case landed on your desk, there were no alarm bells ringing, nothing linking what had happened with your brother?'

'As I said, no. Otherwise I wouldn't have taken the job.'

Torkel turned to her for the first time since he had left the table. 'And you expect me to believe that?'

'You can believe whatever you like, to be honest, but it's true.'

'OK, let me tell you what I think. At the moment,' he said, taking a step forward, placing his hands flat on the table and leaning towards Malin, 'I think that Thomas's financial situation became untenable. I think he borrowed a shotgun from his old hunting buddy Jan Ceder, and used it to shoot the Carlsten family.'

Malin shook her head to indicate that she knew where this was going, but that it was already beyond ridiculous.

'Thomas was afraid that Ceder would tell us who had the gun,' Torkel went on. 'You didn't know how much Ceder hated anyone in authority, and you couldn't take the risk, so you let him go. Thomas was waiting when he got home, and shot him in the dog pen.'

'That's absurd,' Malin said, unable to suppress a little laugh that conveyed her opinion even more effectively. 'Do you have anything, anything at all that proves any of this?'

'We have someone new in charge of the preliminary investigation,' Torkel said, which wasn't an answer to her question.

'I know. Emilio Torres.'

'He's a little more inclined to listen than you were, if I can put it that way.'

There was no mistaking the fact that Torkel was enjoying the situation. He would have liked to think he was bigger than that, but he had to admit that he wanted to give Malin Åkerblad a hard time. She had made his life more difficult, and it was already complicated enough on every possible level.

He fixed his eyes on her, and waited until she looked up.

'I am remanding you in custody, and I am putting out a nationwide call for your brother.'

It had taken a while to find the right place, but this was it.

The black-and-white photograph from the front page of *Expressen* had been enough. That and time. Time he didn't really have.

Once again he compared the photograph with the building facing him. He was convinced it was the same one, but was the girl still there? There was a significant risk that the police had decided to move her when the newspaper published the story, particularly after his failure at the hospital. That would certainly have increased their awareness of the risk to the girl's safety.

He looked up at the third-floor window. He had been sitting in his car for over two hours now, and he hadn't seen any sign of movement behind the glass. In contrast to the picture in the paper, the third-floor window was empty. No pale little face peering out. The blinds weren't even closed, which bothered him. If someone was worried about being found, surely they would have pulled down the blinds?

He decided to get out of the car. It increased his chances of being spotted, but he had to do something. Get closer. Find out more information. He would leave his gun behind, which was in a small black bag on the passenger seat. There were advantages to being armed, of course, but they were outweighed by the disadvantages. It was highly unlikely that he would suddenly have an opportunity to deal with the girl, and the small shotgun would be impossible to explain away if he were searched or, even worse, arrested. He had no idea what kind of security the police had in place if the child was still there; best to assess the situation first. As always.

He got out and walked towards the block, quickly enough to make it look as if he knew where he was going. He thought it looked less suspicious if a person didn't appear to be searching for something.

He was just about to open the main door when he heard a voice behind him.

'Excuse me?'

The man had appeared from nowhere. He was presumably a plain-clothes police officer; he wasn't in uniform. Thank God he'd left the gun in the car. He turned around, trying to look vaguely surprised. He was just an ordinary guy on his way somewhere, that was all.

The man who had stopped him was about thirty; he was wearing a red windbreaker and seemed a little stressed. He must have been sitting in the car that was parked a short distance away.

'Do you live here?' he asked.

The man holding the door didn't quite know which lie to use. He chose the simplest response, the one that would buy him some time.

'Why?'

'Sorry. I'm a freelance journalist, and I'm trying to get a picture of someone who's supposed to be living here, but I haven't seen any sign of her all day.'

'Who's that?'

'A little girl, but I'm starting to think they might have moved her.'

'Who might have moved whom? I really don't know what you're talking about.' The man who could have been armed let go of the door and took a step towards the journalist. This was his chance to find out more.

The reporter suddenly looked weary as he realised he wasn't going to get any answers, just more questions. He shook his head.

'It's just a rumour I picked up, but I thought I'd hang around, see if it was true. Sorry to have bothered you.' He turned to walk away.

'Hang on – how long have you been here?'

'Since this morning, but I'm giving up now.'

'You're probably right.' He raised his hand to bid the journalist farewell. So the police had moved her; if there had been no sign of life all day, that was the most likely scenario. He went inside and waited until the journalist had got in his car and driven off.

Back to square one. Or even worse; now he didn't have a clue where she was. She could be anywhere. He had to find a different way of tackling the problem. The journalist had given him an idea. If he couldn't find the girl, perhaps he could find someone who visited her? Someone who needed her, maybe even cared about her? Someone apart from her mother, he thought as he stood there in the stairwell.

The man he had seen in the cave.

The same man had been the first to arrive at the hospital in Torsby that night. He had seen the car screech into the car park as he lay hiding in the bushes up above, and the tall, slightly over-weight man had got out and run inside. Even then it had occurred to him that this man must be important to the girl in some way. It was hardly a coincidence that he was first on the scene both times.

He didn't think he was a police officer, but he was definitely part of the Riksmord team that had been brought in from Stockholm.

Sebastian – that was how he had introduced himself to the girl in the cave.

There couldn't be many Sebastians working for Riksmord, could there?

After a light lunch at the Railway Hotel, Billy and Jennifer got in the car and continued north along the road to Kurravaara, which according to Jennifer might well be the most beautiful route she had ever seen. Billy called Per Pejok who promised to keep an eye open for them. He was expecting them within the next twenty minutes; otherwise they had gone wrong and would need to call him again.

To start with there wasn't much chance of getting lost: one straight road. When they reached Kurravaara and the inlet that didn't have a name, according to Billy's satnav, they turned left and continued along Norra Vägen following the shore of the lake for a while, then reached the small community which con-sisted of a collection of red buildings that appeared to have been randomly positioned at varying distances from one another and the water, where the ice had already started to break up. However, the snow seemed deeper here, Billy noted with a shudder. There were only 300 inhabitants in Kurravaara, but there were also a number of summer cottages, which made the community seem bigger. North of the inlet they took the second left and followed the road until it ran out. The green door of a small red two-storey house opened as they pulled in, and a weather-beaten man in his forties came towards them. He was wearing a sheepskin-lined leather jacket over a woollen jumper, jeans and heavy boots. A pair of bright blue eyes were the only facial feature visible between an enormous but well-groomed beard and the peak of a cap. Billy could hear dogs barking inside the house as he got out of the car. Hunting dogs, presumably. He could easily picture this man with a shotgun over his shoulder.

'Per Pejok. Welcome to Kurravaara,' the man said in a strong Kiruna accent as he held out his hand. 'You found your way easily enough, then?'

Billy and Jennifer introduced themselves and Jennifer told their host how beautiful she found his village. Billy was expecting to be invited indoors, into the warmth, but instead Per pointed to a red Range Rover parked nearby.

'Would you like to go and see the mine?'

'Yes, please, absolutely,' Jennifer enthused, sounding as if she was off on an adventure. Billy couldn't help but admire her endless enthusiasm.

'We'll take my car – it's better suited to the terrain,' Per said, and Billy could have sworn he saw a scornful little smile as Per glanced at the little Citroën before setting off towards the Range Rover.

Billy sat in the front, Jennifer in the back, and the interior was soon pleasantly warm as they drove through the stunning landscape.

'Matti fought those bastards all the way,' Per explained as he confidently manoeuvred the vehicle along the narrow, snow-covered roads. 'From the very first day when he heard about their plans until . . . well, until he disappeared.'

'But FilboCorp has a contract to buy the land,' Jennifer said. Per Pejok let out a snort that made it clear how much he thought that was worth, spraying the windscreen liberally with saliva at the same time.

'They get what they need.'

'But you reported your brother to the police as a missing person, didn't you?' Billy asked, even though he already knew the answer.

'Of course.'

'And what did they do?'

'Fuck all. The company waved that contract you mentioned, and the police lost interest. Said Matti had probably taken off somewhere with the money.' Per snorted again, and for the first time Billy wondered whether the car should be fitted with a windscreen wiper on the inside. 'But no doubt the boys in blue are on their payroll, just like all those corrupt fucking politicians who gave them permission to dig here.' Per turned to Billy. 'The company reckons they'll make almost five hundred billion over the next twenty years, so they can afford to buy whatever they need.'

He turned onto a wider road that had obviously been resurfaced fairly recently, then after a few kilometres took a smaller track that immediately began to climb steeply. Soon they were driving along something that couldn't even be described as a track, climbing even more steeply.

'We can't get any closer than this,' Per said, stopping at the top of the slope. Seconds later Billy and Jennifer were gazing down on a valley that was totally dominated by a huge grey hole, an opencast mine; to Billy it looked more like a gigantic gravel pit. An ugly wound in the otherwise idyllic landscape.

'Three kilometres long, one kilometre wide and three hundred and ninety metres deep,' Per said without being asked.

'What do they mine here?'

'Copper. They bring up fifteen million tons of ore each year, but there are plans to increase production to more than double that amount.'

Fifteen million tons. Jennifer couldn't even begin to imagine how much that was. How on earth did they get such quantities from a hole in the ground?

'They work twenty-four/seven, all year round,' Per said as if he had read her mind, pointing to a truck down below. 'It takes four hundred litres of diesel an hour just to transport the ore to the crushing shed.' He pointed to a building further down the valley. 'From there the crushed ore goes to the processing plant on a conveyor belt, but you can't see that from here.'

Per turned his attention back to the opencast mine down below.

'As you can see, the mining operation itself destroys the landscape, and they diverted a river not far away which more or less emptied a lake, but that's not the main problem.'

Once again he waved his hand in the direction of the crushing shed and the dark grey mountain of rock beside it, completely different in both shape and colour from everything else around it. Jennifer and Billy immediately understood what he meant.

'Five kilometres long, two kilometres wide – waste rock and tailings left over after processing. Fifty thousand tons are spewed out every day, but when they're exposed to the air, there's a chemical reaction which means that any residual heavy metals are released.'

'Doesn't the company have procedures for dealing with that kind of thing?' Jennifer wondered.

'We get sewage sludge from Stockholm – it's mixed with earth, then used to cover the waste to keep the metals in, but no one knows if it will work, or for how long.'

Per turned to face them, and Billy could have sworn he saw a tear in the corner of his eye.

'The company will be mining here for maybe another twenty years, but that will be there for hundreds, perhaps thousands of years. Who's going to take the responsibility for it?'

The question was rhetorical, but neither Billy nor Jennifer would have been able to provide an answer. This was all new to them – new and slightly scary. Per ran his index finger under his nose and along his cheek; Billy had been right about the tear.

'They say it provides work up here, but the place doesn't employ that many people, and most of those are specialists from overseas. FilboCorp doesn't even pay corporation tax in Sweden. Matti checked.'

Per set off past the parked car, heading for the other end of the plateau on which they were standing. From this viewpoint the unspoilt landscape of the fells and mountains lay before them once more. Jennifer found it difficult to grasp that they had moved no more than fifty metres, yet the prospect was so different. Untouched, magnificent, extending towards the horizon, while behind them there was heavy industry.

'Matti lived just over there,' Per said, pointing to the forest below. Neither Billy nor Jennifer could see a house, so they assumed Per was indicating the general direction rather than a specific spot.

'What will happen when the mine closes in twenty years?'

'The opencast pit will be filled with water – it will become a kind of artificial lake. But it will take a long time for the environment to recover. Everything takes longer up here because of the cold. Matti taught me all this. He made me get involved. Do you really think he would have sold his land, when it looked like this?' His sweeping gesture encompassed the wilderness before them. 'To them?' He jerked a thumb over his shoulder to the mine behind.

Once again the question was rhetorical, but this time both Billy and Jennifer knew the answer.

It was more than unlikely.

Which meant that FilboCorp had a great deal of explaining to do.

FilboCorp's head office was on the second floor at Kungsgatan 36–38. Vanja and Sebastian had given their names on the entry-phone and been buzzed in. The walls of the waiting room in reception were covered with photographs of opencast and deep-shaft mines, with exotic names beneath the pictures. The decor was dark, with plenty of mahogany; ornate, expensive leather sofas and armchairs; and a thick green fitted carpet. Vanja sat down on one of the sofas while Sebastian remained standing, contemplating the photos. One attack after another on the unspoilt beauty of nature, all tastefully displayed in a room that was the very epitome of wealth.

'Who are we supposed to be seeing?' he asked.

'We have an appointment with Carl Henrik Ottosson, head of Information Services,' Vanja replied as she looked around.

'Not with the managing director?' Sebastian sounded disappointed.

'He didn't have time.'

Sebastian shook his head. 'It's hardly likely to be the head of Information Services who asked that lawyer to call Maria, is it?'

'Maybe not, but that's who we're seeing,' Vanja said acidly; she was beginning to regret bringing Sebastian with her. He seemed to be on the warpath.

'His job is to handle the press and give evasive answers. We're police officers. We ought to be talking to the organ grinder, not the monkey.'

'Just leave it, OK? And you're not a police officer, you're a consultant, if we're being picky.'

Sebastian beamed at her.

'So does that mean I can go in a bit harder?'

'As long as you don't get us thrown out.'

'I promise. Trust me.'

Before Vanja had time to reply, a slim man in an expensive suit and matching tie walked in. He was wearing horn-rimmed glasses, his hair was short, well cut and slicked back, and a broad smile revealed white, even teeth. He looked as if he had come straight out of business school. Sebastian took an instant dislike to him.

'Carl Henrik Ottosson, head of Information Services here at FilboCorp. I can promise you we don't throw anyone out,' he said, holding out his hand. Vanja shook it and introduced herself; Sebastian didn't move.

'Don't make promises you can't keep,' he said. The well-dressed man with the Teflon smile took no notice.

'How can I help you?'

'We're investigating a number of murders in Torsby—'Vanja began.

'Although we'd prefer to speak to your boss,' Sebastian interjected.

'Unfortunately he's otherwise engaged. We didn't have very much notice of your visit.' Carl Henrik turned back to Vanja. 'And I don't understand how we can possibly be involved in this tragedy.'

Sebastian took a step forward; surely Carl Henrik didn't think he could be dismissed that easily?

'Which of you asked Rickard Häger to call Maria Carlsten asking to buy her out, just a few days after her sister's entire family was murdered?'

Carl Henrik went pale.

'I'm afraid I don't know.'

'Then perhaps you can understand why we want to talk to the person who does actually know something.'

Carl Henrik did his best to look in control of the situation, but the smile had disappeared.

'As I said, I'm afraid he's otherwise engaged. However, I must stress that FilboCorp always operates within the law. If we have acted insensitively, then I can only apologise, but I can't see that we've done anything illegal, although I'm not familiar with the details of this particular case.'

'No, I don't suppose it is illegal. Unethical, perhaps. Definitely immoral. But no doubt you don't have a problem with that.'

'I can't respond to vague accusations.' Carl Henrik was becoming more and more irritated. 'I thought you had specific questions.'

'Indeed we did,' Vanja shot back. 'Which of you asked Rickard Häger to call Maria Carlsten asking to buy her out, just a few days after her sister's entire family was murdered? But apparently you don't have an answer.'

There was a brief silence. Carl Henrik stared at his visitors; Sebastian decided on a change of tactics.

'I believe you deal with the press?' he began.

'That's part of my remit, yes.'

'Good, then perhaps you can tell me what you think of this headline: *Entire family murdered. This is the mining company that wanted to get its hands on their land*. Then perhaps a few pictures of the murdered children celebrating their birthdays or something – you know the kind of thing, their innocent little faces smiling into the camera.'

Carl Henrik's face lost a little more colour, but at the same time his expression darkened. He was shocked and annoyed by Sebastian and Vanja's uncompromising approach, but he wasn't about to give up.

'It was unfortunate that someone called fru Carlsten so soon after the tragedy, but this is blackmail!'

'Tell that to the local councils when you're applying for exploration permits,' Vanja snapped. 'Or to your shareholders. I'm sure they'll be delighted to hear that you're refusing to assist in a murder inquiry.'

Carl Henrik was getting really angry now, and Sebastian thought he would soon be breaking his promise not to throw anyone out.

'What do you really want?'

'The same thing we wanted in the first place – to speak to the person who can answer our questions,' Sebastian replied calmly. 'But apparently that's not possible. Let's go, Vanja.'

He moved towards the door, thinking he would get halfway before Carl Henrik stopped him. He was wrong. It took only two steps.

'Wait, wait. I'll just check if he's available after all.' Carl Henrik swept out of the room, and Vanja smiled at Sebastian and held up her hand.

'High five!'

★ ★ ★

In less than five minutes Sebastian and Vanja were shown into a room that was even more affluent, if that were possible. The boardroom, Sebastian guessed. It was dominated by a long, highly polished oak table on which several crystal carafes of water were laid out. The dark panelled walls were filled with paintings which gave the impression of being valuable even if they weren't. An elderly man in a dark pinstripe suite and shiny shoes was waiting for them at the far end of the room. He was comparatively short and rotund, but with his rugged features, steady gaze and grey, perfectly groomed hair he seemed much taller than he was. He made no attempt to welcome them, but merely observed them with his ice-cold grey eyes. He seemed less than impressed with what he saw. Carl Henrik made the introductions.

'This is Mr Adrian Cole, CEO of FilboCorp Europe,' he said, his tone suitably obsequious. 'He's just interrupted an important meeting in order to see you.'

'So you're the people who've come here making entirely unfounded accusations,' Cole said in good Swedish, but with a distinct English accent. 'We usually have an excellent working relationship with the authorities, but of course that is reliant on the willingness of those authorities to work with us.'

'We want answers to certain questions relating to a murder inquiry,' Vanja replied.

Cole turned to Carl Henrik. 'You can go. I'll take care of this.' He waited until his subordinate had left the room, then turned back to Vanja.

'We're happy to answer your questions. We deal with difficult issues all the time. Is there copper beneath that mountain? Is it worth extracting thorium? Will the Environmental Court be able to stop us? We're used to questions. And accusations. Would you like some water?'

He pointed to the carafes; Sebastian shook his head. 'No, thanks.'

'But we don't like being threatened,' Cole went on. 'If we're going to provide answers, it has to be done in a spirit of mutual understanding. Otherwise you will need to proceed via our legal team.'

'What exactly do you mean by mutual understanding?' Sebastian asked crossly.

'Whatever we tell you remains confidential, within the bounds of the police investigation. It doesn't turn up in the media. You behave professionally, to put it briefly. Just as we do.'

'OK, but in that case we want answers, not some corporate bullshit,' Vanja said firmly. 'We don't appreciate being fobbed off with that buffoon we met just now.'

'No bullshit, I promise. But that doesn't mean you're going to like what I say. As a general rule, people don't really want the truth.'

'Do you know the area around Storbråten in Torsby?' Vanja asked.

Cole smiled. 'Yes. It's one of the richest veins in northern Värmland. It's worth billions.'

'Is that why you asked your lawyer to call Maria Carlsten and offer to buy her land?'

'You mean Rickard Häger at Lex Legali.'

'That's right.'

'To be perfectly honest, I don't know. It's Lex Legali's job to keep abreast of any possible change of ownership in the areas in which we have an interest. That's how we work.'

'And you don't think it's unethical to contact a grieving woman just days after her sister's entire family has been wiped out?' Sebastian said accusingly.

Cole gazed steadily at him.

'Possibly. But do you know how many times those conversations lead to a sale? Most of the people we speak to feel as if they've won the lottery. They are more than happy to accept our offer – it's a lot of money. But if fru Carlsten was upset, then I apologise. Although I don't actually need to apologise to you, do I? You don't own the land.'

'Do you have to be completely amoral to work here? Is it part of the job description?' Sebastian wondered. Cole smiled at him.

'You want to talk about morals? Do you know what percentage of Sweden's welfare budget comes out of the mountains? An enormous amount, let me tell you. That's what built this country, but people don't want to see it. They want to live in a modern society with everything on tap, and in an unspoilt nature reserve at the same time. It's a nice idea. Sounds good on a chat-show sofa. But I have no intention of apologising for mining rock and making something out of it.' Cole turned to Vanja. 'Was there anything else?'

'Yes. There are other landowners who stood to gain a great deal if the Carlstens sold, is that correct?'

'Absolutely. The Carlstens were the only ones who said no.'

'Have any of them been in touch? Kept asking, that kind of thing?'

'Behaved suspiciously, in other words?'

'Yes.'

Cole seemed to be searching his memory.

'The only person who's come back to us several times wondering if we want to buy his land is the man who owns the area immediately south of the Carlsten property.'

'Thomas Nordgren?' Vanja said quickly. Cole nodded.

'That's right. He's seemed particularly keen over the past couple of years.'

'Have you promised him anything? Done any kind of deal?' Vanja asked with interest.

'We've always given the same answer – we want to buy all the land, or none of it.'

Vanja didn't respond; Thomas Nordgren was now an even more likely suspect.

'Do you think it's him?' Cole asked, correctly interpreting her silence.

'What do you think?'

'I've no idea. But people are capable of doing all kinds of things for money – that's something I've learned. So are we, but we don't commit murder. We don't need to. The land is too valuable. We'll get it one day anyway.'

Billy and Jennifer were sitting in an otherwise empty office on the second floor of the police station in Kiruna, a large square brick building that had nothing else going for it. It could have been council offices, a school, a prison, a former mental hospital, an office block, a storage depot, anything; it was utterly characterless and boring. When Billy drove into the car park and saw it, he sincerely hoped the police station wasn't one of those buildings that was going to be carefully taken down and rebuilt in the new city centre; it ought to be razed to the ground. His colleagues deserved better. The only point in its favour was that it was bigger than he had expected.

They had explained why they were there to the duty officer on the desk downstairs: they wanted to speak to someone who was responsible for the investigation into Matti Pejok's disappearance, or who had some insight into the case. It had taken a series of phone calls, redirections and yet more calls, but eventually they had been shown into this office and asked to wait.

So now they were waiting.

They had been waiting for quite some time.

Billy was just about to go back downstairs to ask if they'd been forgotten when the door opened and a woman aged about fifty and weighing something in the region of 150 kilos walked in carrying a thick folder. She was in uniform, with coal-black shoulder-length hair, distinctive dark eyes, her mouth a slash of bright red lipstick. A woman who wanted to be noticed, or at least had nothing against it. She introduced herself as Renate Stålnacke and sat down opposite them.

'We're interested in Matti Pejok's disappearance,' Billy said.

'Ah, yes, the Pejok brothers,' Renate said with a sigh, making it clear that she had heard enough about those two to last the rest of her life. Billy began to understand why when she spent the next twenty minutes going through all her dealings with them before and after FilboCorp started operating in Kurravaara. 'May I ask why Riksmord is interested in them?' she concluded her lecture, glancing from Billy to Jennifer and back again.

'FilboCorp has come up in another case, and we think Matti Pejok's disappearance could be relevant,' Billy answered honestly.

'Has someone else gone missing?'

'No, a family has been murdered,' Jennifer explained, continuing with the policy of openness.

'And you think the company is involved.'

'We're investigating every possible avenue,' Billy said. 'The mining company is one of them.'

'I don't know why everyone wants to portray them as the bad guys,' Renate said, leaning forward. 'I think we should increase production. We need the metal, there's no disagreement on that point, and surely it's better if we're mining rather than letting kids do the work somewhere in South America, dumping the waste anywhere they like? At least we have rules and regulations to protect the environment, and decent working conditions.'

Neither Billy nor Jennifer felt like getting into a discussion on the pros and cons of the mining industry, so Billy quickly got back to the main point of their visit.

'Do you have a copy of the contract Matti Pejok signed?'

Renate opened the folder and eventually produced a document which she placed on the table in front of her guests, who leaned forward at the same time to study it.

'His brother says that's not Matti's signature,' Billy said, pointing to the bottom of the last page.

'I'm aware of that – we looked into the matter.' Renate took two more documents out of the folder and put them down on the table: a car-rental contract, and a copy of Matti's passport. Both signed.

'They're not exactly the same,' Jennifer said when she had glanced at all three in turn several times.

'Is your signature always exactly the same?' Renate's sceptical look made Jennifer realise she had heard it all before.

'More or less,' she replied confidently.

'Anyway, we didn't think the difference was significant enough to warrant the suspicion that a crime had been committed.'

'Did you consider that he might have signed because he was being tortured?' Even Billy was taken aback. He knew Jennifer pretty well by this stage, and he was well aware that she wished police work consisted entirely of days packed with action and excitement. She wanted to hunt down the bad guys, the smarter and more cunning the better. She wanted to pit her strength against the proponents of evil. The reality of life in Sigtuna was about as far as she could possibly get from her dream of the profession she had chosen, a dream Billy thought she had probably picked up from American movies, to be honest.

Even though he knew all this, he was still surprised by Jennifer's little ray of hope that Matti might have been tortured to make him sign the contract.

'That would explain why the writing on the contract is a bit shaky,' Jennifer went on, clearly interpreting Billy's expression as encouraging.

'It could also be because he found the decision very difficult to make. Or that the document was on top of something that wasn't completely flat,' Renate said, gathering up the papers and putting them back in the folder.

'The Pejok brothers have been responsible for more hours of overtime by this police force than the rest of the residents of Kiruna put together, and I have to admit there have been times when I've been so sick of them that I've considered simply burying anything to do with them, but we investigated Matti's disappearance thoroughly, several times, and there is nothing to indicate that any crime has been committed.' Renate sat back, almost out of breath after her harangue. Billy and Jennifer exchanged a quick glance. Renate Stålnacke seemed more than competent, and from what they had heard and seen, there was nothing that really gave them cause to doubt her conclusion.

'Could I have a copy of the case notes?' Billy asked.

'There's a digital copy waiting for you in reception.'

'Did you follow the money?' Billy wondered as he got to his feet.

'The money went into an account in Matti Pejok's name. It was all there – it remained untouched for several months. We checked from time to time.'

'Have you checked today?'

Renate's expression told him all he needed to know.

She hadn't.

★ ★ ★

Another office. Another wait.

This time they were at the bank along the street from the police station. Billy had called Torkel on the way to update him – not that there was a great deal to report. Per Pejok was still convinced that his brother's disappearance was suspicious; the local police didn't agree. Billy hadn't had time to go through their case notes yet, but it looked as if they had put in the hours and done a good job. However, he had an idea he wanted to follow up, and was intending to contact Malin Åkerblad.

Torkel had interrupted him at that point.

Malin Åkerblad was no longer in charge of the preliminary investigation, in fact Torkel was in the process of trying to get her arrested. Billy would have to speak to her successor, Emilio Torres, instead. Just a minute. Before Billy had the chance to process what he had just been told, a voice with a slight accent came on the line. Emilio Torres introduced himself and asked how he could help.

Billy explained.

Emilio promised to do his best.

Five minutes later Billy and Jennifer arrived at Sparkbanken Nord. They introduced themselves, explained why they were there, and asked for the fax number. They were then shown into the little office where they were now waiting. The odd person walked past on Lars Janssonsgata outside the window, but it would be an exaggeration to say the town was buzzing this afternoon. At least in the area where Billy and Jennifer were.

The door opened and the man who came in was grinning as if he had won the biggest prize of his entire life. He introduced himself as Anton Beringer, manager of the Kiruna branch, in an accent that revealed he wasn't born and bred in the area. His cheerful disposition even extended to his enthusiastic handshake.

'How can I help you?'

'You should have received a fax from the prosecutor's office in Karlstad,' Billy began, and Anton nodded.

'Yes – you want access to one of our client's accounts.'

'There's a chance that he might no longer be a client, but if that's the case I'd like to know where the money has gone.'

'Absolutely, no problem. What's the client's name?' Anton's fingers were already hovering over his computer keyboard.

Billy gave him the name, personal ID number and account number from the contract between Matti Pejok and FilboCorp. Anton quickly entered the details, then pressed Enter with a flourish.

'Yes, he's still a client, and the account is active.' Anton scrolled down the page. 'Wow, that's a lot of money,' he said, turning the screen so that Billy and Jennifer could see while he clarified what they were looking at.

'Not much is actually happening. A huge sum was paid in a little over five years ago – here.' He pointed to the screen. 'Then there were a few minor transactions, but nothing for just over a year.'

'That's when he was reported missing,' Jennifer noted when she saw the date of the last transaction on the screen.

'There has been a monthly transfer of twenty-five thousand kronor for the past four years,' Anton said; this time he was pointing to a row of figures. An account number.

'Can you give me the details of that account?' Billy said, making notes.

'I should think so,' Anton said cheerfully as he turned back the screen and started tapping away on the keyboard.

'He disappears, doesn't touch the money for twelve months, then starts making regular withdrawals,' Billy summarised to himself.

'Twenty-five thousand a month is three hundred thousand a year,' Jennifer said. 'At that rate the money would last him something like fifty years.'

'You mean like a monthly salary?'

'It makes sense, doesn't it?'

'Twenty-five thousand would go quite a long way . . .'

'The account is with Scotiabank in Costa Rica,' Anton announced, his smile growing even broader, if that were possible.

'Twenty-five thousand would go even further over there,' Jennifer commented.

Google and a couple of telephone calls had produced results. It had been easier than expected. Apparently Riksmord and the National Police Board regularly worked with a criminal psychologist by the name of Sebastian Bergman. There wasn't much about him online, but he did have a Wikipedia entry. Sebastian Jacob Bergman had trained at the University of Stockholm and in the USA. He specialised in serial killers, and was one of Sweden's leading profilers. There was also a picture; it was a few years old, but he recognised the tall man with the slightly unruly hair from the mine and the hospital.

There were five Sebastian Bergmans in Stockholm, but only one with the middle name Jacob. Sebastian Jacob Bergman lived at Grev Magnigatan 18, so that was the place to go.

It was difficult to find a parking space, and he had to drive around for a while before he found a spot that would give him a decent view of the apartment block. It was a substantial yellow-stone building with broad white window frames and an imposing main door in the centre. It looked pretty exclusive. He tipped his seat back and made himself comfortable. He wished he had bought more supplies than half a litre of Coca-Cola, but now he was here he didn't want to get out of the car. Not until he had worked out the next stage in his plan.

So far it was simple. Wait until Sebastian Bergman left the apartment, then follow him. With a bit of luck, Bergman would lead him to the girl. There were a number of weaknesses in the plan, but at the moment that was the best he had. He glanced up at the block once again.

Life wasn't fair, he thought.

Not in any way; he had learned that lately.

Those who worried and were cautious suffered.

Children who didn't really deserve it simply had to die.

Life wasn't fair, but you do what you have to do.

That was the way things were.

He had crossed a line with the first shots, and there was no going back. Everything that was happening now was merely the repercussions of those first shots, nothing more. There was only one witness left. Soon this would be over. For a while, at least.

He looked at his watch. Took a swig of the sugary drink and screwed the top back on. He ought to ration it; he would probably have to sit here for quite some time. Only five minutes had passed since he parked; time was passing incredibly slowly. He realised he had to do something. Perhaps he should get out of the car after all, walk over to the door. He had no idea which floor Sebastian lived on. Not that he needed to know, but it was something to do. He might be able to get into the foyer and read the list of residents. It was always good to have an overview.

To be on the safe side, he put the black bag on the floor on the passenger side, pushing it as far forward as possible so that it would be difficult to spot from outside. It might seem silly, but he couldn't risk a passer-by catching sight of the bag, smashing the window and stealing it. Nothing must go wrong.

He was about to open the door when he saw a movement at a window on the third floor. A little face looking out. It reminded him of the grainy picture in *Expressen*, the apartment block in Farsta.

But this time it was in colour, and it was right in front of him.

He didn't need to find out which floor Sebastian Bergman lived on.

It was the third floor, and the girl was with him.

Vanja had reported back to Torkel on the meeting at FilboCorp, and he had informed her that he had started questioning Malin Åkerblad, but had got nowhere so far. He had just put out a nationwide call for Thomas Nordgren, and was hoping to hear something soon. They promised to keep in touch as soon as anything turned up.

It was a lovely spring day, and Stockholm was busy with people strolling around, enjoying the sunshine. Vanja and Sebastian walked along Kungsgatan towards Stureplan. He still seemed irritable and out of sorts; she found it quite sweet that he couldn't let go of the meeting with Adrian Cole.

She felt that having Nicole staying with him was having a profound effect on him; the girl seemed to make him sensitive in a way that Vanja didn't recognise. She quite liked it; he was actually capable of caring about other people. It made him human, and she liked him when he was human. Those were his finest moments.

'Come back and have dinner with me. Us, I mean,' he suggested. 'We're not meeting Stefan Andrén until later.'

'He'll call when he arrives in Stockholm.'

'There you go then – come and eat with us.'

'OK. Sounds good,' she said.

At that moment she spotted him. The man she had been avoiding for months. He was standing outside Hedengren's bookshop, gazing in through the window. Perhaps she had subconsciously chosen to go via Stureplan instead of carrying on along the other side of the street, perhaps old habits had brought her here; they used to go to Hedengren's all the time. Vanja and the man she used to call Dad.

Valdemar.

He caught sight of her seconds later, so she couldn't obey her first instinct, which was to turn her head away and walk straight past him.

'Vanja?' His voice sounded weak, a faint echo of what it used to be. *Dad*, she almost replied, but she managed to change it just in time.

'Valdemar.' She stopped a few paces away from him.

Sebastian didn't seem to know what to do. Should he stay or not? How private was the situation? He moved away as if to give her space, while making sure she knew he was still there. Valdemar took a couple of tentative steps towards her.

'How are you?' he asked, wanting to say so much more.

'Fine. Working hard as usual,' she replied, keeping her tone as neutral as possible. She didn't want to be drawn into an emotional exchange. 'You know Sebastian, don't you?' she went on, gesturing towards her colleague.

'Of course. Hi,' Valdemar said, looking friendlier than was absolutely necessary.

Sebastian nodded. 'Valdemar.'

Vanja was glad Sebastian was there. Otherwise Valdemar would have made the encounter into an emotional circus, she could see that. He had aged. His skin was looser and paler, and there were wrinkles where there had been none just six months ago. But it was his eyes that had changed the most; they were lifeless. All his strength was gone, and the expression that used to make her so happy had been replaced by a resigned sorrow.

He was a pathetic, broken man.

'I've missed you,' he said. It came from the heart.

She had to admit that she took a certain amount of pleasure in his unhappiness. At least she wasn't the only one who had felt the pain of his betrayal; she wasn't the only one who had suffered.

She wasn't sure what to say next.

'I've had a lot to do,' she managed eventually. It was both true and false. 'And I wanted to be left in peace.'

That was definitely true, and it was as far as she was prepared to go, she decided. He was the one who had let her down. She had done nothing wrong.

'I understand,' he said sadly. They looked at one another in silence: one longing to say a great deal, the other desperate to get away as quickly as possible. There was no doubt who was going to win.

'I have to go,' she said, her whole body conveying the same message.

'I thought . . .' Valdemar began, then paused as if he needed to gather his strength before continuing. 'I thought you and Mum went to the graveyard.'

'We did.'

There was a faint spark of hope in Valdemar's eyes. *Now you know the truth*, they seemed to say. *We ought to be able to find a way to move on. Find our way back to one another.*

'I didn't believe her for a second,' Vanja said firmly, determined to crush that little spark.

Valdemar gave a faint nod. He looked as if he wanted to say something else, but couldn't manage it. Something that would change everything and make her stay. But nothing came out. She stared at him, then leaned closer, almost confidentially, but her voice was cold.

'An apology would have been a good start – just so you know.'

Valdemar nodded again. He understood.

'I'm sorry. There's so much I'd like to explain.'

The look in her eyes made it clear that this was too little, too late, then she walked away. Sebastian followed her, and they walked in silence towards Riddargatan.

'Things seem pretty bad between you,' he said eventually. Vanja nodded sadly. The further she got from Valdemar, the more difficult she was finding it to keep her cool.

'It's the lies that kill me,' she said, knowing that her emotions were getting the better of her. 'A whole lifetime of lies.'

'No doubt he thought he had good reason,' Sebastian said gently.

352

'I'm sure he did. But he was my father. Fathers aren't supposed to lie.'

Sebastian gazed at her thoughtfully. The encounter had taken its toll on him too.

'No, but maybe sometimes they do it because they don't know any better.'

'That's no excuse.'

He carried on gazing at her; he too looked as if he wanted to say something, but couldn't find the right words.

Billy was pacing around his hotel room. Whoever was responsible for the decor – and he was pretty sure it had been done at least fifty years ago – certainly liked pine panelling. Everything gave the impression of a rustic mountain chalet from the 1950s. According to the adverts this was Kiruna's oldest hotel, and looking around that wasn't hard to believe. Billy had checked online and had decided to introduce Gunilla to Tripadvisor so that she could avoid hotels with the lowest rating the next time she made a booking. He and Jennifer had finished what they came to do, but there was no flight home tonight, so they would have to stay over.

The last few hours had been intense.

After their visit to the bank, Billy had called Torkel who had promised to pull a few strings. Half an hour later, Ingrid Ericsson from the Economic Crimes Unit had called Billy to ask how she could help. He recognised the name and thought there was some kind of connection with Vanja, but he let it go and explained that they needed to know who owned an account with Scotiabank in Costa Rica, and whether the account was active. Ingrid explained that this could be tricky because of the laws in Costa Rica; Billy wondered if it would be easier if Scotiabank was asked to confirm a name they already had? Possibly – Ingrid couldn't make any promises, but would do her best.

Three hours later, as he and Jennifer were enjoying an early dinner and ranking superhero films, Ingrid had called back. They were in luck. Because they just wanted confirmation of a name, the Costa Rican authorities had been unusually helpful. Yes, Mr Pejok was the account holder, the account was active, and was linked to a Visa card. The latest transaction had taken place two days ago. However, Ingrid didn't know where, and the bank refused to give an address or telephone number for Mr Pejok. She had sent over the photograph of Matti from the passport the police had found at his home after his disappearance, and the bank manager had said that was definitely Mr Pejok.

Billy thanked her and ended the call. The pieces of the jigsaw fell into place one by one, revealing the picture that Billy had been expecting ever since they spoke to Anton Beringer.

Matti had given in.

Allowed himself to be bought.

Everyone and everything has a price.

Apparently Matti's was just over fifteen million kronor.

Billy's only question was how he had got to Costa Rica without a passport, if the Kiruna police had found it after his disappearance? There was a copy in the case notes on the table in his hotel room. Valid until November 2014.

Another phone call, this time to Renate who promised to look urgently into the matter. Before long, just as Jennifer was trying to persuade him to go bowling, Renate came back to him, sounding more than a little embarrassed. Matti Pejok had reported his passport stolen, and had applied for and received a new one less than a month before he went missing. When the police found a passport in his house, they assumed he hadn't gone abroad; Renate openly admitted that they had made a mistake in failing to check whether that passport was in fact the one that had been reported stolen, and cancelled. She made it clear that she was furious, partly because this showed her in a bad light as far as Riksmord was concerned, but mainly because if they had checked right away, they would have had further proof that Matti had disappeared of his own free will, which would have saved her a huge amount of unnecessary work.

Once Billy and Jennifer knew exactly what they were dealing with, they drove back up to see Per Pejok.

They had discussed the matter beforehand; Jennifer wondered if they should actually tell Per the truth. He obviously idolised his brother; did they have the right to destroy that image?

355

However, Billy was of the opinion that it had to be better to know the truth than to spend the rest of his life thinking that Matti was dead and buried somewhere, with no closure.

Billy prevailed.

Per came out to meet them this time too, and showed no sign of inviting them into the house where the dogs were still barking. He wondered why they were back, and they both saw the colour drain from his face when Billy explained what they had found out since their previous visit. He shook his head over and over again, as if he didn't for a second believe the scenario Billy had painted. He clung to the fact that they hadn't actually spoken to Matti. They didn't know for certain that he was in Costa Rica; it could be someone else. He had no suggestions as to who that might be; someone from FilboCorp?

Billy told him the bank in Costa Rica had identified Matti from a photograph.

Per still refused to accept it. Matti had been the very epitome of opposition to the mine.

Exactly, Billy had said. After all his efforts to fight the development, it would have been nigh on impossible for him to stay around after he had sold his land, so Matti had 'disappeared'.

To Costa Rica.

Yes, they were certain.

There wasn't much more to say. Billy and Jennifer were walking back to the car when Per stopped them.

'How much did he get for betraying everyone?'

Billy told him. Just over fifteen million. Per had merely nodded and gone back indoors.

As they drove away, Billy thought that Jennifer had been right. Per would probably have been better off not knowing.

Intensive hours indeed.

Billy's mobile rang. He considered ignoring it; he was sick of phones right now. But of course he took the the call, and brightened up when he saw that it was Jennifer.

'There's a firing range in the basement at the police station. Want to come?'

Surely the police would have the girl under some kind of protection; the only question was how extensive that protection might be. Did they just have people inside the apartment, or were they outside too? He peered at the cars parked nearby, but they all seemed to be empty. On the other hand he couldn't see very far; it was hard to get an overview while sitting in his own car. Feeling frustrated, he decided to check out the area on foot. He would be significantly more exposed, but he couldn't think of an alternative.

He had to know what the opposition looked like.

He opened the door and got out, taking care to make every action as calm and unremarkable as possible. He mustn't stand out or draw attention to himself in any way. He glanced at the parked cars on both sides of the street, searching for a silhouette, a movement.

Nothing so far.

He closed the car door and stretched. It was good to stand up; his back was aching from sitting still for so long. A short distance away on the other side of the street he noticed a black van. It was unmarked apart from an 'S' on the back doors, and was the vehicle most likely to contain police officers keeping the apartment block under surveillance. He needed to take a closer look. He set off, enjoying his first few steps. Decided to keep on going, stay on this side all the way up to Storgatan, then cross over. He would pass the black van on his way back. Then the plan was to continue down to Riddargatan, cross over again, and return to his own car. His focus would be on the cars on the street, and the windows of the buildings opposite number 18. If he had been tasked with protecting the girl, he would have chosen the position that gave him the best view of the apartment.

He strolled towards Storgatan. He didn't want to have to do this too many times, so it was better to take it slowly. An elderly lady came around the corner up ahead and walked towards him. He was pleased to see that every parked car appeared to be empty, and now and again he risked a glance up at the buildings on the left. It was hard to see beyond the reflective surface of the dark windows, and he realised he couldn't be sure there was no one watching.

He passed the elderly lady and ventured a pleasant little nod in her direction. She responded with a smile, which cheered him up. Stupidly. He reached Storgatan, crossed over and made his way back, focusing on the black van. It had a large tinted windscreen which was difficult to see through. He decided on a change of plan; he would cross the street again just in front of it, which would enable him to glance inside in a perfectly natural way. The pavement was empty, but a taxi turned in from Riddargatan and came towards him. Perfect. He increased his speed as he approached the van. Stepped off the kerb right in front of it and turned his head as if to check where the taxi was before crossing. This gave him a good angle to see inside the van; it appeared to be empty. Feeling satisfied, he walked back to his car before continuing down to Riddargatan. That was when he saw them.

The man he had been looking for, and the young woman who was a police officer.

They had just turned into Grev Magnigatan. Fortunately they were on the opposite pavement, and he had seen them first. He ducked behind a car, watched them through the dirty rear window. They were obviously heading for the apartment block. Perhaps they were the solution, he thought as they opened the door and went inside. He decided to wait. He had begun to glimpse the germ of a new plan. He just needed to be sure first.

★ ★ ★

'Maria! It's me!' Sebastian called out from the hallway. Vanja followed him, still a little shaken following the encounter with Valdemar. There was no reply, which worried Sebastian. He hurried into the kitchen where he found Maria sitting in silence next to Nicole, her face pale and drawn.

'Has something happened?' he said as soon as he saw them.

'She's been drawing again,' Maria said, her voice low and anxious as she met his gaze.

'Can I see?' Sebastian picked up the sheet of paper lying face down on the table.

The subject was just as devastating as the last time. Nicole was still moving back in time. This time she was standing in a kitchen, with a skilfully drawn child lying on the floor in front of her. One arm had almost been torn off at the shoulder, and lay at an unnatural angle. There was blood everywhere. The red felt-tip pen had been used so much that the final strokes on the wall were faint, as if it had run out. Maria had tears in her eyes.

'It's Georg, isn't it?'

Sebastian nodded slowly.

'She did another drawing last night – I haven't shown it to you yet.'

'Why not?'

'It was a picture of your sister.'

Maria looked devastated.

'Was it just as horrific?'

Sebastian moved over and put a hand on her shoulder.

'It might have been the wrong decision, but I wanted to protect you,' he said softly.

'I don't want to see it.'

After a moment Maria turned to her silent, motionless daughter, sitting there so small and pale.

'When is this going to end? How long will she have to be in this terrible world? It's unbearable.'

'To be perfectly honest, I don't know,' Sebastian replied, gently caressing her shoulder.

Vanja came in and picked up the drawing. Once again she was struck by Nicole's visual memory; she hadn't omitted any of the key details. Even her own bloody footprints were there.

'I've been thinking,' she said to Sebastian, waving the piece of paper. 'We have to treat this as evidence.'

'Absolutely.'

'Which means I have to take Nicole's drawings with me.'

'No problem.'

Sebastian let go of Maria's shoulder and turned to the child.

'Come on, let's try and think about something else for a while.'

He picked her up and carried her into the living room.

'Shall we see what's on TV?' he said, giving her a big hug. Vanja watched them go, Nicole's arms around his neck, returning the hug.

Perhaps it was because she had just bumped into him, or perhaps it was the way Nicole was clinging to Sebastian. She thought of Valdemar, the man she had once clung to in exactly the same way.

The firing range was smaller than the one where they used to meet back home in Stockholm, but what else could you expect up here? Five booths in a row, five targets twelve metres away. The entire room was covered in pale wood and was reminiscent of an enormous sauna, with fluorescent lights built into the ceiling. The metal door closed behind them once the station officer had informed them of the procedures and safety regulations and laid out the equipment they needed.

'Shall we make this a bit more exciting?' Jennifer said as she went over to collect two pairs of ear defenders. 'Three magazines, the one with the worst shot loses.'

'What are the stakes?' Billy asked with a smile.

'A hundred.' She came back and handed him a pair of yellow defenders.

'Done.'

Billy went into the booth and picked up the gun, then loaded it with one of the magazines in a small box on his right. A stab of pleasure ran through his body when he heard the click that told him the magazine was in place, and he cocked the gun.

He was holding a loaded weapon.

A lethal weapon.

Jennifer had already started firing. He could hear the muted sound of one shot after another, at a steady pace. Every single bullet landed in the inner circle, but it only took a second of wavering concentration. One bullet in the wrong place, and you had lost.

Billy adopted the position, raised his .40 S & W and fired the first shot. Dead centre. He repeated the procedure and rapidly fired the remaining eleven bullets.

He lowered the weapon, removed the empty magazine and reloaded.

Adopt the position, raise the gun.

After the fourth shot Billy noticed that his mind had started to wander. Not that he lost concentration; quite the reverse. It was as if he was transported forward, closer to the target; he could see it more clearly, as if it was suddenly in HD, crystal clear as it changed before his eyes.

Charles Cederkvist, illuminated by the searchlights of the helicopter hovering above.

Covered in blood and disorientated following the car crash.

Billy fired.

The first shot hit Cederkvist in the chest. A round patch of blood on his shirt that quickly spread and lost its shape. The second bullet right in the middle of the red stain. More blood. But Charles Cederkvist was still standing. The bullet in his heart should have killed him, but he was still on his feet. Billy fired again. Six more bullets drilled into his chest, and now Cederkvist's shirt was so drenched in blood that it began to drip onto the ground.

At last he collapsed.

Billy lowered his gun.

Out of breath. His senses on full alert.

He was back in the booth. The distance from the target was twelve metres once again. He inhaled deeply, then slowly exhaled through his mouth as his pulse rate gradually returned to normal. He repeated the exercise, felt his shoulders drop, then changed the magazine with practised movements.

Adopt the position, raise the gun.

This time the target changed as he took aim. A human being. His imagination usually shifted between Cederkvist and Edward Hinde, the man he had actually killed, but this was someone else. He didn't know who it was.

He didn't care.

He fired.

He thought he could hear the bullet thud into the person in front of him. Could see it splintering bone and tearing through

362

tissue on its way through the body before it exploded out through the spine, splashing blood all over the wall behind it. He fired again. Bullet after bullet, right in the middle of the white chest. Nine, ten, eleven . . . Billy inhaled, held his breath, raised the gun a fraction and placed the final bullet in the centre of the forehead. The head jerked back from the impact, the knees gave way. The person in front of him sank to the ground without making a sound.

'That last one is definitely going to cost you a hundred.'

She must have been yelling, he heard her loud and clear in spite of the ear defenders. He turned and pulled them off; Jennifer was leaning against the wall with her arms folded, a victorious smile on her lips. Billy put down the gun and took a step towards her. Without saying a word he grabbed hold of her and pressed his lips to hers.

She made a surprised little noise and he felt her stiffen before she responded to his kiss. She wrapped her arms around him as she opened her mouth and let their tongues meet. Billy pushed closer, not caring if she could feel his erection against her stomach. Her tongue deep in his mouth. He placed one hand on the back of her neck and pulled her head even closer, while the other hand slid down her back and inside her sweater, finding bare skin. She groaned quietly; she was breathing more heavily now. She freed her hands and started to unbutton his shirt without their mouths losing contact for a second. He felt her warm hands on his chest, then they moved down his belly and started to undo the belt of his jeans.

She stopped kissing him and laid her cheek against his. Her warm, shallow breaths in his ear. Their bodies so close together. Billy opened his eyes. It was as if something happened when their lips were no longer touching. He removed his hand from her skin and stepped back.

'Sorry,' he said, moving as far away as he could in the confines of the little booth.

'What's the matter?' Jennifer said, completely at a loss. 'What did I do?'

'Nothing . . . I just can't.' Billy started buttoning up his shirt, which meant he didn't have to look her in the eye.

'It was you who started kissing me . . .'

'I know, but I can't. I'm sorry.'

Jennifer bit her lower lip and slowly took a step closer to him.

'You know what they say – What happens in Kiruna stays in Kiruna.'

'That's not the way it works . . .'

Billy held up his hands defensively, looking at her with a combination of embarrassment and genuine regret.

'OK.' Jennifer stepped back.

'The thing is . . . I'm getting married,' Billy said quietly to break the uncomfortable silence that followed.

'I know.'

'If I didn't have Maya and we weren't getting married, then . . .'

'I know, you don't need to . . . I understand.'

Another silence, so compact that for the first time Jennifer could hear the fans and the faint hum of the fluorescent lights. She cleared her throat and folded her arms once more.

'It's . . .' She paused, allowing her voice to gather strength. 'It was . . . fun is the wrong word, but it's good to know that I'm not the only one who feels that way.'

'No, you're not. But I just can't.' The look in Billy's eyes was more convincing than the words he spoke.

'I know. It's OK.'

Silence once more, but this time it wasn't so uncomfortable; it was a little sad, as if a moment they had both wanted to experience was lost for ever.

'You still owe me a hundred,' Jennifer said, risking a smile.

Billy nodded. He could have suggested double or quits, tried to get their relationship back on a normal footing, back to the way it had been before they kissed, but he'd had enough of guns for one evening.

Sebastian had eventually managed to find the Children's Channel, and was sitting on the sofa with Nicole watching TV. Vanja had never thought she would see Sebastian enjoying cartoons. Maria had pulled herself together and made a start on dinner; Vanja wasn't particularly hungry, but was helping her with spaghetti bolognese. The whole situation felt weird – as if she was meeting Sebastian's new girlfriend, she thought. A nice little girlie chat in the kitchen. Soon they would sit down to eat, have a glass of wine, discuss their plans for the summer or something equally banal. It was somehow typical of Sebastian Bergman. A witness and her mother in need of a safe house had turned into a cosy family dinner.

'Have you known Sebastian long?' Maria asked as she chopped tomatoes for the sauce. Vanja turned to face her.

'Not really. Just over a year.'

'But he's not a police officer, is he?'

'No, he's a criminal psychologist.'

'That's what he said. I've never met anyone like him.'

Vanja merely nodded, feeling slightly uncomfortable with the direction the conversation was taking.

'I think he's fantastic,' Maria went on. 'I don't know what we'd have done without him. The way Nicole has taken to him . . . incredible.'

'Yes, he's good with people,' Vanja said drily, hoping Maria would pick up on the irony in her tone. No such luck.

'And so generous – letting us move in like this.'

'It's fortunate that he has a guest room.'

'We're not actually using the guest room,' Maria said shyly, glancing at Vanja out of the corner of her eye.

'Oh?'

'We're in his room. Nicole sleeps better between the two of us,' Maria clarified.

Vanja stared at her. What was the woman saying? Were they sharing a bed? It was as if Maria suddenly realised how it sounded; she blushed.

'There's nothing going on, we just sleep together. For Nicole's sake.'

'It's none of my business,' Vanja said.

'I've never met anyone like him,' Maria said again, this time in a positively loving tone.

Vanja smiled stiffly.

'No, I don't suppose you have. Excuse me, I just need to go and speak to him. There's something I have to tell him. About the case.'

Vanja walked out, leaving Maria gazing after her in surprise.

'Sebastian? A word, please.'

★ ★ ★

She dragged him into the study and closed the door. Sebastian could see that she was upset, that there was something wrong.

'What is it? What's happened?'

'What the hell are you doing?' she hissed.

'Sorry?'

'With those two out there. The people you're responsible for. The three of you are sleeping together, for fuck's sake!'

This wasn't what he had expected to come out of the cosy little chat in the kitchen. He wasn't ready for this discussion; best to shut it down as quickly as possible.

'It's nothing to do with you,' he said, making it clear that the matter was non-negotiable.

'It has, actually.' Vanja had no intention of letting him get away so easily. 'It's highly unethical. You're supposed to have a professional relationship with the witness and her mother.'

'I rescued Nicole.' Sebastian spread his arms wide and raised his voice. 'She's formed an attachment with me! I'm helping her!'

'This isn't about consideration. This is about you. Your needs.'
Vanja moved closer and lowered her voice. 'I saw you pat the girl
on the head when we left. I heard you call out to her mother
when you walked in. You invited me to dinner "with us". As if
they were your little family.'

'You couldn't be more wrong,' Sebastian objected.

'Really? You're sleeping with them!'

Sebastian was starting to lose patience. He was getting angry
now.

'You're only having a go at me because you met your father
and you can't—'

'This isn't about me,' she snapped. She wasn't going to let him
drag her personal life into the situation. She wasn't like him; she
could separate her private life from her work. 'This is about your
total lack of boundaries. You can't see the difference between
work and your personal life, between your needs and feelings
and those of other people. That's why you sleep with just about
anybody. That's why you've suddenly got yourself a new family.
You're meant to be a support, Sebastian. A fellow human
being. You're not supposed to exploit them when they're at their
most vulnerable. That's just sick, Sebastian!'

He simply stared at her. They could stand here shouting at
one another for the rest of the day, and he didn't want that. He
didn't have the energy. The sudden burst of anger ebbed away,
leaving weariness in its wake.

'I'm not exploiting them,' he said quietly but clearly. 'I'm
helping them, and if you can't see that, it's not my problem.'

Vanja took a deep breath; she was also feeling tired. They were
like two boxers at the end of a round.

'OK, let's say you're doing all this for their sake. You just want
to help. Have you told Maria that you lost your own daughter?
That Nicole is almost the same age as she would have been now?'

'No.'

'Why not?'

'Because it's not relevant. This isn't about that. It's not about
Sabine . . .'

367

He sank down on his desk chair. Sabine pulled him down, made him defenceless. Vanja realised how right she had been. She tried to soften her tone; she wanted to make him understand, not just berate him.

'You lost your family in the most terrible way. The person you are, everything you do, must somehow be affected by that moment. If you can't see that this is about Sabine, then you're blind. And you're not, Sebastian. I know that.'

He didn't answer for a long time; he just gazed at her.

'If you're really fond of those two out there, then be professional. In every way. They need your help. You have to be there for them. They're not supposed to be there for you. Do you understand? Nicole is not Sabine.'

After a brief silence he straightened up and let out a long breath.

'I understand. I understand that you're wrong.'

He got up and walked out. She watched him go; she was about to follow him when her mobile rang. It was Stefan Andrén; he could meet her right away, if she wasn't doing anything more important.

She definitely wasn't.

The door of the apartment block opened and the man in the car sat up straight. The bottom of his back was aching. He didn't even want to think about how long he'd been sitting here watching the place.

You do what you have to do.

It was her. Vanja.

Alone, walking purposefully away. What did that mean? Was Sebastian Bergman the only person in the apartment with the girl and her mother?

He desperately needed to pee.

They had arrived together, Vanja and Sebastian, but not to relieve other officers as far as he could see. People had left the building since they turned up, but no one that he instinctively felt was a police officer.

Could it be that they had no security at all in place?

Perhaps it wasn't so unlikely after all. They had moved the girl from Torsby to a safe address in Stockholm, which had turned out to be anything but safe. *Expressen* had found her, then after the front-page exposure she and her mother had moved in with Sebastian Bergman. Not to another safe address. Could that be because they didn't entirely trust their own organisation? Were they worried about leaks?

God, he really needed a pee.

But he was reluctant to leave the car. He had no idea where there might be a public toilet in the area, and he couldn't really go and piss in someone's doorway. He suddenly noticed the empty Coke bottle next to the black bag in front of the passenger seat.

Vanja reached Strandvägen and turned right. The Radisson Blu Strand Hotel, where Stefan Andrén had already checked in and was waiting for her in the lobby, was on the other side of Nybroviken, no more than ten minutes' walk from Sebastian's apartment.

She passed Svenskt Tenn and glanced in through the window. She didn't own a single thing from there; most of the items they sold were well above her price range. Anna and Valdemar had a tray with Josef Frank elephants on it that had always been used to serve her with breakfast in bed when she was a little girl, and two glass lamps, also with Josef Frank motifs on the shades. They might have more; she didn't know, and to be honest it annoyed her that she was thinking about them now. Wasn't it bad enough that she had bumped into Valdemar earlier on? Couldn't she even walk past a shop without thinking about her lying 'parents'? She was about to cross the road and the tramlines so that she could walk along the side of the street with no shops when her phone rang; it was Torkel.

'Hi, how's it going?'

'Good, I think. I'm just on my way to Stefan Andrén's hotel to have a chat with him.'

'That's great, because we're more or less back to square one.' There was no mistaking the disappointment in Torkel's voice. 'We got hold of Thomas Nordgren.'

'Where was he?'

'He was stopped by customs at Kastrup, and when they ran his details they saw that we were looking for him and called us.'

'What was he doing at Kastrup?'

'He'd just flown back from Turkey. With a little extra baggage in the form of cannabis.'

'For personal use, or to sell?'

'A bit of both, it seems. His finances aren't in particularly good shape, as we know, so I think he was going to sell some, then smoke the rest in the hope of forgetting that he's up shit creek without a paddle.' Torkel paused briefly. 'But that's not why I called.'

Vanja didn't reply; she had a good idea what he was going to say. If they were back to square one, that could mean only one thing.

'Nordgren flew to Turkey on the Tuesday before the murders,' Torkel said, confirming her suspicions.

'So it's not him.'

'It's not him.'

Vanja stopped and sighed deeply. 'Does that mean we have to let Åkerblad go as well?'

'Already done.'

Those two words made it very clear that this was one of the aspects of recent developments that pained him most. Vanja sighed. Back to square one was an understatement. They were in an even worse position. They would have to work hard to make it as far as square one.

'I'll ring you when I've spoken to Andrén,' she said. She ended the call and set off again. She hoped for his sake that Stefan Andrén had something useful to contribute.

371

The man turned and placed the bottle containing the dark yellow liquid on the back seat. He had been surprised at how undignified it felt to piss in a bottle in a car, and he didn't want a reminder.

Instead he returned to his speculation about the apartment block he was watching.

If the police didn't trust their own organisation, then presumably they wanted as few people as possible to know where the girl was.

Two officers on an eight-hour shift in the apartment. Six officers per day. Not the same people every day, for various reasons. That meant ten or twelve people, all of whom could tell God knows how many others that they were guarding the little girl who had witnessed those terrible murders in Torsby.

The more people who knew, the greater the danger of leaks.

Would they risk someone revealing her hiding place, deliberately or otherwise?

After all, he had already tried to kill her twice. He wasn't sure if they knew about the Bear's Cave or not, but they were certainly aware of the incident in the hospital.

The more he thought about it, the more convinced he felt.

There was no extra security inside the building. No armed police officers to protect them. Now Vanja had left, there were only three people in the apartment.

The psychologist, the mother, the girl.

Unarmed, presumably.

Time to do what had to be done.

He leaned forward, picked up the black bag and placed it on the seat beside him. A quick glance around told him that the street was deserted. He unzipped the bag and took out his Serbu Super-Shorty, slipped some extra ammunition in his pocket. The gun was already loaded with four cartridges, but you never knew. He didn't want to risk being unable to complete his mission because he couldn't fire enough shots.

One more glance at the empty street, then he clipped the weapon to the inside of his coat and got out of the car. He locked the door and crossed the street, trying to look as natural as possible. He adjusted his coat as he walked towards the door. An anonymous man paying an ordinary visit to an apartment in Östermalm. Nothing unusual, nothing to attract attention. He could do this, he told himself as he reached the door and pushed down the handle. Nothing happened. He pushed again, then thought that perhaps the door opened outwards, so he pulled instead. Still nothing.

Of course. An entry code.

Fucking Stockholm bastards.

He looked at the little box on the wall with its ten shiny buttons. No entryphone. He needed a code, and he didn't have it.

The alternative was to persuade someone to let him in.

All he could do was wait. Again.

Stefan Andrén was sitting on one of the brown sofas by the big windows in the lobby when Vanja arrived. He got to his feet as soon as he saw her, and they shook hands. Jeans, shirt and jacket. Short, neatly cut hair, clean-shaven. If Vanja hadn't known his age she would have thought he was younger than his forty-five years. There was a glass of beer on the table in front of him, and as they sat down he asked if she would like something. Vanja considered a glass of wine, but she was working after all, plus she hadn't eaten since lunch, so she declined.

'It's about the land you own up in Värmland,' she began, determined to keep the conversation as short as possible.

'What about it?'

'How long is it since you were there?'

Stefan shrugged and reached for his beer.

'I never go there. It's just . . . forest.'

'A mining company proposed a development in the area a few years ago . . .' Vanja went on, but broke off as Stefan snorted and nearly choked on his beer. He swallowed, coughed and put down the glass with a smile that was hard to interpret.

'Yes, I know. That bloody mine. I have to say I was really pleased when the whole thing fell through.'

'What do you mean? You agreed to sell your land.'

'The land I had left, yes.'

Vanja remained silent, making it clear that she wanted to know more.

'Frank came to me, it must be . . . seven or eight years ago wanting to buy land from me.'

374

'Frank? Frank Hedén?'

Stefan nodded. 'I inherited the land, I don't really care about it, so I was happy to sell to him.'

'How much?'

'Quite a lot. He paid me a fair amount of money, but he also conned me.'

'In what way?'

'Nine months later the mining company turned up and started looking at the area. There was talk of selling, at a much better price than I got from Frank, let me tell you. He would have made a fortune.'

Vanja tried to process what she had just heard, marrying it with what she already knew about the events surrounding the mine in Torsby. From her expression, Stefan assumed she hadn't really understood.

'He must have know about the plans for the mine,' he clarified. 'Why else would he have suddenly wanted to buy my land?'

'Excuse me.' Vanja stood up and left the lobby, taking out her phone as she walked. Torkel answered immediately.

'Have we looked at Frank Hedén's finances?'

'Yes – why?'

Vanja went over what she had just been told; she could hear Torkel shuffling through his papers. She remembered the feeling she had had at Frank's house when they talked about Jan Ceder's shotgun: that something wasn't quite right. She hadn't pursued it; perhaps she should have done. Trusted her gut instinct.

'He's up to his ears in debt,' Torkel said. 'Eight years ago he borrowed more than the house and the land were worth.'

'To buy Stefan Andrén's land.' A statement, not a question.

'Yes, but he's also borrowed a lot more on that land over the years,' Torkel went on; Vanja got the feeling he was reading the notes as he spoke to her.

'So what happens when Frank dies? He has cancer . . .'

'There will be virtually nothing left apart from debts. The bank owns more or less everything.'

'He said his friends would sell the land when he was gone, that it would ensure his son's future care. He said there would be plenty of money.'

'There won't,' Torkel said drily. 'Unless FilboCorp buys it at a premium.'

'And in order for them to do that, the Carlstens had to disappear.'

Vanja thought about what she had seen scribbled on the whiteboard in the little office in Torsby. Male, over thirty, local resident, personal connection to the Carlstens, intelligent, planned the murders, believed his hand was forced.

'He fits Sebastian's profile on every single point.' She couldn't hide her excitement.

'We'll bring him in.'

'He's gone to Västerås,' Vanja remembered. Her next comment came without her even needing to think about it. 'At least that's what he said.'

How long had he been outside this bloody door?

A number of people had walked past, and he had the strangest feeling that each one looked at him with growing suspicion.

Was it odd, standing there waiting?

Was he drawing attention to himself?

Surely not. He might be meeting a friend who just happened to live here. Nothing strange about that. Or didn't people wait in the street in Stockholm?

Frank glanced at his watch. How many people lived in this section of the block? No one had come out or gone in during the last twenty minutes. The door remained firmly closed.

He could feel the rage beginning to grow inside him.

It was a door.

He had dealt with so much up to now.

Was an ordinary brown double door with three panes of glass in each side going to be his downfall? For a moment he toyed with the idea of simply smashing the middle pane. It would be quick. A sharp blow with his elbow, reach in and turn the lock, open the door. Ten seconds. But he didn't dare. Someone would hear; the sound of breaking glass might be worse than a car alarm in this upmarket area. Curious faces might appear at every window as soon as the first shards hit the ground.

But he couldn't stay here.

The more uncomfortable he felt, the more unnatural he looked. A little walk might be a good idea, but he mustn't go too far. What if someone emerged from the apartment block when he was thirty, forty, fifty metres away? What would he do then? Run down the street like a lunatic and ask them to hold the door open, as if he were trying to catch the elevator in some American movie? They would definitely notice that, and remember it.

But he couldn't stay here. His rage continued to grow. This wasn't good. If you acted when you were angry, it was easy to make mistakes. It was time to move. Walk off his impatience and irritation. He couldn't afford any mistakes. He set off slowly towards Storgatan, then turned the corner and kept on going. Decided to go all the way around the block, and if no one opened the door for him within five minutes of his return, he would smash the window.

He felt better now.

He had a plan.

Torkel was standing in the little room contemplating the white-board on the wall. He had moved the picture of Frank Hedén into the middle; he studied it closely. It had been taken before the cancer sank its claws into him; he looked strong and pur-poseful. Sharp eyes beneath the cropped steel-grey hair, which made Torkel think of an elite soldier. A hint of stubble on the firm, well-defined chin. If Frank was the guilty party and that picture was published, anyone who saw it would say he was lethal.

And right now everything suggested that Frank was their man.

Most importantly, he had a motive. Money, of course, but combined with the short time Frank had left, it became even stronger. He had to put his house in order, safeguard his son's future, make sure his poor financial decisions weren't the only thing he left behind. However, the other pieces of the puzzle had also fallen into place.

He knew Jan Ceder. They weren't sure of the details of the relationship between the two men, but Frank had admitted that their paths had crossed from time to time. It didn't require a great stretch of the imagination to assume that he had turned a blind eye to the odd breach of the hunting regulations in exchange for the loan of a shotgun.

Frank was also the person who had come to the police and told them about the car he had seen in the forest near the Bear's Cave – the Mercedes. Now it was easy to see why: he had wanted to give a perfectly logical explanation as to why he was in the area, in case someone else turned up at the station and said they had seen *Frank's* car in the forest. Following that particular lead had also taken up time and resources that could have been used to nail Frank instead of chasing after a non-existent car.

Torkel didn't know Frank's shoe size, but he would have put money on 44. He would have the answer very soon; after Vanja's phone call he had sent Fabian to carry out a search of Frank's house that would make yesterday's searches look like a passing glance.

What else did they have?

Torkel thought for a while, but couldn't come up with anything. However, Erik knew Frank. Perhaps not well enough to know his shoe size, but he should be able to contribute something.

He left the room and went along to Erik's office; Erik was just putting down the phone when Torkel walked in.

'Frank never checked into the Best Western in Västerås,' Erik said.

'So he didn't go there.'

'Presumably not.'

'Do you really suspect Frank?'

Torkel spun around to see Pia sitting at one of the other desks. He gave Erik a look, raising his eyebrows.

'She's waiting for me. We're going home together,' Erik explained in response to the unspoken question.

'Do you really suspect Frank?' Pia repeated.

'There are circumstances surrounding Frank Hedén which are a cause for concern,' Torkel said, turning to face her. 'The fact that he isn't where he said he was going to be is one of them.'

'There's probably a simple explanation. Have you called him?'

'Not yet.'

'Would you like me to do it?'

Torkel stared at her with a look of complete incomprehension on his face.

'We've known each other for a long time,' Pia clarified.

'Frank used to do Pia's job,' Erik interjected. 'He's been something of a mentor to her.'

'I could ask him to come in and clear all this up if you like – it's obviously a misunderstanding.'

Torkel didn't respond right away; Pia clearly wasn't impressed. 'What's the problem?'

'I'm not sure I want to warn him,' Torkel said honestly. 'If he finds out we're looking for him, he might take off.'

'He's sixty years old, he has terminal cancer and a disabled adult son at home,' Pia replied acidly. 'Besides which he's innocent.'

Torkel didn't necessarily agree with her final assertion, but the rest made sense. An elderly man under a death sentence with a son who was completely dependent on him: not exactly the most likely person to do a runner. He nodded to Pia.

'OK, but I want to hear the entire conversation.'

'I'll put it on speakerphone,' Pia promised, reaching for her mobile.

'Just tell him we want to speak to him – don't say why,' Torkel insisted, feeling his body tense as the phone began to ring.

For once he had had a bit of luck.

He was only a few metres away from the door when it opened and a young couple with a buggy came out. Frank lengthened his pace and reached the door just before it closed. He smiled and nodded at the couple to indicate that he really did belong here, but they showed no interest in him whatsoever. He stood in the foyer and looked around. He spotted the light switch and pressed it, then checked the list of residents just to make sure he had got it right.

He had.

Bergman, third floor.

He slipped his hand under his coat and felt the gun with the tips of his fingers. Lift or stairs? He opted for the stairs; that would give him a little more time to prepare himself. Should he ring the doorbell? Would they answer if he did? Frank reached the first floor and saw that most apartments were equipped with a spyhole. Sebastian Bergman had never seen Frank, and it was unlikely that he would open the door to a stranger, bearing in mind who was in the apartment with him. Frank was suddenly overwhelmed by a wave of exhaustion. He was going to have to force his way through another door somehow. It had taken him almost half an hour last time, and he had got in by sheer luck. How was he going to tackle this one?

His phone rang.

Frank gave a start and fumbled in his pocket, hoping the sudden noise wouldn't attract curious eyes to every single spyhole in the building.

He grabbed his mobile and checked the display.

Pia calling.

He hesitated; the timing couldn't have been worse, and if it had been anyone else he would have rejected it immediately. But this was Pia. The woman, the person he regarded as his best friend. So many years together, both in the political arena and on a personal level. They had always been there for one another; they had gone through so much together. Perhaps it was a sign, the fact that she was ringing at this particular moment? He took the call.

'Hi,' he said as quietly as he could. He turned and set off back down the stairs; he would be happier talking in the foyer, where there were no doors with people lurking behind them.

'Hi, how are you?' Pia asked in a perfectly normal tone of voice, which felt slightly bizarre given what he was about to do.

'Fine . . . Listen, this isn't very convenient.'

'Where are you?'

Frank thought fast. Erik knew he was supposed to be going to Västerås. Frank couldn't imagine that the Flodins spent their evenings discussing his plans, but there was a distinct possibility that his trip had come up in conversation, so the simplest thing was to stick to the story.

'I'm in Västerås.'

At the police station in Torsby, Pia looked up at her husband and Torkel, who might have been mistaken when he thought he saw a shadow of doubt pass across her face. He nodded to her.

'I'm at the police station,' she said. 'Erik's here, and so is the head of Riksmord. They want you to come in for a chat.'

Silence.

'Frank?'

'What . . .' A lengthy silence; Torkel wondered if they had lost the connection. 'What about?' Frank said eventually.

Pia glanced up at Torkel again; another nod.

'The Carlstens and all that business with the mine . . .'

Silence. Torkel thought he heard a deep sigh on the other end of the line. A weary, resigned sigh.

'Come in and talk to them, Frank,' Pia pleaded.

'I think it's too late for that.'

'What do you mean, too late?'

'I think you know.'

If Pia had had any doubts, Torkel could see that she was now convinced of Frank's guilt. All the strength that naturally emanated from her seemed to disappear in a second. She slumped down, struggling to hold back the tears.

In Stockholm Frank did almost the same thing, although he allowed his suddenly heavy body to drop onto the cold steps, and didn't attempt to hide the fact that he was crying.

'I did it for Hampus,' he said quietly.

'So think about him now,' Pia replied.

Frank didn't say anything. Hampus was all he ever thought about. Everything he had done was for his son. Everything. He had crossed boundaries he had never in his wildest dreams thought he would cross, all for Hampus's sake.

Never thought he could cross.

But he could. Look at him now. A few minutes ago he had been utterly determined to kill three more people, one of whom was a child.

Because he was thinking of Hampus.

Because he was going to have to leave him far too soon, and because there was no one else who would care about the boy in the same way. Unless they were paid to care. It was money that counted. Everything could be bought, you got what you paid for, and he had no intention of settling for anything less than the best when it came to his son's future care. But when he found out that his days were numbered there was no money, because there wasn't going to be a mine. Because the Carlstens refused to sell.

So the Carlstens had to be removed.

For Hampus's sake.

You do what you have to do. Life wasn't fair.

'Think about your son,' Pia said again, and Frank was struck by how gentle she sounded. That wasn't like her . . . 'Think about what could happen to him. And do the right thing.'

Frank didn't even bother to respond. What was he supposed to say? What could he say that would change or improve the situation in which he found himself? Nothing.

'Frank, you know what I can do.' Her voice, a mixture of self-assurance and despair. 'I can help you.'

Suddenly he was overcome with a feeling of emptiness, and let the hand holding the phone drop.

'Do you understand what I'm saying, Frank?' he heard faintly.

Yes, he understood. He understood perfectly.

The brave little girl and her mother would live.

He had had enough. It was over.

The relief at not having to get past that locked door on the third floor. Not having to take more lives.

Not having to take the lives of others.

He reached inside his coat and unhooked the gun.

The shot that echoed through the stone stairwell really did attract curious eyes to every single spyhole.

It was Maria who wanted to attend the memorial service in Torsby, and in a moment of weakness Sebastian had offered to buy a dress for Nicole. He had gone to the only department store he knew: NK on Hamngatan. According to the store guide by the escalator, children's clothing was on the fourth floor. It was still early, so there weren't many customers, and the place felt empty.

At first Maria had thought of coming with him, but Nicole was still affected by the incident in the stairwell, and they decided that the memorial service would be enough of a challenge for her. Otherwise she seemed to be getting better every day, although she still wasn't talking, which both pleased and worried him. Sebastian had tried to talk them out of the service, but Pia Flodin had managed to convince Maria that it would be a chance for everyone to work through their grief together. According to Pia it would be a dignified and peaceful occasion led by the Bishop of Karlstad and herself; there would be thousands of candles.

Pia had been very persuasive, and Sebastian could see why the Social Democrats regarded her as a valuable resource. She was committed, personable and persistent, but she knew exactly when to back off and switch to a softer, more emotional approach. He had no doubt that he could have taken her on, but he had chosen not to, even though he felt that Nicole would be better served by peace and quiet. He had more important things to focus on than some pseudo-sentimental crap in Värmland.

He had started to worry about what was going to happen next.

Frank Hedén was dead. Maria could decide to move back home at any moment, now that the threat to Nicole's safely had gone and the case was closed. How long could he keep insisting that her daughter needed him, from a purely therapeutic point of view? What would happen when Nicole's life had to get back to normal? When she had to return to school? When she started talking? What would happen then? The very thought of the apartment without Nicole and Maria was terrifying.

Vanja had been both right and wrong. He wasn't playing at families, not in any way – Nicole and Maria *were* his family. They had grown close in a very short time. Maria had allowed him to share in every aspect of their lives.

Right or wrong. Crazy or completely normal.

Emotionally, they were his family. That was the truth.

Frank had done everything for his son. All those terrible things, all those deaths, in a bizarre attempt to protect and provide for the person he loved most. However wrong it may have been, Sebastian had a certain amount of understanding for the motive and the driving force behind his actions.

A human being can do a great deal for those he loves.

A great deal.

He had even refrained from seducing Maria. A few times he had been on the point of falling into his old ways, and she had started to approach him over the past few days, but he had controlled himself. It wasn't that he didn't want to sleep with her – quite the reverse – but he had a feeling that sex could destroy what they were slowly building up. That it might somehow make her think this wasn't what he really wanted, in the long term.

Maria had kissed him on the cheek before he went shopping.

Nicole had given him a hug.

However, sometimes he struggled with the idea that this was just a fantasy. A game, as Vanja had hinted. A surrogate for Sabine. It didn't feel that way; emotions couldn't lie like that. But he needed to maintain the change; he couldn't just take what he wanted as he usually did. He had to give back as well, to be there for someone other than himself.

Become a better man.

Nicole and Maria made him a better man.

He wandered aimlessly among the children's clothes. There were lots of different labels and designers; most things seemed overworked and overcomplicated, and it took a while before he spotted a simple black dress with white lace. It was on a mannequin, hidden away in a corner. It would be perfect for Nicole. He searched for the right size; 146, Maria had said. He realised he was enjoying himself. Buying a dress for a little girl. There was something about holding it up, imagining how it would look. It was easy to imagine that this was the kind of ordinary thing dads did for their children.

He paid and went down the escalator. He didn't have much time; Pia would be coming to pick them up soon. She was in the city anyway for some business relating to the Social Democrats, and had offered them a lift to Torsby.

He wondered if he should inform the rest of the team about his plans to go to the memorial service as part of the family, but he quickly rejected the idea. None of them would understand. One day, perhaps, when they realised that Maria and Nicole were a genuine and important part of his life, but it would be a while before that day came. It made no difference to him; with respect, he couldn't give a damn what any of them thought.

Never had done.

Never would.

This was his journey, no one else's, and he intended to enjoy every single moment of it.

He decided to surprise Maria with a beautiful piece of jewellery. Something a little too expensive – Georg Jensen, perhaps. Something that would show her how special she was to him.

It was a long time since he had bought a present for a woman. He couldn't even remember when, but it must have been many years ago.

For Lily, probably.

But now it was time to move on.

388

Vanja was sitting at her desk, sorting out the case notes. Most of them would be archived, but there were a few duplicates that could be thrown away. She already had a substantial pile in front of her, and Billy and Torkel hadn't yet passed everything on.

Erik Flodin had just sent in a final report on the search of Frank Hedén's property, which had been carried out shortly after Frank had shot himself. Hampus had already been registered as a permanent resident at the care facility where he had periodically stayed on a temporary basis, and social services were considering whether he ought to be relocated. He would probably never see his childhood home again. Vanja couldn't help wondering whether Hampus knew how far his ailing father had gone to give him a reasonable life, how many lives he had destroyed in order to make sure his son would be all right when Frank was gone. She hoped his disability meant that he didn't have to experience the guilt that he would otherwise have to live with for the rest of his life. The report was well written; Erik and Fabian seemed to have conducted a very thorough search of the house and surrounding area. A short distance away they had found the burned remains of a Graninge boot in a ditch. Parts of the sole were still visible, and Fabian had been able to confirm that it was a size 44. The Internet history on Frank's computer showed that he had spent a lot of time following the investigation, and that he had been online for almost four hours on the day after the Carlsten murders. He had been meticulous. An ice-cold killer who had followed their every move, skilfully dealing with any information they made public. If Vanja hadn't met up with Stefan Andrén, Nicole would probably have been dead by now. Maria and Sebastian too. That was how narrow the margins had been.

She glanced over at the desk Sebastian normally used. She hadn't seen him since she left the apartment to go and meet Andrén, and they hadn't exactly parted as friends. But if he had died that night, she would have missed him.

Very much.

More than anyone else in the team.

Probably more than anyone else in the world.

He didn't have many friends, Sebastian Bergman, she knew that. People came and went; no one stayed around for long. Everyone was dispensable.

Apart from her.

They had been working together for about a year, and against all the odds they had been good friends – for some of the time at least. For normal people a year was no time at all, but when it came to Sebastian, it was almost an eternity. And in spite of the fact that they were in the middle of a disagreement right now, there was one thing she was sure of: they would find their way back to one another.

That was how their relationship worked, because she liked him. When he was honest. When he didn't mess things up for himself. When he wasn't being an idiot.

Which was exactly what he was doing right now, unfortunately.

Nicole's drawings, which Vanja had brought from Sebastian's apartment, were on top of one of the piles that still had to be sorted. She picked them up; they were so powerful and emotional that she was as deeply affected every time she looked at them. Trapped vulnerability, captured in a few simple strokes of a felt-tip pen. Nicole might not be able to talk, but she could certainly express herself. It felt wrong to archive them; they were therapeutic and personal, not something that should be stored away for years. She would return them to Sebastian; he could decide what to do with them. After all, he was the one who had enabled Nicole to go all the way back to the house in her memory. He was very good at his job, but he had no idea where the boundaries lay, where his role as a psychologist ended and his personal life took over. That was his fundamental problem, the lack of boundaries.

He needed help, she could see that. She was his friend. Sometimes friends had to do things that at first glance might seem unkind, but it was for his own good. And for Nicole and Maria's.

Vanja put the drawings in her bag. She would return them in person, and take the opportunity to pass on a few home truths at the same time.

Nicole was sitting in the bedroom wrapped in two big fluffy towels. Maria had given her a bath and washed her hair. Pia was going to pick them up, and Maria was starting to get a little stressed over whether they would be ready on time. It might have been best if they had chosen a dress that Nicole already owned, rather than Sebastian rushing off to buy something new, but he had insisted and she had appreciated the gesture.

Nicole smelled delicious, a mixture of bubble bath and shampoo, and Maria started to dry her long hair. She loved looking after her little girl; there was something liberating about doing everyday things together.

Simple tasks, reminiscent of another time.

Before everything that had happened.

'I love you, Nicole,' she suddenly felt compelled to say. Those were probably the words she had used most since she got her daughter back, the only words she had found that could act as a bridge between then and now. 'Mummy loves you, never forget that,' she added. Nicole nodded and gazed up at her. She was so innocent, so young, but the look in her eyes had aged, become more troubled, more grown up. It was hardly surprising; Nicole had seen people she loved die. Even if she couldn't put it into words at the moment, she saw the world differently now that she knew how fragile and fleeting life was.

Maria leaned forward and gently kissed Nicole's forehead. Her skin was so soft, so smooth. She smelled of life, of the future. Maria wanted to stay exactly where she was, hoping and believing that everything was going to be all right.

It would be all right. She had decided. She was going to sort out her life, change her job and spend more time at home. Not only for Nicole's sake, but for her own. She hadn't been ready for a child when Nicole came along, and she had tried to cope with her work, her commitment to underdeveloped countries and her difficult relationships while fulfilling her role as a single mother. She didn't think she had been a bad mum, definitely not, but she could have been around a lot more. She could have shifted her priorities.

And that was what she was going to do now.

Perhaps Sebastian would be a part of their future. He wasn't like the other men she had met. He was serious. Decent. And perhaps most importantly of all, he was honest.

The way he had taken care of Nicole was fantastic. None of her previous boyfriends had shown such love for her daughter. It was hard not to be moved by that. Admittedly he was a little older, but she found his manliness attractive, and he was intelligent and funny. Plus she trusted him. The first time they met she had been falling apart, and he had been an enormous support, without trying to exploit the situation in any way. However, they had grown close; they had begun to touch one another.

To hold hands. A gentle pat here, a hug there.

She liked it. She could imagine going further. She smiled to herself; what if something lasting, something good could come out of this tragedy?

It wasn't impossible. She was tired of being alone, and of running after men who were complex, dishonest and difficult. They were usually married, and she ended up having to make demands, while still ending up playing second fiddle. Sebastian was different. He always had time, and he asked very little of her. It was a long time since she had felt so secure with anyone.

A long time since she had trusted someone so completely.

She passed Nicole a blue T-shirt and a pair of velour sweatpants. Hopefully Sebastian wouldn't be too long with the new dress.

She took the wet towels to the bathroom and hung them up. The doorbell rang; she stiffened. Sebastian had his own keys, of course, and never rang the bell. He simply walked in and called out to them.

There was no sound of a key in the lock. The bell rang again. Maria felt her pulse rate increase, although logically she knew there was no danger. Frank Hedén was dead; the threat to her daughter no longer existed.

She took a deep breath, tiptoed into the hallway and peered through the spyhole.

It was Vanja, Sebastian's colleague.

Maria opened the door, trying to look pleased, even though she thought Vanja had behaved very oddly the last time they met. Vanja smiled at her.

'Hi.'

'Sebastian isn't home,' Maria said.

'That doesn't matter – it's actually you I've come to see.'

Maria looked at Vanja in surprise.

'Me? Why?'

'If that's OK.'

Maria nodded and let her in. Closed the door. They stared at one another for a moment.

'I don't really know where to start,' Vanja said.

★ ★ ★

Torkel pulled in by the kerb and switched off the engine.

He leaned forward and looked up at the familiar facade. Was this a bad idea? Probably. What was he actually expecting to get out of the visit? What could they say that hadn't already been said? He glanced at the bag on the passenger seat; it contained two portions of sushi. He could eat one in the office, throw the other away. But no, he would regret it if he didn't go through with this. Somehow it had been in his mind ever since yesterday evening, when he dropped off his eldest daughter.

She was at college out in Johanneshov these days, studying catering and nutrition at the Stockholm Hotel & Restaurant

College. She had decided she wanted to be a chef, or rather her previous school had made the decision for her. She had started a course at the John Bauer school, talking vaguely about 'something to do with tourism', but the place had gone bust. Thirty-six schools had closed down overnight, and almost 11,000 students had been forced to find new places. The Hotel & Restaurant College had stepped up to help resolve the emergency, and taken a lot of students from Elin's old school. She couldn't get onto the hotel and tourism course as she had hoped, and had to settle for catering and nutrition instead. However, according to Yvonne, their daughter had never shown so much interest in her studies as she had since the transfer. She had virtually moved into the kitchen at home, and cooked dinner at least four nights a week.

The students ran a restaurant at the college, and yesterday Torkel had gone there for a three-course meal; Elin had been involved in the preparation. Before the food was served he had been worried that he would have to come up with suitably flattering comments – after all they were only seventeen-year-olds running the kitchen – but he had been pleasantly surprised. It had been absolutely delicious.

He had driven Elin home afterwards and thanked her for the evening once again. Before she got out of the car, she turned to him as if something had just occurred to her.

'Have they told you they're getting married?'

'Who?' It took a second before Torkel realised who she meant. 'Mum and Christoffer?'

Elin nodded.

'When?'

'I don't know, but they're engaged.'

'When did that happen?'

'Easter Saturday. I cooked them a special dinner to celebrate their engagement.'

Torkel merely nodded, waiting to see what emotions would come bubbling up. Would he feel let down? Not because Yvonne was engaged, but because he hadn't been informed, neither before nor after.

Would he feel a sense of loss? Jealousy?

None of the above. He just felt pleased for Yvonne, and both Elin and Vilma really seemed to like Christoffer, so presumably he was pleased for them too.

Yes, he was pleased, but Elin interpreted his silence as an indication that he was downhearted.

'Are you upset? I said she ought to tell you . . .'

'No, no, I'm not upset at all. You know I want nothing more than for all three of you to be happy.' Elin nodded. Torkel placed a hand on her arm, determined to convince her. 'Give Mum my best wishes, and congratulations to both of them.'

'I will. Thanks for coming, Dad.'

She leaned over and kissed him on the cheek, then got out and walked towards the door. Torkel watched her go. She was so tall. Almost grown up. Well on the way to making a life of her own; he hoped he would have the good fortune to continue to be a part of it.

She turned and waved, then she was gone. He waited a moment before starting the car. He really was happy for Yvonne and the girls.

But happiness doesn't last for ever. An old acquaintance was waiting to take over.

Loneliness.

More tangible when others found a way out.

It had still been there when he woke up this morning. When he drove to work. It hadn't gone away in spite of the fact that there was plenty to do following Frank Hedén's suicide, and tying up the loose ends of the case in Torsby. There was also the usual pile of admin that had been neglected while he was away, and was now demanding his attention.

But he had to have lunch, after all.

So did Ursula.

She wasn't expecting him, but she wasn't likely to throw him out, was she?

He picked up the bag of sushi and got out of the car.

★ ★ ★

She seemed genuinely pleased to see him, and invited him in. When he wondered if he was disturbing her, she told him that the most exciting thing that had happened in her life in the last week was seeing who went out in the quarter-final of *Let's Dance*, so he was more than welcome.

They set out lunch in the living room, and he told her about the case even though she already knew most of it. She thanked him for keeping her updated throughout; it had saved her from going completely crazy.

He could hardly stop staring at her.

The new eye looked fantastic.

She looked fantastic.

Everything had changed. He couldn't get enough of her.

He didn't want to leave. He wanted to stay there all day. He wanted them to open a bottle of wine, and when he said he would leave the car and take a taxi home, he wanted her to say she had a better idea. Why didn't he stay over?

But lunch was finished. He had a job to do. Next on the agenda was a meeting with the National Police Board at three o'clock; Torkel had to come up with proposals for making savings within Riksmord. It was the same for every department; last year the board had overspent its budget by over 170 million kronor.

'What are you thinking about?'

Torkel gave a start. Ursula was smiling at him, an enquiring expression on her face. He could hardly say 'the departmental budget', even if it was the truth.

He gazed at her.

She was so beautiful, and he really did love her. He remembered why he had come. The emptiness. The loneliness. Which might, just possibly, be easier to live with if he knew he hadn't been rejected. Replaced. Dismissed as second best.

He had to hear it from her.

'There's something I've been wondering for a long time—' he began.

'What I was doing at Sebastian's place that evening,' she interrupted him. He looked at her in surprise and nodded. 'I was having dinner,' she said simply, as if she had been waiting to tell him ever since he arrived, or perhaps even longer.

'Just dinner?'

'Dinner, and then I got shot before I could drink my coffee.'

'Sorry.'

She leaned forward and took his hand.

'The fact that you and I aren't together has nothing to do with Sebastian. It's to do with me.'

'But you were there because you prefer him to me.' Torkel could hear how it sounded: as if he were a sulky little boy, jealous and bitter. Ursula gave him a warm smile and shook her head.

'I was there because everything is more straightforward with Sebastian. I know it sounds unlikely, but in some ways it's much, much simpler with him.'

'He only wants one thing.'

'That's true, but for me it's . . .' She paused, bit her lip, chose her words with care. 'I'm not going to marry you and live happily ever after, Torkel, but that's because I don't think I can live happily ever after with anyone. I can't give other people what they need in a relationship.'

'Can't I make that decision?'

'They can't give me what I need either.'

Torkel nodded. That was harder to argue against. He could say that he was willing to do anything. The relationship could be entirely on her terms, if only there was a chance, the tiniest possibility, that she might change her mind. But he knew that kind of grovelling wouldn't go down well, so he kept quiet and got to his feet.

'Do you have to go back to work?'

'I've got a budget meeting with the board at three.'

'I just feel we haven't quite finished.'

'I can easily postpone the meeting,' Torkel said quickly, getting out his phone.

It was important to get one's priorities right.

Sebastian was a little stressed when he arrived home; it had taken longer than expected to choose a piece of jewellery for Maria. He immediately realised that something was wrong; Maria's bags were in the hallway, packed and ready to go.

Vanja was sitting in the kitchen.

'What are you doing here?' he said, feeling a surge of both irritation and anxiety at the sight of his colleague. 'Where's Maria?' Vanja glanced towards the bedroom.

'She's calling Pia, asking if she can come a bit earlier,' Vanja replied after a brief silence.

'Why?'

'I think she and Nicole will be going to the service without you . . .'

He didn't really understand what she was saying, but the irritation was definitely outweighing the anxiety right now. Whatever it meant, it wasn't good news. He raised his voice.

'You have no right to come here and interfere in my life—'

'Yes, I have. Maria and Nicole are the victims of a crime. They are Riksmord's responsibility.'

Sebastian didn't know what to say. Was she serious? He struggled to find the right words, but he needn't have bothered.

'Don't be angry with her.' The voice came from behind him. He turned around to see Maria standing in the doorway, her eyes full of disappointment and sorrow. 'When were you intending to tell me?' she said tonelessly.

'Tell you what?'

'The truth.'

Sebastian spread his arms wide.

'I don't know what you're talking about.'

Maria took a step towards him.

'When were you going to tell me that my daughter is some kind of surrogate for the child you lost?'

For a second Sebastian had no idea what to say.

'Is that what Vanja told you?' was the best he could come up with.

'Are we? Some kind of . . . replacement family?' Maria sounded upset rather than angry.

'No, no, absolutely not. Nicole means a great deal to me, you know that. And you . . .'

Maria was staring at him, not a trace of softness in her expression.

'I asked you.'

'I know.'

'Whether you had children.'

'I know.'

'Whether you'd been married.'

'I know.'

'You lied.'

'I know.'

Maria fell silent; Sebastian realised it was up to him to say something.

'I was going to tell you, but it's not the first thing you share with someone. Particularly in view of everything that was going on,' he pleaded.

'You didn't need to tell me, you just needed to answer my questions. I asked you, and you lied.'

What was he supposed to say to that?

'I thought you were honest. I trusted you.'

'You can trust me. You and Nicole mean so much to me,' he said feebly, his voice almost breaking.

Maria was still staring at him, her eyes full of sorrow and disappointment.

'I don't believe you any more. I've heard so much about you. Terrible things.' She let out a sob. Sebastian glanced over at Vanja, who seemed virtually unmoved, bearing in mind what she had done. What the hell had she said about him? He took a couple of steps towards Maria, desperate to make her understand.

'Whatever you've heard, it has nothing to do with us. I've been there for Nicole, one hundred per cent. You know that.'

Maria nodded sadly, wiped away her tears.

'Yes, you have. But why? For your sake, or hers?'

Once again, what could he say? He could feel everything slipping through his fingers. He wanted to explain. Tell her how he felt. What they meant to him. Sabine and Lily were part of it, admittedly, but not a major part. Not a crucial factor. This was something else, something real. He ought to say all of that, but nothing came out.

'Thank you for everything you've done for Nicole, but now we'd like to be left in peace.'

She turned and walked away.

Collected Nicole from the living room.

Picked up her bags in the hallway.

Before the front door closed behind them he sought Nicole's gaze. Found it as easily as he always did. For a few seconds he looked into her eyes.

He followed her.

He had no choice.

He couldn't lose her.

Pia was waiting in the street.

She looked over at the brown door of Grev Magnigatan 18 with mixed emotions. The overriding feeling, the one she wanted to hold on to and never forget, was joy because the meeting with the party executive had gone exactly as she had hoped. Better, in fact. As she left the brown six-storey building on Sveavägen she had been welcomed on board, which could only mean that they were intending to give her the seat on the executive committee.

Now she was going to go home and make sure that tomorrow's memorial service and demonstration against violence was a success. She would work tirelessly for the good of Torsby, even if her trips to Stockholm would be more frequent in the future, and local issues might seem rather trivial now that she suddenly had a direct influence on the Social Democrats' policies on a national level, and on the party's priorities.

She had had her doubts when she left home yesterday. The events involving Frank Hedén had been widely publicised: the mass murderer who killed himself in the stairwell outside the apartment where one of the investigators lived, and where the key witness was staying. It was an unmitigated disaster. The fact that there had been another shooting in the same building just a few months ago, when a female police officer had been seriously injured, didn't exactly improve matters. The tabloids had had a field day. Having a close and important relationship with a mass murderer definitely wasn't good for Pia and her career, which had really taken off now.

But she had come through with flying colours.

Obviously the press had called, wondering how close she and Frank had actually been, whether she had really not suspected anything, and if it was true that Frank had spoken to her just before he shot himself. She had refused to answer any of their questions, and instead had prepared a press release in which she distanced herself from Frank, while at the same time giving due credit to her old friend and mentor. Yes, he had murdered an entire family, which was terrible and indefensible, but people shouldn't forget that he had devoted his life to local politics, and the memory of him as a pillar of the community was still valid. So in spite of recent events, which could be attributed to a temporary state of insanity, he was still well liked, and one didn't simply sell out old friends and colleagues, whatever they had done. Particularly not in order to climb the career ladder in Stockholm; that wouldn't go down well. It was a delicate balancing act, distancing herself from Frank and his actions without speaking badly of him. Condemn the crime not the perpetrator, that had been her strategy over the past few days, and it had worked perfectly during her visit to Sveavägen.

Otherwise she didn't even think about Frank and what they had been involved in together. She was just glad that she seemed to have got away with it, and that he hadn't dragged her down with him.

The door opened and a woman emerged with a little girl. Maria and Nicole Carlsten, presumably. Pia hadn't met either of them, but they were important for tomorrow's demonstration, and she was glad to have a few hours with them in the car so that she could make her introductory speech more personal, give the right sense of commitment to the victims' nearest and dearest. She walked towards them with a welcoming smile and her hand outstretched. Before she reached them the door opened once more and a man she had never seen before came out. Sebastian Bergman, presumably. Erik had complained about him several times: unpleasant, arrogant and boorish, apparently. Pia decided to ignore him completely.

'Pia Flodin. Lovely to meet you,' she said, focusing on Maria. 'My sincere condolences on your loss,' she went on in a subdued tone, giving Maria's hand a little extra squeeze.

Maria nodded her thanks and introduced her daughter. Pia smiled at the girl, whose only response was to edge behind her mother and stare up at Pia with wary eyes. Pia had heard that the girl wasn't talking because of what she had witnessed. She straightened up and looked over Maria's shoulder at the man who was standing by the door.

'I assume this is my third passenger,' she said. She had no intention of revealing that she knew his name; she didn't want to give him any importance.

'Yes, that's Sebastian, but he won't be coming with us,' Maria said. There was no mistaking the ice in her voice.

'No?'

'No. So we can go now.'

'My car's just over there,' Pia said, pointing along the street.

'Maria . . .' Sebastian began, without attempting to approach them.

'I'll send someone to pick up the rest of our things,' Maria said in a way that made it clear to Pia that this was about more than just the drive to Torsby.

'Won't you even let me try to explain? Are you just going to listen to Vanja and believe every word she says?'

'Yes.' Maria took Nicole by the hand and set off towards Pia's car.

★ ★ ★

All Sebastian could do was watch them go. Running after them and trying to get Maria to stop and listen to him wouldn't work, and in any case he didn't want to cause a scene in front of Nicole. The last thing she needed right now was to see the two people she trusted involved in an argument.

'Think of Nicole!' he shouted anyway in a last desperate attempt to make them stay, or at least to allow him to go with them.

Maria didn't respond; she just kept on walking.

Leaving him.

'My car's over there – it was difficult to find a parking space,' Pia said, pointing to a red Volvo on the other side of the road.

Sebastian stayed where he was; every step they took was like a physical blow to his body. He saw Nicole stop as they were about to cross the road; she turned and looked at him. As usual it was hard to interpret her expression, but he thought he could see loss and despair. He was even more convinced when she slowly reached out towards him with the hand her mother wasn't holding. If she had been an adult the gesture would have seemed exaggerated and theatrical, but as Nicole tried to bridge the sudden distance between them with that little outstretched hand, it was simply heart-rending. Sebastian tried to swallow the lump in his throat.

Maria tugged at her daughter and they set off across the road. Nicole didn't take her eyes off Sebastian, and the further away she got, the more pleading and despairing she looked. Sebastian had to turn his head for a moment

When he turned back the three of them were sitting in the red car; Pia started the engine and pulled out into the road. He could see Maria's profile above the blue-and-white sticker portraying the Torsby town logo; Nicole was sitting on the other side of her mother, and he couldn't see her at all.

She was gone. They were gone.

He had lost them.

And the reason was sitting in his kitchen.

★ ★ ★

Sebastian walked into the hallway and kicked off his shoes. He saw a movement in his peripheral vision and glanced up. Vanja emerged from the kitchen and leaned against the wall with her arms folded, as if she thought she might need to shield herself from his fury.

Sebastian merely glared at her.

He hoped the coldness in his eyes would tell her everything she needed to know.

He marched past her into the living room, then stopped just inside the door. For many years it had been nothing more than a room, which happened to be in the apartment where he lived. He had never used it, never had any kind of connection with it. The strongest memory, ironically, was when he had consoled Vanja and tried to bring her closer to him when Valdemar was accused of fraud and embezzlement.

Now he knew what the big room should be used for. That and the rest of the apartment. He had been given a taste of how his life could be.

The lump in his throat had moved down and settled somewhere around his diaphragm. Nicole hadn't lived with him for very long, but long enough for this nagging, gnawing feeling to take root. He recognised the sensation very well; he had lived with it for so many years. It was where the sense of loss sat when it moved in.

He took a deep breath and went over to the coffee table. Coloured pens and pencils, paper, a glass with the remains of a chocolate drink in the bottom, a plate with the crusts from a sandwich. Nicole must have had a snack in front of the TV while he was out. He started to gather everything up; many people were paralysed when they lost someone, but not Sebastian. He had always been good at finding the energy to clear away the physical traces of the people he had lost. After the tsunami he had immediately sold the apartment in Cologne, given away or otherwise disposed of furniture, household equipment and clothes, keeping only a few items. Within weeks he had put an end to their life in Germany and moved back to Sweden.

The fact that he had been completely unable to move on, once all the practicalities had been dealt with, was another matter.

He felt more than saw Vanja appear in the doorway.

'I'm sorry I've upset you, but you know I'm right,' she said softly.

Sebastian didn't reply.

'It was wrong, and you know that,' she went on in the same consoling tone that reminded Sebastian of someone telling small children that their hamster has died and is in a better place now. 'Come on, you're a trained psychologist – you more than anyone must realise how crazy it was.'

Sebastian carried on calmly and methodically picking up felt-tip pens and replacing them neatly in the box in order, from dark colours through to light.

'The silent treatment. Very mature.'

Out of the corner of his eye he saw Vanja move forward and sit down in one of the armchairs. He wanted to yell at her, throw her out, using physical force if necessary, but at the same time he had to stay in control of himself. He couldn't allow this to destroy their slowly blossoming friendship for ever. Any other woman who did what Vanja had done would never have set foot in his home again, but however angry and upset he was right now, he couldn't get away from the fact that a tiny, tiny part of him appreciated the fact that she wouldn't give up, loved the way she curled up in the chair and simply waited him out. She didn't back off from a fight, his daughter.

He straightened up and looked at her for the first time since she came into the living room.

'You had no right to interfere in my life.'

'I didn't. I interfered in Maria and Nicole's lives,' Vanja replied, sounding unusually calm. 'I saw it as an obligation rather than a right.'

'I know you think I only . . .' He didn't finish the sentence, just shook his head. He didn't want to go down that road again, talking about a replacement family, Lily, Sabine . . . not now. 'But I was doing my job – I really did help Nicole.'

He leafed through the sheets of paper he had gathered up and pulled out Nicole's latest – no, her *last* drawing.

'She drew, we talked, the barriers she had put up to protect herself started to break down, she was opening up. Not in words, not yet, but we would have got there. If we'd had a little more time.' He managed to make the final sentence sound every bit as accusatory as he intended as he passed her the picture. Vanja ignored the implication and looked down at the sheet of paper. She recognised the room from the photographs of the scene of the crime: it was the room beyond the kitchen in the Carlsten house.

'What's this?'

'Nicole and her cousin watching television together just before the murders.'

Vanja looked up enquiringly.

'I thought you said she only drew what had happened *after* the murders.'

'No, I said she drew things that were connected to the murders.'

'So why did she draw this?' Vanja nodded at the paper in her hand. 'Everything looks perfectly normal here.'

Sebastian sighed. This wasn't exactly going the way he had hoped. He had shown her the picture to make her understand that he was still working; in spite of the fact that Maria and Nicole had moved in, he was still helping the girl to process the experiences she had gone through. Vanja's actions had put an end to that important task. He wanted to put her under pressure, make her admit that she was wrong and he was right. At the same time, he couldn't help feeling pleased, perhaps even delighted, that she had stayed and made herself at home.

In his apartment. His daughter.

'I don't know,' he said, vaguely irritated with both Vanja and himself. 'In her mind there's a connection to the terrible events that followed, somehow.'

Vanja looked more closely at the picture.

'Frank Hedén had a blue Ford pickup, and the Carlstens had a white hybrid.'

'So?' Sebastian had no idea why Vanja was suddenly showing an interest in cars.

'Nicole has drawn a red car. Outside the window.'

Sebastian reacted immediately; he took the picture from Vanja and stared at it. She was right. Outside the square window with the white curtains pulled back, a red car was clearly visible. How could he have missed it?

'If everything she draws is connected to the murders . . . Could Frank have used a different car?' Vanja said, thinking out loud. 'Or was there more than one person involved?'

Sebastian wasn't really listening. As with everything else Nicole had drawn, there was detail on the red car. A blue-and-white sticker on the back window.

He stared at the image as if he was hoping it could provide answers to all the questions in the world, but his mind was spinning, telling him that he already knew the answer to the most important question.

He could see Nicole right there in front of him, how frightened and desperate she had looked as she crossed the road. But it wasn't because she was leaving him, he realised now, it was because of what she was being dragged towards.

The car.

The red car.

There were two of them again

She was two separate individuals again.

On the outside and on the inside.

★ ★ ★

On the outside she was sitting completely motionless.

There wasn't much else she could do. Mummy was sitting beside her. Just as Fred had been sitting beside her the first time she saw the red car.

Now Fred was dead.

The first time she had been able to hide, but not this time. Mummy put her arm around her and chatted to the woman who was driving. She carried on registering the world outside the car. It had nothing to do with her. She was no longer a part of it. She could have been, she was on her way, but then they ended up here.

In this car.

So she withdrew.

★ ★ ★

On the inside she was also motionless.

Back in the place that was not a place, or a room. She was back there again and it was still empty.

Empty and silent.

Sebastian had talked to her. His words had made the walls that were not walls begin to weaken. It had begun in the cave. A thin thread of his plea to trust him had found its way into that cold,

410

cramped space and she had grabbed hold of it. She hadn't regretted that decision.

The feeling of security had spread, slowly but surely.

For a brief moment, now and again, when Sebastian was talking to her, when she was with him, she felt as if she might even be able to feel safe outside the walls.

Perhaps the terrible thing wouldn't come back if she grew and left the place that was not a place.

Perhaps she might even be able to speak without anything happening.

But that was then.

★ ★ ★

On the outside she sat still and looked out through the car window like any other ten-year-old, the seat belt across her chest and Mummy's arm around her shoulders, adult voices talking, music on the radio.

On the outside she had no way of protecting the inside.

Then again, she didn't need to.

★ ★ ★

The red car had sent her hurtling back.

The bangs, the screams, the terror.

Her own and everyone else's.

★ ★ ★

On the inside she grew smaller and smaller once again, and the walls around her closed in, thicker than ever.

Vanja and Sebastian flew down the stairs. Vanja had just called Torkel to tell him about Nicole's drawing and their sudden suspicions with regard to Pia.

Torkel's response didn't make her feel any better.

He had just finished talking to Adrian Cole at FilboCorp. When he was going through the final report on the case, something connected with Frank's motive had bothered him – something to do with the purchase of Stefan Andrén's land. It wasn't the fact that Frank had bought the land; the financial motive was perfectly clear. It was the timing that didn't fit. The deal had been done long before the mining company's plans were made public. Nine months, in fact. And yet Frank had been confident enough to borrow an enormous amount of money. Adrian Cole had told Torkel something which, combined with Vanja's call just seconds later, made everything fall into place.

According to Cole, the only person who knew about FilboCorp's plans before the official application was the chair of the local council, Pia Flodin. The same person who had just picked up their only witness. Maybe Frank hadn't acted alone after all.

Vanja had found a parking space some distance away on Storgatan, and it took them a while to get there, even at a run.

'Torkel's going to call the control centre and ask them to provide us with full support,' she told Sebastian as they got in the car.

'Good – we're going to need all the help we can get.' Sebastian was breathing heavily; he looked stressed.

Vanja started the car. 'If we assume she's going straight to Torsby, there are two routes to choose from: the E18 north of

Mälaren, or the E4 to the south.' She looked at Sebastian enquiringly. 'Any idea which one she was planning to take?'

He shook his head and took out his phone.

'OK, in that case we'll just have to take a chance. South is easier from here.'

She switched on the blue light and shot away. 'Can you call Control and request a helicopter?'

'Already on it,' Sebastian replied.

Vanja turned down Styrmansgatan and out onto Strandvägen. It was the middle of the day, so the traffic wasn't too bad. Unfortunately – it would have been helpful if Pia had got stuck in a jam. The cars ahead pulled over, and soon Vanja was in the tunnel on Norrlandsgatan. Sebastian spoke to Control and gave Vanja's name and number; he told them about the red Volvo V70, registered keeper either Pia or Erik Flodin. No, he didn't know the registration number, but it had a blue sticker with the Torsby town logo on one of the side windows at the back.

Vanja glanced over at him; she was no longer quite so sure that she had done the right thing. It wasn't her fault that Maria and Nicole were in the Volvo right now, but it was her fault that Sebastian wasn't there with them.

She felt compelled to say something. 'Sorry if I messed up, but I did it for your sake as well as theirs.'

He gazed at her as he sat there with the phone to his ear, waiting for a response from Control. At first she thought he was going to bite her head off, but he simply turned and looked out of the window.

'To be honest I don't understand why it had anything to do with you.'

She nodded. Didn't reply. Put her foot down as if speed could undo what was done.

★ ★ ★

Maria was in the back with Nicole. The car was clean and impersonal, nothing on the floor, not a speck of dust in the compartment between the front seats. Nothing like the cars she usually

413

travelled in; they were always littered with old toys from McDonald's, wrappers and all kinds of rubbish. Pia had switched on the radio, P1; a science programme about the new shipping lanes that were opening up in the Barents Sea due to climate change. Maria wasn't paying any attention. Nicole was curled up beside her; she hadn't moved since they left Grev Magnigatan. She had pressed herself as close as possible to her mother, and after a while she had buried her face in the crook of Maria's arm. As if she wanted to disappear from the surface of the earth. Maria hugged her, hoping to reassure her.

'It's all right, sweetheart,' she whispered. 'Everything will be fine.'

Nicole didn't move.

Maria was regretting her actions. It had been stupid to tackle Sebastian while Nicole was around. She should have thought, protected her from the break-up. Kept some things to herself, not made it so dramatic. But she had been angry, not thinking clearly. She felt so betrayed. She had let him into her life, which was why she had reacted like that to his lies and the revelations that followed. It was hardly surprising, but it wasn't good for Nicole, who had grown even closer to Sebastian. She carried on whispering to her daughter, trying to reach her.

Pia glanced at her enquiringly in the rear-view mirror.

'Has something happened?'

Maria shook her head. 'No, she's just a bit anxious.' There was no reason to say anything about Sebastian to Pia Flodin; she didn't need any more people giving her advice or trying to help. She would solve her own problems from now on.

'But she's still not talking?' Pia went on, trying to sound casual but without success. Maria understood. Nicole's mutism was presumably one of the things that many people would ask her about over and over again in the near future.

'No, unfortunately,' she said, meeting Pia's gaze.

'I'm sure things will improve as time goes on,' Pia replied reassuringly, putting her foot down. Maria thought she was driving a little too fast, but she didn't say anything. Surely they weren't in that much of a hurry to get there?

Suddenly the memorial service seemed like a bad idea. Nicole needed peace and quiet, particularly now that Maria had torn Sebastian from her side in such a brutal way. The security Nicole had felt with him would be hard to replace, and it definitely wasn't to be found among a crowd of strangers trying to express their grief in a town square. It could even have a directly negative effect, reminding her of the terrible things that had happened.

It was Maria who needed the memorial service, Maria who wanted to move on. Not Nicole. She wasn't there yet. Maria had to think of her daughter, not herself. She was ashamed. Everything she had done since she stormed out of Sebastian's apartment had been about her.

'I'm not sure if this is such a good idea,' she said. Once again Pia looked at her in the mirror.

'Sorry? What's not a good idea?'

'The memorial service. I don't think it will help Nicole. I don't think she's ready.'

Pia nodded, sounding as if she understood perfectly.

'It's going to be beautiful – peaceful, dignified, nothing intrusive,' she said warmly. 'I think you'll be surprised by the feeling of support and community.'

'I don't know. I'm sure it will be lovely, but . . .' Maria went on uncertainly.

Pia smiled reassuringly.

'I'll tell you what we'll do. We'll drive down, and if it doesn't feel right, then don't go. I promise I won't nag, but at least you can make up your mind when you're on the spot.'

Maria nodded. She might feel better when they were there; she just didn't know. As on so many other occasions in her life, she wasn't really in control of events, so she sat quietly and allowed herself to be driven towards Torsby.

Perhaps it was because she wanted to fit in, find a context.

Perhaps it was because she didn't want to go back to her apartment, resume her everyday life.

Perhaps it was because she felt the memorial service was a good way of making a fresh start. She wasn't sure.

Her phone rang: Sebastian. She immediately rejected the call. At least she was in control of her mobile.

★ ★ ★

They were on the Central Bridge, blue lights still flashing.

The traffic was getting worse, and Vanja had to slow down a little in order to give the vehicles ahead time to move out of the way. She turned up her police radio to make sure she didn't miss anything. A call asking all cars to look out for a red Volvo V70, registration number Sierra Golf Mike 054 with a blue sticker in one of the rear side windows had just gone out. Control had also diverted a traffic-management helicopter from Nacka; it would be over Söder in a few minutes. Sebastian stared at his mobile in frustration.

'Maria's not answering. She keeps rejecting my calls.'

Vanja's expression was sceptical.

'Do you think it's a good idea to ring her?'

'I was going to warn her.'

'Don't do that. Do you think Maria would be able to keep up the pretence if you tell her about Pia?'

'Maybe not,' he had to admit.

'We could end up with a situation where Pia becomes desperate, and she's got Maria and Nicole in the car.' She tried to calm Sebastian down: 'We do have one advantage – Pia doesn't know that we know. We have to use that advantage for as long as possible.'

Sebastian nodded. Vanja was right, of course, but that didn't make him feel any better.

'I'm such an idiot. I could see from the way Nicole was behaving that something was wrong. I could see it—'

Vanja interrupted him.

'You couldn't possibly have known. None of us could.'

Sebastian didn't reply, but Vanja could see that her words hadn't made a scrap of difference. The radio crackled into life again.

'Car 318 – red Volvo V70, Sierra Golf Mike 054, located south of Hornstull,' said a loud male voice. Vanja grabbed the microphone.

'Repeat, please – precise location?'

The response was immediate.

'Crossing Liljeholmen Bridge. We're heading in the opposite direction and it's going to take a while for us to turn around.'

'OK, turn around but keep your distance. Do not approach,' Vanja said, then threw the microphone to Sebastian. 'Try and contact the helicopter. Send it towards the E4, the Liljeholmen access slip.' Sebastian nodded and picked up the mic.

'South Mälarstrand or Gullmarsplan and the southern link route?' Vanja asked, keeping an eye on the road ahead and the traffic behind.

'No good asking me, I never drive here,' Sebastian said, still trying to get in touch with the helicopter.

'I think South Mälarstrand will be the quickest.' Vanja veered across two lanes at full speed, causing several cars to slam on their brakes. She skilfully manoeuvred them into the tunnel that brought them out by the lake. One lane was closed due to the reconstruction around Slussen, and they were faced with a long queue of vehicles. Vanja pulled out into the lane designated for oncoming traffic, shot past the cars waiting for the red light up ahead to turn green, then pulled back in at the last minute. She was an excellent driver, but in spite of the speed, it felt like a long way to Hornstull.

Sebastian managed to speak to the pilot: good news. He had been listening to the radio, and had already reached Liljeholmen.

'We've located the car. It's in the left-hand lane of the E4 heading south. It's just passing the exit for Västertorp.'

'Excellent,' Sebastian said, glancing at Vanja. 'Anything else I need to say?'

'Ask what speed the car is doing.'

Sebastian nodded; a few seconds later he had the answer.

'About a hundred and five kilometres per hour at the moment.'

'The limit is ninety there; that gives us a reason to pick her up. Tell the helicopter to stay with her, then call car 318 and ask them to drop back so that she doesn't spot them.'

Sebastian nodded. 'OK. And what are we going to do?'

Vanja looked at him, a faint smile playing on her lips.

'We're going to give Pia a little surprise.'

She pressed herself closer to her mother.

The car was moving so fast. Just like that ride she had been so scared of last year at the Gröna Lund amusement park. She had been strapped in then too.

Couldn't stop it or jump out.

The last time she saw the car it had been moving much more slowly.

It had stopped outside the house.

She hadn't paid much attention to it.

Probably a visitor.

A friend of Auntie Karin's.

But it wasn't.

The car had brought screams and death.

The loudest bangs she had ever heard in her whole life.

Louder than thunder. Louder than everything.

They tore bodies apart.

Splashed blood all over the walls.

And now she was sitting in the car that had brought death.

She pressed even closer. Warn Mummy.

She squeezed her eyes tight shut.

She wanted to warn her. But it was impossible.

She couldn't do it. Didn't want to do it.

On the outside she was visible and vulnerable.

On the inside the walls protected her.

As long as she was little.

And silent.

It was Sebastian who spotted the Volvo first. It was still in the left-hand lane, speeding past one car after another in the right-hand lane.

'There,' he said, pointing. Vanja nodded; she had switched off the blue light a couple of minutes ago so that Pia wouldn't notice her. Sebastian glanced at the speedometer: 125 kph.

'She's driving fast,' he said anxiously.

'I'll try and keep my distance.'

She picked up the mic again and called the traffic police controller over in Salem. She had already spoken to a team from the Södertälje traffic division, and the plan was for them to pull Pia over in what would appear to be a routine check, get her out of the car, away from Maria and Nicole, then hold her until Vanja and Sebastian arrived. Hopefully they were already there and had started flagging down vehicles. Vanja had promised to call them if she had visual contact with the Volvo to give them an idea of how much time they had before Pia would be with them.

'I can see her now. She should be there in less than six minutes.'

'We're ready,' came the immediate response.

Vanja turned to Sebastian. She was feeling a little calmer now she could actually see the car they were following.

'Let's just hope Traffic do their job,' she said.

'And what do we do?'

'Hopefully nothing. Turn up and collect Pia from the traffic cops.' Her expression was full of understanding; it was a long time since he had seen that look on her face. 'It's going to be fine, Sebastian.'

He nodded and looked out of the window as Stockholm's southern suburbs whizzed by.

'You're bloody hard work, but you're a good police officer,' he said after a while.

'You're mainly just bloody hard work.'

He burst out laughing.

'Why do I always fuck things up?' The question was meant to be light-hearted and rhetorical, but to his surprise he heard a clear note of self-pity in his words.

'Surely you must know that.'

'No.'

'Because you're arrogant, cynical, don't give a toss about other people, you lie, you cheat, you're condescending . . . Shall I go on?'

'No, there's no need.'

Sebastian gazed at Vanja in silence for a moment before turning his attention back to the red car.

Vanja was right. He had never, ever believed that someone could love him for the person he really was. Not his parents, not his university colleagues, virtually none of the women he had known.

Lily had been the first, and so far the only one. Sabine and Nicole, of course, but they were children.

And Vanja. At least she had the nerve to confront him, to stick around. But there was no one else. He had played so many games, lived with so many half-truths and lies for such a long time that the lies were what he had become. Nothing else.

'Four minutes,' Vanja said, totally focused on the Volvo up ahead.

Sebastian didn't say anything; he was trying to spot Nicole in the back of the car. He could see the dark outlines of Pia and Maria's heads through the rear window, but there was no sign of Nicole.

She was probably hidden by the seat.

The girl he had lost.

Mummy.

She hadn't thought anything for a long, long time.

She had emptied herself completely. She had curled up inside herself, become smaller and smaller.

Hoping that she would disappear completely.

Then it came.

The only thought. The only word.

Mummy. In danger.

She hadn't been able to save Fred.

But he didn't know anything. Neither did she.

Then.

But now she knew.

She had to tell Mummy.

Just as she had had to open the door of the house once more in order to help the man who had saved her, she had to tell Mummy now.

Even if it tore down her walls. Left her unprotected. Exposed her to everything that was wrong and terrible.

Mummy had to be told.

On the outside she slowly raised her face from Mummy's warm jacket. Looked up.

Mummy seemed pleased. Surprised. She was smiling.

On the outside she reached up. Up to Mummy, who lowered her face to Nicole's.

On the inside she found her voice. It was easier than she had expected, as if it had been lying in a corner just waiting for her to have the courage to use it.

'It was her, Mummy,' she whispered. 'It was her.'

Maria stared at her daughter.

Nicole's voice had been weak, yet firm in some strange way. Maria had imagined that those first words would make her rejoice inside, that she would want to scream with sheer joy. Not like now. She wanted to scream with pure fear.

'What did you say?' she whispered back, moving her head closer. She had heard what the child said, but she didn't understand. What did it have to do with the woman whose curious gaze she met in the mirror?

'She was there,' Nicole went on, her voice getting stronger with every syllable. 'When they died.'

Maria followed her daughter's gaze. Pia's expression had changed. Gone was every trace of curiosity, gone was the friendliness and sympathy. All Maria could see now was fury mixed with resolve and energy.

Suddenly she understood.

The eyes in the mirror told her what she really didn't want to know. The truth.

The car swerved dramatically as Pia jerked the wheel to the right. The tyres screeched, Maria and Nicole were thrown to the left, and if they hadn't been wearing seat belts they would have been flung straight across the back seat.

★ ★ ★

The Volvo skidded violently in front of them. Blue smoke rose from the tyres as the car slid across the E4 and zigzagged onto the Vårby exit slip. For a second Vanja was convinced that it was going to carry straight on and come off the carriageway, but Pia seemed to regain control at the last minute and headed down towards Vårby Allé and the traffic lights, still travelling far too fast.

Instinctively Vanja also turned the wheel to the right. She had a better angle than Pia, and the skid wasn't nearly as bad, but she almost lost control. She yelled into the radio mic, steering with one hand:

'Something's happened! The target has turned off for Vårby Allé! Request immediate backup!'

They saw the Volvo force its way past a car waiting at the lights by mounting the grass verge. It scraped the side of the other car, but didn't slow down; it carried on going and soon disappeared from view.

Sebastian held onto the strap above the door as they kept up the pursuit. He stared ahead, but there was no sign of the Volvo. Suddenly he saw a big white van coming towards them, frantically sounding its horn as it came closer and closer. Vanja slammed on the brakes; Sebastian was sure they were going to crash, but Vanja managed to stop at the last minute. The van shot past, the driver gesticulating angrily. Sebastian and Vanja looked for the Volvo, but the viaduct over the motorway was blocking their view. Vanja switched on the blue lights and put her foot down; they had lost the element of surprise anyway. Gone was the feeling that everything would be fine; now anything was possible. Including the worst-case scenario.

Sebastian's face was ashen as he desperately searched for any sign of the red car. All at once the helicopter pilot's voice came over the radio, calm and authoritative, not remotely fazed by what had happened.

'I've got it – travelling along Vårby Allé in the direction of Botkyrkaleden at high speed.' The matter-of-fact tone calmed them both. They hadn't lost Pia; they still had a chance. They reached the straight and saw the red car way up ahead, veering alarmingly from side to side. It looked as if Pia had lost control. It skidded off the road and across the grass on the right, racing down towards the water. For a second they hoped Pia would regain control and stop before it was too late, but her brake lights didn't come on. Instead of slowing down, the car actually seemed to be speeding up, as if gathering itself before it left the shore and flew several metres out into Lake Mälaren. Sebastian let out a panic-stricken yell as Vanja headed for the lake.

At the same time the helicopter pilot made a concise statement:

'The car is in the lake. I repeat, the car is in the lake. Vårby Allé right next to Restaurant Max.'

His voice sounded just as steady and authoritative as before.

Nothing seemed to affect it.

That was probably how a person looked at the world when they were so high above it.

It was a strange feeling. For a millisecond she was in a state of weightlessness. There was no resistance, nothing holding her down apart from the seat belt, and she felt herself and Nicole being pushed up towards the roof. Instinctively she took a firm grip on Nicole and held her tight, preparing for the inevitable impact. The blue-green water was getting closer and closer, dark and impenetrable like a silent wall, just waiting for them. She noticed that Pia had opened the driver's door, that the engine was still running, but there was no sound from the wheels on the road.

That was the strangest thing of all.

The silence.

In spite of the fact that they were moving so fast.

The silence made the bang even more deafening when it came. The surface of the water was hard, brutal. One second it was calm, the next it was white, foaming and all-encompassing. It engulfed the car and the airbags inflated with a dull explosion. Maria's forehead slammed into the headrest of the seat in front. Her whole face hurt, but she held on to Nicole. The car had gone into the lake at an angle, front first, but now the rear section was partially submerged too, and water was beginning to seep in under the doors. Maria could see Pia struggling to escape from the airbag, which was more or less pinning her down. They were sinking fast as water poured in through the open driver's door. Maria realised she had to do something. She quickly undid Nicole's seat belt; the child was pale, but looked confused rather than afraid. In the front of the car Pia managed to push aside the airbag, and she began to wriggle out. So far she hadn't even glanced at her passengers; it was as if they weren't there, as if they had ceased to exist. As a result, Maria was filled with a raging energy. That woman had already obliterated most of her family, but this time she wasn't going to succeed. She and Nicole were going to survive.

She tried to undo her own seat belt, but Nicole was in the way and she couldn't reach the release button. Pia was out of the car and swimming away. The water was ice cold; Maria was already frozen.

'We have to get out,' she said to Nicole, impressed by how calm she managed to sound. 'Trust me.'

She tried to push open her door, but it felt as if it had been welded shut, as if the whole of Lake Mälaren was pressing against the other side. She went back to her seat belt, even lifting Nicole with one arm, but she still couldn't find the button. She was starting to panic as she fumbled around. The water was already up to her stomach, and soon she would have to lift Nicole to keep her head above the surface. She would need both hands to do that, which meant she would have no chance of undoing her belt. The water rose to her chest. The car would be filled with water in seconds. She could see the panic growing in Nicole's eyes, and she could hear her breathing growing shallower all the time.

She had to think. Concentrate. What was it she had heard? Or read? Think! The pressure inside a car full of water was the same as the pressure on the outside, which meant she would be able to open the door. That was right, wasn't it? Not that it really mattered – she had no alternative.

She pressed the button to lower the side window, and to her surprise it worked. The water came gushing in, and she raised her daughter's head; Nicole was shaking with a combination of cold and fear. Maria looked deep into her eyes.

'You're going to have to swim, sweetheart. Just like you did last summer. Swim to the shore. Promise me.'

Nicole stared at her, clearly terrified.

'I'm coming too, I promise.' Maria quickly kissed her forehead. 'Take a big breath, sweetheart. A big deep breath.'

Nicole did as she was told and Maria fumbled for the door catch. She found it, got the door open and pushed Nicole out with all the strength she could muster. It was a terrible sensation, letting go and feeling that little body disappear. Maria tried to catch sight of her, but the swirling, cloudy water made it impossible.

She stretched up as far as she could and managed to get her face in the tiny air pocket just below the roof. She took one last breath, then dived back down to search for her seat-belt button.

★ ★ ★

Vanja had driven off the road, straight through a thicket of bushes, and had managed to stop the car only a metre or so from the edge of the lake. The Volvo was already sinking; only the roof was visible, and it was surrounded by bubbles as the last of the air was forced out.

Someone was swimming towards them. Pia Flodin.

No one else around the car or in the water. Sebastian threw off his jacket, kicked off his shoes and jumped in without a second's thought.

He had been here before.

Back then the water had been warmer, a violent surge throwing him in every direction, but there was no real difference.

He had been here before.

In the water that was taking those he loved away from him.

He swam to the car as fast as he could. Vanja was on the phone, calling an ambulance. A police officer on a motorbike had arrived and was running towards the lake and Pia. Sebastian focused on the car. He could still see the very top of the roof – then it was gone. No sign of life. He dived, but the water was dark and cloudy and he could barely see his own hand in front of his eyes. He came back up and saw someone else break the surface at the same time. It was Maria. She immediately started screaming:

'Nicole!'

She looked all around her, hysterical with fear.

'Is she still in the car?' Sebastian shouted. She turned in his direction; he had never seen such terror in anyone's eyes.

'No, I pushed her out. I pushed her out first!'

She dived back down, and he did the same. It was still dark, still impossible to see anything. But his hand touched the car; he grabbed the edge of the roof above an open window and pulled himself down. He could feel nothing but cold metal, angular industrial shapes.

Nothing living.

No Nicole.

He stayed down there as long as he could before he was forced to come up for air. Maria was there too; she looked terrible. She was shivering with cold and shock.

'Nicole!' she yelled again, weaker this time. She wouldn't last much longer. Sebastian took a deep breath and dived again.

Strong strokes, powerful kicks. He was going to find her.

The pain in his lungs was almost unbearable, and the cold was taking its toll. His ears were hurting, and he tried to equalise the pressure. His hands touched something soft and sticky; the mud at the bottom of the lake turned the water brown, making it even more difficult to see. He fumbled around; his whole body was aching and he could barely think clearly. But he kept on going, even though his lungs were crying out for air.

Back to the surface. A small boat had appeared, and the man sitting in it was calling out to Sebastian and Maria. More and more people had arrived on the shore, mainly police officers in hi-vis jackets. Sebastian tried to take in enough air, then yelled to Maria, who looked as if she had reached the end of her resources: 'Swim to the boat!'

He didn't wait for a response, but took one more breath and went back down. He still couldn't orientate himself underwater, but tried to dive a little further away from the car this time. He didn't really have any idea where he or the car was any longer; everything was water, only water. But one thing was very clear: each time he dived he had less and less time before he was forced to come up. He was getting breathless; soon he wouldn't be able to keep going. Up again. He tried to force in more air, fill his lungs through sheer willpower. Down again. Down into the darkness and the cold.

Suddenly he felt something with his right hand. For a fraction of a second, something swept past. It wasn't hard and metallic, it was something else. He kicked out to the right with every scrap of strength he had left and stretched out his hand as far as he possibly could, searching frantically.

He nudged it again; his fingertips touched something soft.

All at once he was back in the water off Khao Lak.

He had been holding a hand, and he had let go of it.

The same thing was happening now.

It slipped away, disappeared into the gloom just like before.

But it was definitely a hand. Her hand.

Back to the surface, He took in the small amount of air he could manage, then dived again. He no longer felt the cold; he wasn't thinking about the pain in his body and his lungs. There was nothing in his mind except that hand.

He searched, reached out, felt around.

Nothing.

He had lost her again.

The sun must have broken through the cloud cover, because strips of light were shining down into the lake. Everything around him was brighter, and he could see particles of dirt and mud swirling around. Then he saw the outline of her body just a little way off. She was close, just a kick away. He grabbed her hand; it was lifeless. He tried to pull her upwards, but she was heavier than he expected. He managed to get his arm around her waist; he was utterly exhausted, but he would never let her go. Never. He would rather die with her than give up.

As he had so often wished he had done on that December day in Thailand. Disappeared along with his daughter.

He kicked out, summoning up the last of his strength. Up, up towards the sunlight. Towards salvation. But time was running out; it was as if the water was trying to hold on to them.

But he didn't let go. He didn't let go.

Not this time. One more kick, and he felt the sun on his face. Heard himself coughing, gasping for air.

He wanted to shout for help, but he just couldn't do it. He saw Nicole's pale, still face above the water. Strands of hair plastered to her face. He fought to keep her there, kicking, holding her up.

He saw the little boat approaching, with Maria leaning over the gunwale.

'Nicole!' she screamed.

He couldn't go on much longer. He slipped under the water; it was becoming harder and harder to hold her up. The man in the boat reached out his hand, but Sebastian refused to take it. He couldn't. Couldn't let go of Nicole. They both dipped beneath the surface again; it was as if they were being dragged down into the depths.

Then he felt someone by his side. Someone strong. Someone who was lifting him up.

Vanja.

'I've got her,' she yelled in his ear as she took the child from him. He let her do it. He managed to grab the gunwale with one hand, and watched Vanja swimming on her back with Nicole's face above the surface, clasped to her chest. He saw them reach the shore.

Nicole still wasn't moving, but the paramedics were.

They immediately started CPR.

Sebastian let go of the gunwale and swam ashore. His progress was slow, but he didn't give up. He crawled onto the mud and grass, dragging himself along until he reached Nicole. He took her hand and collapsed.

They were still working on her. He was shaking with cold.

Suddenly she coughed, spewing up water. He could barely move or see after all his efforts, but he could hear.

She was alive.

'You can let go now, Sebastian,' said the voice that had saved him.

Vanja.

'I can't. I can't let go again,' he said weakly.

'You have to. They're taking her in the ambulance now. You have to let go. She'll be fine.'

'I don't want to.'

'You have to.'

Vanja and one of the paramedics pulled his hand away with no difficulty whatsoever; he had no resistance left.

They put her on a trolley and ran. He lay on his back and looked up at the sun. He was still shivering, but he had won. The water had lost this time. Someone gave him a blanket, someone else raised him up into a sitting position. Vanja was there, helping him to his feet. He wanted to burst into tears, lean against the woman who was his daughter and perhaps his only friend, and be honest.

But he couldn't do it.

'There's an ambulance waiting for you too,' she said gently.

He nodded. Saw his wet feet shuffling across the grass.

He saw Pia in handcuffs, saw Nicole wearing an oxygen mask in one of the ambulances.

They closed the doors.

Drove off. And he knew.

He knew that was the last time he would see her.

Ever.

'I didn't know he was intending to shoot them.'

Pia Flodin took a sip of water, put down her glass and met Torkel and Vanja's eyes across the table, her expression open and sincere. This was the second time she had repeated those nine words, and Vanja was no more inclined to believe her than the first time. Nor was Torkel, she was sure of it.

They had taken Pia straight to Police HQ in Kungsholmen. She had been given dry clothes and something to eat; a doctor had examined her and agreed that she was fit to be questioned.

Then they made a few calls.

Torkel informed Emilio Torres that they had arrested Pia Flodin, that she had refused legal representation, and that they would send him a copy of the interview transcript. Emilio was happy with that arrangement.

Out of politeness Vanja had called Erik and told him that they had arrested his wife on suspicion of involvement in the murder of the Carlsten family, and on endangering life with the possibility of the attempted murder of Maria and Nicole Carlsten. As she had expected Erik couldn't really take in what she was saying; she actually felt sorry for him as she referred him to Emilio Torres and advised him not to answer the phone for a while unless he recognised the number. There would be a lot of media interest when they found out what had happened. The car crash and subsequent rescue had been witnessed by a lot of people, and journalists were very good at putting together information. Vanja felt a pang of conscience as she put down the phone. She had absolutely nothing against Erik, and in spite of the fact that it was much better for him to hear it from her rather than reading it online or hearing it from a stranger, she knew that her call had changed his life, and his daughter's, for ever.

Speaking of changing someone's life, she had thought it over, then called Sebastian to ask if he could observe Pia's interview. He had seemed unsure, and she had said she would really appreciate it if he could be there. A peace offering. Which had worked.

They had waited for him in the corridor outside the interview room.

'I thought you were staying at the hospital?' Torkel had said when Sebastian turned up, walking with a heavy tread.

'Maria didn't want me there. She wanted to be alone with Nicole. Shall we make a start?'

Without waiting for a response he opened the door and went into the room with a window that looked like a mirror from the other side, but allowed Sebastian to see everything that went on. He watched as Vanja and Torkel entered and sat down without a word to Pia. Torkel switched on the recorder and gave the date, the reason for the interrogation, and the names of those present, while Vanja put in her earphone so that Sebastian could communicate with her.

'I didn't know he was intending to shoot them,' Pia said as soon as Torkel asked her to tell them about the day on which the murders took place. 'You have to believe me,' she added in a voice breaking with emotion, despair written all over her face.

Vanja reminded herself that Pia was a politician. She was used to lying.

'But you drove Frank over there?' she asked, without giving any indication as to whether she believed Pia or not.

'Yes.'

'In your car.'

'Yes.'

'Why? Why were you there?'

Pia subconsciously straightened up, as if she had been asked a question to which she actually knew the answer.

'Torsby needs that mine. It will provide employment, plus an income from taxes which will enable us to invest in health care, education and—'

434

'Skip the election speech and answer the question,' Vanja interrupted her.

Pia gave Vanja a filthy look. As a politician she might be used to interruptions, but she obviously didn't like it. She decided that talking to Vanja was beneath her dignity, and turned to Torkel instead.

'I asked Frank to come with me to visit the Carlstens so that he could provide a more human angle.' She leaned forward, her eyes fixed on Torkel. 'Employment opportunities and income from taxes are just boring politics to most people, but Frank was sick. Dying. He wanted to make sure that his son had a good life after he was gone. Human values, the kind of thing everyone can relate to. I wanted the Carlstens to understand that aspect of the mining development, that it was about helping a fellow human being too.'

She sat back and gave a little nod, as if she had just given an emotional speech to the nation.

'But that's not what happened,' Torkel said, noticeably unmoved.

'No. Frank . . .' Pia shrugged, apparently searching for the right words. 'Frank went . . . crazy, I assume.' She picked up the glass.

'I didn't know he was intending to shoot them,' she said, then she took a sip of water, put down her glass and met Torkel and Vanja's eyes across the table, her expression open and sincere.

'Hang on.' Vanja heard Sebastian's voice in her ear. 'If the plan was for Frank to sit crying into a cup of coffee to make the Carlstens feel like heartless bastards, then why did he have a shotgun with him?'

Vanja was wondering the same thing. She nodded to let Sebastian know she'd heard him.

'Frank had a gun with him,' she said.

'Yes.'

'Why?'

Another shrug.

'He was a gamekeeper. That's who he was. A man with a gun.'

435

'Ask her what she thought was going to happen,' Sebastian said, sure they were on to something.

'Wasn't it a bit strange to turn up with a shotgun if he was supposed to be eliciting sympathy?'

'It was just a gun,' Pia replied, as if she didn't understand the problem. 'It's what he used when he was working. I can see that someone in Stockholm would have reacted, but to us it's no stranger than a carpenter carrying a hammer around.'

'You didn't think it was remotely odd when he got out of the car with the shotgun?'

'No.'

'So the intention wasn't for him to go in and threaten the family?'

Pia looked excessively weary; she let out a loud sigh, making it clear that she doubted whether Vanja was of normal intelligence.

'As I said, he was going to tell them why he hoped they would say yes to the mine. The fact that you're carrying a gun doesn't necessarily mean you're planning to shoot someone.'

She raised her eyebrows at Vanja with an expression that said now-do-you-get-it-how-many-times-do-I-have-to-repeat-myself, and Vanja was suddenly absolutely sure.

She had known.

Pia had known from the start exactly what Frank was intending to do.

Vanja was certain, but there was the small matter of proof.

'Let's say we believe you. What happened?'

'We rang the bell, Karin opened the door and before I had the chance to explain why we were there, Frank raised the gun and shot her.'

'And what did you do then?'

'I screamed, I think. Grabbed hold of his arm, but he shook me off and went inside.'

Vanja opened the folder on the table and took out a number of photographs, which she laid out in front of Pia. Sebastian could see they were pictures of the children.

The children who had been shot.

Shot dead.

Vanja glanced up at Pia, who had fallen silent and seemed to be having some difficulty deciding where to look.

'Go on,' Vanja said encouragingly. 'What did you do next?'

'I ran back to the car.'

'Did you wait for him?'

'No, I drove off right away. Why are you showing me these?' Pia made an irritated gesture towards the photographs.

'Then what?' Vanja gave no sign of having heard Pia's question.

'I just drove, I was panicking. Everything had gone wrong. I was in shock – I needed time to process what I'd seen . . . I drove out into the forest, then I stopped and . . . I just sat there.'

'And you decided not to go to the police,' Torkel stated.

'I couldn't. You know who I am, what I do. I couldn't get involved.' Vanja was still laying out photographs on the table. 'Why are you showing me these?'

'You promised money and jobs for the town before the last election campaign,' Torkel went on, also ignoring her question.

'Yes.'

'Which the mine was supposed to provide.'

'Yes.'

'And now it's election time again. Time to deliver.'

Pia spread her hands wide and took a deep breath in an attempt to control her irritation. Good, Sebastian thought. People who were annoyed were more likely to make mistakes.

'I was trying to sway the Carlstens, I'm not denying that,' Pia said, forcing herself to speak calmly. 'That's why I took Frank with me.'

'And his shotgun,' Vanja interjected.

She might as well not have existed as far as Pia was concerned.

'He was going to help me persuade them. I didn't know he was intending to shoot them.'

437

Vanja glanced at Torkel and realised he had noticed the same thing as her: Pia's defence was beginning to sound more and more like a well-rehearsed story than a spontaneous account of the reality.

'You panicked when you found out there was a witness, and you asked Erik to go and see Frank, get him involved in the investigation in the hope that he would find Nicole first.' Torkel was making an assertion, not asking a question.

'No.'

'I heard your conversation with Frank on the phone. "You know what I can do," you said – you told him to think about his son. It didn't occur to me at the time, but that sounds like a threat. You were reminding him of how vulnerable his son would be if he didn't do the right thing, make sure you got away with it.' That wasn't a question either.

'No. I thought I could help him – you heard me say that too.'

'Yes, after a very long pause.'

'I still said it.'

'Why did you drive off the road?' Vanja suddenly asked.

'I lost control of the car.'

'Maria said Nicole had recognised Pia from the Carlsten house just before she drove off the road,' Sebastian said. That was a lie; he knew nothing about what had happened in the red Volvo, but it seemed like a credible scenario.

'According to Maria, it was because Nicole had recognised you from the scene of the murders,' Vanja repeated.

'That's not true.'

Vanja was getting tired of trying to maintain a professional tone.

'Nicole is still alive. Fred and Georg . . .' She leaned forward, pointing to the pictures of the dead boys. Pia couldn't stop herself from looking down at them. 'Fred and Georg are dead. Frank Hedén might have pulled the trigger, but you're just as guilty.'

'I didn't know he was intending to shoot them,' Pia said yet again, but her tone carried slightly less conviction this time.

438

'Repeating something doesn't make it any more true,' Vanja said.

Pia met her gaze; the younger woman didn't waver, not even a millimetre. In the end Pia was forced to look away, but she refused to admit her defeat; instead she went for a calculated conclusion.

'I want a lawyer.'

'You're going to need one.'

May was showing itself off at its absolute best.

The sun was shining from a clear blue sky on the hotel with its beautiful extensive lawns, leading down to the water where the wedding was to take place. Then there would be a break of a few hours before the reception, which was to be held in one of the largest rooms. The guests had been invited to stay over and meet for brunch the following morning to review the day's experiences before setting off home in various directions.

Two days of celebration in the name of love, as it said on the invitations.

Sebastian had settled into his room, then strolled outside; the wedding would start in less than fifteen minutes. He was wearing a suit and tie, and as soon as he stepped out into the sunshine he knew how much he was going to sweat during the ceremony. He looked around to see if he could spot anyone he knew; Torkel and Ursula were standing a short distance away, deep in conversation, and didn't notice him. He wouldn't be able to avoid them all day, but he wasn't in any great hurry to talk to them. Particularly Ursula; to be honest, he was a little nervous about meeting her again.

The young police officer who had joined them on the case up in Jämtland, Jennifer something-or-other, was chatting with several people he didn't know. That was no good either. He carried on looking around.

Then he saw her, and was slightly taken aback.

Vanja, in high-heeled shoes and a yellow dress that ended just below the knee. He had never seen her in anything other than trousers and a shirt or blouse or whatever it was called when a woman wore it. Unfortunately. She should wear a dress more often, he thought. It gave her a lightness, a girlishness that was enormously attractive, a youthfulness that reflected her age.

He went over and gave her a hug. 'You look lovely,' he said.

'Don't get any ideas,' she replied with a smile, but there was a hint of seriousness in her tone. Sebastian returned the smile and held up his hands in a defensive gesture.

'I said you looked lovely, that's all. That dress really suits you.'

'And I just said I think you're the type who goes to a wedding to see what's on offer.'

'OK, in that case we're both right.'

Brian and Wilma, the evening's toastmasters, rang a bell and asked everyone to take their places. Vanja slipped her arm through Sebastian's and they moved towards the folding chairs which had been arranged in rows on either side of a temporary aisle covered in fine white sand and strewn with rose petals, ending in a pergola covered in white lilies and red roses.

For a while Vanja had been worried that her involvement in what happened with Maria and Nicole would create a permanent distance between her and Sebastian; but their pursuit of Pia, and Sebastian's success in rescuing Nicole from the waters of Lake Mälaren, seemed to have given him closure in some way, and to Vanja's surprise their relationship was now better than it had been for a long time. It was almost as if he didn't want to lose her too.

Just as they sat down the music began to play from hidden speakers and the bridal couple appeared. Billy, in a slim-fitting grey tailcoat with a green waistcoat and tie, looked almost shy as he made his way up the aisle at Maya's side, smiling at their guests. His bride was radiant in a white strapless dress that hugged the curves of her body to her hips, then flared out in a bell-shaped skirt with sparkling silk-embroidered detail down one side.

'It's Vera Wang,' Vanja whispered to Sebastian as the couple walked past. Sebastian nodded. He had no idea who Vera Wang was or what she did, but presumably it was something to do with the dress. He was just wondering how come Vanja knew about wedding-dress designers when the female celebrant began to speak. Sebastian sat back and thanked his lucky stars that it wasn't a church wedding. The woman seemed to know Billy and Maya well, and the ceremony was warm, personal, and nice and short.

When Billy kissed his bride, spontaneous applause broke out.

★ ★ ★

Billy was contemplating his wedding. He had to repeat the words to himself to drive home the fact that it was actually happening.

His wedding.

He had been nervous all day. In spite of the fact that everything was incredibly well organised, more like a military operation than a party, there had naturally been a certain amount of minor firefighting. However, Maya was in control, and her meticulous preparation had paid off.

Everyone appeared to be having a good time. The seating arrangements were a hit. His gaze swept across the tables and fastened on Jennifer, who was next to Maya's brother's boyfriend. She seemed to be enjoying herself. When he got back from Kiruna he had wondered whether there was any way of stopping her from attending the wedding, but he didn't know how to do it without arousing Maya's suspicions. For a while he had hoped that Jennifer might think the situation was too awkward and decline the invitation, but no such luck.

She had come over to them after the ceremony. Billy hadn't seen her beforehand, and was struck by how beautiful she looked in her red dress, with her hair up. Jennifer had introduced herself to Maya and congratulated her. She had sung Billy's praises to an embarrassing degree, then she had hugged him and moved on. Natural, relaxed, as if Kiruna had never happened.

Maya had definitely thought of everything. Every single thing. A photographer called Disa had met them first thing in the morning and followed them all day. To begin with he had felt stiff and uncomfortable, but he had soon forgotten that she was there with her camera, and now he didn't even think about the fact that she was with them wherever they went.

As if that level of documentation wasn't enough, Maya had placed single-use cameras on every table. The settings were bright and colourful, and the decorations were made of leaves, berries and fruit instead of flowers.

Personal and well thought out.

The starter had been served at the tables, but the main course was a buffet that could be approached from several different directions, so in spite of the fact that there were over a hundred guests, everything flowed smoothly and no one had to wait for too long.

Maya had also written a well-received speech, another personal touch in which she explained the reasons behind the choice of food.

The dessert was also served at the tables, there was plenty of wine, and the atmosphere was fantastic.

There had been quite a lot of speeches, mainly by Maya's friends. Hardly surprising, since seventy per cent of the guests were on her side. Billy's parents were there, a few elderly relatives, and some close friends from his school days, military service and the police training academy. And Riksmord, of course. Both Torkel and Ursula had given speeches, and Billy had found it hard to hold back the tears during Ursula's.

He had to admit he was a little disappointed that Vanja hadn't prepared something. He wasn't expecting anything from Sebastian, but he thought Vanja could have made a bit of an effort.

However, on the whole he couldn't help feeling both happy and impressed as he looked out over the room where the meal was just coming to an end. At the same time, he occasionally struggled with the sense that he was a guest at his own wedding.

Which was entirely his own fault.

He had left all the decisions to Maya from start to finish, so it was hardly fair to blame her if he felt like a bit of an . . . outsider. And he had no intention of allowing such a minor detail to spoil this magical evening. He raised his glass to her.

'*Skål*, my darling. I love you,' he said, clinking his glass against hers before he emptied it.

★ ★ ★

After dinner the youngest and smallest guests were led next door where lots of games had been arranged for them and bowls of sweets laid out, while in the main room the staff cleared away and the band got ready to play.

For anyone over ten years old, it was an opportunity to get some fresh air and catch their breath.

Torkel picked up his glass and wandered out in the unusually warm May evening. He caught sight of Sebastian standing alone, and went to join him; Sebastian glanced over, then turned his attention back to the water down below.

'What did you think of my speech?' Torkel wondered, sipping his three-star Cognac.

'Ursula's was better,' Sebastian replied truthfully.

'I agree, but that doesn't necessarily mean mine was bad.'

'No, it doesn't necessarily mean that,' Sebastian agreed in a tone that somehow managed to contradict the words he spoke.

'OK, I get it. You didn't like it.'

'Don't take it personally – I just don't like speeches.'

'None of them? Not even the ones that are about you?'

'No one's ever made a speech about me,' Sebastian stated without a trace of bitterness.

'Not even at your wedding?'

Sebastian gave a start. Where had that come from? How did Torkel know? But then he remembered telling Torkel he had been married when they met in Västerås, the first time he worked with Riksmord again after a long hiatus. A mistake on his part, but what was done was done. He certainly had no intention of expanding on the subject here and now.

'How did it go with Pia?' he asked instead.

'She's been arrested and she'll go to court, but I don't know . . . We're trying to tie her to the murders, but there's absolutely no proof that she knew what was going to happen, or that she was inside the house.'

'What about the car in the lake?'

'Same problem – we can't prove that she didn't simply lose control.'

'So what's going to happen?'

Torkel shrugged.

'At the moment we can charge her with causing actual bodily harm, obstructing an investigation, knowingly protecting an offender . . .'

'Nothing, in other words.'

'She's unlikely to be re-elected, and her high-flying career with the Social Democrats is over – I imagine she'll find it hard to go on living in Torsby. I suppose that's a kind of punishment,' Torkel said.

Both men stood in silence. Everyone around them was fully occupied in having fun. Torkel took another sip of his brandy.

'She sold the house,' he said after a moment, apparently addressing no one in particular. For the first time Sebastian turned and looked at his colleague, genuinely interested.

'Who? Maria? To FilboCorp?'

Torkel nodded, his eyes still fixed on some distant point.

'Does that mean the mining development will go ahead?'

'It looks that way.'

'So Frank's son – what was his name again?'

'Hampus.'

'Hampus will get the money?'

'Yes. He inherits the property and the land regardless of what his father did.'

Sebastian shook his head.

'I'm surprised she sold up.'

'She had no real connection to the house,' Torkel explained. 'There was a reason why her sister bought her out in the first place, and she certainly couldn't have lived in it after what had happened. Nobody was offering as much money as FilboCorp.'

'I gather you're in touch with her,' Sebastian said, hoping his tone sounded neutral.

Torkel gave him a quick glance before he answered. He didn't really know what had gone on between Maria and Sebastian, merely that it hadn't ended well. Maria had made him promise not to talk to Sebastian about her, but after all he was a part of the team and the investigation, and he had the right to be kept informed. Torkel just had to make sure he kept it on the right level.

'Occasionally, yes. I need to know if Nicole decides to say anything else about what happened in the house.'

'Anything else?' This time Sebastian's tone was a mixture of surprise and happiness. 'Is she talking?'

'She's been talking for about a week.'

Sebastian felt a warmth spread through his chest. After everything she had gone through . . . She was the strongest, bravest little girl he had ever met. He missed her. If only he could see her again. Just once. He had been round to their apartment, but there was no one there.

'Where are they now?' he wondered.

'I don't know,' Torkel lied. That was the line he wasn't prepared to cross.

'I'm not the type to turn into a stalker, you know,' Sebastian said, making sure Torkel knew he had seen through him. 'I just want to be sure they're OK. That Nicole is coping, getting better. I promised to hold on to her until she wanted to let go.'

'I genuinely don't know,' Torkel reiterated. 'But she's let go of you, I do know that.' He put his arm around Sebastian's shoulders, and to the surprise of both men, Sebastian didn't move away.

'Time we stopped talking about work.'

As if Torkel were a part of the well-oiled arrangements, Brian appeared on the patio, rang his little bell and informed everyone that it was time for the bride and groom's first dance.

★ ★ ★

This was the only part of the wedding Billy wasn't looking forward to. Maya had insisted that she didn't want a traditional wedding waltz; they were both going to learn to salsa instead. They had followed some films on YouTube, and had had five private lessons at a dance studio in Östermalm. Billy wasn't much of a dancer under normal circumstances, and he knew he had a long way to go before he could say he had mastered the salsa, but here they were, walking towards the middle of the spacious floor and getting into position. He happened to meet Jennifer's eye and she gave him an encouraging smile as she picked up one of the single-use cameras on her table.

Maya had also insisted on a decent dance floor, at least sixty square metres. Billy had expressed some reservations about having live music. Admittedly she had booked a proper band with a crooner rather than some cheesy combo, but it still felt a bit . . . old-fashioned. However, Maya had said they must consider their older guests too, so they had settled on the live band for sixty per cent of the evening, and a DJ for the rest of the time.

The bandleader counted them in, and the music began. Billy was totally shocked; they were playing one of his favourite songs – 'Forgot about Dre' – but in a salsa arrangement. He looked at Maya, who was smiling with satisfaction.

'I love you,' he mimed. She blew him a kiss, and they started to dance. Everyone cheered, and the whole floor was lit up with phone cameras. It went better than Billy had expected. Maya was faultless, of course. She had even changed her shoes so that her feet wouldn't get too tired during the celebrations.

She was perfect and he loved her.

He told her.

'I love you.'

He meant it. He was happy.

★ ★ ★

Later in the evening, when the band came back after a half-hour break, Torkel asked Ursula to dance. They drifted out onto the floor, and neither of them spoke. Torkel at least was enjoying the intimacy, feeling the warmth of her body. Ursula pressed closer and rested her head on his shoulder.

Then he felt something on his other shoulder. A tap. He stopped and turned around.

'May I?' Sebastian said, nodding towards Ursula. Torkel raised an eyebrow; she nodded and Sebastian took over. It didn't take Ursula long to realise that Torkel was a considerably better dancer than Sebastian, and from his position as a reluctant spectator, Torkel could see that she certainly wasn't resting her head on her new partner's shoulder. That's something, he thought as he went to top up his drink.

'I've missed you,' Sebastian said after a moment or two.

'I find that hard to believe.'

'I'm sorry.' It was almost a whisper. Sebastian cleared his throat and looked deep into her eyes. 'For everything. I'm sorry you got shot. I'm sorry I haven't been to see you.'

'Good. So you should be.'

She had no intention of making it easy for him.

'I couldn't.'

'Why not?'

'I just couldn't. It was impossible. I thought about it several times, but . . . I've been gathering my courage all evening, just to ask you to dance.'

Ursula didn't respond. It wasn't down to her to drive this conversation. Instead she quickly drew back her left foot, thereby saving her little toe from a serious bruise.

'We were on our way towards something when . . . when it happened,' Sebastian said after such a long silence that Ursula thought he had nothing more to say.

'Maybe, but that train is long gone.'

Sebastian nodded. Ursula took a deep breath and stopped dancing as a mixture of anger and sympathy came bubbling up. She didn't want to experience either of those emotions tonight.

'I mean, seriously? After everything that's gone on . . . Is that why you wanted to dance with me? To see if you could get me into bed?'

Sebastian didn't answer, but his gaze dropped to the floor, telling Ursula everything she needed to know. The anger took over.

'Thank you for the dance.'

She tried to walk away, but Sebastian held on to her.

'The music isn't over.'

'I know, but Torkel is a better dancer than you.'

'But that's all he's better at.'

'Goodbye, Sebastian.'

Ursula pulled away, turned her back on him and rejoined Torkel, who was chatting to some of the other guests. Sebastian watched as she touched his arm; Torkel's face broke into a big smile and they resumed their dance, her head resting on his shoulder once more.

It was too late. Everything was too late.

If he had been a drinker this would have been the perfect occasion to get roaring drunk, but he couldn't even do that. Was it too late to find some willing distraction? Probably. Besides which, most of them were a bit too young for him. Maya's mother was a widow, but he hadn't exchanged a single word with her all evening. Besides which, she was now Billy's mother-in-law. How unsexy was that?

The band launched into a new song: 'Only the Lonely'.

Oh, the irony . . . Sebastian headed for the table laden with cakes. If he couldn't drink or screw, at least he could consume diabetes-inducing amounts of cake.

Billy and Maya had withdrawn to the bridal suite at half past midnight. Some of the younger female guests had asked whether Maya was going to toss her bouquet over her shoulder, but she had merely stared uncomprehendingly at them. It wasn't a Swedish tradition and she hadn't even thought about it, just as she hadn't considered having someone to 'give her away' at the altar. As if she couldn't manage for a second without a man at her side. Her father had been dead for many years, but even if he'd been alive he wouldn't have been allowed to hand her over. There was no bouquet-tossing either.

There was, however, sex.

Not as carefully planned and neatly packaged as everything else during the course of the evening, thank God – it was spontaneous, lustful, inventive.

And plenty of it.

More than he had thought he could cope with. It was perhaps half an hour before dawn when they finally stopped, and Maya curled up with her head tucked under his chin. 'I love you,' she said, and immediately fell asleep. Billy thought he would do the same, but he lay there wide awake, strangely unsatisfied.

He gently freed himself from Maya and slipped out of bed. Silently he dug a pair of sweatpants out of his overnight bag and pulled on a T-shirt.

When he got outside he took a deep breath. The air was so fresh, and everything was quiet in a way that belonged only to these late-spring mornings when the light was just beginning to creep over the horizon.

He left the main building and crossed the dew-soaked grass, heading for the edge of the forest and the old stable block that stood there. He needed a pee. When he had done what he had to do against a wall, a cat appeared and rubbed around his legs. It was miaowing, wanting a fuss, and the sound mingled with the tinkle of the little bell on its collar. Billy reached into his pocket and took out his gloves. He didn't really remember putting them there, but he must have subconsciously known he would end up here. Hoped he would end up here.

He bent down and picked up the cat. Scratched behind its ears and heard it begin to purr as it pushed its head against him.

Billy let his hand slide down over the head towards the neck, then he squeezed. The cat immediately realised what was happening, and let out a hiss. With his other hand Billy grasped the front paws as best he could. Once or twice the cat jerked its body and managed to use its claws, but the gloves provided protection. He hadn't had any in Torsby, and had got badly scratched. Fortunately he had been out in the woods with the search parties all day, so his injuries had been easily explained away.

He lifted the cat, squeezing the neck as hard as he could with his left hand. It didn't matter whether it suffocated or whether its neck broke.

It was the moment of death he wanted.

The magic moment when life was extinguished.

The moment when he experienced an intoxicating rush of power like nothing he had ever known.

The cat's movements began to slow down, to weaken. Billy leaned closer, staring feverishly into its eyes, breathing heavily. Soon life would be gone. The green eyes would take on a cloudy film, and the body would go limp in his hands.

Simplicity. Purity. Clarity.

The cat stopped struggling and a trickle of blood ran from its nose. Billy stood there and closed his eyes as his breathing slowly returned to normal.

'Was it good for you too?'

Billy spun around and saw Sebastian standing at the corner of the stable block. A single thought flashed like lightning through his brain.

Kill him.

But he pushed it away as quickly as it had appeared.

'How long have you been standing there?' he asked instead, dropping the dead cat on the ground.

'Long enough.'

★ ★ ★

Sebastian hadn't been able to sleep. He was feeling slightly queasy from eating too much, and he regretted the way his encounter with Ursula had gone. Eventually he gave up and got out of bed. He went along to Ursula's room, but just as he was about to tap on the door he heard a deep voice that definitely didn't belong to her. Unlike the laughter that followed. Sebastian deduced that the voice was Torkel's, and walked away.

It was too late. He had missed his chance.

So he went for a walk instead. He saw Billy standing behind the stables, heard noises he couldn't quite place, and now he realised that taking a closer look out of curiosity had been the right thing to do.

Very few people, none in fact, could kill two people without being affected in some way. Sebastian had always been surprised at Billy's lack of reaction, wondered what the young man was doing to deal with the emotions that must have arisen.

Now he knew.

And he didn't like it. He didn't like it at all.

'What do you feel when you do it?' he asked cautiously, well aware that adrenaline and endorphins were coursing around Billy's muscular body.

'How do you know I've done it before?' Billy took a step closer to Sebastian.

'I can see it in you.' Sebastian didn't move. 'Do you want to talk about it?'

Billy stopped. Sebastian could see that he was trying to get a grip on his feelings. Power, sex, pleasure. Feelings he didn't really understand; he couldn't put them into words, but they were so incredibly strong that he just had to experience them again. Everything else, particularly sex, which was supposed to fulfil the same function and provide total satisfaction, seemed grey and boring in comparison. Sebastian nodded to show that he understood, but it was doubtful if Billy noticed.

'It's the ultimate act in many ways. There is power in the thing that is most forbidden,' Sebastian said, taking a step forward. Billy already seemed calmer, more balanced.

'Animals won't be enough to meet your needs for ever. You've embarked on a dangerous journey, and it can only end in one way.' Sebastian's voice was full of genuine anxiety and concern.

'I know where to draw the line.'

'At the moment.'

'I'm not crazy.'

'Yes, you are – just a little bit. Damaged, anyway. Won't you let me help you?'

Billy shook his head emphatically, his breathing becoming heavier again as his anger rose. He pointed at Sebastian with a trembling finger.

'I know things about you too.'

'Like what?'

'I know you're Vanja's father.'

If Billy hadn't already been certain when he received the results of the DNA test last week, Sebastian's reaction would have put the matter beyond doubt.

'Where did you get that idea from?' Sebastian said, making a futile attempt to avoid the inevitable.

'I took items from both your rooms in Torsby and sent them to a DNA lab, one of those that does anonymous paternity tests.'

'The receptionist said you'd been in my room . . .'

'I'll tell Vanja if you take this any further,' Billy said, nodding in the vague direction of the cat.

'So I just forget about all this, otherwise you'll go running to Vanja?'

'And you don't want that, do you?'

'No, I don't.'

'There you go, then.'

'Indeed.'

There wasn't much else to say. Billy turned and walked away, heading back to the main building. Sebastian waited until he could no longer hear his footsteps, then he went over to the cat and kicked it into the bushes by the wall of the stable block. If, or when, someone found it, they might think it had fallen from a window or off the roof and broken its neck.

Or eaten rat poison. Not many people would imagine that the bridegroom had come padding out in the early-morning light and strangled it, anyway.

But he had, and that was a problem. Billy was a problem. Partly because he so clearly linked death with pleasure. Sebastian hadn't been able to help seeing his erection through the thin sweatpants.

And partly because he knew about Vanja.

There wasn't much he could do about the first part right now; therapy and counselling would remove the unhealthy association that had arisen, but it would take time, and first of all Billy had to admit that he had a problem and wanted to do something about it.

That clearly wasn't the case at the moment, because Billy had used his knowledge about Vanja and Sebastian as a tool to make Sebastian keep quiet.

Blackmail worked only if one person had an advantage over the other. If that advantage was removed, the option no longer existed.

Simple in theory, more difficult in reality.

But when had his life ever been simple?

★ ★ ★

Sebastian glanced at his watch.

It was still early, but best to get it over with.

He knocked on the door. No answer. He knocked again, harder this time.

'Come on, open the door!' he hissed, his mouth close to the hinges.

He thought he could hear footsteps approaching from inside. The security chain rattled and the door opened.

'Sebastian — what is it?'

'There's something I have to tell you.'

'Now? Can't it wait until later?'

'No. I've waited too long as it is,' he said, pushing his way into the room uninvited.

Vanja sighed wearily and closed the door.

Acknowledgements

Thanks to everyone at Norstedts and Norstedts Agency who not only devote time and energy to publishing what we write, but also always seem so happy to be doing what they do. That means a lot to us.

Special thanks to Susanna Romanus, Peter Karlsson and Linda Altrov Berg with whom we work most closely and most frequently. So calm, so positive, so good, so important.

Once again we would like to thank all our overseas publishers, who successfully continue to work to bring Sebastian Bergman to a wider international audience. Special thanks to Rowohlt in Germany and Nina Grabe, who not only take care of Sebastian and Riksmord, but also look after us in the best possible way on our – happily – increasingly frequent visits.

Thanks also to all the booksellers, book days, literary festivals and libraries who so generously invite us along to talk about our books and our writing. You commitment is fantastic and invaluable.

Micke:
As always there are so many people I would like to thank for inspiration, help and good advice. Rolf Lassgård, who has always been a part of Sebastian Bergman. Our colleagues at Tre Vänner and Svensk Filmindustri, principally Jonas Fors, Fredrik Wikström, Jon Nohrstedt, Tomas Tivemark, Jenny Stjernströmer Björk, Johan Kindblom and William Diskay. They never question the time and effort I put into the books, and always step up to the plate when things are tight. Above all I want to thank my wonderful family who have been there through thick and thin.

Astrid, Vanessa, William and Caesar – you're absolutely fantastic! You've put up with late nights, and with my absence both physically and at those times when I am thinking more about my fictional characters than those who are closest to me. I am eternally grateful for your patience and love. Without you none of this would have been possible.

A thousand hugs and kisses – you're the best!

Hans:
As usual, as always, the biggest thank you goes to Lotta, Sixten, Alice and Ebba. You are the smartest, funniest and in every way the best family anyone could ever have. Without you: nothing.